Praise for *The Turnout*

'*The Turnout* centres on a ballet school ... a ▓▓▓▓▓ ridden with suppressed hysteria, delineated so convincingly in Abbott's peerless prose that violent death, when it comes, seems not just plausible but inevitable. My thriller of the year' *Daily Telegraph*, Best Books of the Year

'Abbott's novels are often described as crime fiction, and, while indeed she works with mystery and suspense and draws on noir and Gothic tropes, her goal seems less to construct intricate, double-crossing plot problems than to explore the dark side of femininity ... In other words, Megan Abbott is a mood' *New York Times Book Review*

'Imagine *Black Swan* by way of Virginia Andrews' cult *Flowers in the Attic* and you have some idea of the dark nature of *The Turnout* ... A twisting, turning story of revenge and redemption' *Stylist*

'Abbott's exceptional ability to conjure enclosed subcultures is evident again in a richly immersive novel full of tiny bits of dance lore and sharply evoked minor characters. But *The Turnout* seems more ambitious than her previous stories of imploding micro-communities, with a greater resemblance to tragic drama' *Sunday Times*

'Abbott's fiction focuses on femininity's darkest corners and the world of ballet – obsessive and masochistic – is perfect territory for her ... Slow-burning and feverish, with all the intensity of a classic American film noir' *Mail on Sunday*

'[A] taut, suspenseful novel that's anxiety provoking in the best way' *Vogue*

'Abbott captures the blood, sweat, tears and rivalries behind the apparently effortless gra▓▓▓▓▓▓▓▓▓▓▓▓▓▓▓▓▓▓▓▓▓▓▓▓▓ "our friend, our lover" ar▓▓▓▓▓▓▓▓▓▓▓▓▓▓▓▓▓▓▓▓▓▓ *Guardian*

'The queen of crime behind the high school cheerleader thriller *Dare Me* and gymnastics-focused murder mystery *You Will Know Me* turns her insidious eye to the high-stakes world of ballet in her latest novel' *Harper's Bazaar*

'Abbott's prose has never been more impressive than in this whirlpool of psychological suspense, shocking images, well-wrought metaphors – and one final twist that rattles like a serpent's tail in Eden' *Wall Street Journal*

'A story so intensely told that it will haunt your dreams' *Daily Mirror*

'The quality of the writing in this novel is remarkable ... The sublime prose raises the book from psychological thriller towards the realm of classical tragedy ... Abbott skilfully and cumulatively weaves a web of secrets, lies, evasions and insinuations' *Irish Examiner*

'Intoxicatingly intense, with a frisson of suspense and lurking disquiet throughout, those feelings will linger with you long past the last page' *Hello*

'A book that takes a deep dive into the world of ballet, blending nerve-shredding noir plotting with sharp psychological insight ... Abbott has always written brilliantly about the hidden desires of women, and *The Turnout* takes that to new heights' *Big Issue*

'*The Turnout* is a dance that begins slowly and lures the reader in – Abbott's writing is razor sharp, offering a precise dissection of complex relationships, sheltered family, sexuality and secrets. Within the beauty of these dancers' lives is a darkness left to be peeled, layer by layer, until the dying pages' *The Skinny*

'While undoubtedly one of our best crime novelists, Abbott has also always struck me as akin to an anthropologist ... In *The Turnout*, Abbott delves into the rarified world of ballerinas, astutely noting the symbols and signals underlying the romantic image' *Paris Review*

'This dark thriller will suck you in right to the final page' *Sun*

THE
TURNOUT

MEGAN ABBOTT

virago

VIRAGO

First published in the United States in 2021 by Putnam
First published in Great Britain in 2021 by Virago Press
This paperback edition published in 2022 by Virago Press

1 3 5 7 9 10 8 6 4 2

A CIP catalogue record for this book
is available from the British Library.

ISBN 978-0-349-01246-9

Book design by Laura K. Corless

Printed and bound in Great Britain by Clays Ltd, Elcograf S.p.A.

Papers used by Virago are from well-managed forests
and other responsible sources.

Virago Press
An imprint of
Little, Brown Book Group
Carmelite House
50 Victoria Embankment
London EC4Y 0DZ

An Hachette UK Company
www.hachette.co.uk

www.virago.co.uk

For my dad, my hero

Philip Abbott (1944–2019)

Childhood is the fiery furnace in which we are melted down to essentials and that essential shaped for good.

—KATHERINE ANNE PORTER

ONE

WE THREE

They were dancers. Their whole lives, nearly. They were dancers who taught dance and taught it well, as their mother had.

"Every girl wants to be a ballerina . . ."

That's what their brochure said, their posters, their website, the sentence scrolling across the screen in stately cursive.

THE DURANT SCHOOL OF DANCE, EST. 1986 by their mother, a former soloist with the Alberta Ballet, took up the top two floors of a squat, rusty brick office building downtown. It had become theirs after their parents died on a black-ice night more than a dozen years ago, their car caroming across the highway median. When an enterprising local reporter learned it had been their twentieth wedding anniversary, he wrote a story about them, noting their hands were interlocked even in death.

Had one of them reached out to the other in those final moments, the reporter wondered to readers, *or had they been holding hands all along?*

All these years later, the story of their parents' end, passed down like lore, still seemed unbearably romantic to their students—less so to Marie, who, after sobbing violently next to her sister, Dara, through the funeral, insisted, *I never saw them hold hands once.*

* * *

But the Durant family had always been exotic to others, even back when Dara and Marie were little girls floating up and down the front steps of that big old house with the rotting gingerbread trim on Sycamore, the one everyone called the Hansel and Gretel house. Dara and Marie, with their long necks and soft voices. Their matching buns and duckfooted gait, swathed in scratchy winter coats, their pink tights dotting the snow. Even their names set them apart, sounding elegant and continental even though their father was an electrician and a living-room drunk and their mother had grown up eating mayonnaise sandwiches every meal, as she always told her daughters, head shaking with rue.

From kindergarten until fifth and sixth grade, Dara and Marie had attended a spooky old Catholic school on the east side, the one their father had insisted upon. Until the day their mother announced that, going forward, she would be giving them lessons at home, so they wouldn't be beholden to the school's primitive views of life.

Their father resisted at first, but then he came to pick them up at the schoolyard one day and saw a boy—the meanest in fifth grade, with a birthmark over his left eye like a fresh burn—trying to pull Marie's pants down, purple corduroys to Dara's matching pink. Marie just stood there, staring at him, her fingers touching her forehead as though bewildered, transfixed.

Their father swerved over so fast his Buick came up on the curb, the grass. Everyone saw. He grabbed the little boy by the haunches and shook him until the nuns rushed over. *What kind of school,* he wanted to know, *are you running here?*

On the car ride home, Marie announced loudly that she hadn't minded it at all, what the boy had done.

It made my stomach wiggle, she said much more quietly to Dara in the backseat.

Their father wouldn't talk to Marie for days. He telephoned the school and thundered at the principal, so loud they heard him from upstairs, in their bunkbed. Marie's face in the moonlight was shiny with tears. Marie and their father were both mysterious to Dara. Mysterious and alike somehow. *Primitive*, their mother called them privately.

They never went back.

At home, lessons were different every day. You could never guess. Some mornings, they'd get out the great big globe from their father's den and Dara and Marie would spin it and their mother would tell them something about the country on which their finger landed. (*Singapore is the cleanest country in the world. The punishment for vandalism is caning.*) Sometimes, she had to look things up in the mildewed encyclopedia in the den, its covers soft with age. Often, it seemed like she was making things up (*In France, there are two kinds of toilets . . .*), and they would laugh about it, the three of them, their private jokes.

We are three, their mother used to say. (They were three until they were four, but this was before Charlie came, and all of that.)

But mostly, the day—every day—was about ballet.

Their father was away for work so often, and for so long. To this substation, or to that airfield, doing things with fiber optics—none of them knew, really.

When he was gone, they wore leotards all day and danced for hours and hours, in the practice room, along the second-floor landing, in the backyard thick with weeds. They danced all day, until their feet radiated, tingled, went numb. It didn't matter.

That was how Dara remembered it now.

House cats. That's what their mother used to call them, which was funny, if you thought about it, because their mother was the one who kept them home with her. Not one sleepover, nor camping trip, nor a neighbor's birthday party their entire childhood.

They made their own fun. Once, on Valentine's Day, they all cut out valentines from faded construction paper and their mother made a lesson for them about love. She talked about all the different kinds of love and how it changed and turned and you couldn't stop it. Love was always changing on you.

I'm in love, Marie said, like always, talking about the fifth-grade boy with the birthmark who pulled her pants down, who had once hid under her desk and tried to stick a pencil between her legs.

That's not love, their mother said, stroking Marie's babyfine hair, brushing the back of her hand against Marie's forever-pink cheek.

Then she told them their favorite story, the one about a famous ballerina named Marie Taglioni, whose devotees were so passionate they once paid two hundred rubles, a fortune at that time, for a single pair of her discarded pointe shoes. After the purchase, they cooked, garnished, and ate the pointe shoes with a special sauce.

That, their mother told them, *is love*.

Now, more than two decades later, the Durant School of Dance was theirs.

All day, six days a week for the past more-than-a-dozen years, Dara and Marie taught in the cramped, cozy confines of the same ashen building where their mother had once reigned. Steamy and pungent in the summer and frigid, its windows snow-blurred, in the winter, the studio never changed and was forever slowly falling apart. Often thick with must, overnight rain left weeping pockets in every ceiling corner, dripping on students' noses.

But it didn't matter, because the students always came. Over a hundred girls and a few boys, ages three to fifteen, Pre-Ballet I to Advanced IV. And a waitlist for the rest. In the past six years, they'd advanced fourteen girls and three boys to tier-one ballet schools and thirty-six to major competitions.

Every summer, they hired two additional instructors, three on weekends, but during the school year, it was just Dara and Marie. And, of course, Charlie, once their mother's prize student, her surrogate son, her *son of the soul*. And now Dara's husband. Charlie, who couldn't teach anymore because of his injuries but who ran all the business operations from the back office. Charlie, on whom so many students had passing crushes, a rite of passage, like the first time they took a razor blade to their hardened feet, or the first time they achieved turnout, rotating their legs from their hip sockets, bodies pushed to contortion. Pushed so far, the feeling ecstatic. Her first time, Dara felt split open, laid bare.

The Durant School of Dance was an institution. Children, teens came from three counties to take classes with them. They came with sprightly dreams and limber bodies and hard little muscles and hungry, lean bellies and a desire to enter into the fairy tale that is dance to little girls and a few special little boys. They all wanted to participate in the storied Durant tradition set forth by their mother thirty or more years ago. *Encore, échappé, échappé, watch those knees.* Their mother, her voice subdued yet steely, striding across the floor, guiding everything, mastering everything.

But now it was Dara's and Marie's voices—Dara's low and flinty (*Shoulders down, lift that leg, higher, higher . . .*) and Marie's light and lilting, Marie calling out *Here comes the Mouse King!* to all her five-year-olds and bending her feet and hands into claws, the girls screaming with pleasure . . .

Charlie in the back office listening to parents bemoan their child's lack of discipline, the exorbitant cost of pointe shoes, the holiday schedule, Charlie nodding patiently as mothers spoke in hushed tones about their own long-ago ballet aspirations, of the mad fantasy of tutus and rosin, satin and tulle, floodlights and beaming faces, leaping endlessly into a lover's waiting arms.

Everything worked, nothing ever changed.

And yet gradually the Durant School of Dance, decades after opening in a former dry goods store with a drooping ceiling, had become a major success.

"I always knew it could be," Charlie said.

Which one does your daughter have? Dara or Marie?

They look so much alike, but Dara's dark to Marie's fair.

They look so much alike, but Dara has the long swan neck and Marie the long colt legs.

Both carry themselves with such poise. They show our daughters grace and bearing.

They bend and twist our squirmy, pigeon-breasted little girls into lithe and lissome dancers. Our girls walk into the Durant School shrill and strident, with the clatter of phones and the slap of flip-flops, and an hour later, they have been transformed into the strong, sweated stillness of an empress, a czarina, a Durant.

Our daughters love them both, especially Marie.
          Marie, because she taught the younger ones. Because she would get down on the floor with them, would fix their loose braids and, when they burst into tears, secretly give them strawberry sugar wafers. After class, she might even teach them how to do that dance like their favorite pop singer if they showed her first on their phones. At day's end, Dara would peek into Marie's studio, the pastel crush of wafer crumbs, the abandoned hair ribbons and bent bobby pins, and wonder if Marie understood little girls too well.

Dara followed their mother's model. In her studio, she stood queen-like, her chin jutting like a wolf's—that's how Charlie described it—quick to correct, quick to unravel them, the girls with the lazy extension, the girls pirouetting with bent knees.

Someone had to keep up the tradition of rigor, of firm discipline, and it inevitably fell to Dara. Or suited her best. It was hard to tell the difference.

But, for the most part, to all the little girls, their faces upturned, their matching pink tights and scuffed leather slippers—still more to their parents who crowded the lobby, who steamed up the windows, unwrapping their children from fuzzy, puffy coats and nudging them, gently, into the studio—Dara and Marie were the same, but different.

Dara was cool, but Marie was hot.

Dara was dark, but Marie was light.

Dara and Marie, the same but different.

* * *

Every girl wants to be a ballerina . . ."

It was always the photograph that first drew them in. Dark Dara and pale Marie, their heads tilted against each other, matching buns, their feet in *relevé*. The photograph was the first thing you saw when you walked into the studio lobby, or clicked on the website, or picked up the community circular or the sleek lifestyle magazine and saw the glossy ad in the back.

Charlie had taken the photograph and everyone talked about it.

So striking, everyone would say. *E-theeeer-real*, some would even venture. The littlest girls, padding in in their ballet pinks, would stare up at the photo mounted in the lobby, fingers in their mouths.

Like fairy princesses.

So Charlie took more photos. For the local paper, which featured them regularly, for their marketing materials as the school grew in size. But the photos were always, fundamentally, the same. Dark Dara and pale Marie, poised, close, touching.

Once, a marketing person offered them a free consultation. After observing them in the studio one summer day, sweating in the corner, wilting on the high stool they'd given him, he spoke to Charlie under his breath for a long time. That was how they ended up with the photo of Dara and Marie at the end of a long day, after dancing together in the quiet studio, their bodies loose, their leotards soaked through.

Charlie shot them collapsed upon each other on the floor, their faces pink with pleasure.

"Move closer," he said from behind the camera. "Closer still."

Closer still. Back then, it seemed impossible to be any closer. The three of them, so entwined. Charlie was Dara's husband, but he was also so much more. Dara, Marie, and Charlie, their days spent together at the studio, their nights in their childhood home. Back then.

After the shoot, looking at images on Charlie's computer, Dara hesitated, imagining what their mother might say of the photos, their bruises and blisters and blackened toenails hidden, their bodies so smooth and perfect and bare. "Are you sure?" she asked.

"They tell a story," Charlie said.

"They sell a story," Marie added, snapping her leotard against her damp skin.

Dancers have short lives, of course. What happened to Charlie—his crushing injuries, his four painful surgeries—never left their minds. His body, still as lean and marble-cut as the day their mother brought him home, was a living reminder of how quickly things could turn, how beautiful things could be all broken inside. One had to plan, to make a trajectory. That was what made Dara and Charlie different from Marie, from their parents.

Marie always seemed ready to bolt, but never for long and never far. How far could one get if one still struggled to remember a bank card pin number, and left gas burners lit wherever she went.

So, when Dara and Charlie did marry—at city hall, he in an open-collar shirt and back brace and she in a tissue-thin slip dress that made her shudder on the front steps—he brought with him a small trust fund from his long-deceased father, to be broken open at last like a platinum piggy bank on his twenty-first birthday. The amount was modest, but they used it to pay off the mortgage for the studio building, drooping ceiling and all. They owned it outright. It was theirs.

We'll do it together, he said.

And Marie.

Of course, he said. *We three. We means three.*

It was the three of them. Always the three of them. Until it wasn't. And that was when everything went wrong. Starting with the fire. Or before.

THE HAMMER

Is it time? Those were the words humming in her head that morning.

Their mother's kitchen clock, its aluminum yellowed with grease, read six forty-five.

She took a breath, long and wheezing, her body tight and heavy from sleep.

Still, Dara couldn't quite move from her seat, her palms resting on the drop-leaf table, the walnut whorls she'd known since childhood.

That morning, she'd woken fast from a dream about the Fire Eater their father took them to see at the spring carnival when they were very small. The way the woman gripped the bluing torch, how the flames seemed to draw up her throat, her long face, her startled eyes.

The dream was still in her, more or less, still fluttering her eyes, and when she rose from the table to turn off the gas burner, she waited three, four, five seconds to see the blue flame flicker and disappear.

Marie, she thought suddenly. All these months later and she still expected to turn and see Marie, face pleated with sleep, stumbling toward her, empty mug outstretched.

Tea in hand, Dara lowered herself back into her chair, then stretched her torso forward, arms out, her head dropping lower and lower, her arms reaching down her calves, grabbing her ankles, all the blood joining. All the nerves radiating.

We have a different relationship to pain, their mother used to say. *It's our friend, our lover.*

When you wake up and the pain is gone, do you know what that means?

What, they'd ask every time.

You're no longer a dancer.

D ara," Charlie called from upstairs, from their mother's claw-footed tub, "aren't you late?"

"No," Dara replied. *Never,* she wanted to add, reaching to fill her thermos, tea splashing, her joints aching as ever, the only way, some mornings, she knew she was alive.

M adame Durant!" called out a boy's voice, just breaking. "Is it going to be today?"

It was Saturday and not even seven thirty. The front door of the Durant School of Dance wouldn't open for another half hour, but the parking lot was already beginning to fill when Dara arrived, legs vibrating, face burning deliriously from her bracing walk to work.

"Madame Durant!" the voice came again.

Dara turned as the car approached, a porpoise-gray sedan with tinted windows.

Inside, nestled beside his father, was earnest, sloe-eyed, fourteen-year-old Corbin Lesterio, his hair still shower-wet, slicked back like a silent movie actor, or a gangster. "Madame Durant, is it going to be today? The cast announcement?"

"Yes," Dara said, moving past the car, hiding a faint smile at his earnestness, so raw and plain. She picked up her pace, feeling their eyes on her. Corbin, one of the six boys to the one hundred twenty-two girls in the school, didn't know it yet, but they'd chosen him as this year's Nutcracker Prince. Or, rather, Dara had. Charlie hadn't been feeling well and left auditions early, and Marie never interfered in casting, left it always to Dara, who knew it could only be Corbin, with his impossibly long arms and long, lovely neck.

"Madame Durant! Madame!" came other voices, from other idling cars, heaters churning and windows fogging, of eager parents, a dozen mothers, their early morning hair scraped up into clips, their daughters' buns bobbing beside them, their energy high and frantic. "Madame! Madame!" Their excitement as exhausting as their desperation.

The energy—the constant buzzing of anxiety and distress, of hunger and self-critique—was always high at the Durant School, but today it was much higher.

It was inevitable. It happened every year at this time, the chill in the air, the twinkle in all the girls' eyes, their arms high in fifth position.

It was *Nutcracker* season.

A necessary evil, *The Nutcracker* was.

It took over everything. Eight weeks of auditions, in-class rehearsals, on-site rehearsals, costume fittings, and final dress rehearsals with their partner, the Mes Filles Ballet Company led by Madame Sylvie—all leading up to sixteen live performances over two weeks at the Francis J. Ballenger Performing Arts Center, a steel-and-glass eyesore that transformed magically on December nights into a glowing gift box wrapped in dozens of yards of red-velvet ribbon.

Eight weeks of stress headaches and fainting and nervous stomachs. Eight weeks of injuries and near injuries, jumper's knee and growth spurts, bloody blisters and heel spurs.

All of it hidden behind the glitter and cheap satin, the ruffles and netting and tulle, the three dozen wigs, powdered, sprayed, gilded, the backstage pinboard of faux mustaches for the toy soldiers, the wall cubby of caved-in rodent heads for the battle against the Mouse King. And all of it hidden again beneath thirty pounds of flame-retardant paper snow recycled every performance or, in the old days, shredded plastic-bag snow that got stuck in your eyelashes, that flew in your mouth, and at the end of every night, the crew rolled big magnets across the stage to pull out the fallen hairpins.

Most of all, it was eight weeks of tears.

The Nutcracker. The story was so simple, a child's story, but full of mystery and pain. At her family's holiday party, a young girl named Clara finds herself transfixed by her dark and charismatic godfather, Drosselmeier. He gives her a miniature man, a Nutcracker doll she sneaks into bed with her, dreaming him into a young man, a fantasy lover who ushers her into a dream world of unimaginable splendor. And, at ballet's end, she rides off with him on a sleigh into the deep, distant forest. The end of girlhood and the furtive entry into the dark beyond.

All the girls wanted to be Clara, of course. Clara was the star. There were crying jags and stiff upper lips and silent sobs among the dozens forced to play one of many Party Girls, Angels, Candy Canes. They wanted to wear Clara's stiff white party dress, her flowing white nightgown. They wanted to hold the grinning Nutcracker doll like a scepter.

This yearning, so deep among the young girls, was like money in the bank.

Every year, their fall enrollment increased twenty percent because of all these girls wanting to be Clara. Soon after, their winter enrollment increased another ten percent from girls in the audience who fell in love with the tutus and magic.

Never, their mother used to say, that vaguely French frisson in her voice as she collected the fees, *do I feel more American.*

Privately, their mother confided she never cared much for Clara. *She never does anything, a little dormouse of a thing.* And she would read to them the original story, which was much darker, the little girl so much more interesting, intense. And her name in the story was not Clara, which means *bright and clear*, their mother explained, but Marie, which means *rebellious*.

That's me! Marie used to say every time their mother turned to the first page.

Dara's name, alas, had no such story. Their mother could never remember how she picked it, only that it sounded right.

The irony, their mother told Dara once, *is you're the Marie.*

M adame Durant!" squeaked a voice, one of the nine-year-olds, as Dara moved past them all and in the front door of the building. "Madame Durant, who will be Clara? Who?"

Because today was not only one of those nerve-shredding *Nutcracker* season days but, short of opening night, it was *the* day. The cast announcements when everyone would find out what Dara had decided the night before. Who would be their Clara, their Prince, their mechanical dolls, their harlequins, their itty-bitty bonbons and wispy little snowflakes.

"I can barely stand it!" Chloë Lin lisped, clutching at one of her leg warmers, sliding down her shin as she ran. "If I have to wait any longer I'll die!"

The door shutting behind her, Dara took a breath.

But each step Dara took up the staircase throbbed with that same feeling, that jittery energy.

Or, as it turned out, it throbbed with Marie.

B AM! BAM! BAM! BAM!
The Durant School of Dance was full of noise, a sharp, focused banging that felt like a nail gun at Dara's temple.

BAM! BAM! BAM! BAM!

It was a sound Dara knew well. She'd heard it thousands of times, ever since her sister was ten years old and their mother first raised her up on her preternaturally tapered toes. *You, my dear, were made for en pointe.*

"Sister, dear sister," Dara called out.

And there she was, Marie, face flushed, legs spread on the floor of

Studio A, taking their father's rust-red claw hammer to a new pair of pointe shoes.

"The claw returns," Dara said, lifting an eyebrow.

"It's the only thing that works," said Marie, holding out the shoe for Dara to see, its pinkness split open, its soft center exposed.

Even when, as young dancers, they went through three pairs a week, their mother forbid the hammer. It was too rough, too brutal. It was lazy. Instead, one should stick the shoe in the hinge of a door, closing it slowly, softening its hardness, breaking it down. Marie never had the patience.

"Look," Marie said, showing off her handiwork, settling her finger inside the shank, poking it, stroking it. "Look."

Dara felt her stomach turn and she wasn't sure why.

Satin, cardboard, burlap, paper hardened with glue—that's all they were, pointe shoes. But they were so much more, the beating heart of ballet. And the fact that they lasted only weeks or less than an hour made them all the more so, like a skin you shed constantly. Then a new skin arrived, needing to be shaped.

As soon as their dancers went on pointe, Dara and Marie made them learn how to break them in, how to experiment, fail, adapt, customize. They'd sit on the changing room floor, their legs like compasses, their new shoes between them like a pair of slippery fish.

Crush the box, pry up and bend the shank, bend the sole, soften it, make it your own. Thread a needle with dental floss—far thicker than thread—to sew in elastic bands and satin ribbons at just the right spot, a cigarette lighter on the ribbon edges to stop fraying. Pliers to tug out the nail, an X-acto to cut away the satin around the toes to make them less slippery. That was Dara's favorite part, like peeling a soft apple. After, taking the X-acto and, *thwick, thwick, thwick, thwick*, scraping the shoe bottom, X patterns or crosses, giving it grip.

It was all about finding one's own way to fuse the foot to the shoe, the shoe to the foot, the body.

The shoe must become part of you, their mother always said. *A new organ, snug and demanding and yours.*

If you didn't prepare them correctly, if you left out any step, took any shortcuts—too smooth a sole, too low an elastic—it could mean a fall, an injury, worse.

Their mother told them stories of older girls hiding broken glass in other girls' shoes, which sounded like a dark fairy tale, but was there any other kind?

Ballet was full of dark fairy tales, and how a dancer prepared her pointe shoes was a ritual as mysterious and private as how she might pleasure herself. It was often indistinguishable.

*B*AM! BAM! BAM! BAM!
Marie was not going to stop, her teeth sunk into her lip, her eyes unfocused. She was going to prepare one, two, three pairs.

It was all ridiculous, a waste. *Marie,* Dara wanted to say, *what are these even for? Marie, you're a teacher now, not a dancer.*

And the little girls she taught were years away from going on pointe, their feet still clad in pink slippers.

But Dara was too tired to scold. To say what her mother would have said, *You are abusing yourself, ma chère. This is self-abuse.*

BAM! BAM! BAM! BAM!

Marie would not stop until Dara finally unlocked the front door and the first students pushed through, a gaggle of chirpy eight-year-olds, two bursting into tears at the gossamer pile before Marie, at her gutted shoes.

*E*verything was a mad crush that day, Saturdays always were, but especially now, with the class schedule overloaded to make up for audition time and their regular substitute, a sprightly college student named Sandra Shu, felled by a snapping hip that, at long last, popped.

The air was thick with anticipation for the final cast list, which Dara, following their mother's storied tradition, never posted before the end of the day. Otherwise, all afternoon she'd have to endure the crying and mute stares, the sullen faces and despair, the incessant needling of the chosen leads under whispered breaths.

Still, with the pitch of *The Nutcracker* humming all ears, there were more than the usual share of fretful students, a turned ankle, a jammed thumb, two girls fainting from a secret diet of celery and watermelon juice, the student toilet choked with vomit, a boy's dance belt come asunder, one girl teasing another about her body hair, the fine down emerging nearly overnight to keep her floss-thin body warm, and Dara losing her temper with Gracie Hent for crowding the other girls, or with the Neuman sisters for coming to class again in black tights. (*Black tights like an Italian widow,* their mother would say, tsk-tsking.) Pink tights, black leotard, hair fastened for girls; black tights, white tees for boys. The rules were so simple and never changed.

Charlie came in late, moving slowly and warily after a session with his PT. *Helga,* Dara and Marie had dubbed her, with Marie often imitating an imagined Germanic patter at the massage table. (*Elbow sharp as a shiv for my dah-link . . .*) It didn't matter that her name wasn't Helga and she wasn't German but some local mom who, as Charlie loved to tell them, had gone back to school for her degree to support her children and make up for a useless husband. For Dara and Marie, she'd forever be Helga, *built like bull with hands of iron!*

During the hours of his absence, all the problems Charlie typically forestalled had accumulated. There was no one to handle the parents, the niceties, the back office schedule changes, the vomit- and then tampon-clogged toilet, and the boy dancer who wanted to talk, *man to man,* about how to maneuver himself into that dance belt. (*Pull everything up and to the front,* Charlie always explained, *like it's high noon.*)

And then there was Marie. Mercurial Marie, who had become even more mercurial of late. The morning hammering gave way to a kind of dreamy listlessness as she drifted between classes to the third floor, her upstairs bunker, playing raspy old 45s on her windup Cinderella record player with the handle shaped like a glass slipper. Twice, she missed the start of her own class.

Late in the day, when one of Dara's mild corrections made Liv Lockman run into the changing room to cry, Marie knelt down and pulled the girl's sob-racked body close, nearly weeping with her.

"Madame Durant," whispered Pepper Weston, watching the spectacle from behind Dara, "is it true that the other Madame Durant—"

"Mademoiselle Durant," Dara corrected.

"That Mademoiselle Durant sleeps in the attic now?"

Dara didn't say anything for a moment, then, glancing at the metal clock on the wall, announced, *"Depêchez-vous. À la barre."*

Eight months ago, Marie had moved out of their home, the one they grew up in, with its knotty pine and sloping ceilings and time-worn floors and side-sinking stairs and the smell, forever, of their mother's Blue Carnation perfume. The only place they'd ever lived at all, every scuff and scratch their own.

There hadn't been a discussion or even an explanation. Marie just kept saying it felt right, stuffing fistfuls of clothing into a duffel bag and running down the stairs as if, Charlie later said, fleeing a fire.

They both thought she'd be back in a day, a week. After all, she'd left once before, years ago. Left with a moth-eaten velvet rolling trunk of their mother's, intent on traveling the world. But the world had taken a month, more or less.

This time, however, it had been eight months. Yet she hadn't gotten very far, camping out right here in the studio, up the spiral staircase to the third floor, amid the files and glue traps and old recital tutus shivering with dust. Using the powder room and its stand-up shower as her personal toilette, which didn't seem sanitary at all. But Marie often gave off the grimy energy of someone never fully clean.

Only once had Dara climbed the spiral stairs to see what accommodations Marie had made. It turned out she'd made hardly any. The banker boxes were merely shoved in the corner except for one she seemed to be using as a bedside table. There was a metal futon covered with their father's pilling Pendleton blanket, a gooseneck lamp, a jade plant given to her by their longtime *Nutcracker* partner Madame Sylvie in the dormer window, and, on its ledge, a mysterious knot of crystals, a gift from Brandee Hillock's mom, who practiced Reiki and promised to heal Marie's troublesome right ankle.

There was something so sad about the whole setup. *Is this the best you can do, Marie?* As if Marie were forever twelve, weepily dragging her sleeping bag into the backyard when they had a fight.

Since then, Dara had never seen any reason to go up there again. And Marie hadn't invited her anyway.

Dara still thought of the third floor as their mother's domain, her sanctuary, the place she'd retreat to, sometimes for several hours or even a day at a time. It smelled, then, of their mother's perfume, her lily candles, her favorite milled soap. Now it just smelled like Marie.

t's up! It's up!" The screeching and trill, the hush and cursing. While Dara and Marie taught their final classes of the day, Charlie had posted the final *Nutcracker* cast list on the changing room door. Most of the dismissed students had returned for it, and many had never left at all, killing hours on their phones in the changing room, stretching in Studio B, running to the drugstore for contraband soda and sour candies.

By the time Dara approached, a rosy swirl of girls surrounded Bailey Bloom, this year's Clara, the part of all parts, the brave girl venturing into the adult world of dark magic, of broken things, of innocence lost. Dara had targeted her months ago. Knew she had the skills but also the focus, the commitment the part required. Earnest, self-critical, relentless Bailey Bloom, who now stood, eyes darting, among her clambering classmates, their mouths full of congratulations but their eyes twinkling with envy and spite.

"Madame Durant," Bailey said, spotting her, "I can't hardly believe it."

And she smiled widely, showing her dimples—which, Dara realized, in Bailey's four years at the school, she had never seen—like sharp cuts, stigmata deep.

A t six or seven all the parents began arriving, decamping from their parade of heaving SUVs and fogged sedans, Dr. Weston and Ms. Lin, and Mr. Lesterio, looking weary and mildly alarmed after learning his son Corbin would be the Nutcracker Prince, an immediately controversial decision among the other five boys who thought him too old, an ancient fourteen. And Mrs. Bloom, of course, her chest heaving with excitement, calling out her daughter's name. When Bailey ran into her arms, her face nearly collapsed with complicated joy, her mouth opening as if to cry out. Her voice catching and disappearing in her throat.

Watching her, Dara suspected Mrs. Bloom, like so many of the mothers (and, every once in a while, a father), had once harbored ballet fantasies of her own, her fingers curling around Bailey's tidy bun, her eyes full of tears.

J ust as the day's last classes had ended, just as Dara was about to wrench loose the cork from the half-full wine bottle stashed in the deep drawer of the office desk, delivery men arrived and she had to sign for yet another box of new pointe shoes ordered especially for *The Nutcracker*.

Distracted from their changing, jeans half-tugged over their leotards, the eight- and nine-year-olds, a year or two from going on pointe, surrounded the box with *ooohs* and *aaahhhs* as if it were the ark of the covenant. Their feet now so round and pristine, eventually to be like the older girls'. Blood blisters, soles like red onions, feet that peeled fully tip to toe every month or so, calluses thick as canvas, toes curled sidewise, necrotic, ulcerated toes, their nails slipping off, clattering to the floor.

A bold one snuck her hand along the top seam and peered inside, giggling. Wanting in, wanting to touch, to feel this thing that would one day become a part of her, a new organ, tender and virginal, ready to be used, abused, destroyed.

Approaching, Marie took one look at the box, her eyes burning.

"Like lambs to the slaughter," she said softly, before Dara shushed her.

I t was after eight and Dara and Charlie were putting on their coats, or Dara helping Charlie with his, his body stiff and tender.

Watching from the desk, Marie finished the last acidic sludge of wine, turning the bottle over so it balanced on the long spike of their mother's ancient metal bill holder. (*There are few greater pleasures,* she used to say, *than impaling every bill as it comes in.*)

Marie, suddenly so tiny at the big old splintery desk, a cardigan wrapped around herself like a cocoon.

Charlie looked at Dara, who looked back at Charlie.

"Marie," he said, "come over for dinner? I'm making my famous thirty-second omelet."

Dara raised her eyebrows at Charlie, surprised.

Smiling faintly, Marie said no, she didn't think so, propping her dirty feet on the desk, rolling her fingertips over her blood-sick toes.

"She doesn't want to," Dara said briskly to Charlie. "She has plans, I guess."

Marie looked at them and said, "I don't have anything."

Y ou're so prickly with her," Charlie said in the car. "So prickly with each other."

"No, we're not," Dara said, hiding a flinch. "This is how we always are."

"Okay," Charlie said, his hand on hers.

"She left," Dara reminded him. "It changes things."

"We almost left once," he reminded her.

"That doesn't count," Dara said, putting on her sunglasses even though it was dark out. "That was years ago."

"It was," Charlie conceded, pulling his hand away to turn the steering wheel.

WHEN I WAS A CHILD
AND SHE WAS A CHILD

That night, Charlie and Dara spent hours with the big calendar clipped to the old, brass-tarnished easel stand and planned the *Nutcracker* schedule, from early practices through the final, New Year's Day performance, just as their mother always had.

They tried to account for everything that might arise—the errant injuries, strep throat epidemics, the death of a grandparent, any and all disruptions.

They spoke their shorthand, standing back and studying the calendar, Dara raising an eyebrow, pointing at a particular date, a particular name, and Charlie replying, "Fixed, fixed," as he struck his pencil across one date, drew an arrow to another.

They had tea from the Merry Mushroom teakettle, its '70s orange and brown softened with age. They smoked cigarette after cigarette and didn't feel bad about it, and then they curled on the bed in their master bedroom and watched an old movie with the sound off until they drifted to sleep.

So many nights like this with Marie and it felt funny she wasn't there.

So many nights like this, Marie thumping the TV top with the heel of her hand, like their father used to with his TV downstairs (both likely the last antenna TVs in three counties by now), the images shuddering into focus—an old musical from black-and-white days, pretty girls dressed in feathers, their bodies slicked with jewels.

So many nights like this with Marie, who was now gone, curled instead on her futon at the studio, like some itinerant hobo, grateful for the roof over her head.

"She'll come back," Charlie kept saying, but there was something nice in this too. For Dara. Something nice in being, for the first time in their marriage, for the first time ever, living alone with Charlie in the big old house, drafty and familiar and theirs.

Something nice in bed that night, nuzzling herself against Charlie's back and knowing they were all alone and it was their house now. It was only theirs, all theirs.

We were three and then . . . not.

After all, Charlie had been in their lives for more than twenty years, since he first showed up in their mother's ballet class at eleven years old, the prettiest boy any of them had ever seen.

The prettiest girl too, joked their father, batting his eyelashes.

Their mother doted on Charlie—her star student, her favorite, her *cher Charlie*—one of the few boys, the most wildly talented, and eventually he came to be a part of the family, too, staying over for dinner several nights a week when his mother, a nurse, worked late.

Their mother loved having a young man in the house. Their father worked long hours. When he was home, he disappeared into his den. Through the crack in the door, Dara would watch him collapse in his recliner for the ten o'clock news, a six-pack of Old Style on the quaking TV tray beside him.

When Charlie was thirteen, his mother had to move to some damp, distant corner of England to take care of her ailing parents. There was a day of tears in the house until Dara and Marie's mother decided Charlie should simply stay with them in order to continue his work with the studio. A boy was a valuable thing.

So, for a month, which became nearly a year, which became forever, Charlie moved in with them.

Dara and Marie could barely handle having a boy in the house. Marie began peeing in the neighbors' yard, too afraid that Charlie might hear her.

How strange to have him in their private space of dotted underpants slung over the shower rod, the stench from the mounded ballet slippers, their mother walking around in her silky robe—her "glamour gown," the girls called it—her legs bare and mashed and mauled dancer's feet, feet like a day laborer's hands, their father used to say.

How their father agreed to the new arrangement was a mystery. Once, they heard him grumble to their mother that she better be prepared because *a boy that age is just gonna be jerking himself off the minute the lights go out.*

Dara's mother said nothing, coughing lightly.

You'll see when you wash the sheets.

C harlie slept on the pullout sofa in the living room.

In the morning, before Charlie slid the mattress back into the sofa's mouth, Dara would press her face against the sheets. Marie would look for telltale stains.

Dara liked to go into the bathroom right after Charlie showered, to smell his smells, to touch the sink counter and imagine Charlie's clothes set there, his undershorts.

Dara liked to stand in the shower and imagine Charlie standing there.

T hey had been each other's firsts, age fourteen. It happened in the basement, the makeshift studio next to the chugging washer and dryer. Each of them stretching on the floor, watching each other from opposite corners, watching each other in the mirrors their mother had mounted on the walls with electrical tape.

It happened in a blur of heat, Dara's breath catching, and suddenly, she was crawling toward him, her palms slapping on the floor. Her form divine. It was like a moment in a dance. The serpent attacks. The lion seizes its prey.

She crawled toward him and then on top of him, pushing his shoulders to the floor, and he looked surprised the whole time and she wasn't even sure it had happened until they were both shaking and wet.

Dara should never have told Marie, who immediately told their mother, the words slipping helplessly from her mouth, or so she claimed. Their mother, however, only tilted her head and murmured, *C'est logique, c'est logique.*

(Later, their mother confided to Dara, *If it had been Marie, I would have worried. With you, ma fille mature, I never worry.*)

Marie wouldn't speak to Dara for days, abandoning their bunkbed and sleeping instead in the TV room, on the carpet next to their father's recliner, the two of them watching late-night talk shows, their father letting Marie sip his beer.

Every evening when he wasn't traveling, he'd come home from work and navigate stacks of pointe shoes, towers of them in the corners, tights hanging on doorknobs. Music, forever, from the old stereo console, from the turntable upstairs. The sound, forever, of the barre squeaking, Dara's or Marie's eager hands on it, their mother's voice intoning, *Lift through the leg! Turn that foot out!* Their house was all ballet, all the time.

The only room left untouched was the den, their father's sanctuary, with the cabinet TV he refused to throw away, insisting even the tubes were valuable antiques, and the shag carpet that offended their mother and the Igloo cooler alongside the furry nubbed recliner, the autumn floral with the corduroy ridges that Marie liked to run her hands along, sitting on their father's lap, sharing popcorn from the foil dome and watching their dad's monster movies, dubbed to English and with great spouts of the thickest, reddest blood she'd ever seen.

Marie was the only one allowed to join him in there, the only one permitted to talk to their father at all while he was "unwinding" from his day and it was best to avoid him. Marie, who would curl up in his Pendleton blanket and watch *Night Stalker* reruns until their father drifted into a beery snore and their mother dispatched Dara to get her sister to bed.

Dara didn't want to spend time in there anyway. The room smelled funny and there were always crumbs in the carpet that she felt under her feet. Dara would so rather sit at their mother's dressing table and put her fingers in all the lotions and creams and tonics and watch their mother do stretches on the floor and tell her stories about the time she danced at the Royal Opera House in London and drown in the perfumes and loveliness of their mother's attentions.

S oon enough, Dara began sneaking Charlie into the bunkbed with her, both of them curled together, their bodies locked. They did all kinds of things, figuring it all out. If their mother knew, she never said.

Marie sleeping like a kitten in the bunk above.

Or so they thought. A few weeks later, Marie spilled all to their father too. He raged for days, telling their mother she had only herself to blame, turning their house into a brothel. Their father took Charlie into the garage and had a long talk with him and Charlie returned an hour later, his face white and his wrists red.

He told me, Charlie confided to Dara years later, *that I would never be any kind of man if I stayed here. He told me that no man could be any kind of man in this house. And then he started to cry.*

A boy was a valuable thing.

C harlie had moved in and never left. *Finally,* Dara always said, explaining it to others, *one of us had to marry him.*

And so, they went to city hall one year to the day of the car accident, their father's Buick drifting across the icy-ribbed highway into oncoming traffic.

The driver behind them dazedly told a reporter it would have been beautiful if it hadn't been so terrible. Watching, he said, it looked like their parents' car was almost flying.

*W*hen I was a child and she was a child, recited Charlie, the poem that became their vow. It was their mother's favorite poem and you didn't usually read poems at city hall weddings, but Charlie insisted.

We loved with a love that was more than love—

*M*arie had served as witness, wearing glitter on her eyes and their mother's rabbit blanket as a fur stole, and had cried endlessly at the Italian restaurant after. Had cried and held on to her sister and crawled onto her lap.

Marie, who they promised would live with them forever.

Dara and Charlie moved into her parents' room, even slept on their sheets that first night, their wedding night, before Dara took them all to Goodwill the next day.

FIRE, FIRE

It happened sometime in the night. That very night, the *Nutcracker* schedule finalized and the air outside crisp and cutting.

It happened while Dara, unable to sleep, was pacing their mother's familiar insomniac route from the master bedroom to the sewing room, to their dusty childhood bedroom, its maple bunkbed gleaming from the hall light, their old furnace chugging as the temperature fell.

It happened while Charlie was lost in slumber, the dreamy haze of his sleeping pill, flat on his back, hands folded on his chest like a tragic young prince in his burial state.

Exactly two miles away, all the lights off at the studio except the gooseneck lamp on the third floor where Marie was squatting, it happened.

The fire was a big mouth," Marie had said on the phone, her voice dizzy with shock. "A big mouth swallowing everything."

By that point, the firefighters were already there and the sprinkler system spouting old brown water everywhere.

And by the time Dara and Charlie had pulled into the parking lot, there was only smoke left, a great fog from which emerged a baby-faced fireman carrying an old metal space heater, its center mussel-black.

Now, hours later, they stood in the morning mist, the parking lot slowly filling. Charlie's arm around Dara, Marie shuddering under the Pendleton blanket, all three of them soaked from the fire hoses. Charlie on the phone with the insurance company, some humorless agent named Van who kept asking about candles and flat irons, cigarettes and kitchen grease.

It was the space heater, of course. That ancient contraption their father used to drag from room to room when he'd forgotten the heating bill. The one with the coils that ran so lovely red that you wanted to touch them until you did. Their mother had eventually brought it to the studio, keeping it on the third floor, where she liked to take naps and think. The third floor that Marie had now made her own.

"Isn't it cold up there?" Charlie had been asking lately, worried as the nights grew cooler, as fall wore on.

But, Dara supposed, Marie would figure something out. She did, of course. Charlie found her one recent morning sleeping in Studio B, shivering in a sleeping bag, and the Pendleton blanket curled with dust.

That evening, he'd brought down the space heater and planted it beside her.

He told her she was being foolish. Dara heard them through the doorway.

"Who's the fool here," Marie had replied, taking the space heater under her arm.

There had been a coolness between Charlie and Marie ever since she'd left, a distance. It wasn't only with Dara. *She's being silly and stubborn,* Charlie kept insisting. *She should just come home.*

Marie claimed she didn't even remember turning the space heater on. She'd been sleeping when she smelled smoke. The curtains had gone up in a glorious flash, ashes catching across her face.

"But not Dad's blanket," Dara said, curling her fingers around the Pendleton's scratchy wool, pulling it off Marie's shoulders with a hard yank, letting it fall to the ground.

The fire investigators stayed for hours. Marie followed them around the studio, smoking the loose cigarettes she bought from the deli with all the cats on Fourth Street.

"Maybe now is not the time to smoke," Charlie kept saying under his breath.

The investigators told them they were lucky the firefighters had arrived so quickly, containing the blaze mostly to Studio B. They put little flags and big cones on the floor and up the walls. They took photographs and video. They bagged up the space heater, its coils rattling, now harmless as a child's toy.

They gave Marie a lecture about the three-feet rule and frayed cords and sparks.

Dara could tell the investigators didn't like the look of it. Who could?

But Marie merely nodded obediently. Marie, who, their whole childhood, was always knocking over house plants, breaking things, leaving the water running in the claw-foot tub until the ceiling bulged below.

It was so big I was sure they couldn't stop it," Marie said later as they surveyed the damage, the floorboards like wet paper.

"If you wanted them to stop it," Dara asked Marie, "why did you start it?"

"Dara," Charlie said, surprised, "that's not what happened."

But Marie only gazed up at the ceiling sticky with smoke, a shine on her lip like she'd just eaten something very fast, or was about to.

* * *

All around them, all day, were swarms of incoming parents and students, even ones without Sunday classes but who'd heard about the fire, or some, recalling the death of the original Madame Durant and her husband, looking for fresh evidence of some kind of "Durant Curse."

Oh, no and *my god* and *no one's safe* as they snuck peeks into Studio B, its volcanic core.

"We'll get everything back to normal as quickly as possible," Charlie assured them. "We have contractors coming today."

"But, Madame Durant," Bailey Bloom said, echoing what was surely a pervasive fear, "what about *The Nutcracker*? What about Clara?"

"Bailey," Dara said, loud enough so everyone could hear, "have you ever heard of a year without a *Nutcracker*?"

"No, Madame Durant," Bailey said.

"Nothing will change," Marie added, slinking up to them, her hair smelling like smoke. "Nothing changes here."

It reminded Dara of something their mother used to say, *Ballerinas are girls forever*. Nothing ever changes. Ballet is like Eden that way.

ENTER DEREK

He was coming at seven A.M.

There was no time to waste. Despite their assurances to parents, they couldn't afford to lose one of their three studios, not during *Nutcracker* season. Something had to be done to Studio B, streaked black, its floorboards like a soaked sponge.

He was coming at seven, Dara and Charlie arriving early and opening all the windows, the smell of the fire and the fresh mold mingling with the usual smells of sweat and adolescence, of feet and urine and funk.

They'd already had appointments with two other contractors, one of whom was ninety minutes late before staying for ten minutes only to jot down a series of astonishing figures on a Post-it and slap it in Charlie's hand. The other never showed at all, then requested they send him photos of the damage first, making some joke about them needing more space for tutus.

"Third time's a charm, right?" Charlie said nervously, lighting a cigarette in the back office, waving away the telltale smoke.

He was coming, the contractor was on his way. Derek something.

Someone recommended him. Dara couldn't remember at first, but wasn't it Mrs. Bloom? Bailey's mother, more vested than any other parent, given her daughter was this year's Clara and thus was everything.

"She said he's the only honest contractor she's ever worked with," Charlie had said. "Which probably means just honest enough."

All they wanted was someone to repair the blackened floor, to ferret out any mold, to get rid of the soot and the ash that burned in their throats constantly, but first to deliver a fair estimate to their insurance company, to their claims adjuster, a humorless woman named Bambi, who was immune to any charms.

"Mrs. Bloom said he can do anything," Charlie said. "She was extravagant in her praise."

Dara thought about Mrs. Bloom, her crested blazers, her impeccably manicured nails, perfect half-moons, her bountiful donations to the annual *Nutcracker* fund, the care taken over her daughter Bailey's immaculate bun, never a hair loose, not even a slim tendril.

She thought, *He must be good.*

D o I have to be there?" Marie asked, calling down the spiral staircase from the third floor. "I don't think I need to be there."

Charlie made a face to Dara, a face that said, *Maybe she doesn't have to . . .*

"You have to be there," Dara said, standing at the foot of the stairs, Marie's face hovering above. "Because you nearly burned us all down."

T he contractor arrived on time. His name was Derek something, a big man, maybe fifty, fifty-two, with a face and neck tan as a butterscotch candy, in an ill-fitting blazer with chalk marks on both sleeves, belt pulled too tight, giving him the overall look of a former high school athlete gone to seed. On his feet were a pair of natty Chelsea boots caked with mud that he tracked through the studio like a deer hunter.

He held two phones in one outsize hand—a bear paw but fuzzier, Dara thought—and extended the other immediately to Charlie, all the while raking his eyes across Dara and Marie once, then twice, before smiling with hundreds of teeth.

"Nice place, nice place," he said, striding through their mirror-lined space with its pointe-shoe posters and graying walls. Arriving in Studio B, its floor charred, its walls soot-scattered, he looked around and sucked his teeth. The spot where the space heater had sat was a mean scorch Marie kept stroking with one foot.

"It's a damn shame, isn't it?" he said, shaking his head, looking at Marie. "What nature can do."

The fire, brilliant and bright, had gnawed its way through Studio B and the storage room behind it, eating the floor and spitting out kindling shards in its wake. It had mercifully been extinguished before it reached the changing room, where, every day, hundreds of little girls with bobbing buns slipped in and out of downy wool coats and softly fraying leg warmers, rubbing their palms anxiously on puckered leotards and scratchy tights.

They needed it all fixed, Charlie explained to the contractor, they needed it now. They couldn't cancel any more classes, couldn't hang tarps and open windows and hope they weren't giving their pin-thin students, their tender-lunged kindergartners emphysema.

I think it smells nice, Marie had whispered that very morning, and Dara had wanted to smack her.

"I get it," the contractor said, rolling back on his natty heels after he'd walked through the entire studio once, clicking his pen, clicking his tongue. "Short-term, quick fix. You gotta; you're small businesspeople. You want to be fully operational as quickly as possible. I can do that. I can do that for you. But first . . . can I ask you a question?"

"Okay," Charlie said warily.

"Have you ever heard the one about the Phoenix rising from the ashes?"

"Sure."

"Why can't that be you?"

He explained that he could remove and replace the sooted drywall, the blistered floorboards, the burned window casings, the radiator covers now melted to the crumply black of a tin ashtray. He could clean the HVAC system ducts of smoke, have the whole studio smoke-lacquered. These were easy things. Surface solutions.

But, given the ample check sure to come from the insurance company and given his own estimate, which would be fair, of course, but that would obviously point out various concerns (*These old buildings, they're tinderboxes, aren't they?*) . . .

. . . why not think bigger?

Had they thought of expanding? Knock down that wall and get rid of the storage room behind it, make Studio B nearly twice its size. Even raise the ceiling. There were so many possibilities.

"Why sell yourself short?" he said, clicking his pen. "Grab that brass ring."

*M*y, *what a big voice you have,* Dara thought. Big and booming. And the way he stalked their careworn, dust-moted space with his pointy, muddy boots, leaving mud membranes across the soft-beaten floor.

Marie didn't even seem to be paying attention, forever tugging at the cuff of her sweater, fingers tangling in its fray. *Such a child,* Dara thought, *forever a six-year-old girl.*

know it's your job to upsell," Charlie said. "But even with the insurance—"

"You make the money back twice over," the contractor said, spinning around the space on one heel. Squinting at the pocket doors that didn't pull shut and up at the spreading brown stain on the ceiling, the one Marie thought looked like a king rat. *The rat,* she said every snowfall, *is collecting more followers.*

"You have a little inconvenience, but after, you throw a big champagne-busting, get a little notice in the local paper, you got more new customers than you got tutus."

He smiled at all three of them. Dara folded her arms.

He paused a moment, eyes on Dara. Then he began talking again, but this time he looked only at her.

"I'll be honest: What I know about ballet you could fit on the head of a nail. But I do know this: Every little girl loves it. They're all born with it—the same big pink dream. And their mommys have it, too, and will pay big bucks to walk into a place that feels special. That feels, well, magical."

Charlie cleared his throat, sneaking a glance at Dara.

"You're not just businesspeople. You're artists," the contractor continued, eyes still flickering on Dara. "I'm just a guy who works with his hands, but I like to think there's a creativity to what I do. An art, maybe."

Charlie nodded politely. Dara was looking over at Marie, whose eyes were fixed on the ceiling, the king rat stain.

"Bottom line," the contractor continued, "I don't think artists should have a limit—a timeline, a dollar figure—on their dreams. I don't think you should.

"So why not dream bigger?

"I can give you all the things you want."

As he talked, their Studio B—the smallest of the three—seemed even smaller. *Maybe because he's so big*, she told herself, twice as thick as each of them and dwarfing even Charlie. And now that he'd directed their eyes to the ceiling's brown weeping corners, it reminded Dara how, the prior year, the eaves leaked into the studio all winter long.

He knew how to talk. He knew how to flatter, to play the humble service worker, the clumsy male amid a space so . . . *female*, he noted, nodding respectfully at Dara and Marie. Dara, who kept her arms folded across her chest.

Marie, who turned her head away.

Marie, who seemed even quieter than usual, more recessed, head bowed, like an empty bowl.

They ended up in the back office, the strong smell of the cigarettes all three of them snuck there between classes and at day's end, the rickety wooden desk, its blotter studded with errant scorches. Mingling still with the distinctive scent of their mother's Gauloises, *like burning tires on a black night*, she once said. A relief from the contractor's aftershave, like pressing one's face into a bucket of limes.

"This," the contractor said, reaching out, wrapping his hand around the rail of the narrow spiral staircase that snaked up to the third floor, the dormer space. "This should be the first to go."

"No," Dara said immediately. "Absolutely not."

He looked at her, and then at the staircase—iron, spiky, relentless.

Dara could feel Marie watching her intently.

"We'll get you a new one," he said. "With a warm wood, real nice. Smooth on your feet, smooth like a baby's bottom."

"No," Dara repeated. "That stays."

Charlie cleared his throat, shifting his feet uncomfortably.

"It's unsafe," the contractor said, sliding his finger along the slender rail, the pad of his index finger landing in the sunken dent that had been there a decade, more. "And busted."

He gave it a hard tug, the railing rattling in his hands.

A gasp—quick and high—escaped from Marie's mouth. Marie, who had not said a single word since the contractor arrived.

And one more tug, as if he might tear the whole staircase loose like a fairy-tale monster.

"The staircase stays," Dara said.

It was the only time she saw his mask drop, the contractor. That little slash of something—overreach? Irritation? Anger?—stamping his brow.

It was there, then it was gone, the smile returning. The big teeth.

D ara excused herself. Said she needed to take a call.

Walking to the lobby, she felt her breath catching, but she didn't know why.

Their mother loved that spiral staircase. Their mother said it was *cosmopolitan. Bohemian. Recherché.*

Their mother, that swan neck, those elegant arms. Her dark hair gathered up tightly with her grandmother's dragonfly combs. So dignified, so refined, carrying so much inside all the time. Surrounded all day by mirrors and never letting anyone see.

W hen she returned to the office, the contractor was writing something on a pad of paper, looming over slight Marie and slender Charlie as they waited, two pale figurines, cut like glass.

"I got a tight, lean crew that works like beasts," he was saying as he wrote. "Sweetheart deals with the best suppliers. They trust me. Your insurance company trusts me. Your claims adjuster, Bambi, we go way back."

"That's fine, but—" Charlie started.

"You can go cheap and easy," he said, slapping the paper into Charlie's hand. "Or you can transform your little school into that ballet palace you always wanted. Make every little girl's fantasy come true."

S uddenly, he had to go, he was in a hurry. His phones were ringing, his beeper. He shook his head like, *What can I do, so popular, everyone wants me.*

"We'll let you know," Charlie said, walking him out. "But it sounds like more than we have in mind."

Halfway out the door, the contractor stopped, hand on the jamb, one last aftershave gust.

"So," he said, grinning, eyes dragging across all three of them, "who decides?"

"We're partners," Dara said. "We make decisions as a—"

"I do," Marie said, her voice low but insistent. "I decide."

Derek looked at her and laughed.

Then Charlie laughed, too, the hollow, soundless laugh he used when mothers asked if he could help them correct their posture. Dara didn't laugh. Marie didn't laugh either.

"I thought so," Derek said to Marie, grinning, opening the door, his eyes now only on her. "I thought you were the one."

So you're the big boss now," Dara said after, her lip curled, both of them smoking feverishly, the visit feeling so big, "Princess Marie?"

"I wanted him to look at me," Marie said.

Dara looked at her.

"The Big Bad Wolf," Marie said, her cigarette shaking slightly in her hand.

Dara shook her head. "Well, it's all over now."

"Yes," Marie said, flicking tobacco from her trembling thumb. Taking another long drag. Smoking for dear life.

He was gone more than an hour before Dara felt her shoulders relax, her arms hanging lamely at her sides.

Strangers were in and out of the studio all the time, new parents, servicemen, the mail carrier. But this felt different, invasive. *You show some-one your damage and they know all your weak spots. They know everything.*

For the next hour, Dara dragged a mop and bucket and she scrubbed all the floors, every place he'd stepped, the gray sludge his shoes left behind.

T hat night, at home, the itchy feeling in her palms she'd felt all day was finally gone.

Taking the kettle off the stove, she poured Charlie a cup of white tea. She sat down and put her feet, thick and throbbing, in his lap and he rubbed them delicately.

Everything was right again. Dara hadn't even bothered to look at the estimate the contractor had left them, a sheet of paper torn from a spiral notebook like a schoolboy.

"I'll get some more contractor recommendations," Charlie said. "I'll find us someone good who can just do the job we asked for."

"I know you will," Dara said. Charlie always fixed everything.

"Unless you think maybe . . ." Charlie said, glancing at the estimate on the table.

Dara felt a stab in the arch of her foot, a nerve firing.

"It's just," Charlie started, "he had some good ideas. Things we've been talking about for years. More space. A real expansion. Room to breathe."

Dara didn't say anything, pulling her feet away swiftly, drawing them close.

"Maybe this is what we've been waiting for," Charlie said. "Maybe the fire wasn't such a bad thing. We rise from the ashes."

Dara wrapped her hands around her feet and squeezed them until they hurt.

"Maybe it's a mistake," Charlie continued, "to always play it safe."

HOTHOUSE

It wasn't like they hadn't considered renovating, expanding before, Dara thought in bed that night, her hand on Charlie's back, smooth as an ivory tusk. Smooth and cool and pure.

"Just think about it," Charlie murmured. "See how it feels."

Designed to accommodate sixty or seventy students, the school now served twice that. And there were always new competitors—two new competition dance schools in the past year alone, splashy and mercenary, crowded with aspirants, sparkled, sprayed, and glued together like party dolls, offering up a promise of YouTube stardom and hot, fleeting fame.

You had to compete with that. And you were competing with what some considered a dying art. The misty pink hothouse of ballet.

And did you stand a chance when your space was cramped with only three studios and a floor in Studio B that, even before the fire, was pocked with age, warped with spring-thaw leaks? Maybe, while they were already making repairs, it was time to pull it up, to put in a new sprung floor with layers of wood and padding to absorb shock and enhance performance. To patch up the ice-dam damage, the king rat stain on the ceiling before winter arrived.

And there was Charlie. Dara and Marie spent their days turning out the knees, pointing the feet, bending the backs, pushing in the pert bottoms of endless little girls. To them, any business matter was a blur in the background. Charlie, however, could see the big picture.

And Charlie, after all, needed something. Something other than bookkeeping, designing little display ads for the local paper, soothing anxious parents, seeing his doctors—all his doctors—about his half-broken body. That magnificent, blinding marble thing that had, slowly and then all at once, cracked.

"It could be just what we need," Charlie said. "What your mother would have wanted."

Slowly, Dara felt the certainty rising in her chest, like a sharp stone her lungs brushed up against with every breath.

Maybe Charlie was right. Maybe their mother—who'd put twenty years of toil and affliction into their cramped, sweaty, stenchy place, ripe as the hollow of a dancer's pointed foot—would want this.

Marie will be hard to convince," Dara said. Marie didn't like disruption or change or intruders from *out there*. None of the Durants did. Dara could only remember a handful of occasions—a meter reader once, an animal control officer that time a raccoon got caught in the screen door—when anyone outside of their family set foot inside their house their entire childhood.

Still, Charlie pointed out, Marie was the one who had in fact moved out of the house, taken a leap.

But, Dara replied, look how far she got.

* * *

Charlie kept asking Dara and Dara kept saying it was best not to pressure Marie, which Charlie should know by now.

Marie didn't like to think about things. Business decisions, all decisions, hung like a weight around her neck.

Marie didn't like to sign papers, to put her name on things, to have too many keys.

Marie, who had so few attachments, obligations, connections that sometimes she felt like she was going to float away, ascend. But Dara could never tell if this was what she wanted, or her greatest fear.

Marie, who'd slept in their childhood bunkbed for years, only moving down the hall to the sewing room when she began having back pain from the slender mattress. She still said she didn't know what to do in a full-size bed. She said she felt lost.

I'm the one who has to live with it," Marie said, later that day.

Dara was watching Marie at the barre, stretching, her skin ruddy with heat.

"We'll all be living with it," Dara said. "We'll have to rearrange our whole schedule around it. We might have to rent space at the Y to cover classes."

The parents wouldn't like it, and the younger girls—the five-, six-, seven-year-olds Marie taught—would use it as an opportunity for laziness, every disruption an excuse to giggle and play rather than practice.

"So then," Marie said, "why do it?"

Marie watched herself in the mirror. Her body pulling itself into long, stretchy pieces of taffy. *Not very elegant, Marie,* Dara thought.

"Don't you want more space," Dara said. "Isn't that why you moved here to begin with."

Neither of them were questions exactly.

"Maybe this way," Dara said, staring at Marie, bent over at the waist now, the whiteness near her scalp, so white against the ruby face, "we can avoid any more fires."

Marie didn't say anything. What could she say?

Later, Dara was tidying the changing room, collecting abandoned sweaters, twirls of toe tape, curls of elastic ribbon, scruffs of lamb's wool popped loose from pointe shoes.

She could hear Charlie talking to Marie in the back office.

"It's time," Charlie was saying.

"Is it," Marie said.

There was a pause, Dara leaning closer, trying to hear.

"It's time for something," Charlie said finally. "We need something."

In the middle of the day, their claims adjuster, Bambi, a petite, solidly built woman of indeterminate middle age, arrived to review the damage.

She moved quickly, taking pictures with her phone.

"Have you hired someone yet?" she asked Charlie.

"No," he said, but then he mentioned Derek and that maybe the adjuster knew him.

"Sure," Bambi said, blinking. "I'm surprised you can get him. He's in high demand."

"Really?" Charlie said.

"He must've liked you," Bambi said, handing Charlie her card as she began to leave. "He must've seen something he liked."

That evening, Dara stayed late with a few students, including her Clara and her Nutcracker Prince, Bailey Bloom and Corbin Lesterio, both of whom wanted extra practice.

But even with all the windows open, one by one, they started coughing, Bailey's peashoot body shaking from it.

The smoke was gone from the air, but it had tunneled in deep, sunk itself into the wood, the drywall. Corbin's big dark eyes blurred with tears. The fire was gone, but it wasn't.

It made Dara think about a story their mother told them once. About the famous ballerina in the nineteenth century, a gas lamp catching on her skirt, enveloping her in flames before the entire audience's eyes. How she spun and spun, the blaze consuming her until she was rescued.

She lingered a few months after, her corset melted to her ribs.

The surviving scraps of her costume still hung in the Musée de l'Opéra in Paris.

That, their mother told them, *is love*.

The following morning, Dara and Charlie arrived to find Marie sitting on the floor of Studio B, her face sweaty, her long neck and chest glistening, her legs tangled up.

Spread around her were the proposed plans. The design layout, the sketches, Derek's scribbled estimate, his slashing hand, the frill of the schoolbook paper.

She was still catching her breath, palm pressed on the papers.

"Marie," Charlie said, "what say you?"

She looked up, bewildered somehow, as if they had appeared suddenly from inside her own head, her own dream. She turned her face up, staring up at the skylight, and whispered something softly.

"Yes, Your Highness?" Dara asked, looking down at her sister.

"I say it's time," Marie said softly, tapping her toe once on the scuffed floor. Dara nodded and Marie lifted her head, her face pink and decisive. "It's past time."

There was a toast with champagne—the bubbly pink kind from the corner store, in paper cups with blue flowers—and cigarettes on the fire escape. Those pink sugared biscuits their mother ordered in bulk from France and stockpiled in the pantry, these at least a decade old.

Charlie kissed them both on their cheeks, his lips cool and lovely.

Dara watched Marie enjoying her bubbles, her moment. It was infuriating. Why had she given Marie such power? Marie wasn't a full partner anyway. Marie was squatting here, a non-residential space not fit for living. But was Marie living at all, or merely burrowing in?

Marie, that foxlike face of hers, running her tongue along the waxy rim of her cup.

When Charlie went inside to get fresh matches, Dara said, "What are you so happy about?"

Marie looked at her a moment, then leaned closer, her lips smelling like Dixie-cup wax.

"Just remember," she whispered, a quiver in her voice, "you're the one who invited him in."

The next morning, when Dara and Charlie arrived at the studio at seven thirty, Derek the contractor was already there, standing in the middle of Studio B, legs astride like the figure on the cover of their mother's copy of *The Fountainhead*.

In the corner, Marie stood, watching. Watching as Derek gave instructions to his crew: two young men with heavy tool belts and tape measures, one with drop cloths looped around his arm, his arm braided with muscles.

Dara squinted. Something was different about Marie.

And then Marie turned and she saw it. Marie's forever-pale mouth was painted fire engine red. Like a warning, a five-alarm.

Dara pictured Marie strolling to the drugstore late the night before, or early that morning, trying on lipsticks under the fluorescent, fly-specked lights.

"Good morning," Charlie said, nudging Dara forward, moving to shake hands with Derek. "Looks like things have already started."

A HAMMER OVER MY HEART

I t was fast, so fast. Faster than the fire even.

They were watching the walls come down.

Dara and Marie wore the safety goggles and dust masks he handed them, though Derek himself went barefaced. They stood at the spot on the floor he dictated, a safe distance.

The two workers, Benny and Gaspar, watched too. Stood back and observed. Benny, lithe and goateed, and Gaspar, thick and sinewy, saying things to each other in Portuguese under their breath.

Derek lifted a long-frame hammer from the floor.

"It only hurts the first time," he said, winking at Dara and Marie.

Like a caveman and his club, he began swinging the hammer, punching starter holes into the wall.

Punching again, nearly bursting through his shirt, wiggling the drywall back and forth.

The holes looked like dark pinwheels. Looked like bruises.

Marie covered her ears with the heels of her hands.

Next came the saw. The one with the long blade—how he hoisted it up high, making a long vertical cut from the ceiling down, down, down, splitting the wall. Tearing the bisected panel with his big catcher's mitt hands.

It was as if, somehow, the saw were sinking down her own spine, Dara thought. That was how it felt.

Beside her, Marie was breathing so hard, her dust mask puffing up, then disappearing into her mouth.

Next came the crowbar, prying the baseboards and trim free, great splintering sounds that made you want to scream. Made Dara want to scream.

Knocking the studs free, the veins in his arms straining.

The long hammer back, its claw tearing a monstrous hole, his hands plunging inside, ripping, rending. Tearing again, tearing everything. Everything. Until there was nothing left.

Until Derek set down the hammer to answer his phone—one of his phones—disappearing into the stairwell, shaking the dust from his hair.

Dara looked where the wall had been moments before, now only an ugly seam on the ground, the subfloor thick with sawdust sneaking through.

Her safety goggles fogging, Dara thought for a second she might cry. *What is wrong with me?* she thought. *What is wrong?*

"Is it over?" Dara asked, clawing the goggles from her face.

But Marie wasn't listening, tearing off her dust mask as if suffocating. She was looking at the hammer, leaning against the wall now. "It's still hot," she said, her fingers on its rubber handle. "It's still hot."

That afternoon, as the students began to arrive, Dara distracted herself from everything going on in Studio B, the huffs of debris, the makeshift tarp path taped to the molding floors so one could pass through.

She tried not to think about the wall, the wreckage. The dust on her eyelashes, the smell of rot at the center of their beloved space. Second to their home, the most beloved space.

"It's the right thing," Charlie assured her. He'd spent the morning filling out insurance paperwork. There was a lot of paperwork and Derek seemed to keep giving them more.

"I know," Dara said. Besides, there was no time for sentiment. Her three o'clock students were arriving, Level III boys, the soft slap of their canvas shoes against the floor in the dressing room, faces blazing from the cold, earnest and anxious footsteps pad-padding to the barre, side glances at Dara, enthralled by Dara.

I t wasn't long before she lost herself in the churn of the day. In her first class, the boys in their black tights and white tees, straining. She devoted so much more of herself to the boys. After Charlie couldn't teach anymore, she'd taken over them and found she liked it. They were always so intently focused—they had to be—the boys. They faced so much social dismissal. It gave them a special intensity, especially Malik, Tony, and, of course, her Nutcracker Prince Corbin, thoughtful and quiet, their voices softly breaking, their faces faintly dotted with acne, their chests like ship prows yet waists so dainty, like prim bows.

M ore than once, the floor shook with a rumbling from Studio B. Some kind of enormous drill or maybe a pneumatic device thundering through the walls.

The boys pretended not to notice, focused on their *grands battements* at the barre.

But it was impossible not to notice and Dara, pacing, counting off, felt each pulse from the machine ripple up her spine.

After, she peered into Studio B, a cloud of smoke and Derek the contractor covered in soft gray powder, wiping his brow, drinking heartily from a tumbler of some kind.

* * *

The day skittered along, the crushes of girls bolting into the changing room, unwinding scarves, kicking off boots, tearing off coats, yanking down jeans, stripping down to sameness, lining up in their identical black leotards, pink tights, tight buns knotted atop their worried faces.

Dara led the advanced students in their mother's beloved Studio C while Marie taught her little darlings in the cramped but serviceable Studio A.

Meanwhile, in Studio B, the carnage took hold. Dust, debris, ash, grit, thunder, fury. The slick-slack of tape, the hard thunk of nail guns, the grinding rage of the drill, the tinny drone of box fans. The younger girls couldn't concentrate, the six-year-olds slapping their chubby palms over their ears. But the older ones continued to pretend to be untouched by any of it, their devotion to the dance far greater than any squalid disruption.

As the day closed, Marie, mysteriously in high spirits, gave all the students an unplanned lesson in swordplay, showing her Level IIs how to handle the cardboard foils for the Mouse King battle. Marie, her sweater a swirl on the floor, wearing a filmy white leotard Dara had never seen before.

Soon enough, Dara's students, changing to leave, were drawn in, too, watching Marie play the Sword Swallower, lifting the sword above her head and then taking it into her mouth.

She wants everyone to see, Dara thought, and she thought she even spotted Derek lingering by the doorway, watching as Marie sank one, two, three cardboard foils into her mouth, head thrown back, her throat like a pale lily.

At the end of the day, Dara hurried to the back office to find Charlie, wanting, so badly, to go home.

But Charlie wasn't alone. Seated at his desk, he was signing something, a coffee-stained contract. And, looming over him, was Derek, his shoulders hunched, cologne swirling, his hair powdered with soot.

"Hello," Dara said, stopping short.

"Got a lot done today," Derek said, grinning, tugging his damp shirt from his chest, the fleshy chest of one of those old-time wrestlers, beefy and staggering around the ring.

Beside him, Charlie looked so small and wan, a wilting petal.

"I think that's it," Charlie said, handing over the sheaf of papers.

Derek began looking them over. "So you own the building?"

"We do," Dara said, walking in, Derek's eyes lifting to her. "It's been good for us. Plenty of space. Close to home."

"You live on Sycamore?" he said, eyes still on the papers.

"Yes," Charlie said. "That cul-de-sac behind the old train tracks."

"I know that street," Derek said, looking up, eyes newly bright. "Big old houses. Red brick, gables, low stoops. Built in the twenties for the white-collar types working at the mill. Until the neighborhood turned."

"Well, it's different now," Dara said, bristling at the word *turned*, remembering when they were the only ones on their street who didn't have a car on blocks in the front yard.

"It sure is," Derek said. "I worked deconstruction over there once, years ago."

"Deconstruction?"

"I was just a kid, dumb but big. Our job was working those abandoned houses over on Van Buren, strip 'em one by one for parts. Leaded glass, copper piping, mantelpieces. Once we found a human leg. Just the knee down. We left that there. R.I.P."

Derek looked at Dara like he was waiting for her to laugh. She didn't.

"Boss taught us all kinds of things. How to pry loose a perfect piece of old-growth pine without splitting it. *Like unhooking your mother's bra,* boss used to say. Then we'd get out the backhoe and take the whole house down."

The office felt far too small with him in there. Dara stepped toward the window, open a crack. The way he'd looked at her when he said *unhooking your mother's bra*.

"After," he continued, "we'd take the remaining rubble and fill the basement with it. Choke the whole thing up. Drop some dirt down, some seed. Go by a month later, there's a little grass growing there. It's like prairie. Like the house was never there at all."

Dara didn't say anything. Her eyes were on the spiral staircase behind him. He was leaning against it. It was like the other day, his hand on its railing, the way he'd yanked it, the feeling she had like he might yank one more time and bring everything down.

"Kinda sounds like you were a vulture," Charlie said, reaching for his coat. "Licking the bones of the dead."

Derek smiled, showing all his teeth. "Except we didn't lick them. We sold them."

Dara stayed late, arranging a ride home for Bailey Bloom, whose mother failed to appear at pickup.

"I guess she forgot," Bailey said, her brow pinched. "My dad can come. Or something."

When Mrs. Bloom finally answered her phone, she sounded frazzled, teary.

"I'm so sorry, Madame Durant. Is it just you two left there?"

"Yes. But—"

"I'm on my way. Please forgive me. I thought her father . . . well, I'm sorry."

Dara assured her it was not a problem. At least not yet. It was the first week of *Nutcracker* season. The hand-wringing, tears, drama, had only just begun.

She's always been an odd one," Charlie reminded Dara later. "Remember last year? The hair?"

Then Dara did remember. For a few weeks, Mrs. Bloom had gone from a sleek brunette to an icy, near platinum blonde. How embarrassed she seemed, her locks pulled back tightly, slicked with spray to hide their brightness.

The girl at the salon had talked her into it, she swore.

It reminded Dara of something their mother, whose hair fell nearly to her waist, always said: *Never let anyone under thirty touch your hair.*

The worst part is the name, Mrs. Bloom had confided to Dara, blushing and tucking phantom wisps into her chignon.

Hot Buttered Blonde, she whispered, blushing again.

As she was leaving, Dara spotted Marie lingering in the darkened Studio B, creeping along the tarp, her bony feet coated in dust.

She watched as her sister knelt down and ran her finger along the snaky seam where the wall had stood, the one the contractor had torn through, like a sideshow dare.

"Boo," Dara said, sneaking behind her.

Marie looked up, her face aflame, that morning's lipstick on her teeth.

I think Marie's got a crush," Charlie said that night. "On the contractor."

"What do you mean?" Dara asked, shaking loose Charlie's vitamins and herbal remedies, setting out his daily allotment.

Charlie shrugged. "Just the way she looks at him."

"That's impossible," Dara said. Marie was a person who kept to herself. After a few semi-tragic romances with fellow dancers in her early twenties, after a prolonged fixation on a married cellist of some note who passed through town a few times a year and dallied with her heart, Marie was a lone wolf.

"Marie's bored," Dara said. "Or something."

"Marie," Charlie said softly, "is lonely."

Dara looked up from the pile of pills and said nothing.

THE PINK

Within a few days, it was quieter, the initial demolition past and the air heavy with new smells, sulfurous plaster, chalky dry wall, the tang of mildew.

Dara was sure the parents would protest, but there were few complaints. They were too consumed with *The Nutcracker*, when they would receive the rehearsal schedule, whether or not last year's sound system issues would be resolved, and *isn't it time to replace the mouse heads? That glue is definitely toxic.*

She smoked restlessly between classes and marveled at Marie, who seemed to be unaffected, leading her four-year-olds through hops and jumps. The endless plonk-plonk of the piano and Marie's faint, high voice, *arms up, fingers, fingers to the sky.*

"He'll move fast," Charlie kept saying. "He's in high demand."

But Dara didn't see how that was possible based on the state of Studio B, which resembled the scooped-clean inside of a volcano.

"I promise," Charlie said.

The plonk-plonk and Marie flitting from corner to corner with her little girls, and not noticing the clouds of dust wafting in, or the occasional trills of the drill, the sharp punch of the hammer.

And poor Bailey Bloom, her eyelids covered with dust, approaching them. "My mom can't come here anymore," she said dolefully, which was how she said everything. "Construction makes her sick."

"Well," Charlie said, "she can start coming again when rehearsals start at the Ballenger."

"Everything will be better then," Dara said. "Everything."

You wanted this," Charlie reminded her later. "It's only been a few days."

"You wanted this," Dara reminded him. "And then we all did."

Maybe it was because he was always there, the contractor. And you always knew it, whether he was shouting instructions to Benny and Gaspar ("Get that hot mud, it shapes up nice and quick") or enmeshed in one of his long phone calls conducted as he sat on the open windowsill or paced the entrance area ("So I told her, put it in an envelope if it looks that good . . ."), his wheezing laugh echoing through every studio.

And then the meal times, delivery boys streaming in and out, their faces red from the chill, delivering greasy breakfast sandwiches, submarines for lunch, the mid-afternoon pizza whose oily smell made all the students sick with disgust and longing.

The students staring with such yearning, half of them subsisting on strange diets Dara did not support—lettuce leaves with hot sauce, cotton balls coated with ranch.

There was no time for distractions. The growing *Nutcracker* pressures, the urgency on the students' faces—it was consuming, and Dara could hear their mother's voice in her head. *Never forget, ma chère, each year is someone's first* Nutcracker. Then adding, *If you can give them that, you have them for life.*

Dara knew it was true. She still remembered every exquisite detail of her first year dancing in it, four years old, playing one of the Kingdom of Sweets Polichinelles, the dozen little clowns who pop loose—*surprise!*—from under Mother Ginger's giant hoop skirt to the audience's delighted gasps.

How, for so long, it seemed—though it was surely less than a minute—she scurried blindly beneath Mother's hoops, crinolines hot against her face, hidden from the audience but feeling their presence, their anticipation.

How she could barely breathe, how she couldn't wait to burst out, leaping forward and bounding across the stage, drunk from the escape, and, somehow, from that captivity.

I t just breaks my heart," Mr. Lesterio said, furrowing his brow.

Dara hadn't even noticed him standing in the doorway. She'd been lost in concentration, watching his son Corbin, feet like sparrow wings, as he practiced his *pas de chat*, his knees apart, legs high.

"The guys on the soccer team found out," Mr. Lesterio said discreetly. "They call him Dancing Queen. That's the nicest thing they call him."

"He really shouldn't be playing soccer," Dara said. "He's our Nutcracker Prince. He could injure himself."

Mr. Lesterio shook his head, curling his hands around his coffee thermos. It wasn't the response he'd expected. Dara thought about what Charlie always said, about softening her tone with the parents. Their mother never had, she'd remind him.

"Ms. Durant, you have to understand," Mr. Lesterio was saying as Corbin, distracted, was watching them both now, stuttering through his glissade. "I lettered in four sports and spent two years in the U.S. Army Reserve."

"If he were injured in a game," Dara said, "you'd never forgive yourself."

You must be firm, their mother always said about parents, *or they will dominate you.*

Mr. Lesterio didn't say anything for a moment.

They both looked as Corbin landed, sweeping his hair from his eyes as a pink frill of girls in the back of the room snuck glances, whispering behind their hands.

"It embarrasses him," Mr. Lesterio said, nearly under his breath. "Being looked at like that."

"He wouldn't be dancing if he didn't want to be looked at," Dara said.

But of course Corbin—his fine features and frame, the way he moved—would have been noticed anywhere, under any circumstances. Those things, however, fathers were blind to.

"Every day," Mr. Lesterio said, cradling the thermos now, holding it close to his chest, "I expect him to come home and say, *I can't take the pink anymore.*"

Dara looked at him. "Don't count on it."

You showed him," someone said, low and intimate.

Dara, standing at the barre, looked in the mirror and there was Derek the contractor, emerging from Studio B, running his hand through his dark scrubby hair.

"*I can't take the pink anymore,*" Derek said, imitating Mr. Lesterio's gruff tone, his squeamishness. "Get a load of that."

"Can I help you with something?" Dara said. His ingratiation worse, somehow, than his thoughtlessness, his careless swings with his drill, his sledgehammer.

"Your John Hancock," he said, handing her a sheaf of papers. Their construction contract, barely more than a computer template, something called "Contractor Services," its corners bent, a copy of a copy.

"I thought we were done with the paperwork," Dara said.

"Bureaucrats," Derek said. An answer that wasn't an answer.

"I'll show these to my husband," Dara said. "He handles the administration."

Derek nodded and tipped his head. He did a funny little backward dance like a courtier bidding adieu to the queen.

Dara turned, heading toward the back office, away from his aftershave smog and the bigness of him.

But she could still see him in the mirror. Derek, tilting his head knowingly, and saying something to her in a voice so low and tawdry, she'd wonder later if she'd misheard.

"Me," Derek said. "I like the pink."

He didn't belong in her studio, in Studio C, which was hers.

Why was he even here at all when Benny and Gaspar were doing all the work, the spectacle of the wall-demolishing now past. And yet a dozen times a day, he seemed to find an excuse to saunter through every room, clipboard clasped, his too-tight dress shirts, his dual phones, his throbbing beeper.

I think you should tell him," Dara told Charlie later, "there should be some kind of divider. A barrier between Studio B and our studios. To protect the students."

Charlie looked at her.

"A few of the parents have mentioned it," Dara said. A white lie, she told herself. They were sure to complain soon. And didn't Mrs. Bloom's refusal to set foot inside count?

"I'll say something to Derek," Charlie said. "I'll take care of it."

In the back office, Dara sat at the desk, going through the invoices impaled on the metal bill holder. Three hundred pounds of artificial snow for *The Nutcracker*, wigmaster services, two replacement toy soldier uniforms, four replacement mouse heads.

"Were you talking to him earlier?"

Dara looked up. It was Marie, skin pink with heat, that white leotard now sweated through, translucent. You could see everything.

"To Derek. What were you talking about?" Marie said. "Tell me."

Dara raised an eyebrow, a gesture inherited from their mother.

"Nothing," she said, setting down the bill holder. "It was nothing." There was a sneaking pleasure in this, a flash of jealousy from her sister.

Marie paused, touching her neck with an open hand.

"I could never talk to him," she whispered.

Dara looked at her. "That's ridiculous."

"When he comes near me," Marie said, her neck instantly red, "I can't breathe."

THE CURTAIN

The next morning, Dara woke up with a thought of Marie, that perennial swirl of her fine hair caught in the drain of their mother's old claw-foot tub.

Marie never let you forget she was there, even when she wasn't. Even when she didn't live there anymore.

Marie, who'd wasted an hour or more on that cardboard sword stunt the other day, making such a spectacle of herself. In that obscenely sheer leotard, feigning the Sword Swallower, plunging the foils into her mouth as the contractor watched.

When he comes near me, I can't breathe.

It didn't make sense. Marie liked softness, gentleness, refinement in men. The ones she'd dallied with in her twenties, tousle-haired golden boys who played guitar for her and padded around her studio in bare feet so as not to scuff the maple floor. The studio dads with the wool blazers and the smooth hands who thanked her so very much for the elegance and refinement she'd given their daughters.

These were the men Marie liked.

* * *

I can't feel," Charlie said, leaning over at the kitchen table.

Dara looked down at his feet, long and marbled. Six years after he'd been forced to stop, his feet were still dancer's feet. Hard and gnarled and hoof-like. But not half as mangled as hers, ugly like a crow's, or Marie's, which their father used to call *the boomerangs*.

Jolie-laide, their mother always insisted. To her, all dancers' feet were beautiful, beautiful not in spite of but because of their hardness, their contortions, their battle against nature, against the body itself. *What could be more beautiful,* she used to say, *than a will like that?*

Kneeling down, Dara wrapped her hand around one of Charlie's feet. It felt like the bedpost on her parents' bed.

"Can you feel this?" she asked Charlie, gently squeezing his arch. After the last surgery, he was supposed to get sensation back. They always said he'd get sensation back.

"I can't feel anything," he said, looking down at her, at Dara on her knees before him.

All day, there were thunderous tremors from Studio B, leaving a haze of debris, the smell of mold, mice. The silt from decades of young girls: stray earring studs, hair elastics, dusted ribbons, Band-Aids curled with browned blood.

Charlie holed up in the back office with heating pads and ibuprofen; Dara had to manage alone. Would have to explain the way the floors shook to parents. To instruct the girls not to be distracted by the tiny earthquakes under their feet.

You gotta watch that. Believe me, I know."

It was Derek's smoke-thick voice. She could hear it the minute the last of the fourteen-year-olds filed out of class and the strains of *Giselle* ceased.

She followed his voice through the sooty brume of Studio B, past Benny and Gaspar, their faces covered by safety masks so large and thick that Dara wondered what she and her little students were inhaling every day.

"This is the sweet stuff," Derek was saying. "Sweet as mom's milk. Well, not as sweet as my mom's, but she was neighborhood tops."

The laugh—the cartoonish *har-dee-har-har*—making Dara's teeth grind as she opened the office door to see Derek and Charlie.

Derek inexplicably lifting Charlie's shirt up, examining him under the desk lamp. On the felt blotter were two pill bottles, penny-orange.

"You gotta get 'em to hit this spot," he said, his Hawaiian Tropic hands splayed on Charlie's blue-white back. "They put the needles right here. But in the meantime, try those pills."

"Dara," Charlie said, eyes wide with surprise. *This,* she thought, *is what it would feel like to catch him at something.* It was a funny kind of feeling.

"Comparing war wounds," Derek said, spotting Dara.

"So you're a doctor too," Dara said, picking up one of the pill bottles. "I guess you fix everything."

"Dr. Feelgood," Derek said, smiling as ever while Charlie tugged his shirt down. "Old rotator cuff tear, high school football. Used to have nerve pain so bad I'd get tears in my eyes. My ex knew some tricks." He stretched his shoulder, his shirt straining. So big in their small office, the wingspan of an eagle or vulture. "I try to spread the wealth. Just for friends."

Dara handed him back the pill bottles, watched him closing his palm over them, the big lion's paw. His hands, in that brief brushing of hers against his, felt like the bottom of those pointe shoes after sixty strokes with her X-acto.

Dara adding, finally, "We don't have friends."

Charlie's body was a glorious wreck—his jumper's knee, the rotator cuff tendonitis, the hip arthritis from overuse, and most of all his spine, which had never been the same since the surgeries. Since they put his spine back together with wires, plates, screws.

They didn't even know when he'd done it, but it could have happened at any performance, any rehearsal. They wouldn't have believed it if the X-rays hadn't been right before them like that old Lite-Brite game their father picked up for them at a garage sale once.

They called it a hangman's fracture because of the way your neck snapped back.

It started with a broken bone—C2, a neck bone second from the skull, a bad one to break. Typically, it was the result of a very bad fall, or a very bad car crash.

Charlie wasn't even certain how it happened. It could have been any number of falls, collisions, a dancer aloft in his arms crashing down into him. That was how it was for a dancer.

When he himself was a boy, the doctor told them, his best friend sustained a hangman's fracture his very first time at the high dive.

What a thing, he told them. *What a thing.*

The problems started with the broken bone, but it affected everything else. Nerve damage doesn't discriminate. Sensation tentative. Arousal too. Everything was connected, you see. All the parts—each so delicate— forming a precarious whole.

You don't know anything about his injuries," Dara told Derek later, finding him in the stairwell, texting with one hand, other hand on a tilting cup of takeout coffee.

"True," he said, finishing his text before looking up. "But I know about pain. You don't work long in my business without your fair share of that."

"You should never touch a dancer's body."

He lifted his eyebrows. "Only dancers get to touch dancers, that how it works?"

He gave her a look full of meaning, a meaning she couldn't grasp.

"Pain is different for us," Dara said. The pain threshold of ballet dancers was three times greater than that of anyone else. That was what their mother always said, told her pupils, told them. Three times greater, maybe four. Maybe ten.

"I guess you know a lot about it," Derek said, putting his phone in his pocket as if the conversation interested him at last. "Pain. I guess you come to like it."

"No," Dara said, her face warm, the stairwell starting to fill with incoming students. "We just make it our friend."

"So," he said, as if catching her in something, "you have a friend, after all." Students were passing, but he tried to hold her gaze, to catch it at all.

She would not give it to him but couldn't seem to make herself move. Couldn't seem to draw her face into a scowl, a dismissal. Couldn't seem to, maybe, breathe.

Hearing a creak, she turned. Looking up the stairwell, she saw a shadow she knew was Marie.

When he comes near me, I can't breathe.

All afternoon, the hammer-slapping, the slow drone of a hundred machines next door, Dara puzzled over it. Over Marie.

Though she herself had lost her breath with him, it was different. It was because he'd overstepped his boundaries. But to be so . . . taken with that man. That backslapper, glad-hander, noisemaker with his white teeth, like the dusty mints they used to have at nice restaurants? That smell beneath the aftershave, like crushed cigarettes and Speed Stick. The telltale white spots of a tanning booth rash, the furry forearms of a primate.

But then she remembered the way Marie looked at him, so shy, recessed even, as if his presence, the expanse of him, was overwhelming. His big, aging footballer shoulders, that heavy cologne, his stomping feet and his constant jiggling of the keys in his pocket. A lumberjack who could take down a wall, could crack anything in half with his bare hands.

They were all strong. Dara, Charlie, Marie. Everyone there was strong. Charlie, in his heyday, could lift dancers above his head as if they were mere butterflies, fluttering between his hands.

Still, looking at the contractor, Dara felt certain he could snap her in two like a wishbone.

It made her pause. It made her need to sit down a moment.

The next morning, Dara brought it up to Marie again. It had been bothering her.

"He's not attractive," Dara said.

Marie didn't say anything.

They were sitting on the floor of Studio A, Dara helping Marie rub ointment on her legs, vibrating with old nerve pain.

"He's really not," Dara continued, pushing her thumbs into her sister's narrow thighs. Pushing as hard as she could. It was the only way it worked.

"Maybe," Marie said, "we have different ideas about attractive."

Later, Dara spotted Marie contemplating Derek's work boots, abandoned on the tarp when he disappeared for a two-hour lunch, swapped for his fancy bit loafers, shined to butterscotch. The boots were big, like Herman Munster shoes. Brown and mottled like a baked potato. Speckled with milky paint, or chemicals, thick orange laces snaking up the center.

They were so big, like another person in the room. Like a man in the room, demanding to be noticed. Assuming he would be.

Marie's eyes stayed on them as she walked slowly around the tarp, as if circling.

They'd feel hard and crusty beneath your fingers, Dara knew that.

It looked like Marie wanted to touch them, badly, but they were too big for her small hands.

You always," Dara said later, when they were hunting among the lobby chairs, searching for Brielle Katz's lost muffler, "found Charlie handsome. You said he looked like the groom on the top of the wedding cake."

"I did," Marie said, reaching for something, an abandoned winter hat studded with dust motes, "say the thing about the wedding cake."

By any objective measure, Charlie was handsome. His body so slender and beautiful, his features so delicate, his gleaming blondness, like the handsomest boy ever at the cotillion in an F. Scott Fitzgerald story.

He was handsome to everyone. Everyone.

How could anyone look at Derek, his wooly arms and spreading belly, his whitened teeth and his winking ways, and at Charlie and think they were both the same anything?

We don't have to like him," Charlie said as they prepared to leave that night, sawdust thick in the air and the thumps of Europop still galloping from the boom box in Studio B. "No one likes their contractor."

Dara didn't say anything.

"Besides," Charlie said, gesturing to the clear vinyl curtain now hanging in the doorway to Studio B, "he takes orders pretty well."

Dara walked over. She'd imagined something more discreet, a zip door or a tented partition. But it was only strips of heavy plastic, like at the car wash.

It made everything inside Studio B look a little like a funhouse.

She could see Derek, stripped to his T-shirt white as his whitened teeth. The plastic rippling, he looked enormous, a funhouse Derek, holding a large rubber mallet, swinging it like a caveman club.

"I didn't say I didn't like him," Dara said.

Charlie smiled, one hand on Dara's shoulder, lightly kneading it.

"But," Dara said, "I don't like him."

"Here's an idea," Charlie said, hands on both her shoulders now, turning her away. "Don't look behind the curtain."

* * *

That night, Charlie's back spasmed.

Dara had been watching him sleep, his bare, broad back, the V of his waist. She couldn't help herself, her hand reaching out to touch his shoulder blade, to draw him close, that skin so cool and soothing to her. The instant her fingers touched his skin, it came: a violent stiffening, and immediate, urgent, violent retreat.

A terrific jolt, reminding Dara of sleeping with Marie, who resided in the bunk above her all those years. Marie and her restless legs. *Ma chère Marie's dancing in her sleep,* their mother used to say.

She yanked her hand back as if she'd touched an open flame.

Seeing the look on her face, he apologized even as he was instantly immobile with pain.

"It's not your fault," he said, closing his eyes. "I knew it was coming. I tried to get in to see my PT today, but . . ."

"Let me," Dara said. "Please."

He paused a moment, mouth tight in a grimace. But then, surprisingly, he let her.

Gingerly, she helped him flip over on his stomach.

"I'll be so careful," she said.

"I know." His voice muffled in the pillow.

And he let her, her fingers hard on his hot mangled back, the heel of her hand driving hard between his shoulder blades, white and wide like wings cresting.

She liked touching it and it was the only time she felt allowed, as if his spine were so delicate—like a slender fishbone—after the four surgeries, the halo neck brace, the rehabilitation.

She liked to run her fingertips across it, liked to dig her clenched fist into it.

She went harder that night, grinding herself into him, elbows forging downward, sharp and relentless.

She was chasing the pain, she told him sternly.

It made her dizzy, and damp between the legs.

You, he murmured finally, his feet arching with pleasure, his forehead sticky, hands reaching behind for her, finding that place between her legs. *You have all the power.*

I n the morning, she slid his shirt over his head, tentatively dressing him, his body rigid and afraid. This part was always sad.

It was like he'd given her something and then taken it away.

It would, she knew, be weeks or months before it came again. The lightning bolt splitting his shoulder blades. The lightning bolt that brought them, fleetingly, right to the center of things, shuddering them both to life. You shouldn't wish for such things. Yet Dara did.

Y *ou will never have to reckon with pain,* their mother told them long ago. *You both understood it from the start.*

They never even thought of it as pain.

Once in a while, their mother came to breakfast with a purple hinge of skin over one eye, or a bruised cheek. Their father at the coffee maker with tiny marks like red stitches up his neck, blaming the cat, even though the cat had no claws and had disappeared days ago anyway.

No one said anything, though sometimes Marie would want to touch their mother's face, her heavy-lidded eye, her twisted elbow, and then she would cry.

Never cry over pain, their mother told them. *Those are wasted tears.*

She explained how, if you were a dancer, you were always protected.

Feet strapped into pointe shoes, body strapped into a leotard and tights, hair strapped into a bun—no one could touch you, your entire life.

ANIMALS

A week, more or less.

That was all the time it took, Dara would marvel later.

That was all the time it took to eat the apple, for Eden to fall.

It was the following morning, a week after he'd started with them. The contractor. Derek.

Dara arrived at the studio early, and alone.

She'd fantasized Charlie might wake cured, thanks to her ministrations. But when he'd sat down that morning to put on his shoes, his face went white and stricken. Dara settled him on the worn chaise in the bedroom (*the fainting sofa*, their mother called it), its tufts settling to flatness, its velvet shiny with age. There, he awaited a call from his PT, hoping she could fit him in today, could soothe him with her firm hands, a mysterious knuckle technique that left him breathless.

Dara arrived at the studio early, and alone, and immediately heard the sounds.

* * *

The thick plastic curtain across Studio B, its strips rippling from the furnace huffs.

Approaching, her pace slowing, Dara could see something behind it.

Approaching, she heard the sounds.

The sounds of her sister, sounds she knew so well. The short, nervous breaths like after a near fall. Soft groans like when she hyperextended her knee. But then a low moan she'd never heard before, ever.

She moved closer and thought, *Oh, no, she's hurt herself.*

The blur of her sister's body—the flesh of her flesh, the sweated sheer of that white leotard—moving.

Like animals, she said to herself later. *Like animals.*

Dara's finger V-ing, splitting the plastic strips, squinting between them to see.

Her sister's palms slapped on the floor, her knees grinding against it, head thrown back, her neck long and snaky, her hips narrow and relentless.

That's not how she looks, Dara thought, but she wasn't sure. She wasn't sure of anything.

That's not how I look.

Dara's fingers on the curtain, hot to the touch from the breathless furnace.

Her sister on all fours and behind her, that thing, grunting. Red T-shirt rippling like a bullfighter's cape. The laugh that seemed caught in his throat.

The whir of her leotard, bone-white, its crotch wrenched to one side.

71

One breast slipping loose from the half-tugged leotard, his belt buckle clack-clack-clacking.

His blue hands clamped on her shoulders, the bright blue nitrile gloves coated in dust.

Oh, Marie's mouth open like a baby doll's, her eyes clicking back like a baby doll's.

And the sounds coming from her mouth, sweet and surprised.

The curtain, turning everything into a funhouse mirror.

And through its rippled plastic, her sister, face tight with feeling. Her knees blazing red the rest of the day.

Give me that, he was saying. Red Riding Hood's wolf. Grunting words. *Show me. Wider. Let me see all of it.*

The gloves falling to the floor like blue birds. His hands, the slap of his undone belt.

Now here, here. Open, open. All those pretty teeth. Pretty tongue.

Marie turning, her mouth wide, waiting.

Marie. Marie. What did he do to you?
Marie. What have you done.

Dara hid in the stairwell, palms clammy, mind racing, until she heard a door closing, the fan in the powder room burring to life. Marie's footsteps like a feral cat's claws on smooth wood. She imagined it. Marie in the powder room, its fan wailing now, a spin and tug of the towel dispenser. Marie cleaning herself, running a scratchy towel between her trembling thighs. Marie dirty. Dirty Marie.

I like the pink, she thought suddenly, then covered her mouth. She might be sick.

Minutes passed. Dara hurried, head down, to the back office. Then came the sudden, piercing fuzz of a drill, and, moments later, the hum of Benny's motor scooter outside, the chattering of arriving students, some mild changing-room teasing of Bailey Bloom, that slippery whiff of a girl, now dubbed Bailey Boom after falling three times yesterday while practicing jumping from Clara's bed, and, somehow, everything kept going.

Within an hour, Dara was standing amid the whorls of smooth-haired girls in their pattering pink slippers, the "Waltz of the Flowers" plinking through the speakers, the crush of parents in overcoats with phones and tall cups of takeout coffee and hands reaching to smooth their daughters' hair, to unstick the leotards from the clefts of their bottoms.

A ll day, Dara taught in Studio C, barking instructions (*I see rubber legs. They should be scissors!*), adjusting the girls with her hands, shaping a foot, turning a leg, as the power saw next door thundered, the floor shaking from it. *We can't have this. We can't do this. We must correct this.*

The girls' teeth rattling, and their laughter, giddy and confused.

All day, Dara taught, she made corrections, she issued commands.

Get that leg behind. Eyes up. Rib cage closed. Chin up, lift, lift . . .

She vowed to think about none of it, focusing instead on the rhythm of class, the unending, unbending flow of repetition. *Tendu, front, side, back.* The same *Nutcracker* movement, strings echoing jollily through the speaker. *Il faut le répéter,* as their mother always said, *pour affiner.*

Still, it sat in her brain like a spider.

Sneaking glances into Studio A. Sneaking glances at Marie, standing before her bumblebee throng of six-year-olds, their errant hands always running up and down the soft front of their leotards, their downy skin quilling beneath.

Marie, with what seemed a slight curl of her lip as though smiling to herself. A slight tremor to her hands, the way she kept touching herself discreetly, her hand on her neck, her arm across her chest, brushing against her breasts.

When Dara passed her at one point, she caught a whiff of it, of them. She covered her nose, her mouth.

Marie at the mirror, teaching the little girls. But all Dara could think of was Marie in Studio B that morning, with her red, rubbed-raw knees and her plaster-spackled palms and that sly little smile on her face that made Dara feel hot and enraged.

In Studio B, Benny and Gaspar had covered all the mirrors with some kind of protective film that looked like smoke. Like there was smoke everywhere from some kind of fire no one could see. Was that how Marie could do it? Could let her body—make her body—do those things with that man? She, who was trained, raised to make her body only do beautiful things.

If she had caught a glimpse of herself, of him, could she have possibly let herself participate in such animal horrors?

Her body crouching, his tan-mottled hands on her, his chest a big coffin, twisting and turning her, swiveling her around so roughly. Turning her inside out. Turning her out. That impeccable body—*a golden hummingbird*, she was called by the director of the regional ballet company they were invited to join and then, after two years of uneventful service in the corps, asked to leave—that exquisite body humiliated and grotesque. Revealing itself, laying itself so bare. Her golden throat stretched, her mouth open, begging for it.

M adame Durant, like this?"

Corbin Lesterio's face pinched as he stood at the mirror, unhappy with himself, his perennial weakness a slight swayback, his pelvis tipped forward ever so little.

"Tilt that tailbone down," she said. It was her usual correction for him. Often, he corrected himself the minute he saw her head turn.

"Can you," he said, his voice cracking, "show me?"

Dara paused, looking at his hips, his hips pressed too far forward. It would be so easy.

"You know what to do," Dara said. "Do it."

That was how their mother had been with her students. Aloof, remote. *A marionette does not become a dancer,* she used to say. She never touched her male students, their bodies, after age seven or eight. *Never touch them once they're old enough to know better.* And, most of all, *Never touch the ones who want to be touched.*

She stepped back to watch Corbin start again.

It was only then that she saw Derek standing in the doorway. She wondered how long he'd been there, shaking soot from his hair.

He had a look on his face she couldn't place. Something smug, insinuating.

I like the pink, she thought suddenly.

"I need a signature," he said, smiling a little. "For the insurance papers. Last one, I promise."

She caught a fleeting glance of the pages, another template agreement. This time titled "Assignment of Benefits."

"Ask Charlie," Dara said, as firmly as she did with Corbin. "He'll be back tomorrow. I told you to ask him."

I thought you said he wouldn't be here much," Dara said to Charlie, calling him after cutting her final class short, the hum of the power saw thundering through Studio B, setting the nervous twelve-year-olds on edge, their teeth chattering from the vibrations.

"He's always here," Dara said. "Always."

"I guess he likes to be hands on."

Dara paused. No, she told herself. He couldn't know. Because if he knew, he would feel like Dara felt. Except worse.

"It's just been a long day. The girls are picking on Bailey Bloom," Dara said, dumping Nespresso into her chipped coffee cup, her hands shaking. "Usual *Nutcracker* bullshit."

"Fuck that Tchaikovsky guy," Charlie said, making her smile, promising her he'd be back to help her tomorrow, that day's PT session leaving him "liquid-y and grand."

It was hard not to marvel at the magic Charlie's PT seemed to conjure. Dara remembered Mrs. Bloom raving about her once, later recommending her to Charlie.

No, she couldn't tell Charlie. She couldn't bear it, to have him know. Charlie, who loved Marie like his sister, and protected her—from assailing parents, from telemarketers, from aggressive drivers, from street leers when they'd go into town, Marie in her cropped top, her bodysuit. Like his sister.

No, Charlie couldn't know.

Besides, it was probably already over, an impulsive act, like so many of Marie's impulsive acts. Like that first time she'd left five years ago, her big "trip around the world." Once she'd landed on the idea, she *wanted, needed* to go immediately. The Acropolis could be gone one day. The Spanish Steps in Rome might close. And wasn't Venice sinking? She would not be stopped. *Don't you dare*, she kept saying whenever Charlie tried to reason with her, to caution her against rash decisions. *Don't you dare stop me.*

They didn't stop her and, less than a month later, she came back. Marie always came back.

Standing at the office window, Dara watched the final straggling students scurry or limp off to waiting cars, their tailpipes pluming exhaust, followed by Benny and Gaspar, hurrying to their motor scooters. And finally, Derek himself walking to his truck, that slightly limpy gait— like John Wayne gone to seed, Dara thought. She could've sworn that before disappearing inside that truck, he looked up once, to the studio, to the office window open just enough for Dara to sneak a smoke. To watch.

"I'm staying late tonight," Dara told Charlie, having decided something. "I have one more thing I have to do."

ME AND MY SHADOW

Dara waited outside the powder room, pouncing on Marie as she opened the door, pulling her wrap sweater across her chest.

"Oh!" Marie said, startled. "I thought you left."

For a moment, Dara couldn't speak, her eyes fixed on two vivid bruises between her sister's collar bones.

The bruises were yellow, like she'd run a buttercup across herself. Like when they were little, standing in the weedy yard, *hold the buttercup beneath your chin* . . .

In an instant, she pictured the hard thrust of the contractor's fingers and thumb that morning. That very morning.

Except, Dara thought, *except*. It took more than a day for a bruise to look like that. It took many days for a bruise to fade to yellow. Every dancer knows that, always one or more toenails gone black and blue, forever spreading arnica on the starburst over an elbow that hit the floor.

What she'd seen behind that plastic curtain had not been the first time.

"What have you done?" Dara said so loudly Marie instinctively backed against the powder room door, her head hitting it hard. "What have you done, sister?"

O h, the look on Marie's face. Dara had never seen it. Thirty years of watching her sister's face and she'd never seen this look.

Her skin. Like it was radiating. Like it was on fire. Like it had been pressed in acid and shorn itself and formed itself anew.

I t's been going on for days," Marie was saying, rubbing her wrists, a smile creeping up her face.

They were in the back office now, Marie seated on top of the desk, red knees, her legs hanging like the limbs were all broken.

"Your exploits don't interest me," Dara said.

Dealing with Marie was like dealing with a disruptive student, a student who demanded all the attention and would do anything to get it.

"It's happened three times," Marie said, grinning. "My god. I bled the first time. I bled."

Dara gave her a cool stare and began packing her bag, her misty water bottle, bobby pins, toe pads, her calf compression sleeves.

Inside, though, Dara could cry from it. From seeing Marie on that desk, saying such filthy things. Their family desk, black cherry mahogany with three cigar marks on the top and front edge from their grandfather's Cohibas. From the sight of Marie sprawled so crudely on that desk, no tights, only her bare thighs so lately used by rough hands.

"I could barely walk after," Marie said, her legs swinging off the desk like a metronome. "I can barely walk now."

"Did you think I'd be shocked," Dara said, her face growing hot, zipping her bag shut, then unzipping it again. The bag was packed.

"I didn't think about you at all," Marie said, a vague shrug.

"Nothing you do shocks me. You're really very boring."

The truth was Marie had shocked her many times.

"It's unprofessional. Déclassé," Dara went on. She couldn't stop the words from coming. "Couldn't you control yourself at all? A half hour later and children might've seen."

Marie looked puzzled, dazed.

"I never thought of that," she said. "I never thought of that at all."

D ara could have left, could have plugged her ears. She had already un- packed and repacked and unpacked her bag three times. She wanted to leave to show Marie how little she cared.

In the end, though, she merely stood there, watching Marie pull two cigarettes from the secret stash in the potted snake plant because there was no smoking at the Durant School of Dance, their mother's oldest rule.

The matches shook in Dara's hand.

They both lit up and Marie told everything.

I t started two mornings ago, just after six. Unable to sleep, Marie had slunk down the spiral stairs.

She didn't know anyone was there. No one should have been there.

She started warming up in Studio A, circling her ankles, hips, and shoulders, stretching herself.

First, she heard the echoey sound of a phone vibrating on the floor. It was coming from Studio B, from behind the plastic curtain.

Then she heard the contractor saying something, talking to someone. Talking about how he's got a lock on something and no one's going to fuck it up for him and she can say whatever she wants and play the holy martyr, the virgin bride, but he has the texts to—

There was something in the gruffness of his tone that set her pulse rac- ing, that sent her on her feet. Sent her skittering to the pocket powder room, where she set her hands on the corners of the vanity and took a breath.

She could still hear the voice, his voice, and it was making her feel funny inside, like that time she stuck her hand in the hole in the wall at a haunted house and felt a snaky tongue reach her fingers.

But the voice was swiftly louder: *Hold up, I'll call you back, I think one of the sisters is here . . .* and his footsteps like a monster movie.

She pressed the toilet handle gently so it barely flushed.

The cheap door popped open like a cork and he was suddenly there.

She thought maybe she let out a sharp cry of surprise, but maybe she didn't.

It was so fast, after all, the smile on his face, his blistering cologne, the heel of his hand on her shoulder.

What —she started.

I can't wait any longer, he said, or she did.

He twirled her around like they were dancing.

Tugging her sweatpants down, hand pressed on her leotard, and her heart going like a chop saw.

The mirror, limescaled, showed her herself and she had never seen herself look like this.

She grasped the vanity edges, bracing herself. It was so exciting, she couldn't bear it.

When he hooked his finger around the loop of her leotard crotch, tearing it cleanly, she gasped.

Everything was going and the vanity shook and she felt so strong like she might tear it loose from its foundation.

The feeling of him, so immense, ten times too big for that tiny pocket, for tiny her, and he pushed himself into her, growling in her ear, *Is this what you want?*

And it turned out it was. It was, it was.

He assaulted you," Dara said, her voice throaty, the cigarette blooming.

"No," Marie said. Pausing, trying to find more words. Giving up. "No."

* * *

He left first, smiling and grabbing her face for their first smeary kiss. The kiss felt more intimate than anything else, the smack of his bristle, the heat of his breath—mint and tar.

("Oh, that kiss, wet and rough," Marie said now, tightening her legs, her hands on her thighs.)

The door shut behind him soundlessly, the pocket open, then shut.

She sat down on the toilet seat, her right leg shaking so hard she couldn't do anything.

Her right leg shaking like a newborn foal trying to stand, trying to make the limbs work.

The paper towel up and down her thighs, the smell of everything in that tiny space.

She sat down again.

She couldn't stop grinning.

When she came out a few minutes later, she heard him tell Gaspar to go and fix the bathroom vanity. *It got busted and you got no idea how.*

She saw him through the plastic, a red curl on his neck, which she knew was the red curl from her own fingernail, pressing into him, gouging.

You're burning."

"What?" Dara said.

Marie reached out with licked fingers and snuffed Dara's burning cigarette. It was only then Dara felt it, shaking it off, sitting up straight.

There was something wrong about the story—or a hundred things wrong, but also something missing. Dara couldn't figure it out until she did.

"Why were you wearing a leotard?" Dara said, remembering Marie's white leotard the other day, and that very morning. Pearl white, bone white. Degas white.

"What?"

"Nearly every day this week. You never wear one to warm up. Or to teach. You wear leggings, shorts. Not a leotard. And not a white one."

Marie looked at her, blinking her eyes.

"You wanted him to look at you," Dara said. "You wanted to entice him."

"It's just a leotard," Marie said, averting her eyes.

Dara was thinking of something else. The day before, after an exhausting fouetté demonstration, a dozen whipping pirouettes, for all the potential Sugar Plum Fairies (*Leg higher, whip, whip, whip, relax that hip*), she'd seen Derek staring at her from the doorway, the plastic curtain draped over one shoulder like a counterfeit cape. The stare was hard and insistent and it was only later, turning, that she saw what he'd been looking at: the sweat on her leotard, under her arms, between and under her breasts and blooming darkly between her legs. And, as she turned again, a slow fouetté, a dark line between her buttocks.

It reminded her of something. How when they were twelve, thirteen, fourteen, Dara and Marie would sweat so much down there their mother would only let them wear black leotards so you couldn't see it. So it looked not like a stain but a shadow.

Me and my shadow, Marie used to say.

Remember when he tore down the wall?" Marie was saying, clasping Dara's hands, pressing Dara's ash-scorched knuckles.

Dara pulled her hands back. She rose. She said she had to leave.

But Marie was not done with her yet. Rising, she followed Dara as she gathered her things once more. As she put on her coat and closed the window and checked the ashtray for burning stubs. She followed Dara, explaining how she'd snuck down to Studio B late that night after the walls came down, after everyone was gone and the air still thick with dust. How she'd stepped barefoot across the plastic sheeting to the far corner where it sat, the thing.

Derek's long-frame hammer, leaning against the wall, hickory handled, its steel head glinting.

She (*Can you believe this, Dara?*) dropped to her knees, touching it. Finally, lifting it, feeling its weight. It tingled under her fingertips.

What must it be like, she wondered, *to so utterly destroy something?*

told him," Marie said. "I told him later. What it felt like. Watching him take it down. Do you know what I said?"

"I don't care," Dara said, her fingers to her brow.

But she knew what Marie had said.

I want you to tear me open.

It made Dara want to laugh, to gag, to cry.

Dara looked at her sister, this little pervert, and said nothing.

I want you to tear me apart.

GASH

After, Dara was so happy to leave the studio, to retreat to the house, to leave them to it, to whatever they did and would do, Marie and that man.

The studio was tainted now, and home forever felt safe, reassuring. Setting foot inside, she felt her shoulders settle, her hand touching all the familiar doorknobs, the light cord in the hallway that you had to pull twice.

The more she thought about it, the angrier she was at herself. For listening to Marie, for indulging her in this troubling behavior. Taunting behavior.

But then Marie hadn't been herself in a long time, since she moved out of the house and became a squatter in their own place of business. Since she left in the middle of the night, heaving a pair of milk crates and one overstuffed shopping bag out the front door of their home, onto the uneven pavement, stumbling into the waiting Shamrock cab. Later, they found the message taped on their bedroom door. *"Gone for air. Not coming back."*

* * *

Who needs her here anyway, Dara thought, walking through the front door, that familiar scent of mildew, paste, old perfume. Who needed Marie's buzzy, antic energy, her nighttime pacing and her bad dreams, the way she used all Dara's tampons and ate all the sardines?

Instead, Dara could do what she did. Sit for a while in the kitchen with her fenugreek tea and give Charlie his anti-convulsant pill for his nerve pain and take her arnica tablets for sore muscles and warm up their hot-water bottles and pad off to bed.

And, as she adjusted the pillows to help Charlie find the best position for his back, she was doubly glad she hadn't told him about Marie. If she had, they'd be talking about her sister now—all those conversations they'd had to have over the years about Marie and her troublesome behavior and her impulsiveness and willfulness—instead of turning off all the lights together, the great old house slowly darkening. Retreating to the bedroom, the old woven cane bed and the fireplace that smelled like hickory.

It was such a respite from the churn inside her, the hot splotches that came the minute she closed her eyes: images of Marie and that man . . . Marie and her strange little colt body and her neck thick and ringed red, his hands on her shoulders, wringing them red.

Looking over at him, she only wished Charlie weren't having to treat his body with such care, propped up on pillows, a homemade heating pad packed with rice. She only wished that, in bed that night, she could touch the cool alabaster of Charlie's muscled back again, like slipping beneath a museum's velvet rope to lay hands on the smooth marble of a Greek god.

"I'm so happy," she whispered from across the expanse of the bed, "to be home."

Sleep came very late, not until she toe-tap-touched her feet five hundred times on the footrest, an old trick, a compulsion from childhood, from those nights in the wagon-wheel bunkbed, her body awake, her brain awake, her body itching.

Every night, bunkbed top to bunkbed bottom, Dara and Marie twitched and fidgeted, stretching the growing pains from their narrow, muscled limbs, their faces pressed against the bedpost, its shellacked wood cool on their cheeks.

The bunkbed had arrived in a kit when they were very little, still sleeping with their mother every night. It was a big jumbly box of pieces, popped into place by their father. Their father who could fix anything, lift anything, barrel-chested and forever hotted up on something, some inner unhappiness, entombed in a house filled with tutus, with dangling tights and nervous females. Back then, whenever he came in to kiss them good night with beery breath or to tell them to turn their goddamn lights off, to stop giggling and go to sleep, he seemed to take up the whole room. When he set a hand on the bunkbed post, you felt like he could lift the whole thing into the air, could tear the bunkbed into kindling, could crush the whole thing with one swoop.

But by the time they were ten or eleven, he no longer came in to kiss them good night, rarely came upstairs at all, and the bunkbed was only theirs, the forever of their childhood. Dara had probed every groove and beetle hole with her fingers. Thousands of nights, she'd lain there, trying to sleep, listening to their mother pacing the hallways, listening to their father's TV crackling old movies into the night, reciting her French conjugations for tomorrow's lessons, cracking her toes and doing *dégagés*.

And everything shared from bunkbed top to bunkbed bottom was sacrosanct, never to be discussed elsewhere.

So many nights, half sleeping, they whispered secrets about their bodies.

About the thing Dara heard an old man at the drugstore call a "gash," a dirty magazine open in his hands. *Look at that gash*, he said to the weary cashier, his hands shaking, waving the centerfold in the air, its fleshy center. *Great big slit between her legs, looks like murder.*

Or that night Marie confided that she had an extra part of her anatomy that no one else had. Something inside, hidden, that she could coax out if she thought a certain way, or imagined that boy who always skateboarded by their house.

Dara didn't believe her and explained the things she'd figured out, touching herself down there, dreaming about Harry Perez, the only boy in her ballet class, and how he'd lifted her over his head, his fingers finding things he hadn't known to find, her leotard soaked through at the crotch by class's end.

But I have something no one else has, Marie insisted.

We all have it, Dara kept saying, but Marie wouldn't stop.

I'm touching it now, she said. And Dara kept making faces even though Marie couldn't see.

Dara even threatened to sneak down to their father's TV room and bring back the *Encyclopaedia Britannica* and show her a picture of what it looked like *down there*, pink and accordioned like the most elaborate tutu in the world.

But Marie insisted that she was different and she said if Dara didn't believe her she could come up and see for herself.

Marie never stopped insisting and Dara was never really sure.

BREATHE

The old floor was coming up; it was coming up, tooth by tooth. That's what it reminded Dara of, like their childhood dentist and his tangly forceps. Their father always told them they were lucky they didn't face the squeaky pliers he'd endured as a boy.

The old floor was coming up that day, and Dara still had not told Charlie.

She'd planned to, over breakfast, on the way to the studio. But something kept stopping her, an inexplicable panic about what the look on Charlie's face might be like. There was something she was afraid of seeing, though she wasn't sure what it was.

In the past, Marie's romances were always intense and brief. There'd only been three as far as Dara knew. (But who knew what had happened on her trip around the world? For years after Marie would refer vaguely to her *European experiences*, her eyes going soft.) There had been Claude, the French Canadian boy who first nestled his head between Marie's legs, an act they knew about only from a few stolen glimpses of cable TV, peeping into the next-door neighbor's house. *But I had no idea what it would feel like,* Marie said after. No one told her it would feel like *that*. Claude came to rehearsal the next day with a bruise on his cheek like a wet slap, Marie's thigh snapping against his face like she might never let him free again. Alas, like the two to follow, it was over nearly before it began, Marie too distracted to make sense of the bus schedule to get to his apartment, two transfers, for a quick clinch, wilted deli roses, and then having to listen to Claude recite his poetry while they sat on the floor of his basement apartment. A week later it was over. Marie couldn't manage most things.

This, too, will be over soon, Dara told herself. Maybe it already was.

One day, she told herself, *Marie will learn to control herself.*

B esides, there was no time for it. No time at all. As soon as they arrived at the studio, Charlie rushed to the back office to catch up on paperwork and Dara faced the gauntlet. *Nutcracker* preparations were already dominating their days, the frenzy of auditions past and performance panic already setting in, all alongside the low grumble of a hundred disappointed or resentful girls bemoaning the loss of Clara, the role they were all born to dance, to that little nothing Bailey Bloom.

Immediately when Dara arrived, it emerged that, the day before, Bailey had found a razor blade cunningly hidden in her demi-pointe shoe. Fishing it out with her fingers, she'd shorn off a flap of skin.

"Why did it take you so long to tell?" Dara asked gravely as she inspected the girl's foot, tender and pulped.

"I was afraid," Bailey said, "you'd take Clara away."

"Bailey," Dara said, "Clara is yours to lose."

What she wanted to say was, *Bailey, steel yourself.*

It happened every year. There would have to be a meeting to discuss company loyalty, spirit, healthy competition. Another thing to do.

Marie and the contractor. Maybe it would go away.

* * *

Mrs. Cartwright, you knew the schedule before we even began auditions," Dara was explaining to one of her most frustrating mothers, always swooping in in her camel-hair coat and gold-rimmed sunglasses, striding over to Dara with *My life is crazy right now, Ms. Durant, you must understand* . . .

"But these rehearsals," she said, "why, they press right up against Thanksgiving. We always go to Bermuda for Thanksgiving. Iris is counting on it." Then, lowering her voice, "And, well, she's just a Candy Cane. Which was, of course, your choice, not mine."

And there it was. It was never really about the schedule demands, Saturday rehearsals. It wasn't about the weeknight costume fittings or the shared carpool duties. It was about who was Clara, and who was not.

"Mrs. Cartwright," Dara said, snapping her fingers at the dawdling Level II students, Marie's pigeon-breasted seven-year-olds, ushering them into Studio A, "we made it clear that all the parts bring the same demands. Even the Candy Canes."

Mrs. Cartwright paused, eyebrows lifting.

"You know," she said, "your sister is more polite."

Past the gauntlet, Dara finally approached Studio A and Marie. You couldn't miss her with that garish lipstick she persisted in wearing but also, today, with an improbable scarf flung around her neck. Garish polka dots and fringe, like something she'd dug out of the lost-and-found bin.

"You can't teach like that," Dara said. Charlie appeared in the doorway, his posture stiff.

"I can and I have," Marie said.

"She can't teach like that," Dara said to Charlie, making a face.

"I can do anything," Marie replied, looking at Charlie in a way that irritated Dara. And what was it with that lipstick, like a red gash across her face.

"She can do anything," Charlie said wryly to Dara, with a shrug.

S o Dara threw herself into the day, trying to avoid Studio B, avoid seeing him. Twice, she saw Marie lingering at the plastic curtain between classes, her fingers tangled in the edges of that ridiculous scarf of hers, the little ones scrumming past her. She wasn't doing anything, but Dara didn't like it.

N o, no," Dara said, watching dear, long-lashed Corbin Lesterio struggling with his entrechats, his legs scissoring with dizzying speed but no form. "No flapping like a duck."

"I'm sorry, Madame Durant. I'm so sorry."

"Don't be sorry. Just be better."

He tried again.

"Where is my flutter?" Dara called out. "Your legs should be moving sideways, not swinging back and forth."

She had no intention of touching him, but he didn't seem to understand, and when she approached, he stepped back abruptly, his face coloring. His voice, half-broken, stuttering an apology.

"I didn't know. I mean, you can, but I . . ." he began, then stepped back again, his arms twined around each other, his hands spread as if covering himself, as if Adam with his fig leaf. His eyes darted all around, catching on the plastic curtain to Studio B. "Please, I want you to show me. I just . . ."

Dara looked at him, his radiant blush. His hands hovering beneath his waist.

She understood now. "Do you want to talk to Monsieur Charlie?" she asked.

Every boy ended up needing to talk to Charlie about certain things—the particularities of the male body, puberty. Not all of them felt comfortable explaining to their mothers about needing support, about dance belts, those filmy thongs with the pouches meant to keep everything in place.

It's the only favor ballet ever granted its men, Charlie once told her. Brushing and pressing up against bodies all day, the heat and closeness, it was impossible to hide anything. Worn under tights, the dance belt concealed every adolescent boy's secrets. Too slender a garment to protect them from a misplaced foot, an errant elbow, it protected them only from fleeting boy shame.

"Class is over anyway," Dara said gently, "and he'd be happy to talk to you—"

"Madame Durant," Corbin said, his face as red as Marie's mouth, "I don't want to talk to anybody."

M oments later, she was in the parking lot, smoking, when Derek appeared, pulling out a drugstore vape. She had the feeling he'd followed her out.

It felt strange being alone with him after what she'd seen. After the things Marie had told her. And the way he was looking at her now. She drew her sweater tight across her chest.

"Can't be easy for a boy," he said, shaking his head. "Jesus."

"What?" Dara said. Then realizing he must have seen her with Corbin. Must have been watching from behind the plastic curtain.

"I almost feel sorry for the kid," he said, a whisper of a smile. "Quite a spot you put him in."

Dara felt her face grow hot.

B ack in the stairwell, she took three long breaths, shook the forgotten cigarette free from her hand, the ash burning her knuckles.

She would simply have to tell Charlie. Marie had emboldened him, this contractor. Now he felt like he could say anything, do as he pleased. Charlie had to know. She would have to tell him.

Tonight, she resolved, smearing the cigarette butt with her shoe, a black smudge the shape of an X.

B ut it turned out she didn't need to.

Just before the late-afternoon crush, Dara was heading to the back office when she heard his voice.

"Who do you think you are," Charlie was saying, a laugh in his voice, light and delicious like she seldom heard anymore, "Isadora Duncan?"

Dara stood outside the door for a moment. That laugh, that tone—it reminded her of the sneaky elation they once felt, after the grief over their parents' death, after a year or more of nightly check-ins from Madame Sylvie and quarterly visits from the nice woman with the thick brown shoes from Child Protective Services. Suddenly, they were grown-ups, with an entire big house to themselves, and they'd spend those evenings, bodies loose and muscles springy and hot, making pots of spaghetti they'd barely eat, drinking party-store wine, trying on their mother's dressing gowns, Charlie wearing that foil top hat from the party-store spin rack.

She opened the door just as Charlie's hand reached out, his fingers tangling in the fringe on Marie's scarf.

"Dara," Charlie said, straightening himself. "You're just in time. Can you remind your sister of Isadora's fate?" He made a jerking motion across his neck.

Dara winced. A hangman's fracture. There were so many ways to injure yourself. Like poor Isadora, one of her famous long scarves caught in the wheels of a car.

"I'm not afraid," Marie said, smiling faintly, moving away from Charlie, smoothing her scarf, untangling its fringe. "Of that, at least."

"Your back must be feeling better," Dara said to Charlie, reaching for his mug and dumping his tea bag into the trash, cold tea splashing.

"Stop!" Marie let out a gasp and Dara looked over in time to see Charlie yanking Marie's hideous scarf free. ("Free Marie! Liberate the neck!")

Charlie, teasing Marie like he used to years ago in dance class, calling her Snap-Crackle because of the way her hips used to *pop-pop-pop*.

Abruptly, Charlie froze, Marie's scarf still in his hand, drooping and forlorn.

Dara turned and saw too. Marie, the marks on Marie. On her neck this time, and fresh. They were violet and obscene. Dara couldn't stop looking at them. Fleshy dabs from Derek's fleshy thumbs. Like little Jack Horner, his finger in the pie.

"Jesus," Charlie said, voice low. "Did Tessa Shen kick-spin you again?"

"No," Marie said, running her hand across her throat, stroking it.

The gesture undid something in Dara, who could feel her chest burning. This whole business, the scarf—another way of drawing all the attention. Marie and her body, *like a golden hummingbird*. Marie and her mysterious sex organs, the part she had that no other woman had. Marie, Dara thought, the freak. Marie and her freakshow.

"Stop showing off," Dara said, fingers to her temples. "Nobody cares."

Charlie turned and looked at Dara.

"What is this?" he asked, gesturing to the bruises. "Did you know about this?"

Both of them looked at Dara, as if she were the problem.

"Didn't you?" Dara said. Then, "Marie likes it rough."

Charlie's gaze wobbled to Marie, a look on his face like a lost child's.

"What are you talking about?"

"Ask her," Dara said, her eyes fixed on the violet, imagining the contractor's meaty fingers pressing. She thought she might choke from the thought, from the picture in her head.

"Someone better tell me," Charlie said.

Marie looked at him, both her hands wrung around her neck.

"My sister's screwing the help," Dara said.

* * *

H is hands," Marie whispered, both of them lying on their backs in the empty studio in between classes, holding on to their ankles, feeling like they might crack, "remind me of that belt Dad used to have, remember? The leather splintered, but he wouldn't stop wearing it. He said it was made from gators. Maybe it was."

"I don't want to hear about it." Dara didn't want to hear about hands like belts, like their father.

"If I had to hurt him," Marie said, eyes shining. "I'd hurt his hands. I'd break his fingers, one by one."

"Smash them with a hammer," Dara said dryly. "Like your poor pointe shoes."

But Marie only nodded, breathless. "Because of all the things they do to me—I never want him to do those things to anyone else."

And she smiled and smiled.

Jesus, Dara thought.

"You're like a teenage girl," Dara said. "After her first fuck."

C harlie hadn't wanted to talk about it, about Marie. They'd talk about it later. *But, really, what is there to talk about,* he'd said, reaching for his jacket. *She's a grown woman.*

Leaving Dara the car, he took a Shamrock cab to Helga for a last-minute PT session. Helga always understood the pressures of *Nutcracker* season, even once sending Charlie home with a paper plate of peppermint cookies tied with yarn ribbon. (*She's very thoughtful,* Charlie said. *Or she has a crush,* Dara teased.)

But with Charlie gone, the students had chosen that day to be little monsters, all except Bailey Bloom, who snuck in the powder room before and after classes, not wanting to change in front of the other girls, their snipes.

At day's end, Dara and Marie retired to the fire escape, tarry and quivering, the sun burning through the skyline.

They'd been drinking. Mr. Higham had left them a champagne split four-pack as a thank-you for his little Jamie's entry into the City Academy of Dance. The splits were chilled and he warned Dara they'd "skunk" if they didn't drink them right away. And Dara didn't want to go home anyway, feeling strange about the day, about the marks on her sister and about Charlie and about everything changing, slowly and all at once.

"It *is* my first fuck," Marie said, tripping slightly over the word. "In a way."

"I don't want to hear any more about it."

"I disagree," Marie said.

They sipped their tiny straws. Dara could feel her thighs inflating, her belly blooming. Sugar, sugar. She couldn't stop.

"Maybe," Marie said, lying on her back, her hands on herself. "Maybe I'm in love."

*D*oes *he only take you from behind? Like an animal? It's not very attractive, you know.*

It's not a good look for you. Bone and rope, that's all you've got back there. Not all, Dara . . .

*T*hey were drunk, they were drunk and Charlie finally called Dara. He was home and making their fenugreek tea. He was home and getting ready for bed. Where was she.

"Marie," Dara said, finally, rising shakily to her feet, "I hope you know what you're doing."

Her sister looked up, her hair falling from her face, and slowly smiled.

"Dara," Marie confided, "the things he does to me . . ."

The violet splotches on her neck, they seemed to move and dance and Dara wanted, suddenly, to touch them. She wanted to—

"But *what*?" Dara said, her head throbbing. "What does he do?"

* * *

No one ever really did anything you hadn't thought of before, Dara kept saying to herself. In the bedroom, wherever, with bodies in the dark. There were only so many ways bodies fit together or didn't.

Oh, Dara, Marie kept saying, *I can only tell you how it feels.*

But then Marie started to talk about the things—about the trick with fingers, and the heel of his hand on her throat until—

Stop.

And best of all that thumb. Had she seen his thumb? The curve in it that was just the right shape and size—

Marie, I need you to stop.

Marie, don't you know you can never let them know.

Let them know what?

How much we . . . how much we . . .

Oh, Dara, she said. *Oh, Dara, he knows. That's what I'm talking about. He looks at you and he knows. . . .*

That was when she knew. Right there on the fire escape. It wasn't going to be a fling. It wasn't going to be a passing affair, a pickup, a sex thing. Not for Marie at least.

Whatever it was, it was already happening. And there was no stopping it.

That night, Dara dreamt she was walking through the studio and it was ten times its size, the renovation far beyond their budget or the laws of physics, gravity, the ceiling four stories high with stained-glass windows at the top like a cathedral.

Walking through it, wending from empty room to empty room, its mirrors shimmering, she began to hear something, like a few years ago when Marie left the water running in their mother's old claw-foot tub. The kitchen ceiling puckering above Dara's head, the smell of rotten wood and rust.

It was like that, a straining. Like the beams holding the ceiling aloft might snap. Like everything had been put together with cardboard and paste, like pointe shoes, the smell of mentholated spirits emanating from them, dead after every use.

She dreamt she finally reached Studio B, where, inexplicably, her classes were now to be held. The plastic curtain still hung across the threshold and she was excited to look.

Blood rushing through her, she watched, pressing her face against the plastic, her nose poking it. She tried to see. She squinted and tried to see.

She felt her heart beating, a dampness between her legs.

But instead of bodies, instead of secrets, something lurched forward, a dark blur and a pair of eyes looking straight back at her. Looking at her as if excited and appalled.

UP THE SPIRAL STEPS

t'll pass," Charlie said over soft-boiled eggs the following morning. "It's a fling."

Dara didn't say anything.

She'd come home late after drinking with Marie and crawled into bed, pushing herself against him, her head hot. She tried to wake him, her hands gently roving, but he didn't move, the thick brume of his meds. So she made herself so small, curling into a ball, feeling—under the crinkly duvet—like a fetus, lima-bean size.

He was sleeping. He was sleeping and didn't care to talk about it. *It's Marie's business. She's a grown woman.*

After a fashion, Dara had thought.

And now they were eating soft-boiled eggs in their mother's chipped porcelain egg cups. The ones their father used to make fun of, holding them with one pinkie perched. *Your mother thinks she's a grand lady,* he'd say. *Some kind of aristocrat kidnapped by a piggish pauper.*

The eggs that morning smelled funny. A puff of sulfur when she cracked the shell.

"It'll run its course," Charlie said again, resting his head on his hand. "It doesn't mean anything."

Dara still didn't say anything, just let him go on, the sulfur thick between them.

"He has to finish that renovation sometime," Charlie was saying now. "The floor is gone."

The floor is gone, Dara thought.

S he's already got one family member keeping close watch," he said as they stepped outside, the late October air sharp, stinging. "She doesn't need another."

W hen they arrived at the studio, the stairwell was choked, Benny and Gaspar heaving enormous sprung floor panels up the steps, great maple hardwood bands to be woven together like a basket.

Dara lowered her head and moved quickly, bracing herself to see him, to have to pass through Studio B, a temporary path made of narrow mats strewn over the old subfloor.

But Derek, it turned out, was nowhere to be found and her sister was hungover, sprawled on the floor of Studio A, drinking coconut water from a box, squeezing it until nothing was left.

"What's wrong?" Dara asked, because it was so clear Marie was dying to be asked, nearly reaching for Dara's ankle as she walked past.

"I called him all night," she said. "He never called me back."

"Did you try his beeper?" Dara said. "Or his other beeper?" Charlie gave her a scolding look and continued on into the back office.

Marie looked up and Dara saw her eyes were pink, swollen, like wet buds.

Pathetic, Dara thought, a coldness settling in her. This was all too much to ask. Too much. Why did everything Marie do have to be so big, so all-consuming? *Look at me! Look at me!*

As if on cue, the grumble of a truck came from outside.

Marie jumped to her feet, tossing the coconut water into the trash. Smoothing her hair back. Heading for the window like an excitable bird. Like a desperate thing.

"It's not . . ." she said, peering out the window, her fingers pressed on the cloudy glass. "It's just the delivery man."

"You're humiliating yourself," Dara said, moving toward the back office, seeing Charlie there, giving her another look.

"I don't care."

"You're humiliating us."

But Marie didn't say anything, her head down. Her thoughts remote, mysterious.

Dara couldn't help finding a sneaking pleasure in it. In Derek standing her up, abandoning her. Missing a late-night rendezvous with a very drunk Marie, her bruises ready for re-bruising. Aching for it.

Maybe he had other girlfriends. No wedding band, but that didn't mean there weren't girlfriends. Maybe a live-in one, or even a common-law wife, who knew. Men like that, who knew.

And when Derek eventually showed up for work, hours later, mirrored sunglasses on, like a cop, and looking distracted, it was even more satisfying to see him stroll right to Benny and Gaspar, to never make it to Studio A at all, to Marie, who stood in the doorway, her five-year-olds clustered behind her like a pile of downy dandelion heads.

Maybe, Dara thought, *Charlie was right, after all.*

Maybe it will pass.

Clatter, clatter, the silver-sprayed swords unsheathed for the mice.

In Studio C, Dara was walking students through *The Nutcracker*'s fight scene, Clara's battle with the Mouse King and his furry legion.

But the thud-thud-thudding from Studio B didn't stop, and three times the lights flickered, the circuits strained from all the power tools.

"Madame Durant," Bailey Bloom was saying, as five "mice" surrounded her, batting her, swatting her like a piñata, nearly pressing her jonquil body into the corner, trapping her, indeed, like a rat. "When do I get to throw my slipper at the Mouse King?"

"No swordplay," Dara called out to the aggressive mice. "You're not there yet."

Szzzzzt. The lights flickered above and then dimmed to brown.

"Taking care of it," Charlie said, emerging from the back office, one hand on his ailing back, and moving quickly to Studio B.

Dara looked around at the students all staring at her in the semi-darkness, hands wrapped around the cardboard swords, four of them drooping, one bent from being packed hastily after last year's production.

"Madame Durant, when do we get to do it with the mouse heads?" peeped Carly Mendel, her brow pinched. "Because I heard they make it hard to breathe."

There was a clamor of voices from Studio B, Charlie's low tones and Gaspar's hurried apologies, and the whir of Benny rushing past to the circuit box.

Finally, the lights rose again and Charlie left for the hardware store to buy a new fuse, or maybe just to leave, to have some respite. Dara could hardly blame him.

"*Vite, vite,*" Dara called out, quickly directing the Mouse King, Oliver Perez, his sword the largest but its tip creased and bent, to the center of the space for his dramatic fall after Clara hurls her slipper at him. "Take your positions."

"Madame Durant," Bailey said and Dara turned, exasperated.

"What now?"

Bailey pointed to the doorway, where a trio of seven-year-olds stood, clutching one another, shaken by the gravity of stepping over the threshold into Studio C, the older-girl studio, the forbidden space for which they longed.

"Why aren't you in class?" Dara asked them. "You three should be in Studio A with Mademoiselle Durant."

The seven-year-olds looked at one another before pushing forth the tallest one, a bowlegged girl whose name Dara couldn't recall.

"But, Madame," she lisped, her arms interlocked with the girl beside her, *where is Mademoiselle Durant?*"

Dara pushed past the students entering for her three o'clock class. Pushed into Studio B, through the plastic curtain, which tangled her arm.

Benny and Gaspar looked up, surprised, a pneumatic tool of some kind shuddering in Benny's hand, both their faces covered in masks.

"Where is he?" Dara asked. "Your boss."

But Benny only gestured at his ear guards helplessly and Gaspar looked away.

She wouldn't dare, Dara thought, her head tilting up to the third floor. *She wouldn't.*

Running back through Studio A, past her whispering, eager pupils, Dara took long breaths. She pushed into the empty back office and pinned her hand on the railing of the spiral staircase that led upstairs. One foot on its bottom step. But she could feel it. The iron rail vibrating, its steps vibrating, slithering up to the third floor, where her sister was fucking the afternoon away with this stranger in their mother's private-most space.

Ms. Durant, we need to talk."

It was only moments later, and Dara pretended to not quite hear Dr. Weston, keeping her gaze on her students across the room, warming up in what seemed an appallingly lazy manner.

Upstairs, she could hear Marie moving, could hear her little cat feet.

"Ms. Durant." Dr. Weston lowered his voice discreetly. "I can't be the only one concerned about what's going on in there."

Dara pursed her lips, her eyes on Chloë Lin's sickled foot.

"Mademoiselle Lin," she called out, poker-faced, "inside of your heel forward, *s'il vous plait*. Do not give me ugly feet."

Inside, her mind raced. *Had Dr. Weston heard? Had one or more parents—and they all talked, ceaselessly in that gossip nest of a waiting room—spotted Marie and Derek together? Caught them in one of their slippery and grotesque ruttings.*

That would be the end of it, of course. The school, everything.

"Ms. Durant," Dr. Weston said again, his neediness so insistent, so abrasive.

Putting on her parent face, Dara turned to him at last.

"Dr. Weston," she said quietly, moving closer to him, "now is not the time."

In her head, she was frantically conjuring excuses. (*My sister's become deranged, she's having a psychotic break . . .*)

"But tomorrow's November first!" Dr. Weston said, more loudly now, a sheen of sweat on his brow.

"Pardon?"

"And how will my Pepper—or, of course, any of her fellow dancers—have time to truly prepare the Waltz of the Snowflakes when one studio is unusable?"

The Nutcracker. The goddamned *Nutcracker.* Dara took a sharp breath of relief. That's all it was about. Of course. That's all they cared about, these parents.

They were relentless and Dr. Weston, a dermatologist with the tight, tan face of a stock photo dad, was one of the worst, worse even than Mrs. Cartwright, almost never missing a chance to explain why his ungraceful twelve-year-old daughter, Pepper, would be the Clara for the ages. (*Innocent but spirited! Refined yet feisty! Pepper has all those qualities, Ms. Durant.*)

Marie could be running a whorehouse out of the third floor as long as the show went on. . . .

"I assure you, Dr. Weston," Dara said, "it'll all be over very soon."

'm sure it's fine," Charlie said later, when Dara called him. He was at the hardware store and she imagined him standing, paralyzed, before a display of fuses as long as a Christmas tree.

"It's unprofessional. There were students downstairs. *Her students*."

"Maybe . . . maybe she felt sick."

In fact, descending the spiral stairs, Marie had tried to claim to Dara that she had suddenly felt weak in the knees. She'd had the nerve to tell Dara that with her skin still flushed, her lipstick blurred and, Dara knew, that man still inside her, dripping down her leg.

"I could hear them," Dara said to Charlie.

"You think you could. You didn't go up there, did you?"

"No," Dara said after a pause. "Dr. Weston was there."

"I don't see why it bothers you so much," Charlie said.

"Doesn't it bother you?" Dara said.

Charlie didn't say anything for a moment, and Dara could hear the sound of the store speaker announcing a big sale on big tools for big men.

"Is it because he works with his hands?" Charlie said. "After all, your father—"

"That's not it," Dara said. "And he doesn't work with his hands. Does he even work at all? He's on that phone all day long when he's supposed to be—"

"So what is it? Because he's older? Because he's not handsome or—"

"She's making a spectacle of herself. She's making a fool of herself." Though Dara couldn't say why, exactly. It was so clear. She shouldn't have to explain.

Besides, she knew it bothered Charlie too. He had barely looked at Marie since the bruises. He avoided her like she was contagious.

"I guess," Dara ventured, "I guess I thought you'd be more upset."

There was a silence between them, the line almost crackling. It was like the sulfur that morning, Dara thought. Still hovering.

"It won't last," Charlie said finally. "I promise."

It was time to begin her five o'clock class, but Dara wasn't ready yet.

"Fifteen minutes at the barre," Dara told her assembled students and ducked into the office. "I'll be back."

Charlie had gone to meet with Madame Sylvie and the directors at the Francis J. Ballenger Performing Arts Center to talk about *Nutcracker* promotion, marketing.

Marie was playing catch-up in Studio A, working with this year's *Nutcracker* tiny Polichinelles who emerge from beneath Mother Ginger's enormous hoop skirt and gambol across the stage.

"*Écoutez, mes petite chéris . . .*" she was saying, her voice with such a lightness to it, so carefree, so pleased with herself. "*Oui, oui, plus rapide!* Faster!"

There was now an electrician in Studio B, yet another bill to add to the teetering pile, and Dara could hear Derek's running commentary on prewar buildings and archaic fuses and the dangers of the grid.

"Are you sure," Dara could hear the electrician ask, "you prepped this site according to code?"

Sitting in the back office, Dara sorted mail. She smoked a cigarette. The furnace came on, everything rumbling. The spiral staircase trembling behind her.

Moments later, a scent caught her. She looked behind and noticed Marie's scarf, that ugly fringed thing, flung across the radiator. A singeing smell wafting.

Dara reached out and grabbed it, curling it into her fist. *Marie will burn this place down if it kills her.*

That was when she saw it. Proof, as if she needed any. A mud track on the third step of the spiral staircase that led to the third floor, to Marie's futon, her hideout, her love nest. The third step, and the fifth too. It was a sight Dara knew well, mud tracks, his signature tattoo, his imprint all over the studio every day. The tread of natty boots, of a man who goes as he pleases, who knows no boundaries, who leaves messes in his wake.

D ara stood on the first step, the stairs shuddering beneath her as she stared at the ugly shoe treads. Then she found herself taking another step.

There was no one up there, not now.

From Studio A, she could hear the shaking of the tambourines and Marie's voice a faint, lilting hum as she guided her girls through the "Mother Ginger" routine.

She took two more steps, nearing the spiral's final coil.

Are you there, she thought suddenly. She nearly said it aloud without knowing what it meant. *Are you there? Is* who *there?*

Stepping backward, she flashed on their mother swaddled up on the third floor after a fight at home with their father. Dara, age fifteen, rushing to the studio with good news (*Mother, I'm going to be one of the Dewdrops in* The Nutcracker), hearing their mother's voice upstairs and taking one tentative step after another, the staircase shivering as she did. *So unsafe*, their mother used to say. *Not for you*.

And another voice, a voice saying her mother's name.

And she held tight and tighter, her hand gripping the steel so tight it might cut her.

Mother . . .

D ara."

Dara turned to the door with a start, jerking her hand from the railing.

It was Marie, waiting like a cat.

It was then that she realized she still had Marie's scarf in her hand, curled up into a ball. Discreetly, she dropped it into her sweater pocket, damp and crushed.

"What are you doing?" Marie asked, biting her thumbnail, a nervous habit since childhood, but one Dara hadn't seen in a long time.

"Nothing," Dara said, walking back down the steps. "Cleaning the mud tracks maybe."

"That's mine, up there," Marie said, gesturing to the third floor. "That's my space."

"Is it now," Dara said, pushing past her. Not liking her tone. "Funny. Because we own the building. Charlie and me. Just like we own the house."

Marie stepped back slightly, teetering on one heel.

"So," Dara continued, "guess who's trespassing?"

Marie stood, her thumb between her teeth, like a child who knows there's nothing she can say.

Dara hadn't intended to say it. She tried never to mention that kind of thing, the business arrangements. Just like when Marie sold her share of the house to them five years ago to go to Europe. When she returned, Dara was careful never to remind Marie that she was technically now their guest.

Marie didn't really have a home, Dara thought suddenly. A wave of something—sadness—coming over her before she fought it off. Pushed it away.

That night, she told Charlie as they sat at the kitchen table drinking refrigerator wine.

"Well," Charlie said, "she can do what she wants up there, can't she?"

"It's not appropriate. It's our place of business."

"I don't know, Dara. But you really shouldn't be up there. I mean, that's her home."

"That's not her home," Dara said. "This is her home."

"She left," Charlie said with a new coolness, his mouth slightly slack, his muscle relaxants taking hold. "Remember."

Dara was getting ready for bed that night when Marie's scarf fell from her pocket and landed on the carpet like a sad rag, its red polka dots like a clown.

Swiftly, she picked it up and threw it in the trash. Then reached down and buried the scarf beneath the trash, the old Band-Aids, the bent bobby pins.

HOT BLONDE

Early the next morning, at the studio, Dara was able to forget everything.

It was a lovely moment of stillness, of dancer and dancer, the mirrors, the movement, a body arching, turning, flying.

All she heard was the soft *thrush* of Corbin Lesterio's feet on the floor. The occasional crunch of his knee, the pop of an arching foot. Corbin's breath, nervous and then calmer. His form strong and then stronger. His bearing becoming, slowly, the bearing of a prince.

He'd persuaded his father to pay for private lessons to help him with his *Nutcracker* audition, and then with the part itself. And Corbin was so eager to please, showing her again and again his *tour en l'air. Legs together*, Dara called out again and again, studying him.

After, she found herself talking to Corbin in the changing room, chatting about the role of the Nutcracker Prince, helping him with his coat, his hands fumbling with the buttons. Teasing him a little bit about his Adam's apple, and how it might ruin his form.

He was so nervous the whole time, his voice speeding up, cracking. He was so nervous and forever blushing, which was so charming.

For the first time in days and days, she felt like herself, her studio free of intrusions, the speakers soundless, the drills unplugged, her focus fixed and intent. She wanted to hold on to it.

Before the arrivals began, the needy, anxious students, whispered chattering and endless preening. Before the parents—Mrs. Briscombe, whose seven-year-old had taken up the habit of eating the drywall, paper, and dirt in Studio B, the endless queries from Dr. Weston, whose daughter Pepper had been caught breaking the shanks of Bailey Bloom's pointe shoes, which was better than the razor blade but hardly ideal.

Before Derek. The sound of his lumbering gait, the raucous ring tone, his voice barking or cooing into his phone, talking to parties unknown, or sometimes, loudly, to Bambi, their insurance adjuster and apparently everyone's, given how much Derek spoke to her and with such familiarity. (*Oh-ho! Next time you gotta go to Aruba. Trust me, cocktails on Pelican Pier and you'll be in heaven. I can get you a deal . . .*)

Before Derek might be watching her from behind the plastic curtain.

Instead, everything was so innocent, and right.

It ended quickly, however. Marie descended, her hair tousled and collarbone splotched pink, exuding après-sex smugness.

Behind her was Derek, wearing yesterday's shirt untucked, the collar points spread, in stocking feet with gold toes, prim loafers looped by his thick fingers.

"Sorry," he said, his voice still thick with sleep, when he spotted Dara saying goodbye to Corbin. "Was hoping to find a coffeepot or something." Then a pause before looking at Corbin, then back at Dara.

"Didn't mean to interrupt," he added, smiling.

Dara looked at him, said nothing.

"Madame Durant, look," Corbin was saying, his left leg extended backward, his center line strong, his swayback now gone, a perfect *piqué arabesque*, a thing of beauty that made Dara's hands tremble at her sides. "Look at me."

The rain came all day that day, painting the windows, shuddering along the awnings, filling the building's swollen gutters.

From Studio B, its windows forever open to release the dust, came the incessant metallic plink of drops against all the plastic sheeting. Surely, Dara thought, they could close the windows for a few hours. Surely, because she couldn't even hear any work being done.

Finally, when Dara noticed Chloë Lin nearly slip on a growing puddle, she traversed the matted path to Studio B, where she found only Gaspar, sweeping the foam-and-wood subfloor with long, methodical strokes, his headphones on.

"What's going on?" Dara said.

Gaspar explained that a delivery of subflooring had ended up at the Durant house rather than the studio, so Mr. Derek and Benny had gone to retrieve it.

"Yes," Charlie confirmed, arriving late after a trip to the bank. "Some kind of mix-up with the vendor."

"A half day that cost us," Dara said. "And I still haven't seen anything from the insurance company. How are we paying for all this?"

"We're not, yet," Charlie said. Then turning, his hand on his wool scarf. "Is it me or is it damp in here?"

The maritime conditions did not forestall more Clara drama, Dara eventually ordering a sobbing Pepper Weston from rehearsal. Bailey Bloom was not pretty enough, Pepper insisted, wringing her eyes, and she hyperextended. *She* should be Clara, she was *supposed* to be Clara, and it was not too late to make a change. Her father told her so.

112

"There's always next Christmas," Dara said, nudging her into the changing room, "if you work hard. Much harder than you are now."

Later, she ran into Derek in the parking lot, one of his phones forever at his ear, gesturing commands at Benny and Gaspar ahead of him carrying heavy bags of grout, cement, whatever else had somehow ended up at their house, clogging their driveway, the truck bed filling with rain.

She tried to move around him, but he kept blocking her, like a little boy might do, a little boy with a crush he didn't understand.

Up close, she saw a signet ring gleaming from his right hand, his ring finger.

Up close, the leather from his car coat reminded her of something. She couldn't name it, but she pulled back quickly, turning away.

So rare that she was so close to him, but he was standing so close to her, the smell of the leather, the powder room's oozing soap.

"Nice house you got over there, on Sycamore," he said. "Big, a beast. They don't make 'em like that anymore, eh?"

Forever that blinding white smile, that signet ring flashing. Aftershave like burying your head in animal hide, in fur.

Dara nodded, trying to move past. *Why is he talking about our house?*

"Was that the house you grew up in?" he asked, tilting his head. Making conversation as if they were friendly, as if everything was fine and he wasn't debasing her sister nightly.

"Yes," Dara said. "I need to get back inside—"

"It's awfully big for just the two of you. Have you ever thought of selling it?"

"No. Never."

"You may not see its value on the open market," he continued. "That part of town is no longer the wrong side of the tracks. The tracks moved. You could flip it like a flapjack. Make a pretty penny."

"Absolutely not," Dara said. "That's our family home. We would never sell it."

Derek lifted his eyebrows.

"I'm starting to get the feeling you don't like me," he said, smiling again, this time almost as though embarrassed, or something. "But there's no reason we can't be friends. And your sister . . ."

"I don't have to like you," Dara said, moving past him, a blast of the leather scent in her face. "You'll be gone soon."

The look on his face, surprise and something else, a wounded look, something.

It was satisfying, unexpected. A little boy's face, his mother abandoning him at the mall.

She could feel him looking at her even as she walked away, walking as fast as she could.

The conversation hummed in her ear unpleasantly long after. What did he know about their house anyway? Yes, it was old, leaky, drafty, their house. There were uneven floors, windows painted shut, plaster crumbling, and roots growing in the pipes.

And it was big, far too big, their parents managing a down payment when the neighborhood was on its heels. No grocery store in five miles but at least three bars. No streetlights their first ten years there, no matter how many times their father called the city.

And it was true that the neighborhood had transformed in recent years, the corner deli replaced with a light and bright café, the public pool filled with concrete and replaced with a health spa, and all those creaky, charming prewar houses sold, razed, and replaced overnight with gaudy palaces.

The house was nothing to a man like Derek. The land was everything.

A man like Derek, he could never understand it was their home. It was their whole childhood. More than that, Dara thought, her eyes blurring.

Suddenly, she remembered something Marie had said, months ago, before she moved out.

They had been looking out the front window at the old weather-beaten colonial across the street, the SOLD sign on the weedy lawn. The latest of many.

"We could do that," she'd said. "We don't have to live here forever."

"Is that so?" Dara had said. "You wanna run away with the circus?"

But Marie kept looking, her fingers on the windowpane like when she was little.

"We could put it up for sale."

It hurt to hear. That house of their childhood, however varied and unsettled, their mother crying at her vanity table, her chignon slipping loose, their father raging down the hall, knocking his fist into that peeling plaster and demanding respect in his own home, or at least attention.

"*We* could," Dara said pointedly, reminding Marie of the facts. "Charlie and I could. Because it's our house. But we wouldn't."

Did you say something to Derek?" Marie asked later.

"About what?" Dara replied. Her sister had come upon her as she exited the powder room—the one she could never set foot in without thinking of her sister and Derek in there. The way the sink now wobbled on its base.

"I don't know. He left early. He didn't even say goodbye."

Dara didn't say anything, suppressing an unexpected smile.

"What if he's done with me?"

"Marie. Marie." There was something so desperate about it. Her sister who knew how she felt, her disapproval over this entanglement. But who else could Marie talk to?

"When he says he has to go, I follow him out the door. I chase him down the spiral stairs. I beg him to stay."

"Pathetic," Dara said as coolly as she could even though Marie's intensity—her face pressed so close, her mascara sweat-stippled—was making her hot, confused.

"I don't care. I don't care. I have no shame. He ate away all my shame."

"No wonder he's getting tired of you," Dara said. "I'm tired of you."

"I need to hear his voice at night. I can't sleep without his voice in my ear, talking and talking, all night."

It was just like when they were little, Marie always begging to sit with their father while he drank his beers and watched *Columbo* reruns, old movies. How she would ask him to explain everything and he would, on and on. *See, he looks like a magician, but he's really a Nazi. I mean, Christ, look how clean he is.*

"He'd promised he'd stay over tonight." She looked up at Dara, her eyes bewildered like a child's. "Why is he doing this to me?"

Dara shook her head. Everything he said was a con.

"I've done everything he asked me to. Such filthy things," she said, voice rising, "I've done it all and liked it."

Dara paused a moment, pictures flashing in her head. Marie's degradation. Hairy and ugly and splotchy, his great tufted back, his made-to-order teeth, the marks his socks left on his ankles. Battering away at her, splitting her open, slapping her softness, fist wrapped in her hair.

"That was your mistake," Dara said. "You have to hold something back. Now you're no longer his conquest. Now you're just his whore."

But Marie wasn't listening.

The next morning, Dara approached the back office, following the sound of Marie's lilting titter.

She saw the look on Charlie's face first.

She heard him say, "Marie, what did you do? What did you *do?*"

And Dara thought she might walk into the back office to find Marie with a black eye like out of a cartoon, a pink slab of steak pitched over it.

"I don't know, Charlie," Marie was saying, her voice softly shrugging. "I just did it. I just did it."

That was when Dara saw it. Marie's hair. Caught up in a ponytail and stripped from sandy blond to near whiteness.

The whole office smelled sweet and chemical.

"You look ridiculous," Dara said.

"Only to you," Marie replied coolly. Then touching her hair a little nervously, patting it.

Seated at the desk, Charlie didn't say anything, just kept staring.

Well, it was impossible not to. She looked like an old-time pinup who should be lounging in silver lingerie, in bright lamé. A gangster's moll. Or maybe a hooker, high-end. The kind their dad, when he had a load on, talked about seeing in the port cities when he was in the Merchant Marines. *Always a few with a fancy doll look you'd pay extra for just to come in their faces.*

"Derek likes it," she said, touching the nape of her neck, slipping the elastic free. "I like it." Leaning down, whispering hotly in Dara's ear, "He liked it so much he fucked me all night."

Dara coughed loudly, feeling sick. That wasn't a word Marie used, or didn't use without stumbling over it, like she had the other night.

"Well," Charlie said. "That's that." And reaching for his back pills, shaking the container, pills tumbling across the desk felt.

Something was hovering near the front of Dara's head, but she couldn't name it.

Suddenly: A phrase floated forward in her brain.

Hot Buttered Blonde.

She couldn't get it out of her head, every time she saw Marie that day, her head like the fizzy top of a dandelion, a daffodil's crimped corona.

It was many hours later that it came to her. That time last year, Mrs. Bloom submitting to the hairdresser, to the tantalizing name: *Hot Buttered Blonde.*

A coincidence, surely.

Mrs. Bloom, the year before, a brazen blonde. Her shame over it.

Marie, of course, had no shame.

*H**e tells me things, Dara. He tells me what I do to him.*

  He says when he leaves here, he smells of it. All the heat and cunning. The smell of the studio, which is the smell of me. Musk, baby powder, sweat.

He says he can smell it on his shirt cuffs, in the creases of his shoes. All the bodies so close, daring eyes and straining limbs. The salty brine of hunger and pain. Bodies, he never knew they could be so complicated, so tortured. He never knew how much girls like to torture themselves.

It was impossible. That man, with his two phones and his big voice and his swagger. A cliché of what women supposedly liked, secretly, under the skin.

This man—he was a nothing. There was no center to him. No feeling. And he didn't care about Marie and would toss her aside soon enough or already had because a man like that—

He says he thinks about me when he's driving home on the highway. When he's pumping gas or rolling a cart down the grocery store aisle, the pink stacks of meat.

He thinks about having me again. Spreading me open. Pinning me like a butterfly.

His glove compartment—did you know, Dara—he keeps one of my leotards in there. He pulled it off my bedroom floor, pressed his face against its soft, wet crotch. Stuffed it in his pocket when I wasn't looking. At stoplights, when he's stuck in traffic, when the light goes red, he pops it open, puts his hand in there, thinks of me.

Maybe we should call someone," Dara said to Charlie that night, finally home from his PT appointment, the Shamrock taxi pulling up just after nine.

"Like who?" he said, a muzzy look in his eye. "The sex police?"

"You don't get it. You don't get Marie."

Charlie looked her.

"I get Marie," he said. "Believe me."

You never really knew what went on in other people's bedrooms, in their heads, Dara thought.

But this thing, this desire to be bossed around, dominated—such a cliché. Such an old, dusty woman thing she'd never understand. She'd never felt it herself.

But with Marie, it made sense, in a way.

She'd always been willful, resistant.

Yet it turned out she couldn't wait to be bent, broken, split in two.

The stronger they are, the harder they fall.

That's what their mother used to say about dancers. How you had to break them. Their stubborn bodies, their stubborn wills. The more defiant and resistant they were, the harder you must be. The more violent, the stronger hands on their bodies, bending them, pressing, turning them out.

The stronger they are, the faster to their knees.

But, Dara thought, *no one is stronger than me.*

TWO

THE TURNOUT

———————

Every ballet dancer must achieve her turnout. The ability to rotate her body one-hundred-eighty degrees, from the hips down to the toes.

Imagine your thigh muscles wrapping around your bones, their mother always told them. *Imagine your leg as a spinning barber pole.*

She loved to tell them how, when she was ten years old, she was one of four dancers in her province to undertake special training with a Great Diva, a severe Russian beauty famous for having her feet surgically broken, her bones realigned so she might have a more natural line, a more perfect pointe.

Every day for the six weeks of the program the Great Diva scolded and berated their mother for her turnout.

Every day she yanked and dragged their mother's legs, twisting them, muscles straining, bones nearly twanging until they rotated so far at the hips that the knees, the feet turned outward. But still, it was not enough.

Mademoiselle Durant, entendez! Tailbone down! Over toes, not over heels!

Every night, their mother sobbed into her pillow, sobbed from the pain of cranking her body like an old motor.

Then, one day, when the Great Diva demanded once more that she *turn, turn, turn*, their mother felt something rise inside her, something powerful.

Suddenly, something snapped inside and her hips and legs felt infinitely pliable, soft taffy, a slinky expanding.

Her hips, hot and newly supple, opened like a book from the center of her body. It felt glorious and so painful she saw stars.

But she did not stop.

Why would she? That feeling, that sensation hot in the center of her.

She kept turning until her feet pushed past one-hundred-eighty degrees, until they turned backward like a doll with its legs put on backward. Like a circus freak.

It was, she told them, *the greatest feeling of my life.*

It will be, she told them, *for you too.*

When Dara achieved her turnout at age ten years, six months, she saw the same stars. It was a feeling she recognized from her own furtive confusions, in the claw-foot bathtub, under her bunkbed blankets, her hands tingling, her thighs gaping like a keyhole, and that feeling after, like her whole fist would not be enough.

It's the dancer's body opening itself to the audience, their mother always told them.

Giving them everything.

The moment you achieve it, you've become a dancer. You've become a woman.

BRAZEN

The bruise was very high up Marie's inner thigh, ringlet-shaped, florid, a cherry bursting.

Dara was trying to lead Corbin Lesterio and Oliver Perez, her Nutcracker Prince and the Mouse King, through their epic swordfight, the climactic clash in the first act.

But there was a visitor lurking in the doorway. And this time it wasn't Derek. Inexplicably, it was Marie, her bright new hair like a queen's crown, you could not miss her. Nor could you miss the monstrous bruise on the inside of her thigh. Standing there with one leg turned out, flashing it like a hooker flashing her garter.

"It appears we have a surprise guest," Dara said tightly. "Or a Peeping Tom."

Marie took this as an invitation, strolling in, still panting a little from leading her four-year-olds, sweat wreathed beneath her breasts.

The purple neck marks from the week before had grown yellow, a sticky highlighter across her collarbones. But now there was this, fresh. On her thigh. Open. Impossible to miss.

Corbin looked away discreetly, but Oliver seemed rapt, his sword falling to his side.

"Let's start from the top," Dara said, drawing the boys' roaming eyes back to her.

Marie watched for a few moments, Corbin and Oliver circling each other, their arms lifted, then swooping, all leading up to Corbin's double *saut de basque* before landing the death blow.

"You know what?" Marie interjected suddenly. Corbin and Oliver looked at her, alarmed. No one ever spoke in Dara's studio but Dara. "I think the change could be faster. Like this."

And Dara watched as Marie moved toward Corbin and Oliver and reached out to position Oliver's arm. Making a correction to Corbin's hip.

Unlike Dara, Marie always touched her students, but Marie's students were all little girls. Yet Marie, now, had one hand on each of their narrow hips. *Get up on your legs. Don't sink those hips on me.* Her hands like tiny white moths fluttering around them both. Their hard bodies, their stiff energy. The boys red-faced, eager.

Dara watched.

Oliver pressing Corbin, Corbin swaying backward before pitching forward, coming back stronger, the force of his body, the swoop of it, straight into his turns.

Marie's change made it more dynamic. Marie's change felt frenetic, surprising. When Oliver lunged, the sword tip pressed against the hollow in Corbin's neck, Dara felt herself gasp.

She was remembering that Sword Swallower they used to see at the carnival as children. How she crossed two swords down her throat at the same time. Her head thrown back, her throat like an elegant vase, the swords' round handles like bright flowers blooming forth. Dara covering her eyes, while beside her Marie kept saying, *Look! Look!*

The boys finished, breathless, looking over to Dara for approval.

"Well, then. We must set Mademoiselle Durant free," Dara said, walking past Marie. "She's done enough."

* * *

"D o you want me coming in your studio?" Dara asked later. "Do you want me to advise your little moppets on how to play Candy Canes, to do cartwheels?"

But Marie didn't say anything, cross-legged on her studio floor, licking her finger and turning the pages of some kind of flashy brochure.

"What is that?" Dara asked.

Marie spread open the brochure like a centerfold, revealing an array of cars shiny as candy wrappers gliding across a great expanse, a desert, or climbing up a grand terrain. Everest. *"Luxury in motion,"* it read.

"Why are you looking at cars?"

Marie shrugged maddeningly, her eyes on the shiny pages, fingers digging into that silky silvery hair of hers.

Behind them, the drill started up again in Studio B, the floors shaking suddenly.

Dara covered her ears, hopelessly.

Marie looked up and smiled at her, like she was the crazy one.

I 'm trying, Madame Durant. I swear."

They were rehearsing a hallowed moment in their *Nutcracker* when Clara slowly, beautifully, goes into an *arabesque*, standing on one leg, the other extended behind her in a perfect line, as she lifts the Nutcracker doll—or, for now, a paper towel roll because Dara couldn't find the prop— like a torch. It's the moment in which, in some way, she gives herself over to the Nutcracker, this funny little man with his funny big teeth who will become her prince.

If a dancer hasn't mastered her turnout, there's no hiding it in the *arabesque en pointe.*

And Bailey Bloom was flailing. All the Level IVs tittering behind their hands. Her *balancé* was somehow both wobbly and tense, her body keeling backward.

"Mademoiselle Bloom," Dara said, "would you rather have a broken nose or a broken back?"

Bailey lifted herself upright. "Neither," she said tentatively. "I mean—"

"Weight forward," Dara said, moving toward her, Bailey's eyes now dinner-plate wide. "Remember your turnout. The more you rotate that hip, the higher the leg. You must open yourself out to the audience."

"I am," Bailey said. "I mean, yes, Madame Durant."

Pa-thet-ick, came the stage whisper from Pepper Weston, flicking a bobby pin in the air in the far corner of the studio. *The ringleader,* Dara thought, *of that little pink pack.* Glancing over at them. Pepper, Iris Cartwright, Gracie Hent and her extravagant sighs. One or more of them had planted the razor blade in Bailey's shoe, had filled another of her shoes with rubber cement. Little monsters.

"Again," Dara said, twirling her finger at Bailey, who scurried back to position.

"Imagine a string tied around your sternum," Dara said, watching Bailey raise her leg. "Someone is gently pulling that string. Lifting your chest upward and out. Back wide. No shoulder blade creep. Keep breathing."

The other girls watched, waited.

"Rotate that hip," Dara said. "Give yourself over."

Bailey's body steadied, her arms outstretched, the paper towel roll damp in her hand. Dara moved closer.

"Shut them out," Dara said, her voice low and stern at Bailey's ear. "Listen to me. They don't exist. Listen only to me."

Dara and Marie had done well enough as dancers. Both had been in the corps of the same small regional company. Once, Marie accepted an offer from a larger touring company—only to return three weeks later after fainting in a hotel lobby, her body whittled down to wishbone. (*I forgot about eating,* she told Dara. *I couldn't remember to do it.*)

Their mother once confided to Dara that Marie was not a lovely dancer—*not like you, my dear*—but she was a memorable one. She danced, their mother said, with the intensity of a bad dream. You did not forget her.

Dara had known she was more technically skilled. That her body—two inches taller (*all of it in the neck*, Charlie used to say, stroking it, long ago)—was more "ballerina" than Marie's coiled frame. But she had not known until that moment that their mother thought Marie was the real dancer. It was better, after all, to be memorable than lovely.

L ater that day, Dara peeked in her sister's studio, Marie again seated on the floor, her legs splayed wide, the bruise a ring of fire.

Leaning forward, her face resting on her elbows, she was talking, low and slow, to two of her seven-year-old girls, both sitting cross-legged across from her and listening intently.

The hammering from Studio B was loud, the plastic curtain vibrating, so Dara couldn't hear what Marie was saying, but she couldn't stop watching.

Suddenly, a shadow appeared behind the curtain, large enough to fill the frame.

Dara knew who it was and knew he was watching Marie, her legs spread wide, the bruise, like an open mouth, red and hungry.

Marie, who was posing for him, showing herself to him, exposing herself, laying herself bare.

Dara would not stand for it.

She charged across the studio, Marie's head lifting, watching as Dara stalked over to the plastic curtain, pulling it back.

Derek giving her a look, a whiff of dismissal, one finger pressed against his ear, pushing a plug back into place.

I don't understand why it's taking so long," Dara said.

Derek nodded vaguely, infuriatingly, a long copper pipe in his hand, holding it like a baseball bat, twirling it like a baton.

"All these weeks," Dara continued, voice scraping now over the noise, "and I'm still standing on plywood."

"Subfloor," Derek clarified, smiling a little. "We hit a few stumbling blocks. Some surprises with the pipe grid. You own an old house, so you know. It's always something with those big shambling places built before the code—"

"This has nothing to do with our house. I'm talking about the job we hired you for," Dara said, her voice so loud she surprised herself, a stirring from Benny in the far corner unrolling plastic sheeting. He and Gaspar exchanged looks. "You may be fooling my sister, but you're not fooling me."

"I would be disappointed if I did," Derek said. His tone, his demeanor felt new, felt smug, less salesman, more something else. Dara watched as he choked up on the copper pipe, gripping it like a bat, swung it casually, like a ballplayer on deck.

"You know what my old man used to say?" he said, the whir of the pipe in his hands. "Watch out for a bad woman, and never trust a good one."

Derek was gone by lunch, disappearing for the rest of the day, leaving everything to Benny and Gaspar, who spent the afternoon working with what felt like heightened velocity, their baseball caps damp with sweat.

Dara felt badly, except she didn't.

Later, Dara came upon Charlie and Marie arguing near the electrical kettle.

All day, Charlie had been enmeshed in some low-level disagreement with Marie over her failure to keep attendance, which made it hard for him to bill.

"Why don't you just admit," Charlie was saying to Marie now, "you took that box of Assam red. The one I special-ordered."

It didn't make sense. Marie never drank tea. Only canned coffee that looked like tobacco spit.

"And when was this?" Marie replied, caressing her neck flagrantly, like a child wondering at her body.

"When you left. When you moved out. When you left us," Charlie said. "Did you take that too?"

Marie stared at him a moment, her teeth tugging into her lip.

It was a standoff of some cryptic kind and Dara chose not to get involved.

That night, Dara couldn't sleep and wandered the house, no creaking floorboard loud enough to wake Charlie from his sleeping pills.

Nice house you got over there, on Sycamore, Derek had said. And he'd mentioned it again, that day. She didn't like the idea of him looking at their house, evaluating it. She didn't like the idea of him even thinking of their house, its insides. It felt like there was something behind it.

She moved from room to room, her hands on every splintery doorframe, every wiggly doorknob. Last was their old bedroom, its door closed. She always kept it closed.

Any time she spent more than a few minutes inside, she felt sweaty and unsettled. With its sloping dormer walls, the space was so small it could only fit a dresser, a lamp, and their bunkbed, its wood shellacked to a lustrous shimmer, the wagon-wheel headboard with the spindle spokes you could hold on to or fondle, reading a scary story, waking from a bad dream.

Even through the door, she could smell it, a room redolent of their girl selves, the must of sweat-stiff leotards, the sting of balms, their bodies, budding and fulsome, their clammy underarms and thighs. The sounds, the squeaking bunkbed, the click-click of Marie's teeth while she slept.

For each of them, it was their most private space, which, of course, they shared. The hidden cove where Dara dreamt and wondered, her body always aching and changing and fighting itself.

"Are you thinking about a boy?" Marie would whisper from the bunk above. Long summer nights, the click of the beetles, the soft grind of the cicadas, all those crickets rubbing their legs together, the low moan of the mosquitoes at the screen.

"I'm not telling you," Dara would say, even if she was always thinking of a boy—Peter Garcia, who pressed against her once at recital, the Marshall brothers at school—or even more just thinking of herself, her own body, hard and scraped raw from dancing.

Her own body, its secrets she was just beginning to unfold, slowly, with quivering fingers.

Marie figured out how to do it before Dara. Dara could hear her above, the little panting sounds. She could picture Marie's face pressed against the slats, red and veiny.

Dara did it differently, though.

Dara couldn't be as quiet as Marie. Because, she decided, she felt it so much more deeply.

Because, every time, Dara thought she just might die from the feeling.

Every time, she saw stars, just like with the turnout. *You don't see stars, Marie? Are you sure you're doing it right?*

Marie wanted to see them too. Wanted Dara to show her.

But Dara kept it for herself. Marie was always bragging that her body was different. That she had *something no one else has*. Well, maybe Dara did too. Once, the feeling came through her so strongly she kicked her right leg hard against the footboard, snapping one of the slats in half, shooting it across the room.

Giggling in the dark, Dara and Marie crouched over the carpet, trying to find the pieces.

They Elmer's-glued it back into place and no one knew until, a few weeks later, Dara knocked it loose again, her ankle caught between the slats, her body drenched and shaking.

* * *

For weeks after the slat broke, Marie liked to sit on the floor at the foot of Dara's bed while Dara tried to sleep. She liked to finger the spot the broken slat had occupied. The roughness, the scatter of sawdust. She liked to crouch down behind the footboard and squeeze her fist through the empty space between the slats. Or push her hand through and point her index finger at Dara while she tried to sleep. Her eyes glowing, wolflike, in the dark, she liked to point her finger at Dara as if to say *I know you.*

THICK AS THIEVES

Two Weeks Later

*T*he Nutcracker performances began in twenty-six days.

Twenty-six days, which is nothing, a blink. Twenty-six days, which is everything, is two dozen rehearsals, hundreds of corrections (*Elbows up! Rib cage in!*), thousands of *tendus* and *jetés*, the endless repetitions that make ballet.

The Nutcracker began in twenty-six days and Studio B seemed no closer to completion. In fact it seemed less, its subfloor still exposed, the new flooring still not yet arrived, an unmistakable smell of mold hovering hotly in the air.

The Nutcracker began in twenty-six days and Studio B was still a hazard site, wires hanging from the walls, floorboards piled, tarps slipping loose, the windows forever flung open, the air thick with plaster and dust.

The Nutcracker began in twenty-six days and her sister was destroying herself.

* * *

And everyone was cold. The temperature had dropped overnight, a warning bell from the coming winter, and the radiator pipes were shushing and singing, spitting brown water and smelling of dust and hair, of skin peels and toenails.

And they still had to keep the windows open in Studio B for this stage of the renovation. For the smells, mysterious and clinging.

You never wanted the studios to be too warm. A little chill helped keep the energy up, to offset the natural heat emitted by bundles of young girls. But now it was so frigid that, before class began, the youngest girls shivered in their leotards, skin dimpled, huddling together for warmth. Rows of them, pink and paler pink—like a rabbit's ear.

"Hey," Derek said when Dara and Charlie arrived, all their studio layers wrapped around their bodies like mummies, "how's that furnace holding out on you over on Sycamore?"

Here he was again, talking about their house.

"It's fine," Charlie said, walking past Derek, his eyes catching on the state of Studio B, which seemed to have remained in the subfloor stage for days and days now. What work were they doing?

Derek turned to Dara. "Those big Victorians gotta land you a heating bill in four digits," he said.

Dara didn't say anything, draping her coat over her arm, navigating the cords, the chaos.

"Or maybe I'm wrong," he said finally. Men like this, she thought, had to fill the air, fill the space. Any room they were in. "Maybe you never even have to turn on the heat."

Lifting a power cord from her path, leaning close as she tried to pass. "I bet you don't."

He put his hand on her coat, her coat on her arm.

"I bet your house is hot, hot, hot."

The house again," Dara said to Charlie later that morning. "See how he keeps talking about it."

"He'll be done soon," Charlie said, staring at a stack of bills, "and out of our lives."

"We still haven't received a dime from the insurance company," Dara said. "I don't even know how we're paying for this. Or how he is."

"I'll call them again," Charlie said. "It keeps changing. The estimate keeps changing."

"The parents . . ." Dara said. "I'm hearing complaints."

Once word got around that Mrs. Bloom couldn't be around the construction dust, a coterie of parents—well, at least a few—had begun expressing concern that their daughters were breathing dangerous particulates, possibly mold. *I assure you,* Dara always said, *there's no risk. But if you're concerned, we can give your daughter's part to another girl,* which always stopped them cold. Several of the younger girls began showing up with dust masks strapped to their bobbly heads, tearing them off the minute their parents left, shoving them in coat pockets before Dara could see.

"Parents always complain," Charlie said. "That's what makes them parents."

"It's going to get worse," Dara said.

Charlie looked at her. "She'll get tired of him," he said, turning away.

"You're wrong," Dara said.

Every night that week, Dara had walked by the studio late, trying to burn off all the tension, everything. And every night but one, the only lights on were Marie's on the third floor. A tiny octagon glowing. And Derek's truck was in the private driveway, parked deeper than during the day.

In the morning, he snaked down those spiral stairs, sometimes with a toothbrush hanging from his mouth, or buttoning his cuffs.

The day hurdled forward, three long hours with her alternating Dewdrops, two earnest, impossibly big-eyed sisters named, also impossibly, Holly and Ivy, a year apart in age but with nearly identical bodies, long, scythe-like feet, and small sleek heads with throats like long scarves, stretching forever.

In the next studio, she heard Marie all day, the low hum of her sing-songy voice, *plié, tendu, port de bras*, all her little ballerinas fluttering around her, dipping up and down, dreaming of one day being as elegant as Mademoiselle Durant, her technicolor bruises, the red of her red, red mouth.

Marie didn't appear for their usual lunch break, a forty-minute window between classes and rehearsals for a banana, tea, plucking figs or almonds from a shared baggie, Charlie smoking on the windowsill.

"Where is she?" Dara asked Charlie.

He gave her a look.

"Where is she?" Dara moved to the spiral staircase, peering up. *She wouldn't dare, would she?*

"No," Charlie said. "He took her to lunch."

"The contractor."

"I saw them leaving," he said, his brow creased. "She was wearing a skirt."

Dara shook her tea bag, Earl Grey spattering.

"I told you," she said.

Charlie raised an eyebrow, looked away.

An hour later, Marie had not returned, forcing Charlie to lead her six-year-olds through their barre work, trying not to strain himself, planting himself in the corner, all the girls sneaking peeks in the mirror.

Another half hour passed before Marie appeared. She was indeed in an ill-fitting skirt, the kind a secretary in a movie might wear, and a new jacket, leather like Derek's, but with a chic sash. It was two sizes too big and seemed to swallow her.

Dara spotted her watching herself in the mirror, swanning about in it for a minute before she made her entrance in Studio A.

Apologizing to her excitable students (*Mademoiselle Durant, you look so pretty!*) as she passed them, she stripped the jacket loose, its new leathery smell choking everyone. She unzipped the skirt, letting it fall to the floor, leaving her back in her usual thick tights.

Dara watched from the door. Watched the whole spectacle.

H e took me to that Italian place with all the red awnings," Marie was saying to Charlie as Dara walked into the office later. "We had fried calamari big as curtain rings and a lobster we picked right out of the tank."

Charlie sat, silently writing checks at the desk, an odd look on his face, like he was thinking of things but wouldn't say them.

It was surprising, really. All of it. The lunch, the production of it, even that Marie had chosen to tell Charlie about it first. Rather than Dara.

"Is that why you were so late?" Dara asked. "Couldn't pick your lobster?"

Marie turned and looked at Dara.

"And then you know what we did, Charlie?" she said, her eyes still on Dara. "We went to a luxury showroom and looked at cars."

"Cars?" Charlie said, looking up. "Why?"

"I think I might need one," she said.

"It's ridiculous," Dara said. "You live where you work. You need a car to come down the stairs in the morning?"

"If you need to go anywhere," Charlie said, "you can take the Chrysler."

"You barely know how to drive, Marie," Dara said. "Remember?"

"Well," Marie said, her face changing, that fox look it could sometimes get, "I didn't know a lot of things until I did."

Dara looked at her, feeling a chill.

A s Dara walked away, she could hear Marie returning to her conversation with Charlie. Charlie, pondering the stack of mail in front of him. Charlie looking far-off, unreachable.

"Big, snazzy cars," Marie was saying. "They give you champagne while you browse. You can sit behind the wheel." Then, her voice softer, "They all smelled like Dad."

Whatever had seemed to be turning now seemed turned. Marie and the contractor. They were a thing, together. And it was changing things. Derek's new cockiness, cock of the walk. Marie dyeing her hair, wearing a skirt, looking at snazzy cars. Marie flagrant and unrepentant, fornicating on the floor above while her seven-year-old students waited below.

"So, what did you talk about at this lunch today? Power tools?" Dara asked, unable to stop herself from returning to the doorway. "Spray tans?"

But Marie, standing behind Charlie seated at the desk, didn't say a word. And that fox look coming back to her face as she snaked her arm down past Charlie's cheek and neck and into his shirt pocket, pulling a cigarette from the pack snug there.

Sliding it into her mouth like some kind of femme fatale, disappearing into Studio A, the click of a lighter, a cloud of smoke trailing behind her.

That evening, Marie climbed in Derek's big oil-slick truck and headed off to parts unknown. Together they went, both in their leather jackets like a motorcycle gang, off into the sunlight, and Dara knew now that something had changed. Marie had shut her out. This was the new stage.

The next morning, her fears were confirmed.

She'd arrived at the studio before seven and he was tumbling down the spiral stairs from Marie's lair, his hair still gleaming from the stand-up shower, his breath mints blasting—it made her sick.

His smell, his cleanness made her sick.

She so preferred the smells of the studio—sweat and feet and tiger balm, the musk of feet and boys' crotches and the occasional whiff of ammonia from the little ones, their tights stinging with urine—and the smells of the house, their home—camphor and tea and wet plaster and the burnt furnace stench and, still, in every carpet fiber, every pine whorl, their mother's scent. Perfume and desperation.

"Morning, sis," he said, bolder than ever.

"I'm not your sister," Dara said.

"I guess no one has a chance, do they?"

"Pardon?"

"You three," he said, his voice wet from sleep, "thick as thieves."

He was standing before her now, coffee cup half crushed in his big meaty hand.

"I'm busy," Dara said, on hold with the insurance company, trying to get some answers about their claim payment.

"Hey, I get it. Family is everything," he said, leaning against the jamb. "Marie explained."

Explained? Dara thought. *What does that mean?* And she didn't like the way he was watching her. It felt like he was poking her with his manicured fingers.

What kind of man gets a manicure, she'd said to Marie.

A man who cares about where he puts his hands, Marie had replied.

"I'm busy," Dara repeated abruptly. "Do you mind?"

He took a sip from his coffee cup and made no move to leave.

"You all used to live together, right? In that big old spookhouse on Sycamore?"

There was something strange about the phrasing of it. *Live together.* Or maybe it was just the way he said it, sotto voce, like a sly secret.

"We grew up there," Dara said. "Is this about the house again? Because—"

"You and Marie. You two grew up there."

"And Charlie."

"You know, when I first got here, I couldn't tell. Is Charlie your husband," he said, tossing his cup in the trash, "or your brother?"

Dara looked at him. "Is that supposed to be funny?"

"I'm just curious," he said. "It's kind of unusual. Two sisters, one husband. How's the math work there?"

She didn't like the way he was watching her.

"For years," he said, tilting his head, resting it on the door jamb, "the three of you playing house. Kinda an odd setup. Non-traditional, if you will."

Dara didn't say anything.

"So close. So private," he said. "I guess it worked until it didn't."

Dara stood up, began moving.

"Your sister told me about it." He paused a second, looking at Dara, waiting for something. "She told me you wanted her to leave."

Dara's mouth opened, then closed.

"No," she said, shaking her head. Feeling dizzy all of a sudden, the smack of Derek's aftershave.

"No," she repeated, stepping backward, uneasy on her feet. "I didn't want her to leave. And she didn't leave." Then, more softly, "She abandoned us."

FOXY

She told me you wanted her to leave.

All day it buzzed in Dara's brain. Was he lying, bluffing? Or was Marie, foxy Marie?

Dara stood in her studio, hands clawed around her tea mug, calling out commands to her Clara and her Nutcracker Prince—*Lengthen the spine, don't tuck. Lengthen the neck and lower the shoulders. Turn the head without tilting. Bailey. Bailey. Bailey, attendu!*—but all she could think of was Marie.

She thought about calling Charlie, who was over at the Ballenger Center meeting with Madame Sylvie, but she didn't know what she would say. She wasn't sure she could make him understand.

Later that day, the rain-heavy gutter in the front of the building gave way, tumbling dead leaves, twigs, mud, to the parking lot below, spattering three exiting students in ballerina pink.

Later, Gaspar found a dead bat among the debris, wings splayed. It had gotten caught, snared.

* * *

In Studio A, she found Marie stretched on the floor, her arms above her head, her barely-breasts disappearing into her bony chest.

Dara stood above her, her hands drifting down to her own breastbone, feeling the hard chop of her rib cage. Their strange, strange bodies. All the heat and fire was in the feet, stamped and lined and mangled and engorged. . . .

"Why did you talk to him about us?" Dara said, her feet near Marie's head. "Why?"

Marie looked up at Dara but didn't say anything. That cool blond hair of hers—the talk of the studio for days after—was already starting to look strangely green, frayed.

"Derek. Why did you tell him personal things?"

"What things?"

"About your moving out of the house. He said you told him I wanted you to leave."

The corners of Marie's mouth seemed to lift ever so slightly, a ghost smile.

"I didn't tell him that," she said. "That's not what I told him."

Now Dara couldn't stop, an awful feeling in her chest.

"And about the way we lived," she said, stumbling over the words.

"What about the way we lived, Dara?" Marie said, looking up at Dara, her palms across her breasts. Her eyes vacant, guileless.

Dara paused, watching her sister. Was it her sister, even. This creature possessed.

"The way he said it, the way you told him about us," Dara continued. "He twisted it all around like there was something wrong about it. Something . . ." She fumbled to find the word. "Unseemly."

Marie looked at her, a faux blankness that made Dara want to scream.

"What?" Dara said, her voice rising. Marie and her little silences, her cryptic smiles. "What are you thinking?"

"I'm not thinking anything," Marie said, rubbing her arms with her hands, a giddy look on her face.

Dara's arm thrust out, grabbing Marie's elbow hard, yanking it.

"Don't worry," Marie said, staring down at Dara's fingers, red on her skin. "I won't tell him about you."

That night, Dara couldn't sleep. She kept thinking of the two of them—that snide contractor and her remote sister—sharing confidences. Whispering about her, about their private matters. This was new, Dara thought. This was the turning, the deepening she'd been feeling.

It was a breach. A betrayal.

"I suppose you and Charlie never talk about me when I'm not around," Marie had said later.

"That's not the same," Dara had replied loudly, her voice strangling up her throat. "He's my husband."

Marie started shaking her head, over and over, as Dara went on, "And you know Charlie. Charlie loves you. We've all known each other since we were children. We grew up together. There's nothing wrong with that. It's family, it's . . ."

She went on and on, hating the sound of her own voice, high and strained and nothing like their mother's. She always tried to match their mother's soft, lush alto.

"We grew up together," Dara finally repeated.

But Marie only looked at her and said quietly, "Did we? Grow up?"

That night, back in the warm confines of the house, cluttered and smelly and familiar, she wanted to tell Charlie everything. She wanted him to calm her down, to make her tea, to rub her feet with his strong hands.

But she couldn't. They never talked about when Marie moved out, or why. It had been a strained time for all of them and there was no need to stir it all up again. That's what was so enraging about it all, about that contractor bringing it up. About Marie having told him things.

I didn't tell him that, Marie had insisted. But in that vague way that left you to wonder what she did tell him. And why.

When Dara finally fell asleep, two of Charlie's yellow-and-green pills sinking her into some kind of swampy dream place, she had bad dreams. She dreamt she could hear them, Derek's sly voice, Marie's tittering laugh. Snide, insinuating, both of them. They were in the room, in her bedroom. They were standing in the bedroom door. No. They were huddled at the foot of the bed, their eyes dancing, hands over their mouths, snickering. They were right there! Watching!

Charlie, Charlie, she said, shaking him, hands clawing at his back.

But he didn't wake up and she was never sure if he was in the dream or not. If he was in the dream and couldn't hear her, or she'd woken up and he was lost in his own yellow-and-green-pill sleep, the sludge of Charlie's sleep world, which was a distant place she longed to go.

THE FLOOD THIS TIME

Studio B was full of water, three inches in the corners, the brand-new floorboards soaked soft as tissue paper.

Dara could smell it before she saw what it had done. An unwell smell, an unhealthy one, like the dunk tank at the spring carnival when they were kids, the one their mother forbid their father from letting them in or they'd definitely get polio and never dance again.

She'd already been running late, struggling to get out of bed that morning. Charlie had gone to the studio ahead of her. He told her the walk would be good for his back anyway.

Take an extra half hour, he said. *The studio will go on without you.*

"It's not as bad as it looks, ma'am," Benny said as Dara walked in, an even stronger swampy stench in the air. He and Gaspar were ankle deep in brown water, working a utility pump and wet-vac over the half-finished floor, the freshly installed sprung panels submerged, water-logged and buckling.

"Where is he?" Dara said, covering her mouth and nose.

"Ma'am, please, don't be alarmed," Benny kept saying as she stood in the corner of Studio B, her shoes filling with warm, murky water.

The feeling came over her.

"He'll be here forever," Dara said, to herself, to anyone. "We'll never be rid of him."

n the back office, she found Charlie on the phone, his face white.

"What happened?" Dara asked. "Why didn't you call?"

"Busted pipe," Charlie whispered, hand over the mouthpiece.

Derek had explained everything. It turned out someone—though both Benny and Gaspar denied it and Dara believed them—must've driven a nail into a pipe in Studio B. It must have been leaking all night, the sub-floor now a sponge beneath their feet, an adjacent floor panel water-buckled. They would have to drill holes into it to dry out the cavity inside.

"And where is he now?" Dara asked, leaning against the door.

"Off to rent an industrial dehumidifier," Charlie said miserably. "Before we get mold."

Pipe repair, parts, and labor. Time. More time. Starting over with the new floor installation, waiting for a replacement panel. There were overruns already. And twelve hundred dollars for the permit Derek said they wouldn't need but did and then had to pay a penalty too.

"This is what they do," Charlie said, reaching for the stack of bills they'd been avoiding: equipment rental, concrete sealer, special adhesive specially ordered, something called polyplastic. "Con artists, all of them."

Then, one by one, Charlie began impaling them on their mother's ancient bill holder, its rusty metal spike.

Something has finally turned for him too, Dara thought.

"We made a mistake," Charlie said, leaning back in the chair. His face so pale it looked like stage makeup, his eyes dark blotches. "With him."

At last, Dara thought. *At last he sees.*

He looked at her. "We made a terrible mistake."

* * *

Mrs. Durant, we are very sorry," Benny told her later, pulling up the subfloor with a crowbar. Everything smelled marshy, waterlogged. "We did everything we could."

Dara said that she was sure he had.

Marie didn't want to talk about it.

She told Charlie that Derek had nearly been hurt while trying to stanch the leak, a pipe hitting his head, spraying scalding water over him, his arm pink and blistered.

"What a shame," Charlie said dryly. "You would think a contractor would know better."

There was something thrilling about Charlie's new chilliness.

But Marie didn't seem to notice, plundering the ancient metal first-aid kit for ointments, salves.

As the day wore on, however, Dara noticed a new contentment on Marie's face as she led her students through their barre work, through *sur le cou-de-pied*, Marie crouching beside her seven-year-olds, reaching over and manually adjusting their pink feet, squeezing the toes around the ankle.

"Wrap that leg, that foot. Like a scarf, you see? Rotate from your hip to your toenail. And no sickling, *mes anges*. Pristine pointed toes, *s'il vous plait*."

Of course, Dara thought with a chill. *She thinks now he'll stay longer. She's trapped him here in her sticky Marie web.*

These things happen," Derek explained to Charlie later. "But that's what insurance is for."

Dara could hear them in the back office, Derek's big-man voice, his reassurances. She stood at the door, listening.

"Is that so?" Charlie said. "Because we don't have that kind of insurance. We're just a small business."

"Don't you worry, friend," Derek said. "Between my liability insurance and your policy, we'll be rock solid. I'll talk to your adjuster myself. Bambi and I go way back. Hasn't everything worked out so far?"

"What, like the flood?"

"Listen," Derek said, "I hear your worry. But I'm gonna do you right, friend. That's a promise. I'm gonna do you right. And your wife. And, of course, your sister-in-law. All of you."

It felt like a sucker pledge, a con man's guarantee. But then also something else.

And your wife. And, of course, your sister-in-law.

Charlie didn't say anything. Dara thought she could hear him through the door, breathing.

We have to fire him," Dara said later. "You see it now. How he is. We have to fire him."

Charlie looked at her, then leaned back into his chair.

"In the middle of *Nutcracker* season?"

"That's exactly why we need to fire him," Dara said. "Fires, floods. Why wait for the locusts? We can't get through the season like this."

"I'm not any happier about it than you are, but I don't see what choice we have. Do you want to spend the day calling up new contractors? Getting bids? Starting from scratch?"

Dara didn't say anything. She was looking at the new raft of *Nutcracker* bills on the desk. The costume rentals, the tailoring services, the backdrop rental, the photographer, a new sound technician this year, the heaping mound of pointe shoes and on and on.

"He says he's going to front us all the expenses," Charlie said.

"To pay for the damage he did?" Dara said. "And why would he do that?"

"Because he quote-unquote trusts us," Charlie said wryly. "That's what he said."

Dara's head was still throbbing from last night's yellow-and-green pills, from Marie's impish laughter all day, that mood she'd been in, flittering around her six-year-olds like she was one of them, loud and silly as she showed them how to scurry, paws in the air, as the *Nutcracker* mice.

Marie, who seemed elated at the setback that would keep her lover on-site for even longer, for what seemed to Dara to be an infinite time. She could nearly picture Marie taking the hammer she used to demolish her pointe shoes and punching it into that pipe itself.

"He trusts us," Dara said coolly. "Lucky us."

The flood became an excuse for chaos, for falling behind. For a huddle of Level IVs dawdling in the changing room, for the Neuman sisters sneaking out for a donut from the deli, for the contraband gum Dara found stuck to her studio floor, purple and obscene looking and leading to a fruitless sweep of all students' cubbies that took another twenty minutes from their day.

This was why you needed routine, rigidity, timeliness. One slip, a wrist turned too far, a pointe shoe sliding from a dancer's heel, a faulty space heater, and everything could change in an instant. Everything could fall apart.

"Eyes in front! Attention!" Dara said firmly, her ten-year-olds distracted, whispering to one another between exercises. Grave looks and rolling eyes.

"Is this it?" Dara said, folding her arms, giving them all a look, walking alongside them, their legs like pink pistils trembling. "Is this what you intend to do onstage, with hundreds of audience members, all dressed up in suits and ties and holiday velvet? Because I have a studio full of Level Threes who would be happy to take your spots."

"No, Madame Durant," they all said.

As if on cue, they all heard the faint screech from the changing room.

Dara moved quickly to the doorway and, amid the piles of coats and backpacks, denim and purple corduroy, saw Bailey Bloom bending down in front of her cubbyhole, her hands trembling, her face stricken.

The dead rat inside looked waterlogged, its fur quilled.

Huddling around Bailey with sympathetic coos and paper towels from the powder room, the girls had many theories—too many, really. The rat must've arrived with the flood, washed from some secret eddy in the building into the cubbyhole, so low to the ground. Or the rat, fleeing the flood, found safe harbor in the cubby only to die there.

"Maybe Bailey was keeping food in her cubby," Iris Cartwright speculated. "Some people like their snacks."

"Gross," Gracie Hent said, shaking her head. "That's nasty, Bailey."

You're telling me," Charlie said after, "a rat emerged from the subfloor in Studio B and climbed into this cubbyhole two feet off the ground?"

Dara made a note to call Mrs. Bloom, or to have Charlie do it.

It was all very unfortunate and Marie spent an hour calming Bailey in the back office, the girl's face green and her hands still shaking.

"Clara suffered too," Bailey said. "She had to face the Mouse King. This will only make my Clara better."

"That's the spirit," Marie said, stroking Bailey's hair in that way Marie had that made everyone feel like a most beloved dog. "That's the way."

Dara didn't have time for the escalating Clara drama. She had bigger problems.

She had the contractor, who seemed to grow larger every day. Not his girth, which was not insignificant, but his presence. He was never not there, from when Dara arrived until, it seemed, after she left—Marie taking his hand and slinking up the spiral staircase with him to her attic hovel.

* * *

That night, Benny and Gaspar worked late, their arms sunk deep in polyplastic. Derek was nowhere to be seen.

"You two should go home," Dara told them finally.

They looked at her dubiously, pulling the masks from their faces.

"I won't tell him," she added discreetly. "Go home."

Benny nodded knowingly, but Gaspar, sliding his mask back on, added, under his breath, "He comes back sometimes. You know."

Dara let out a tangled cough and wished suddenly that she had a mask too.

It was after eight. Dara had sent Marie and Charlie to the Ballenger Center to meet with Madame Sylvie and the set designer and prop master to get approvals on the Christmas tree preparations. Neither appeared too eager about their task. They increasingly seemed to avoid each other lately. *Shouldn't Dara go,* they both said, *not me?*

"You know all the important things," Marie said glumly. "And I have plans . . ."

"I have a private session tonight," Dara said. "*Faites votre devoir.* Do your duty."

Marie looked at her, her shoulders drawing back in surprise.

"You sound just like her," she said, her voice suddenly small. "Mother."

Dara paused. "No, I don't," she said. "You better get moving."

And so Marie left.

If Derek returns, Dara thought smugly, *he'll be out of luck.*

I hope I make you proud," Corbin kept saying, blinking nervously.

"I hope so too," Dara said, eyes on his *port de bras*, his arms droopy, weak. The simplest things were always the hardest.

She'd promised some extra time to Corbin, her struggling Nutcracker

Prince. He came back to the studio late, his face ruddy from the cold, and pled with her.

How could she say no? It was a challenging role. He had to do battle and to woo and, in that famous moment when the Nutcracker costume, attached with cables, is whisked away to reveal the Prince behind the festive carapace, he had to make sure he wasn't swept away with it.

But, as always with the Nutcracker Prince, the big moments were never the problem. It was the small, the elemental things. The *port de bras*. The movement of the arms, fluid, elegant.

"Watch those hands," Dara said, shaking her head. "I want to see a pocket of air between the thumb and fingers. And straight spine, please."

"Yes, Madame Durant," he replied, half-breathless.

He lifted his arms again and immediately over-rotated, his shoulder blade jutting unnaturally. *Chicken wings,* Charlie had said earlier that day, watching him. *Tsk tsk.*

"Can you—might you show me?" he said.

Dara shook her head dismissively. Because you didn't touch students. Not past eleven or twelve. Other than rotating or softening a hand. It was a shame because the boys in particular would benefit from it. Many had a tendency to be too hard, too rough. To compensate, overcompensate for the fact that they were boys who were dancing, who stretched tights over their bodies and strapped on dance belts. It was so difficult anywhere, anytime, to be a boy who wanted to dance.

Charlie knew that.

At one time, teachers used to touch all the time, used to manhandle. Their mother used to tell them her former teachers would be appalled to know it was now considered unsuitable, worse. *Épater la bourgeoisie,* she used to mutter. *They're the ones with the filthy minds.*

And poor Corbin seemed so fretful, seeking. Again, it was like he wanted to be touched, his need so great it ached. *Show me. Might you show me.*

Instead, Dara began to demonstrate.

"Your arms as an extension of your back," she said, moving her arms, turning her wrists. Airy, light, from first position to second, third, fourth to fifth, her arms ending above her head, her breastbone lifting, his eyes on her. "Like wings."

"Yes, Madame," Corbin said softly, watching.

"You must understand, Corbin," she said, "that you have wings."

His eyelids fluttered a moment and then stuttered to a stop. He watched her. He watched her *shoulders out, arms in, wrists and hands out* once, twice, three times in succession. He watched with those heavy-lidded, drowsy eyes of his, their pupils tight and bright now.

He watched her, and Dara could hear him swallowing. Could see his Adam's apple jumping.

The space was that quiet. They were that still.

"Do you see now?" she said, her breath even, her body hot and orderly.

"I see," the boy said. "Yes, I see."

Dara smiled and held her pose. He kept watching.

There was something so precious, always, in the shyness of the boys.

It was only moments after Corbin left, Dara still gathering her water bottle, her sweater from the floor.

"Private sessions, now, eh?"

Dara turned to see Derek in the doorway, one arm holding the plastic curtain back.

"What?" Dara said. "What are you doing here? Haven't you done enough damage for one day?"

"Came back to check on the fellas' work," he said. "And I couldn't help but catch some of that. You and the boy. What is he, fifteen? Gotta feel good being around that. The way he looks at you."

"I'm leaving," Dara said, turning away from him, her face inexplicably hot.

But Derek merely leaned against the wall, jingling his keys, ruminating. "Hell, nothing can stop you when you're a fifteen-year-old boy, can it? When you're fresh and unspoiled and strong."

This again, Dara thought. She pretended not to listen, tucking her water bottle under her arm, slinging her sweater over her shoulder. He was just trying to provoke. He wasn't making any sense.

"And you have all this energy, so you'll go crazy from it. Your brain running hot, your body even hotter. You just want everything."

He stopped and looked at her. She could smell him. That sharp, clean smell. Breath mints, aftershave, that big bar of Lava soap from the powder room. And something else. Beer, and something more intimate. She stepped back.

"You must like feeling that near you," he said.

Dara backed up, shifted, turned her torso away from him, but it didn't matter. He still felt too close, as if his mouth were on her ear, in her head.

"Don't worry. He likes it too," Derek said. "He's gonna dream about you tonight, tucked in his Spider-Man sheets. That must feel good."

Dara turned and began walking, her body tight and not her own. In the mirror, she could see him watching her.

"I thought so," he called out after, a soft chuckle echoing after her.

What is it, Dara kept asking herself. *What is it we've let in our studio, our mother's studio. My sister's bed. My sister's body. Our lives.*

In the back office, trying to catch her breath.

She wanted to go home but couldn't yet. Charlie was picking her up. It was too late to walk. She didn't want to run into Derek in the parking lot, worse.

Popping the dust-brown window open, Dara took a long breath of cold, hard air.

Glancing down into the parking lot, she saw his truck, like a dark puddle.

And a figure darting quickly past the dumpsters and toward the truck.

Dara leaned out and saw her, a petite woman in a princess wool coat, poppy-red wool gloves, and enormous Jackie-O sunglasses swathing her face. She was moving slowly, furtively.

One of the mothers, Dara figured. Any of three dozen of the wealthier mothers. *My Emily forgot her algebra homework. Can I check her cubby?*

But this woman was walking in such a funny way, as if the pavement were covered with black ice, or fire.

Then Dara watched as she approached Derek's truck.

What is she doing? Dara thought, watching as the woman reached out with something in her hand—an envelope, white—which she slid beneath the windshield wiper in one swift gesture.

The woman paused, then reached out again and laid her hand on the vast hood, rested her palm there. Nearly stroking it, like the belly of a large cat.

Dara felt her palms itch, her hands grow sticky.

It was only when the woman turned, removing her sunglasses and moving away, that Dara realized it was Bailey's mom, Mrs. Bloom.

Mrs. Bloom, whom she hadn't seen in more than a month, since the renovation began. Because, as Bailey had explained, the construction made her sick.

Mrs. Bloom, who always held her expensive handbag across her chest in the studio, shielding it from the dust, the bobby-pinned buns, twitching little girl heads all around. Mrs. Bloom, who slathered sanitizer on her hands constantly. Mrs. Bloom, who never let Bailey remove even her leg warmers in front of the boys.

But this too: Mrs. Bloom who'd dyed her hair platinum blond just like Marie.

Mrs. Bloom, Dara suddenly remembered, the very one who'd brought Derek into their lives. Her referral, her recommendation.

What is she doing? Dara thought, rapt.

A heavy metal door slammed somewhere and Mrs. Bloom seemed to jump to life, turning, ducking behind the truck for a moment. Her whole body in an animal crouch.

Dara turned and looked through the open door to see if Derek had left. The lights were finally off in Studio B.

When she returned to the window, Mrs. Bloom was gone. And there was Derek striding to his truck, that John Wayne swagger of his. That rooster strut.

Mrs. Bloom.

Sinking down to the desk chair, she took three breaths and wondered if she'd imagined the whole thing.

Six, seven, eight, she counted until she was jolted, the sound of Derek's truck starting like a shotgun pressed between her shoulder blades.

W ell," Charlie said at home that night, "he worked for her."

"So she doesn't show up at the studio for a month, then sneaks up to his car after dark like some kind of Peeping Tom?"

He shrugged, his eyes rung brown with weariness. He was so tired. And his back . . .

"Maybe she owed him money," he said. "Doesn't everyone owe him money? People just keep sending him checks. Our insurance company, his. That guy's really got it all figured out."

"You say it like there's nothing we can do about it," Dara said.

Charlie looked at her, palming his pills, lifting them to his mouth.

"You want to do something, Dara," he said, like ice, "do it."

A fter, Dara took a bath. She wondered if she should tell Charlie about the things Derek had said, about Corbin. The insinuations. But Charlie wouldn't see it the way it was, she thought. That was Derek's greatest trick. You could never prove anything. But every provocation felt like a deeper threat. You couldn't prove it, so he was going to just keep going. Until he got what he wanted.

They prepared for bed in silence, Charlie doing his stretches, Dara with their mother's pearl-backed hairbrush in hand, doing her nightly one hundred strokes.

It wasn't until late into the night that Charlie's hand found hers under the sheets, the duvet. His hand cool and clamped over hers. Clamped tight.

His breath so familiar, the same as hers. All his smells, her smells.

She moved against him, her right hand in his, her left palm on his chest.

She could feel his heart beating, slow and sluggish, but there.

A BUTCHER'S THUMB

The next morning, Dara and Charlie arrived at seven and saw an unfamiliar car in the lot, its girth straddling two spots. So new it still had the window sticker.

Low slung and burnt orange, it was impossible to miss. It looked, obscurely, like a big, wide thumb. Like Derek's thick tanned thumb, a butcher's thumb. That's what their father would have called it. Outsized and curved like a scythe. There was something obscene about it.

"Derek," Dara said, approaching the car.

"But he drives a truck . . ." Charlie started, his voice trailing off.

"He told her to do it," Dara said, peeking in the car windows, smoked and ridiculous, "and she did it."

She looked up at the building, all the way up to the third-floor dormer window.

"Marie!" Dara called out. "Sister dearest!"

"Dara," Charlie cautioned, hand on Dara's shoulder. "Dara, don't—"

"Marie, explain yourself!"

Explain yourself, the words echoed in her head, their mother's old dictum—to tardy students, to disruptive ones. Sometimes, when she was feeling dangerous, to their father. That time she found him passed out in the garage, seated behind the wheel, having driven home from his local, high on Molson and maple whiskey. The car still on, the garage full of exhaust.

Explain yourself, she kept saying over and over, pounding the car window with the heel of her hand. Dara, standing behind their mother, watched him shake himself awake, his handsome chin and jaw streaked with vomit, something.

Explain yourself and nearly crying as she said it and Dara would never forget the look on her father's face: One of bewilderment and shame. One that would turn in moments to something else, jumping out of the car, pulling their mother by the hair—her long, shining swoop—even as she didn't stop. *Explain yourself, explain yourself.*

Who, Marie once said, an aside to Dara, *could ever explain oneself?*

"This car," Charlie was saying, walking around the vehicle, "looks really expensive."

But Dara was barely listening. Neck arched, she gazed up at the third floor again, feeling suddenly drunk in the frigid morning, her wool cap covering her ears, the heat in her face and the dizziness of gazing up, up, up.

"Explain yourself!"

Bam! The dormer window popped open at last and Marie's bombshell-blond hair shaking itself loose, Marie's fox face eyeing her. The look on it, gloating.

It's mine, she seemed to say. *All mine.*

"It's mine," she then said, smiling proudly. "All mine."

There's no way she can afford this," Charlie said. "Is there?"

"No," Dara said.

* * *

Maybe it was in the air, Dara would think later. The feeling of reck-lessness, profligacy. Because that afternoon, Dr. Weston took Dara aside to bemoan *The Nutcracker* fees, larger this year to account for new costumes to replace the most threadbare ones, some of the tulle stiff and cracked with age, for the repairs to the backdrop and the elaborate and tu-mescent Christmas tree. The increase in the facility agreement, the payroll.

Operating the wet-vac nearby, Benny gave her a sympathetic look as Dr. Weston went on and on about how the fees should be a sliding scale based on the roles their children were granted.

After, she found Charlie at his desk, making a list of delinquent par-ents who had yet to ante up for some holiday magic.

"Good thing Dr. Weston doesn't know this," Charlie said, looking at his paper. "Our Clara's mama hasn't paid her share."

"Mrs. Bloom?" Dara asked.

"Mrs. Bloom of the emerald-green Mercedes," Charlie said. "I'll call her."

"No," Dara said, "I will."

Charlie looked at her. "You're not going to ask her about last night, are you? We need her to pay up."

"She'll pay up," Dara said, swiping the number from his hand.

Besides, she needed to talk to Mrs. Bloom anyway, about Bailey. Ner-vous, fearful Bailey, who began *Nutcracker* season with a throng of friendly classmates happy to braid her bun, to invite her for hot chocolate at Dreus-ser's after class, and who now faced straight pins in her shoes, ketchup on the crotch of her stowed leotard, cold stares around the rehearsal space.

Poor Bailey, who now stood, like Clara, on the dark stage alone.

But when Dara tried to call Mrs. Bloom, a recording asserted, *The num-ber you have dialed is not in service. . . .* On some old paperwork, she found a landline number from years ago. But when Dara tried it, a recording announced, *This number is no longer in service or has been disconnected. . . .*

Afterrehearsal, Dara asked Bailey if she could help her get in touch with her mother. But the girl kept insisting she didn't have the number, didn't know it. She looked embarrassed.

"Bailey," Dara said, "we need to be able to contact her."

"But why?" Bailey said, twitching in the costume, Clara's filmy nightgown, which she would have to wear in the nightmare scene. "Did I do something wrong?"

"No," Dara said, and from the corner of her eye she saw a shadow in the doorway. Smelled that thick, sweet smell of his aftershave, the menthol snap of his vape.

"I'm still gonna be Clara, right?" Bailey asked, her eyes glossy.

"Of course," Dara said, her eyes on the shadow. *Why is he hovering here?*

Bailey nodded cautiously, then shook the staticky nightgown from her tights and began spinning, pirouetting, her hair coming loose from its pins.

Dara looked over at the doorway, but Derek, if he'd been there, was gone.

Within the hour, Dara's phone illuminated with a private number. It was Mrs. Bloom, her voice slight and careful.

"I understand you're trying to reach me," she said quickly. "If it's about my . . . obligation . . ."

It was all a little embarrassing. Dara assured her that everything could be settled simply.

"Surely it's just an oversight because you're such an ardent supporter of *The Nutcracker*. But it seems you've also missed the last billing cycle for classes too."

There was a pause on the other end. Dara could hear Mrs. Bloom breathing. Little, short breaths like a nervous animal.

"Yes, well," Mrs. Bloom said, clearing her throat, "I'm a little cash poor right now. The house—there were repairs."

"Yes, I know. We have the same contractor, remember? You rec—"

"How long will he be there?" Mrs. Bloom said. "Is he . . . how long do you expect it to go on?"

"The dust, I know," Dara said. "I'm sorry about that. We've had some setbacks. A flood. So we're a little behind. But I assure you, we want it over as soon as possible."

"Is he there now?" Mrs. Bloom said, her voice newly low, husky.

"Um, yes," Dara said, finding herself lowering her voice too.

"I should go," she said abruptly. "I have to go." Her voice almost forlorn, like her daughter's. *I'm still gonna be Clara, right?*

"Mrs. Bloom," Dara said quickly, "did I see you last night? In the studio parking lot?"

There was a choked sound from the other end of the phone.

"Me?" Mrs. Bloom said. "Oh, no."

"Because I thought I saw you. At Derek's truck. You were—"

"His truck," Mrs. Bloom said bitterly. "Hardly."

"Pardon?"

There was a brief silence, Mrs. Bloom breathing antically.

Then saying softly, "Is it true about Mademoiselle Durant?"

"Is what true?" Dara said, her head throbbing now. Afraid of what Mrs. Bloom might say, might mean.

"That she . . . she went blond?"

At that moment, the thundering wet-vac in Studio B started up again, the lights flickering with the surge.

"Mrs. Bloom," Dara said, raising her voice, holding the earpiece close, "is there something you want to tell me?"

The whisper came frantic, tight, the words sliding together: "Listen to me. Listen."

"I am listening," Dara said, though she could barely make out Mrs. Bloom's voice, so faint and strained.

"He has something he wants," she said, her voice sliding in Dara's ear like a blade. "He'll hold it close until he's ready."

"What?" Dara said, not sure she'd even heard her right. "What?"

But Mrs. Bloom had hung up.

"Did she pay up?" Charlie asked. She set the phone down and felt something cold go over her, a chilled hand laid on her neck, her collarbone.

"What? No."

"Not anything at all?" Charlie asked.

But Dara didn't answer, her head lost in thought. Charlie wouldn't understand. He hadn't heard Mrs. Bloom's voice. He hadn't seen her down there in the parking lot, the fear in her crouch.

All day, Mrs. Bloom's voice shivered in Dara's ear.
  Is it true? That she went blond.
He'll hold it close until he's ready.

But there was no time to think it through, not with sixty ten- to twelve-year-olds filling the studios, all getting fitted by two harried tailors, their mouths full of pins.

There was no time to think and there was that car in the parking lot, its brilliant orange already dimmed by mud and salt spray. By late afternoon, when Dara stole a glance, it looked shabby, a tired pencil eraser, a crushed safety cone.

That car.

It wasn't until the end of the day that Dara caught Marie alone, sitting on the fire escape with a cigarette, that ridiculous leather jacket enclosing her, legs wrapped upon herself like a spider.

"I talked to Mrs. Bloom today."

"Oh," Marie said, gripping her feet, bare and beaten. Marie's feet were the worst of any of their feet, like twisted slabs of raw meat. Dara never noticed unless she saw others staring. To her, they were a forever reminder of how hard Marie went, how relentless she'd been as a dancer, how she now carried that relentlessness elsewhere.

"She seemed to be implying things," Dara said. "About Derek."

"Really," Marie said, studying her blackened toenail. "Did she finally pay her fees?"

Dara paused. "Do you know something about Mrs. Bloom and Derek?"

"No," Marie said.

Dara didn't believe her.

"How did you pay for that car, Marie?"

"I have money," Marie said. "I just never had anything to spend it on before."

"You mean anyone. You bought this because he told you to."

"I bought it for myself," Marie said, lifting her chin. "I needed it."

"You needed it. For what, Marie."

Marie didn't say anything, scratching her forehead, the skin at her temple still pink and tender from whatever she'd used to bleach it, to bleach herself bare.

"Do you even remember how to drive?" Dara said. "It's been years—"

"Derek's helping me with the stick," Marie said, her hand dropping to her lap, her eyes fixed on Dara now. "I should have done this years ago."

She could see Marie was trying to make her understand something. It felt like Marie was accusing her of something.

"People have cars," Marie continued, a new steeliness to her voice. "That's what they do. They move away. They buy a car, fuck other people, buy a house."

She stopped herself and looked at Dara. A look like she was accusing Dara of something.

"Are you sure?" Dara said. "Because some people seem to never do that. Who move away only to come back. Who move out only to hide in an attic like a little mouse."

"You have a car," Marie said. "You have a house."

Dara looked at her, a chill behind her ears. A memory of something.

"Why are you bringing up the house now?" Dara asked, but Marie didn't say anything.

Marie, her legs like a spider's, head lowered, hiding itself, or something else.

EN GARDE

All evening, Dara thought about Marie. The car. Marie had rarely driven. Had never liked it, not after their parents. The last time she drove had been five years ago.

Dara still remembered the phone call in the middle of the night. A nurse from the local Methodist hospital called to say Marie had been in an accident.

Charlie told her it had to be a mistake. Marie was asleep down the hall, as she was every night. Every night the three of them padding up the stairs.

But Marie wasn't asleep down the hall. Instead, she'd taken their shared Chrysler for a nighttime drive on some county road, her brights blaring, and ended up shearing off the front bumper on a guardrail only a few miles from the highway median their parents' Buick had waltzed across ten years before.

It was a miracle, really, that she emerged with only a few bumps and bruises, and a sprained thumb.

That's what the highway patrol officer told Dara at the hospital.

Seated on the gurney, Marie displayed for Dara her thumb, newly outfitted in an outsize splint, a neoprene glove with hooks and loops like a falconer or a fencer.

En garde, Marie said, as if reading her mind.

I saw them, she said after when they asked her what had happened. *Mother and Father. They were ahead of me in the old Buick. They were going so fast. I had to keep up.*

Dara felt herself grow cold.

I wanted to warn them. But it was like they were trying to lose me, leave me behind.

Marie's legs shaking, her pupils jitterbugging.

But how can you rescue someone, she said, *who doesn't want to be saved?*

Dara said she wasn't making any sense and that she'd better start. *Why did you crash into the guardrail, Marie? Where were you going anyway?*

But Marie couldn't answer, the pills making her silly, sick.

Her forehead was bulging, a goose egg right between her eyes, and Charlie kept trying to make her laugh, feigning to touch it, asking if it was soft- or hardboiled.

They didn't want her to start talking about their parents again.

Don't worry, Marie told Dara later. *It wasn't really about them.*

It's always about them, Dara thought, a realization that hovered there a moment, then was gone.

Less than a week after, Marie made her announcement. She was going to go on a trip. A trip to far-off places. She needed to. Places like Budapest, maybe Croatia, or Trieste.

It was alarming, but maybe it wasn't. Maybe it was time.

Dara herself had almost left once, years ago. It was that time just before their parents died, and she and Charlie were so freshly in love. It was the kind of thing that seemed so urgent when you were very young. Far younger than Marie was now.

And it nearly happened. Until it didn't.

But Marie was going, and maybe it was time.

It seems to you like I just decided, Marie kept saying to them. *It seems impulsive to you. It seems reckless to you. To you.*

Just let her, Dara finally said to Charlie. *Just let her.*

Because Dara realized, suddenly, that she wanted Marie to go. A flicker in her head, the house without Marie. A family of only two. It was unimaginable and it made her heart go fast.

She doesn't have any money, Charlie kept insisting. *She can't go anywhere.*

We'll give her money, Dara said. The studio wasn't yet in the black, but Charlie had a little money left from his trust fund.

That was how they came to the arrangement. They'd buy out Marie's stake in the house, based on a fair estimate of their devising. Their parents had left it to both of them, but what did Marie need with a house if she was going to be traveling around the world?

It's her choice, after all, Dara told Charlie, who wasn't so sure.

And, of course, Dara said to Marie, *we hope you'll come back to us, come home.*

A deed is just a piece of paper, Charlie added more urgently to Marie. *You belong here.*

There was a big party before she left—all the studio parents came, and the former students now grown—and Marie drank a bottle of champagne herself and ended up kissing one of Dara's former students in the pantry, a twenty-year-old boy with a dashing blond forelock, and generally causing mayhem before collapsing in tears at the kitchen table after everyone had left. Charlie put her to bed, laid a cold washcloth on her face, a trash basket nearby in case.

She's not going, Charlie told Dara. *You'll see.*

* * *

But Marie did go, dragging their mother's rolling trunk behind her.

"First stop, Greeeece!" That's what the first postcard said, a week later.

The second one, from Rome, came a week after that and had only a few words scrawled across: *"BEING GOOD. LOVE TO MY DARLINGS."*

There was no third one and, twenty-five days after she left, they woke to the sound of Marie's battered feet pittering along the upstairs hallway, a duty-free bag with a half-eaten box of mandoles and three cans of halva ringed around her wrist. Their mother's velvet trunk abandoned at the foot of the stairs, its wheels now stripped.

I had it all wrong, she said, clinging to Dara in bed that night, the two of them twinning, making Marie feel safe. *I thought the voices inside were saying to go, go, go!*

And what, Dara asked, *did they really say?*

They said don't listen to the voices, Marie said and laughed, laughed so hard that she shook in Dara's hands, in her arms, Dara holding her, this little bird, its beak sharp and cries small.

We're glad you're home, said Charlie, who always knew what to say and said it, his eyes glassy and relieved, Marie clambering into his arms, staying there.

That night, they piled together in the master bed like they'd always done when their mother was still alive, like on the final nights of *The Nut-cracker*.

They snuggled against one another, one hand over another's foot, a tickle to the ribs, a smoothing of one's hair. Charlie loved to stroke their hair, one hand on each mane.

What, Dara thought, *could anyone find in that other than love?*

They loved Marie. They had helped her. They owned the house, but it was hers to live in. Forever if she liked. Except she didn't like it, in the end. She'd left again, abandoned them. But what if, suddenly, she might want it back? Because he did.

THE SETUP

I t was the blue of four A.M., the furnace clanging.

Dara couldn't sleep and had embarked on a *Nutcracker* task that meant digging through the creasy, mold-thick boxes in the basement, tripping over the heavy, pungent carton with their father's old hockey equipment, warped wooden sticks, faded jerseys still stiff with years of sweat.

Nearly tripping over an old banker's box, she found her foot landing in damp hair and almost cried out. But it was only their mother's old rabbit fur blanket, crawling loose from a soggy wardrobe box tipped on its side.

She paused. She had no memory of putting it down here. Had Marie? She bent down to reach for it, its smell cloying, both familiar and forgotten.

Their mother had many holiday traditions: sprinkling holy water on the barre before the first new class, stringing popcorn-and-cranberry garlands before Midnight Mass, and eating milk bread with sugar in bed if you were sick.

But their favorite took place every year after the final performance of *The Nutcracker*.

The end of such a grueling haul, a dozen performances or more, every year more substantial parts for Dara and Marie, moving from mice and party guests to harlequins and flowers. Neither ever played Clara because that wouldn't be fair, their mother said.

(It wouldn't be good business, Dara later realized.)

Eleven, twelve o'clock at night and their father invariably on the road or asleep in his lounger downstairs, monster movies flickering on the TV, they returned from the Ballenger Center, tiptoeing through the house, following their mother to the master bedroom, unpeeling themselves, unsticking themselves, their eyes raccoon black, their feet full of masses, their color high.

Black nails, purpling skin, flesh stippled. Sore legs sunk in ice or cracked feet dunked in mouthwash, arnica slathered, then cling-wrap tight around throbbing muscles.

No more stuffy mice suits, no more crawling under Mother Ginger's hoop skirt!

No more fake snow in my mouth, up my nose!

No more simpering Clara and her teary face!

And they'd curl up in their mother's bed and drink warm eggnog heated gently over the stove, and watch videotapes of old *Nutcrackers* on the tiny portable black-and-white. The last one would always be their mother herself as Clara, age twelve, in the Alberta Ballet's beloved *Nutcracker* season.

And their mother would bring out that fur blanket, the one Dara had just found—wet and musky—on the basement floor. She'd remove it from her velvet trunk and tell them it had once been her own mother's and was made from the fur of genuine Vienna Blue rabbits.

The blanket came out only once a year and smelled like lavender and olden days and felt on your fingers like the inside of a bunny ear. Dara could feel it now, how it felt then. Plush and electric, kicking off sparks.

Snuggling underneath it, drinking eggnog and laughing and tussling legs against one another and their eyes always still dusted with snow from the performance, it was their favorite night of the year, every year.

When Charlie came into their lives, he became part of it too. He carried the tray with the eggnog in the red reindeer goblets from the kitchen to the bedroom, never spilling a drop.

That very first year it was strange, maybe. But then it never was again.

Here was Charlie, a very shy thirteen with his Adam's apple conscious on such an impossibly long neck, anxiously swinging his impossibly long arms.

Their mother lifting the edge of the blanket and inviting Charlie in.

Their mother's raising it with such flourish, the white of her arm against the blue of the fur. The fur electric and irresistible, her eyes trained on Charlie.

Come in, come in, come in.

At last, Dara found the box she was looking for, the one with *NUT-CRACKER (OLD)* written on the side in their mother's familiar scrawl.

Inside was their rotting papier-mâché Nutcracker head, the one they'd used for a dozen or more years of performances, every Nutcracker Prince sliding it over his boyish head.

In recent years, they'd turned to a newer one, its shellac chipping after only a dozen performances, its quality suspect. *I will find the original one, le vrai bonheur,* Dara had promised Corbin Lesterio.

Looking at it now, she thought of how happy he would be.

Distracted, she was hurrying for the stairs, the papier-mâché head over her raised fist, when she nearly tripped on that fur blanket again, her foot sinking into it, warm with mold.

Her stomach turned.

Hurriedly, she kicked it away, to the far corner by the wheezing furnace.

At the living-room window, she examined the Nutcracker head in the early morning light. It wasn't as she remembered at all, its skull sunken slightly, dented on one side, its smell of dried paste, the fading red of his hat, the features on his face dulling, the twirling mustache rubbed away, the mesh over one eye torn.

But his bared-teeth grin loomed just as large. When the Prince turned his head for the first time, flashing that grin, it always sent all the little children in the theater hiding under their seats.

She supposed it was like all children's stories, all fairy tales—always much darker, stranger than you guessed. Children themselves much darker, stranger than you guessed.

That was when she thought she saw something through the front windows, smeary with morning mist.

An orange flare, like maybe the neighbor burning leaves in his trash can again. But, moving closer, her hands curling around the Nutcracker head, she saw it was that car, Marie's, its orange even more so amid the grim morning, the orange of an Elmer's glue top.

"Marie . . ." she said aloud, her right hand reached out to the fogged window as if her sister could hear her. *Is she coming home, is she . . .*

There was an awful feeling in her chest, and before she could name it, the idling car leapt to life again.

As it hurtled past, into the morning mist, she saw him. She saw Derek behind the wheel. Derek alone.

'm telling you," she told Charlie the minute he woke up, "he was in her car and he was watching us. Spying on us."

"Or the house," Charlie said, rubbing his temples. He walked over to the window, drawing back one of their mother's French-pleated drapes, the damask gray with dust.

"What do you mean?" Dara said, the Nutcracker head still in hand, the way little girls held baby dolls, resting on their forearms, their alarmed baby-doll faces forever staring up, eyes painted open, wondering, fearful.

"I don't know," Charlie said, his brow furrowed. "He asked me some questions about it. What year it was built. Had we ever thought of selling it. That kind of thing."

"You didn't tell me that," Dara said.

"I didn't think . . . I mean, it's his field," Charlie says. "Maybe he . . ."

But Charlie's voice trailed off, a slightly puzzled look on his face.

He has something he wants. That's what Mrs. Bloom had said. The house. The things he seemed to know about it. And then there'd been Marie, just the day before: *People have cars. That's what they do. They move away. They buy a car, buy a house.*

"It was just strange because we also got a call yesterday," Charlie said, more awake now, more alert. "Some woman called for you. Something about the house."

"What about the house?" Dara said. "Wait—"

"She was from the city or something," he said. "I wrote her number down."

"Why didn't you tell me?"

"It wasn't important. I mean, it didn't seem important."

"Where's the number?"

"At the studio."

Dara sat down beside Charlie, the Nutcracker head between them. Both saying nothing.

She couldn't tell what Charlie was thinking. She couldn't tell how he felt. His eyes were cool blue and empty. It was how he'd always been as a dancer. All those years, all those bone spurs and labral tears, the stress fractures and torn tendons. Grinding his body to a fine powder. He didn't let himself feel it, or anything. Or at least he never showed it.

You're dancing yourself to death, his doctor said once, under his breath.

But Charlie wouldn't stop. Until his body stopped for him. Until the hangman's fracture that, surgery by surgery, forced him to stop dancing at all.

But it wasn't that he didn't feel things. When their parents died, Charlie was the one who broke the news to Dara and Marie. The state trooper punted it to him. And Charlie, older than his years, told them so gently, so cleanly.

A day later, while Dara and Marie were upstairs dressing for the funeral, he drove his hand through the kitchen window. He still had a scar the shape of a seashell in the meaty bit between his thumb and forefinger.

And, once a month, he still put lilies on their mother's grave.

RICH AS CREAM

need to talk to you later," Dara said as she watched Marie slip down the spiral staircase that morning, her face blurry with sleep.

"Sure, boss," she said, brushing past Dara. "But do we really have time? Don't we need to get cracking those nuts?"

Insolent, Dara thought.

Even her voice didn't sound like Marie's voice. It was more gruff, throaty.

It was the things he was saying to her. The ideas he was putting into her head.

He's like a mesmer, Dara thought. *It's like mind control.*

It reminded her of those ads they used to have in the backs of her father's magazines.

WANT THE THRILL OF IMPOSING YOUR WILL ON SOMEONE?
HOW TO CONTROL WOMEN'S MINDS!

* * *

The only succor the day offered was that Derek didn't appear at all.

"Where is he?" Dara asked Benny, who shrugged, his face dark with sweat.

"He makes you do all the work," Dara added.

Benny took off his cap, wiping his face.

"Madame Durant," he said, "I'm sorry."

"Sorry for what?" Dara asked.

Gaspar, working the belt sander in the corner, looked at Benny, who then paused. Taking a breath.

"For this," he said, shaking his head.

And it was unclear if he was referring to Studio B, a space that now looked as if it had swallowed itself, the floor sunken and the air above heavy with grit, or something else, something larger, and deathless, of which Dara could only see the dark corners, the creeping edges. The growing thing that had sunk its claws into the studio, into Marie, into everything.

All day, Dara waited for a chance to get Marie alone, but they were both consumed with rehearsals, with the one-on-one and small-group work as they slowly stitched the ballet together.

The older ones were truly Dara's now, giving themselves over to the throbbing feet, the blistered blood, the smell everywhere of bandages, rot.

Mademoiselle, entendez! Swiftly, Dara moved from correction to correction. *Tailbone down! Over toes, not over heels!* There was no more room for error. They were all hungry for correction. Desperate to be stretched, yanked.

All eyes on her all day, all those eager faces, those plaintive expressions, those hungry looks. The twitchy neediness of the girls, their bodies never leaner, never stronger, but a darkness hovering behind their eyes. *This is what happens,* Dara thought, *when you've entered the ballet. When you've finally gone beyond your old ideas of your body's limits, of what you would push yourself through.*

The pain is real and abiding.

The pain is bracing and makes you feel alive.

The pain is your friend. The pain is you.

The pleasure came later, when Dara brought out the Nutcracker head, which she'd set on the windowsill all day to air out the mold, the basement funk.

Its painted face was slick with condensation.

"Madame Durant," Corbin Lesterio said, taking it from her, holding it in his hands like an enormous gem. "I've been waiting for this for so long."

"Don't get too excited," Dara said, trying not to smile. "Like everything else in ballet, it's hot and it smells."

Corbin lifted it over his head with trembling fingers. Remembering all the young men who'd worn it, Dara felt a heat behind her eyes.

That was when she heard the faint sound of laughter. In the far corner, several of the Level IVs had gathered to watch, a few hiding giggles behind their hands.

"What's funny here?" Dara said. "I'd like to know."

Everyone went quiet, heads down, except Pepper Weston, who said, "It's just . . . it's silly."

"No, it's not," someone said.

It was Bailey Bloom. A rare interjection from their Clara, who was mostly mute these days, avoiding the wrath of her rivals.

Pepper looked at her, clicking her tongue malevolently.

"I think," Bailey said, more shyly now, "it's beautiful."

Corbin turned his bobble head toward her. The painted grin seemed to smile at her.

Dara watched as Bailey blushed.

* * *

It was nearly two before Charlie finally found the phone message he'd jotted down from the day before. It was just a phone number with *"House?"* scrawled next to it.

The noise from Studio B a constant rumble, Dara ducked downstairs to sneak a smoke in the narrow space between their building and its neighbor while she returned the call.

But after she punched the number into her phone, she was met with a tinny message announcing the user's mailbox was full.

Sighing, she put the phone away and plucked the cigarette she'd tucked beneath her tank strap.

"Spying on me?"

Dara looked up, startled. It was Derek, lurking behind a dumpster, vape pen in his hand like her emaciated sixteen-year-olds.

"Who's the spy?" she said, whipping around. "Asks the person sitting outside our house this morning."

His eyebrows lifted. She'd surprised him.

As if stalling for time, he pulled a handsome brass lighter from his pocket and extended it to her. Reluctantly, she took the light.

"This is what I miss most about cigarettes," he said, looking at the lighter. Then, gesturing to his vape pen. "No class."

But Dara was in no mood, her phone hot in her hand.

"I saw you," she said. "In my sister's car this morning. I think you saw me. That's why you drove off."

He paused a second, then seemed to gather himself, to put on something like a mask, his features softening, a smile forming itself—easy and winning.

"Guilty as charged," he said, hands in the air. "Your house interests me."

Dara's hand shook, the cigarette ashing. She wished she hadn't started things. Now it was too late.

"We're not interested in your thoughts about our house," Dara said.

"Look, we got off on the wrong foot. I know that house is special to you. But it could be so much more. Maybe you're too close to see it."

"We fell for your upsell once," Dara said. "Not again."

Derek smiled, his teeth like an accordion, unstretched.

"No upsell. I promise. You know, I own some properties downriver. It's in my interest to keep my eye on the market. I did some research. A hobby of mine. That's a house with marquee value. High ceilings. Original plaster, that big old fireplace, louvered doors, good light if you ever pulled back those Addams Family drapes over there," he said. "Sure, we'd have to knock down a lot of walls—that house is all walls. We build out a big open modern kitchen, en suite bathrooms . . ."

"We're not knocking down any walls," Dara said, throwing her cigarette to the ground. "And how do you know so much about our house? You've never been inside it."

"I know what Marie's told me."

"What did she tell you?" Dara demanded.

But Derek was already talking over her, insisting, "I've been in other houses just like it. You lift the ceiling, lose those old beams, strip out the wooden window sashes and panes, install modern ones. Strip out the knotty pine and all this old-fashioned gingerbread trim. People don't want that. They want things new and shiny, like the wrapping's still on. We take that big old drafty coffin and make it look new and shiny, you know what happens?

"We all get rich as cream."

Dara felt something cold pass up her body, her cigarette tightening in her hand.

"There is no *we* here," she said.

"No?" Derek said, moving closer to her. Moving very close and lowering his voice, a sudden confidence. "Because there's only room for three in a marriage?"

Dara felt herself stumble back one, two steps.

"If you're under the impression that we have any interest in ever working with you again—" she started.

"I know it's tricky," he said quickly, smiling again. "Family stuff always is. I didn't mean to step on any toes. Excuse the pun."

Dara threw her cigarette to the pavement and moved past him.

"Worked out pretty good for you and Charlie, though," he said, his smile going flat now. "Marie moves out and now you two are sitting on a pot of gold, aren't you? Why not work together, make that pot even bigger?"

Dara began walking away.

"Hey, I don't judge," he said as she walked to the fire exit. "And I respect a smart dealmaker."

Dara pulled open the old metal door, a gust of steam-heated air in her face. She could picture Marie, her lips pressed to his ear. What had she told him; it could be anything.

"I don't judge," Derek repeated. "I only look for new opportunities, new partnerships."

Inside now, she rested herself flat against the door, the cigarette stealing her breath.

W here is she?" Dara asked, moving among the seven- and eight-year-olds spilling from the changing room, little-girl sweat that smelled oddly sweet, their mouths open and aching for air. "Where's Mademoiselle Durant?"

"She let us go," a braided redhead lisped. "She said we'd worked hard enough."

A dubious look fell across her face and Dara sighed, moving toward the back office.

W hy are you doing this?" she said to Marie, finding her perched on the fire escape.

"Doing what?" Marie said.

"He was in your car this morning."

"My car is his car," she said, her hand on her thigh, a new bruise there, red and tight. "He can do anything he wants with it."

"Like stalking our house?"

Marie paused, clamping her fingers over her toes. This was news to her sister. Dara could tell.

"What did you tell him about the house?" Dara asked. "He seemed to know an awful lot about it. You know there's no way we'd ever hire him to do anything after this. You know damn well we'd never sell that house."

Marie was looking at her thigh, pressing her fingers into the bruise. Her fingers where his had been, her eyes closing.

"Marie," Dara said, "he's using you. He wants something."

He has something he wants. He'll hold it close until he's ready.

"Everyone," Marie said, staring at her bruise, stroking it with one finger, "wants something. Even you."

"What did you tell him?" Dara said, more loudly now. "About the house."

"I tell him everything, Dara," she said. "I tell him everything he wants to know. Everything he asks."

"He's a thief."

"And what are you?"

The question felt like a sharp smack. "What does that mean?" Dara said. "Marie, you wanted out. You wanted the money. And you don't even live there anymore."

But Marie only smiled mysteriously, smugly.

Dara reached out and grabbed her sister's face in her hand. She held it tight, Marie's eyes big with surprise, fear. It was something their mother had done, and only a few times but enough that they never forgot it.

"You're lucky," Dara said, her voice strange and heavy, "I don't throw you down those stairs. You're lucky I don't kick you out of this studio, our school. Our life. Everything you have is because of me. You don't have anything of your own. You have nothing."

The words kept coming and both of them couldn't wait for them to stop.

* * *

After, Dara locked herself in the powder room, her shoulders shaking. She couldn't leave, couldn't let anyone see.

She hated this feeling, this wild thing inside. Something was inside her. *Control yourself,* she thought. *For god's sake, control yourself.*

He's brainwashing her," Dara said that night. "Trying to convince her we ... *took* something from her."

"Dara," Charlie said, touching her wrist, "he can't do anything we don't want to. It's our house."

She looked at him. She was thinking of the things she hadn't told him. The implication that Marie somehow had the house taken away. And those insinuations. *For years, the three of you playing house. Kinda an odd setup.*

"He said other things too."

Charlie paused a second, his body stiffening. "What kinds of things?"

Dara paused, looking at Charlie's back, its beautiful shape, its secret fragility.

"Never mind," she said. "I don't remember."

But Charlie was no longer listening, staring at a piece of paper.

"What is it?"

"I called to see why we still haven't received any checks from the insurance company," he said, brow tight.

"And?"

"Apparently," Charlie said, not looking at her, "we did."

"Apparently? Did you deposit them?"

"The money doesn't go to us," Charlie said, still reading the paper in his hand. "In these cases."

"What cases? Who does it go to?" even as she felt a sinking feeling inside.

"To the contractor."

"Wait, why? We would never agree to that."

But it turned out they had.

Charlie handed her the piece of paper. A copy of a form that read "Assignment of Benefits." Dara recognized it. Remembered telling him to give it to Charlie. Charlie signed for everything.

"He said it was standard," Charlie said, shaking his head helplessly.

"So it all went straight into his pocket," Dara said, feeling her body sinking, too, a weight hovering inside. "All the insurance money so far. It's all his."

Charlie nodded. "I mean, he was laying out money for all this material, the flooring . . ."

"How could you . . ." she started, her voice shaking. But what could she say? She hadn't read the form either. She never looked at forms, there were so many.

"Dara," Charlie started, but he didn't finish.

Dara was on the phone for hours with the insurance company, an endless touch-tone maze, one chirpy voice after another, all assuring her they could change the payee, they could give her a record of payments made, but it would take time and would delay further payments, possibly incur new charges . . .

"I don't care," she said. "We're long past caring about that."

A trap had been set. They were in it. Dara was sure of it now.

Charlie didn't say anything, taking a stack of new bills and piercing them on the spike of the bill holder.

"It's escalating, don't you see?" Dara said to Charlie, stiff-backed behind his desk, heating pad steaming while he snuck a smoke, the cigarette perched on an open drawer.

Couldn't he see?

Looking at her, she saw, finally, he could.

THE FIRE EATER
AND THE SWORD SWALLOWER

That night, Dara sat in the bathtub a long time, running her fingers along its chipped rim, the dent when their mother slipped that one time, after too much wine.

This was all she had left, their home. Her home.

It was big and old, but all that bigness and age mattered. It was their whole world, their whole history. The Durant history.

The contractor had taken over the studio, an invasion and a deconstruction. He had taken over Marie, an invasion and a deconstruction.

But this. He couldn't touch this. He never would.

It was where everything had begun, everything. For the first few years of the Durant School of Dance, their mother even taught classes in the house, in its sprawling damp basement, its floors laid with special vinyl.

Upstairs, Dara and Marie shared a bedroom so the two other bedrooms could be combined into yet another studio space, their father knocking down the wall with his claw hammer. Drinking Narragansett all day, crunching cans under his work boots, he kept going, swinging and swinging until there was nothing left, finally catching the claw on his cheek.

Marie found them in the bathroom, blood on the sink, the towels, the bath mat, their mother sewing up her father's face. (*The skin was like crinkly brown paper,* she told Dara after.)

After, they disappeared into the bedroom, their mother's turntable stuttering *chansons,* Dara and Marie huddled on Dara's bunk, trying to listen through the wall, but there were too many walls and they couldn't hear anything except once their mother's laughter, like a bell, and then crying after, for hours. Crying after their father had stomped back downstairs and disappeared into the dark of the front lawn. Dara and Marie watched him from the window, the streetlamp like a spotlight, the neon flare of a cigarette, his face in his hands.

The house stirred with past moments like these, good and bad, dark and fulsome.

The house was a living, breathing, saggy, and gasping thing.

They would never sell it. They would never leave it. And Marie should not have taken the money. Marie should not have left.

Late into the night, Dara woke to find Charlie had slipped from bed.

It turned out he couldn't sleep and had spent the night downstairs, on the pullout sofa that was ruinous for his back, the pullout sofa he slept on when he first came to live with them, all those years ago.

In the morning, she saw the tumbler stained with wine on the kitchen table.

"I don't understand," he said when she walked past him on her way to the car. "What's happening to us?"

Dara stopped and put her hand on his shoulder.

"We were all so happy here," he said, voice foggy and lost.

The studio felt heavy with worry.

The first full dress rehearsal at the Ballenger was only days away, so Saturday brought no rest, no birthday parties, no family activities, no playdates. Instead, the studio was open and everyone was expected, even the Grayson sisters, whose baby brother was being baptized four blocks away.

It was Saturday and they had nothing inconvenient like school to get in the way.

They could work all day until they all burned from it.

"Is that really necessary?" Marie asked after Dara announced that they should expect to be here all day, no complaints, no excuses.

Dara didn't say anything, pushing past her sister. If Marie wanted to spend the day lolling around in filthy sheets with the contractor, that wasn't her problem.

The girls were fidgety, nervous. Several lost their footing, one fell. One of the twelve-year-olds accused another of kicking the backs of her legs and the two began shouting, one of them slapping the other in the face with such high drama that one of Marie's six-year-olds watching from the doorway began to cry.

"*Pas de larmes.* Dry your eyes," Dara said, snapping her fingers. It was the only way with the little ones. "Regal. Untouchable."

The six-year-old clung to Marie's legs and cried more, her face pink and unbearable. "I hate it," she whispered, hysterical. "I hate it."

"Don't worry," Marie said, hand cupping the girl's russet head, "it'll all be over soon."

Dara tried to stay in her own studio, away from Marie. It would be bad enough that evening, when they had to go to the Ballenger to work with the stage manager on all the cues. It would take hours.

And Marie was now avoiding Dara too. There were no stealth smokes on the fire escape, or anything that might mean she had to pass through Dara's studio.

Late in the day, Dara ducked her head in Studio A, but Marie wouldn't look up from the Polichinelles, the four- and five-year-olds playing the cartwheeling clowns that emerge from Mother Ginger's enormous hoop skirt in Act II.

They bounded past her and Marie swiveled and turned and only once gave a glance Dara's way. That face, foxlike. Sly.

And then there was the problem of Bailey Bloom. Every time Dara looked at her, she thought of the girl's mother. Mrs. Bloom, the choke of her voice. The fear in it.

Mrs. Bloom was entirely missing her daughter's drama. The curse of Clara upon her, Bailey had arrived that morning in a Shamrock cab, her tights grimy from the seat. It seemed she was no longer welcome in the carpool by her peers, though Gracie Hent claimed there was simply no room in her mother's hatchback for another girl.

"Plus," Dara heard Gracie say under her breath, "she sheds."

Dara walked over, hands on her hips.

"What was that?"

"She sheds," Gracie repeated, more hesitantly now, her head dipping.

The true terrorism of girls is the accuracy of their aim. Bailey's hair had become so thin and spare it slipped forever from her meager bun. The day before Dara had found her in the changing room staring at her paddle brush, tufted with a mound of stray hair.

"Mademoiselle Hent," Dara said sternly, "move to the back row. You're no longer needed up front."

Gracie Hent's look of surprise was gratifying, even as Bailey looked stricken, even as Dara knew it would get worse before it got better.

Back in the office, the phone was ringing and Dara answered it without thinking.

"Ms. Durant?"

"Yes," Dara said, her chest tightening, the woman's official tone, something.

"This is Maggie at the county recorder's office returning your call."

"Right," Dara said, alert now. "Are you the one that called the other day? Something about the house?"

"This is Ms. Durant of 1221 Sycamore Avenue, correct?"

"Yes," Dara said.

"I suppose we've been playing phone tag. You'd called about the deed to your property? And you are correct. Your name is still on the deed, along with a Ms. Dara Durant. So if you'd like to record a transfer of ownership, all you need to do is file a quit claim deed."

Dara held on to the edge of the desk.

"This is Dara," she said. "I think you're trying to reach my sister. Marie."

"Oh, dear," the woman said. "My apologies."

"My sister shouldn't be on that deed anymore. Not for five years. And why is she calling you?"

"Ms. Durant, I'm afraid I can't answer these questions."

"Transfer of ownership—is that what you said? Transfer to who? A family member can't just push another off the deed."

"Ms. Durant," the woman said, "we can't get involved in family disputes."

"That's my home. My husband and me. Her boyfriend put her up to this. It's fraud—"

"Ms. Durant, I'm going to hang up now. But you may want to speak to your sister." The woman paused. "Or your attorney."

Dara locked herself in the back office and called Charlie, whose voice sounded faint and groggy. He'd been running *Nutcracker* errands all day in the Chrysler, picking up an extra box of "snow," the slippery confetti that would dust and swirl and cover the stage every night, and all the dancer's heads, too, at the end of Act II, the Waltz of the Snowflakes.

"And Marie started all this?" Charlie kept saying, again and again. "She called them?"

"Yes," Dara said. She thought of the insurance form Derek had hustled past them. "Or she did, without understanding what she was doing. What does Marie know about deeds?"

She could hear Charlie's throat clicking nervously on the other end.

"I don't understand," Charlie said. "Anyone can just file something and take away your own property?"

"Not anyone. She's still on the deed. We must not have done the paperwork. Putting you on the deed, taking her off."

"Oh," Charlie said. "I guess I don't remember."

Everything had happened so fast, Marie so eager to take their money and run. *The world was waiting!* Everything became about getting her out of there, getting her the money for her share of the house, getting her shots, getting her passport photo taken at the drugstore, her face in that passport so vibrant, almost manic, smiling with all her teeth but a funny wander of her right eye, like, *Are we done yet, are we done because I gotta go, go, go . . . or I'll never go at all.*

But the moment Marie left, Dara marveled at how empty the house felt.

Charlie, she'd said that night at dinner, raising her glass, trying to smile. *At last, it's just we two. Like we wanted, all those years ago.*

We didn't want to be left here, he reminded her. *We wanted to leave.*

Are you going to talk to her tonight?" Charlie asked when she called again. "I mean, we have to. We . . ."

"We have to," she said. "After. Later."

She was thinking of the long hours she would be sitting with Marie at the Ballenger Center that evening. Marie and her vulpine face and her guile and deceit.

"I should be there," he said. "I'll come."

He sounded urgent, warm. She felt close to him for the first time in days and weeks. A tenderness that almost ached.

"Stay there," Dara said. "We need you upright. We need you."

Charlie paused. "Okay. We'll talk when you come home."

Dara looked at her watch. It was late. So late. But she didn't want to hang up. She wanted him to reassure her, something.

"Oh," Charlie said, "I dropped off the snow, so it should be there."

The snow for the Waltz of the Snowflakes. It came by the crate and it was never enough. And after every performance, parent volunteers, if they were lucky, would sift through it all for the next performance, digging out bobby pins, a stray button, an earring back, all the hazards every dancer faced under their feet. The stage floor had to be pristine, even in a paper snowstorm. A single errant hairpin might bring down a dancer, might take everything away.

But it was worth it, the snow. It was the *ahhhhh* moment everyone always remembered.

"How's it look?" she asked, holding the phone against her ear. His voice, hushed and reedy, still soothed her, summoning up safe, warm places.

"Like snow," he said. Then, after a pause, he added, "Remember how your mother always kept some, after every performance?"

Dara smiled. "For her Clara and her Nutcracker Prince as a souvenir."

"*Our special secret*," Charlie said, his voice so soft now. "When I was the Prince, she gave it to me."

It was nearly seven, long past when they were supposed to be at the Ballenger.

She hadn't laid eyes on Marie in an hour or more. Chloë Lin told Dara she saw her smoking in the parking lot and talking into her phone.

"She looked funny," Chloë said, pulling on her coat.

"Funny how? Be precise."

But Chloë only gave her a look of mild panic and would say no more.

Running back to the office, Dara called up the spiral stairs, but there was no answer. She had planned to talk to her on the drive over, or at the theater itself if she had to.

She didn't know what she would say, but she would do it. Marie would have to answer for her actions. Was she really going to let this monster devour them?

Dara was reaching for her bag when she heard an engine starting outside. Looking out the window, she saw the orange car under the streetlamp, Marie at the wheel, her face so stark and white. Turning the engine, grinding the gears. A stutter start, a brake screech, the car finally lurching forward, Marie's blond head shuddering behind the windshield.

Marie driving, Dara thought, a pinch in her chest. An old twinge, like when they first learned their jumps, watching Marie throwing herself into the air—turning, turning—for her partner to catch her. A blind turn, a blind leap into safety or the abyss.

Marie shouldn't be driving.

Marie shouldn't be out there, alone.

The Ballenger Center was a lit box flickering on the horizon. Like an enormous circus tent promising excitement inside.

Seeing it always reminded her of their father taking them to the traveling carnival that appeared one weekend every year in the parking lot of St. Joan's. This was when she and Marie were very young and he still did things like that. Darkness would always be just falling and you could see the tents like great bright blobs on the horizon. When they walked past the ticket takers, they gasped because it was all so dazzling, the colorful costumes and the guess-your-weight booth and the ball-and-basket games their father said were a scam even before he sank sixteen dollars into one to win a two-dollar beanie toy for Marie.

There was, always, the sound of eyelash-curling screams coming from the dark ride, Deathbone Alley, where couples disappeared into the shadowy center of an enormous painted mouth lined with glistening silver teeth. Their father did not permit them to go inside.

The sideshow tent was their favorite anyway. Dara favored the Fire Eater, but Marie only had eyes for the Sword Swallower, swinging her golden hair back, in her hands an electrified sword made of glass that lit up her throat. How she threw her head so far back, it seemed to disappear. How she looked like she had no head at all, just throat, gullet.

I could do it, Marie kept saying, trying to shove her whole fist into her mouth. Experimenting for days with paintbrushes and wooden spoons.

Marie, who kept trying until she stuck a kitchen skewer down there, gagged, and threw up blood.

For years, she dreamt of objects caught in her throat: a knitting needle, the back-scratcher their father kept in the side pocket of his recliner.

For years, she'd wake up gasping for air.

Marie loved the Sword Swallower, but Dara loved the Fire Eater.

Flinging her head back, that curtain of black hair, tongue stuck out wide and flat, setting the wick of the torch on its pink center, her mouth forming an O.

How she tilted her head so far back, you could see all the flames climb up her throat. The flames like a scarf swallowing her throat.

The Fire Eater, the Sword Swallower. They were both women, dark and fair and fearless, their heads pitched back, their mouths wide open, everything laid bare.

They could take these things inside them and emerge unscathed. Dangerous things, deadly things. They could take these things inside and remain untouched, immaculate. The same forever. Forever the same.

THE DOOR FROM CHILDHOOD

All evening, Dara and Marie sat two rows apart, going over *The Nut-cracker* cues with the Ballenger stage manager and with silver-haired Madame Sylvie, the head of the Mes Filles Ballet Company, their partner for more than a dozen holiday seasons and with their mother long before that. Madame Sylvie, who served as their legal guardian when their parents died and who signed the consent to let Charlie and Dara marry at the tender age of sixteen. *Anyone who's been through what you three have,* she'd said, *has wisdom far beyond your years.*

Every year, Madame Sylvie's dancers performed the "adult" roles and the most technically advanced ones: Clara's parents, the adult partygoers, the luminous Sugar Plum Fairy, and Clara's godfather, the enigmatic Drosselmeier, who appears in his white wig and his eyepatch to give Clara the Nutcracker doll and launch her dark, shimmering adventure.

"I think you're going to love this year's Drosselmeier," she whispered to Dara with a wink. "He's quite beguiling."

Every year, Madame Sylvie, with her deep maple-syrup tan and silver bangles from her annual trip to Anguilla, would sit with them through the cues, through the treacherous early tech rehearsals and the frantic dress rehearsals. She always watched with such calm, her knitting needles in hand, endlessly clacking, a pile of wool, her eyes scanning the stage over the top of her reading glasses.

The cues, there were hundreds of them, and they rarely changed. Everyone had their expectations, many of these parents having seen their first *Nutcracker* when their mother still led the school. It was foolish to amend anything, to redo what worked so well, what made everyone so happy. Everything the same as it always was.

Except this year, Dara sat with Madame Sylvie while Marie crouched two rows ahead, jotting notes with a dull pencil and doodling countless sketches of pointe shoes, a habit since childhood, the toes of her shoes always sharp as blades, like a guillotine falling.

To Dara, it was conspicuous, even aggressive, but Madame Sylvie didn't appear to notice, needles rattling, eyes lifting again and again to the stage.

C harlie couldn't join us?" Madame Sylvie asked.

"No," Dara said. "His back's been bothering him."

Dara noticed Marie's head twitch two rows ahead, roots showing now beneath the snowy dye.

"Every time I see your husband," Madame Sylvie said, "I think of how much your mother adored him. *Mon garçon chéri!*"

"Yes," Dara said. "She did."

The dancer playing Drosselmeier had taken center stage, adjusting his black eyepatch as the lighting crew, somewhere up above, experimented with gels, with top lights, so that the white of his powdered wig glowed, drawing the eye, holding it.

"See! Isn't he something?" Madame Sylvie whispered, feigning to fan herself with a free hand. "But then Drosselmeier's always been my favorite."

Dara squinted up at the stage. He was older for a dancer, maybe thirty—maybe even as old as Charlie—but with a heavy brow and thicker neck. He reminded her of so many other Drosselmeiers over the years, with their felt eyepatches and their wigs like great clouds, how scary they were when she was very young, in the way children love to be scared.

"When he makes his first entrance, you think he's the villain. I mean, the eyepatch!" Madame Sylvie said. "But then little Clara is drawn to him. It confuses her. It excites her. It confuses us, excites us. It's a seduction."

"I suppose," Dara said, her eyes flashing on Marie, also watching the stage now, her fingers curled around the top of her notepad.

At age four or five, Marie would shove her fingers into her mouth, her chin shaking, at the sight of Drosselmeier. *What's he going to do?* she'd ask, jerking Dara's arm. *Don't take it!* she once cried out when that year's Clara reached for the proffered Nutcracker doll in Drosselmeier's spindly white hands.

"I mean, he's no Freddy, but . . ." Madame Sylvie said with a wink.

Dara smiled faintly. A young dancer named Freddy had played Drosselmeier four years in a row beginning when Dara was ten or eleven. How she and Marie desired him, so handsome in his waistcoat, so elegant in his dark cape. How they would talk about him at night in their bunkbed, Marie on top, legs twitching all night, Dara on the bottom, her foot dangling through the footboard, stretching her feet, her blackened toes. How Marie wanted to, inexplicably, pull Drosselmeier's eyepatch from his face and run her hand over the sunken hole she imagined there. How Dara liked to place herself near him in the party scene and brush against him, to feel his hipbone jutting, to push herself into his waistcoat.

"Can we get him the prop?" Madame Sylvie called out.

And someone appeared onstage to hand Drosselmeier one of the six Nutcracker dolls they would have on hand for the performances.

"Much better," Madame Sylvie said. "What is Drosselmeier without his Nutcracker?"

Dara remembered watching their mother tell a dozen Claras that, when Drosselmeier gives her the Nutcracker, she must *feel as if it comes alive in her hand.*

Dara remembered wanting to hold the Nutcracker too. It seemed like a magic totem. A totem that becomes a boy, the Nutcracker Prince.

"*C'est très érotique*," Madame Sylvie was saying, voice low and cracking now. "She becomes fixated with her little Nutcracker. So fixated she sneaks back out to find him after the family goes to bed. She falls asleep with it in her arms, lost in fantasy until the doll comes alive as a full-size man. It's a parable, no? Of first sexual experience. The pleasure and danger. Drosselmeier seduced her. And she is glad."

Madame Sylvie's needles tick-ticked and Marie's pencil flew.

"But you can't let the Claras know any of this, of course," Madame Sylvie said. "We must keep their innocence intact. That's what we must do with our Claras. But on some level they already know, don't they?"

Two rows apart, but Dara could hear Marie breathing. She could feel her like a little girl panting, overworked. Like their father used to say to Marie, a day of dancing, her body whirring and unstoppable, *Little girl, you run so hot, you're gonna burn up.*

"You know who he is? Drosselmeier?" Madame Sylvie said, smiling into her knitwork.

Dara wanted to leave suddenly.

"He's the promise of what's beyond the door," Madame Sylvie said, her voice husky now, pointed. "The door from childhood."

When they were finally finished, close to ten o'clock, Madame Sylvie pulled Dara aside and said, smiling, "I lost a husband and two lovers during *Nutcracker* season. I'm sure you and Marie will make up on the other side of Clara."

All Dara wanted was to get Marie alone, to get some answers. *What did she mean by calling the county register? What do you—what does he want with our house?*

But by the time they moved through the last set of cues, the elaborate sleigh flight that takes Clara away to unknown lands, she couldn't find her.

Hurrying to the lobby, she looked through the large glass walls only to see Marie disappearing into the evening mist like a phantom. Her orange car receding in the distance, like a faint flame.

HE'S IN THE HOUSE

Moments later, Dara turned down Sycamore, the street fogged and furtive, inching along until she saw their big old house, its bleary windows, roof tiles loose like whiskers.

It made her chest ache suddenly. Most of the time, you never truly saw your own house from the outside. It was impossible. But she was seeing it now. Seeing her home, her childhood, her family. Drafty, pocked, hungry.

This is ours. It is ours. No one can take it. Never.

She needed, urgently, to be inside. To sit with Charlie at the kitchen table, with their tumblers of wine, now fully replacing the fenugreek, the chamomile, their new nightly routine, Charlie's shiny orange medicine bottles, his pills and vitamins plotted on the table like a tic-tac-toe game. Together, they were a family. Together, they would protect their home, everything.

But when she arrived at the front door, she saw the note taped to the graying green paint. Charlie had gotten the last available PT appointment. He wouldn't be home for another hour or more.

* * *

She poured some wine for herself then, balancing the tumbler in the crook of her arm, headed upstairs to wait in the bedroom. They had to band together now. They had to. And she'd felt so close to him on the phone earlier, remembering about the snow.

Maybe Charlie's back would feel better. Maybe he would come back into the bed that night. Maybe he'd let her hands rest on him, find him again in the blue-dark of the late night, his pills working their gentle ministrations.

The thought made her instantly feverish, and the warmth dipped to her hips, between her legs as she climbed the stairs. *Charlie.*

Halfway up, in the band of light from a second-floor window, she saw the first one.

A footprint, faint but muddy, on one of the carpeted steps.

Looking up, she saw another. Tracks, like tracking a mountain lion, a great black bear.

But these tracks were familiar, the gray-brown slurry she knew so well, trailed daily across the floors of their studio. She even recognized the shoe print, the natty toes of the contractor's natty boots.

He's in the house, a cry racing up her throat.

Reaching the top step, she saw the open door at the end of the dark hall. Their childhood bedroom.

She never left that door open. She seldom went in there at all, except maybe once a year to dust it, to polish the old wood of the furniture set—the dresser and, of course, the bunkbed. The bunkbed, Marie on top, Dara on the bottom, like a pair of twins pressed tight in the womb. The bunkbed, with Marie's teeth clicking in her sleep, and Dara, restless, her foot kicking against the footboard slats, her arches wrapping around them, her thoughts drifting to that year's Drosselmeier, the feel of his hipbone against hers as she brushed past, her foot pressing, pressing on the slat, as she pushed into the feeling . . .

Standing there, Dara saw the open door. She saw the shadow thrown on the floor.

He's in the house. He's in the bedroom.

Dara set the tumbler of wine on the banister and took a few steps.

The streetlamp outside made the door unnaturally bright, beckoning to her.

Who's there," she called out, her voice like a bark.

He appeared suddenly, his body taking up the entire doorframe. Like a monster in a dollhouse, like he could reach his arm up and take the whole thing apart in one glancing blow.

"Hey," he said, swiveling. "Sorry. Did I scare you?"

He looked surprised, he was surprised. But not that surprised.

"I gotta tell you, it's a trip, being here," he said. "Marie talks about this house all the time."

He was enormous, looming, his shadow making him twice his size, and the only light from the streetlamp outside.

"Easy, easy," he kept saying.

"What are you doing in our house?" Her voice low, tremulous. "How dare you come into our house."

"I'm sorry I scared you. I thought Charlie would be home," he said. "I wanted to talk to him about my idea. This house, its potential. But he wasn't here, and it's just so damn good-looking—well, great bones at least—I had to take a peek."

"Trespassing. Breaking and entering," Dara said, steadying herself. "I want you out now, or I'm calling the police."

"It's only trespassing," he said, lifting his arms above his head, resting his fingertips on the top of the doorframe, "if you aren't given a key."

Fucking Marie, Dara thought. *Goddammit, Marie.* It was so much worse, every time, than she thought it could be.

"Your sister wanted me to see it," Derek said. "She wanted an outsider's take. Someone with some expertise, some perspective. Given everything. Given how it all went down."

"How what went down?"

"How she came to lose it. Her piece of it."

Here it is, Dara thought. It had been coming for so long. Dara saw it now. If he couldn't win it, he'd try to take it.

"You don't know what you're talking about."

"I know what she told me," he said. There was something heavy in his voice even though he was smiling. "She was in a vulnerable state. That's how it sounded to me."

"Marie's lived her whole life in a vulnerable state," Dara said. "And this is none of your business."

"Marie's business is my business," he said quickly, icily—a tone Dara had never heard from him before.

"Why?" she replied. "Because she opens her legs to you? She opens her legs forty times a day for a living and it doesn't mean a goddamned thing."

"You got a mouth on you," he said, tight and cool. "Quite a mouth."

"Get out," Dara repeated. "Go. Or I call the police."

Derek looked at her. For the first time, she thought she could feel a little desperation on him, a slick of dampness growing on his brow.

"I've seen everything I need to," he said. Dara let herself breathe.

But as he turned, he took one last look into the bedroom behind him. His eyes darting.

"I like to imagine you two in there," he said wetly, like his mouth was resting on a bottle neck. "Two of you, two little ballerinas, like the tops of a music box. Pink and perfect, tucked tight into a little boy's bunkbed."

How do I get him to leave? How will I ever get him to leave? Dara thought, suddenly, of their mother crying over her father, all those nights. *How can I get him to leave,* which always sounded like, *Will he never come home?* Those two, their endless tango . . .

"My brother and me had a bunkbed just like it," he said. "Except it was a ship's wheel instead of a wagon wheel."

He paused, then grinned widely. "We had this routine. My brother would do this voice, Miss Touissant, the hot French teacher at De La Salle.

Parlez en français, mes garcons! And we'd both jack off—lower bunk, upper bunk—in time."

He looked at her, then added, "One time, I came so hard I kicked out a slat on the footboard."

Dara's breath caught. In a flash, she was ten again, her own foot snapping, the crack of the wood, the slat darting across the room like a bat.

"Snapped it right in half," he continued, watching her. "How about that? Told a girlfriend once and she said there was something sick about it. My brother and me. Something unnatural. I told her, if that's unnatural, sign me up." He paused. "Do you, Madame Durant, think that's unnatural? Any of it?"

Dara reached out for the wall, her legs shaking. Thinking of the broken slat, Marie's face peeking through.

Marie, she thought, her mind racing, *Marie, you gave it all away. You gave us all away.*

T hat's the greatest trick women ever pulled on us," he said. "Making us believe they're different."

He was halfway down, the old steps groaning beneath him.

"She's using you," Dara called out, running to the top of the stairs. "She's using you and when she's done, she'll come home to us."

Derek stopped, turned.

"Come home to you?" he said. "Is that what you think is gonna happen? That poor kid. That poor goddamned kid."

Dara felt a sharp pain in her back suddenly, profoundly. "What does that mean?" she asked, her voice gritty and strained. "What did she tell you?"

"Family secrets," Derek said, his parting shot, "are the very worst kind, aren't they?"

S he watched from the hallway window until his truck pulled away, like an oil slick spreading.

When she was sure he was gone, she stood in the bedroom doorway where he'd stood. The Big Bad Wolf. She wanted to see what he'd seen. That most private space. That space of countless intimacies.

But all she saw was the shabby blond dresser and the bunkbed, which took up nearly the whole room, its footboard glinting from the hallway light.

Is this, she thought, *what it looks like from the outside?*

Is this all it looks like?

But then she couldn't sit with the thought. The idea.

So she let it flit past and focused instead on what was in front of her: the gleam of Derek's smeary palm print on the bunkbed, on its headboard.

Her fingers fumbling over the keys, she texted Charlie and he called immediately. He was nearly home, only blocks away, but he called, the sound of him clambering for a dropped phone on the other end.

What?" Charlie said, rushing through the front door, his breath still fogged from the night air. "I don't . . ."

"He was in our bedroom."

"Our bedroom?"

"No, *our* bedroom," Dara said, confusing herself. "Marie and me. But he could have been everywhere."

"How did he get in here? I mean—"

"Marie," Dara said.

His coat half off, Charlie's arms dropped.

"Is that what he told you? Does she even still have a key?"

"Of course. We didn't force her to surrender her key to us."

Then she remembered Marie earlier that evening, her head twitching when Dara explained to Madame Sylvie that Charlie wouldn't be joining them that night.

"She thought we'd both be at the Ballenger. She gave him her key."

"Dara, I don't . . ." Charlie started but then stopped.

"He wasn't getting anywhere with us on partnering to sell the house," Dara said, "and now he's got a new angle. She's filled his head with crazy ideas."

"Like what?"

"Like we took advantage of her. Like we stole the house out from under her."

"Dara," Charlie said, hands on her shoulders now, "we'll fix this. We'll . . . I'll fix it."

"We have to fire him," Dara said. "Tomorrow."

"Of course," Charlie said, but he wouldn't quite look at her.

How tentatively he walked, his back arched, his coat dragging behind him. His gait strained, stilted. His body stiff, like—as they used to joke years ago when it all still felt like it would go away soon—Frankenstein's monster.

"I just need to think," he said, heading for the stairs.

She waited for him to come to bed, but first he took a bath. Then she heard him moving through the house, checking all the locks, attaching the door chains.

Finally, late into the night, Dara crept downstairs and found Charlie sitting at the kitchen table. His back curved, the whiteness of his shoulders hunched. His legs spread wide and, before him, a plate of blobby pasta, untouched, spattered up the napkin tucked in his undershirt.

Something was wrong. He shouldn't sit like that, not with his injuries. His half-broken body. But also a dancer—especially a dancer like Charlie—never sat like that, crooked, humped.

"I figured it out," he said, not even turning around, his angel-blond head bowed.

Dara stepped inside, her eyes on the stove, red-spattered, broken sticks of stale spaghetti scattered across the its top. Spaghetti that likely dated back more than a decade, her father's love of Mueller's with canned clams, or a pat of butter, ten raps from the grated-cheese can, emerald green and jumbo-size.

"Figured out what?" she said, spaghetti cracking like twigs under her feet.

He turned around, his head bobbing in a way that made her wonder if he'd taken too many of his pain meds, like he had once in the spring, after Marie left and they were fighting a lot and he'd torn the gutter off the side of the house and pulled a dead raccoon from inside. For months the smell had haunted them. They couldn't find the source. Charlie kept saying it was the smell of death, death, and something was dead inside if he could only find it.

"Figured out what?" Dara repeated. But even as she asked, she realized, urgently, she didn't want to hear what he might say. She found herself suddenly afraid of what he might say.

"He's hypnotized her."

"What?"

"The contractor. He's hypnotized her. I read about it. It happens."

Dara looked at him, wanting to pull that spattered napkin loose from his undershirt. She wanted to clean him up, straighten him up.

"Charlie, please," she said. "Let me—"

She pulled the napkin with a hard yank and moved to the sink, turning on the hot water. Holding the napkin beneath it.

He looked up at her curiously, like a little boy waiting for his mother to wipe his mouth.

She watched as the napkin slid from her red hand, slid through the hungry black flaps of the garbage disposal. She looked down the black hole as Charlie kept talking, his words slipping from him before they were finished forming.

"But the good news is we can fix it. Like deprogramming. We just need to take her to a shrink, a therapist of some kind."

She flipped the switch and the garbage disposal clattered on, the corner of the napkin slipping into the hole, the motor grinding, grinding, shredding the fabric until the napkin must've caught itself in its gears and the whole thing shuddered and stopped.

"Okay," Dara said. "Maybe."

She reached out, fingers on the switch again, trying to restart it, a current of electricity fuzzing through her hand, jolting her.

"Either that or we're the ones," Charlie said, more softly now, more like himself. "Either that or we've been hypnotized. Been hypnotized our whole lives."

Dara turned and looked at him. She wanted to put her hands over her ears. *These are the things I don't want to hear.*

"Dara," he said, "we have to do something."

Dara nodded, her hand shaking.

"Dara," he said, "we have to do it *now*."

Once, years ago, tucked in bed, they'd heard their father, drunk and ragged, cry out to their mother that he could do whatever he wanted in his house, that he could set the house on fire if he wanted.

I will do it, woman!

And their mother, cool and weary, smoking cigarette after cigarette at the kitchen table, saying, *Stop waving that lighter at me, old man.*

What if he does it, Marie whispered from above, her little hand clawed around her bunk.

He doesn't have the guts, Dara told her, though she wasn't sure herself.

You never knew what people would do. You never knew when blood ran hot. That was why it was always best, like their mother always said, *to keep it cool.* To not let it get to you. To still your heart, or slow it down.

I can't, Marie said, taking Dara's hand from above, pulling it to her chest, the beating sound beneath her breastbone like a rabbit's, fast and out of control.

UNNATURAL

The car ride—five minutes, less—pressing her hands against the heating vent on the dashboard, her breath catching and the air so cold it felt like sharp points against their faces.

Pressing her hands there and Charlie driving, his face blue under the streetlight, fingers clamped to whiteness on the steering wheel. Charlie driving, his arms moving to steer as if they were in an ocean liner, loose and wide, tires caterwauling and that feeling that the car was hovering above the ground, and Dara's hands against the vents until they burned, the scorch in the air and Charlie telling her it all has to *stop, stop, stop*.

We have to stop him, he was saying. *She'll let him ruin everything.*

He was saying things about Marie, and how they had to get her, had to go in and pull her out like she had fallen into quicksand*, but hadn't she?*

Staring out at the darkness ahead, Dara could almost see her there, in the distance. Marie, emerging from the pitch black, waving her hands above her head like an SOS and crying.

Like Clara in her nightgown on the blackened stage, lost in her dream world, no way out, no way home.

* * *

The fog made everything shimmer.

The third-floor window of the studio glowed like a church steeple and below Derek's truck glowed, too, a brilliant black marble alongside the hot candle of Marie's car.

Everything looked slightly exaggerated, like the time Dara tried on another girl's glasses and the world instantly drew into unimaginable focus. (*Haven't you had your eyes checked lately?* the girl asked and Dara didn't dare tell her, *No, never.*)

She couldn't wait to take off the glasses, everything too bright, too sharp, everything hurting her eyes. *Does the world look like this?*

Charlie was ahead of her, a streak of white across the asphalt. His body moving as she hadn't seen it in years, since before his injuries, since the days their mother would sigh and whisper, *comme une panthère* . . .

Inside, the gust of sawdust, sealants, spray foam everywhere, the radiators chugging, Charlie called out for Marie.

As they charged toward the back office, Derek emerged from the mouth at the top of the spiral stairs.

"Who's there?" he called out as he wended down, the staircase vibrating beneath him. Dara feeling it under her feet, up her spine.

And then Marie emerged from behind him. An old cardigan wrapped around her, her legs bare and her feet, too, forever pink and pulpy.

Slowly, slowly she descended, her feet nearly missing every step, her eyes stunned, glossy.

It was hard to believe it was happening, the radiator filling the small space with gasps of heat, the smell of burning things, forgotten cigarettes on the windowsill, mittens left too long on the radiator pipes, the stench, still, of Marie's tortured space heater, the fire that started it all.

"Now, what's this all about?" Derek asked, picking up the old metal bill holder from their mother's desk, spinning the wooden base with his meaty fingers. *So much performance,* Dara thought. *So much stagecraft, this con artist, this swindler.*

Did you think," Dara was asking Marie, who had curled up in a corner, sweater and underpants, her legs red and scaly, "we'd just give it over to you, to him? Our family home. Like you gave away everything else."

"What? No. That's not—" Marie started, but then Derek lifted his arm in front of her, and Marie's mouth closed.

It made Dara, suddenly, so sad. Seeing Marie's mouth close.

Suddenly, Dara wanted to cry from it.

"Look, let's just settle down here, friends," Derek was saying, his thick fingers around the bill holder's spike. "I think there's been a little misunderstanding. And maybe a little alcohol."

He was looking at Charlie and she knew he could smell it on him, all that wine, the jug from the fridge empty when they left. The room so small and Charlie's face red from it.

"Charlie, my friend," he said, "you're the business corner of this little triangle, right? You're the sweat and spit behind the Durant School of Dance. So I present this to you as a business opportunity. We can make that house of yours into a pot of gold. It's not too late for us all to partner up. But it will be soon."

"We're not interested," Charlie said. He had an expression that made Dara nervous, his jaw rigid.

"But your sister is," Derek said. "And she's the one who gets to decide, right?"

Like that first day, Dara thought. Derek asking them who decides and Marie, mute for the entire meeting, insisting, *I do. I decide.*

Except now she was silent, her head bowed, her cardigan slipping, her bare body beneath smeared with acid-bright bruises, baggy blisters, stage scars, a painter's palette.

Oh, Marie, but you wanted it . . . you let him in. You whispered all our secrets in his ear.

"She's a partner in the business," Charlie said. "But not in the house. She sold her share."

"She sold her share, you say?" Derek asked, wrapping his hand around the bill holder again, splaying his big jointy knuckles.

"You know she did," Dara said.

"Are you sure?" he said. "Because, from what I hear, you gave her an itty-bitty amount of money. A few table scraps to get her out of your hair, but are you sure that was all aboveboard? I'm just curious because, according to the county register, there's no record of a transfer of property."

Ah, Dara thought, *here it is.* The call from earlier that day.

"Are you talking about your attempt to defraud us?" she said.

Derek's eyebrows lifted.

"I know you called them," Dara continued. "I know what you're trying to do."

"Not me," Derek said, looking over at Marie. "She."

Dara's eyes darted to Marie, her head still bowed. Dara wanted to strangle her.

"You need to leave," said Charlie, his face flushing now. His body tightening before Dara's eyes.

Derek smiled grimly, shaking his head. "I read up on this. A little legal concept. Undue influence. Do you know it? It's when a trusted person uses said influence to get another person, a vulnerable person, to sign over their rights."

"I'm sure you know everything about undue influence," Dara said. She could feel herself ramping up to something, an excitement in her chest. "You saw how she was that very first day. You saw your mark and you swooped in. And look at her now."

They all turned to Marie, her bare-legged crouch. Her hands flew to her face like when she was ten, shutting her eyes, plugging her ears like they were still in their bunkbed, hearing everything, seeing everything, their father yelling, their father crying.

"They're doing it again," Marie said, turning to Derek. "They're doing it."

"What are we doing?" Charlie asked Marie, a stunned look on his face. Stumbling toward her now. "Jesus Christ, Marie—"

And Marie's face folding ever so slightly, her hand trembling toward Charlie just as Derek swooped in.

"I don't think you get it, friend," he said, moving in between them as if Charlie were threatening Marie, as if Derek were the gallant. "What belongs to Marie belongs to me. You steal from her, you steal from me."

"Jesus, Marie," Dara said, "don't you see what he's doing?"

"Don't talk to her," Derek said. "Talk to me. If you're not interested in a partnership, then we're gonna have to make a deal. Some kind of arrangement. A reparation of sorts. For how little you paid Marie the first time."

So that was it, Dara thought. Right in the open at last.

"No," Marie said, turning to Derek, voice rising, her hands fisted. "This isn't what I wanted. I wanted out. Out. Out. Out. It took me thirty years to get out of that house. Thirty years and I . . ."

Dara moved toward her. "Marie . . ."

"I think I'm going to be sick," Marie said, moving toward the spiral staircase, Dara following. "I think I'm going to be so sick."

On the third floor, Dara stood over Marie, Marie retching rusty saliva into a wire trash can, her voice scraping.

It was so strange being up there again after all these months, her eyes scanning the dark space—all their mother's things from when this space was hers, her hideaway: the gooseneck lamp, the brittle old futon, their father's pilling Pendleton flung across.

"Dara, I didn't know. I didn't know how bad it was. I . . ."

"Stop it," said Dara, her ears ringing, all of it too much.

She didn't want to be up there anymore, or ever, the heavy scent of bodies, of Derek's body. Of Marie's. Like sharing a room all those years, knowing even the smell of her tampons, stuffed in the trash. And most of all, the smell still of their mother's Blue Carnation perfume.

Mother . . .

"Stop it," Dara repeated, turning away, "while we clean up your mess."

They could hear them in the office below, the fuzz of Derek's voice.

"I have just as much an interest in that house as you," Derek was saying. "And just as much a right. We both happen to be involved with women whose names are on that deed."

"Dara's my wife," Charlie said, his voice strange and strangled, a voice she didn't recognize. "Marie's my sister."

There was a pause. "You three, so close. Snug as three bugs in a rug. What guy stands a chance?"

"What does that mean?" Charlie said. "We're family."

"So it's true, then?" Derek asked.

"What's true?"

Marie, on her knees over the trash can, looked up at Dara. A sudden alertness, a knowingness. *We need to go back down there. We need to go.*

They were on opposite sides of the office, Derek spinning that bill holder again, spinning it by its rusty spike.

"Derek, stop this," Marie was saying from the staircase, Dara pushing past her down the steps toward Charlie. "Come upstairs."

"What's true?" Charlie repeated, louder now. On his face that expression again, the one that made Dara nervous because she hadn't seen it since they were teenagers, overhearing Dara's parents fighting, her father smashing dishes, their mother threatening to throw herself out the window.

But Derek didn't see it, didn't know. "That you three," he said, a funny kind of glitter in his eyes, "over on Sycamore, that you shared . . . things?"

"Shared things," Charlie said. "Of course we—"

"Like a bed," he said. "Like you shared a bed."

"I don't know what you—"

"Charlie, don't," Dara blurted. The feeling suddenly of a death blow coming.

"I mean, what do you even call that?" Derek said. "Tell me how it worked. 'Cause I'm picturing—"

"Derek, stop," Marie called out from the top stair. "Derek, come up here, okay?"

Derek paused, the air heavy and stifling, before slowly curving his lips into a smile.

And then he set down the bill holder and moved toward the stairs. Dara let herself breathe again.

"Sure, honey," he said. "I'll come up."

Starting up the stairs now, his gaze moving from Dara to Charlie to Marie at the top of the stairs and back again. "But, boy, I gotta say, watching the three of you here, those bodies of yours, always stripped half naked, touching each other all the time. Flesh pressing flesh."

"No, no," Marie called out. "Derek, come—"

"Ménage à Durant," Derek continued, his tree-trunk arms pressing on the quivering stair rail. "It was bound to happen."

"Shut up," Charlie said, his voice suddenly icy cool, his gaze fixed on Derek. "Shut your mouth. I know about you. I know more than they do. I know who you are."

There was a flicker of panic in Derek's eyes.

Dara looked at Charlie, taken aback. "What do you know?"

"I know about *you*, brother," Derek said, a ripple of anger in his voice now as he leaned over the stair rail. "I've seen some things. Served two years in Stuttgart. Spent a few lost weeks in Thailand. But the three of you—that's a new one for me. I mean, the last taboo, right? Or is that cannibalism?"

He had a look, not a smirk, not even a smile. It was something else. It was very serious. He was very serious.

"And you," he continued, turning to Dara now, his gaze hot. "You, my Dark Durant, are full of surprises."

"Derek, don't!" Marie was saying from the top of the stairs.

"Let me ask you," Derek said to Dara, leaning over the railing, "did you give Marie to Charlie to keep him there, or Charlie to Marie to keep her—"

I t was all so fast, Charlie charging up the stairs after Derek.

Charlie and Derek hurtling into each other, a crash of bravado, of machismo, of huffing and puffing and blowing the house down. Derek's boot clacking against Charlie's jaw, and Charlie butting hard into Derek's crankcase chest, knocking him back, the slick bottom of Derek's slick boots clattering down one, two steps.

His balance lost and Charlie reaching down for him with ropy arms, lifting him, improbably, Derek's legs scrambling beneath him and the stair rail bending against his weight.

Heaving Derek up, ramming him against the rail, Charlie's face like it used to look long ago, when he was dancing. Intent, afire. Before the injuries, the haze of pain, the chemical stupor. Before Marie left and left again, like a ghost in the night. Before their parents' deaths, before their wedding, before everything. When he was only a boy, dancing.

L ater, when she remembered it, when she pressed her fingers to her closed eyes and tried to remember it, it was as if, in those final seconds, they were dancing a pas de deux.

Their mother used to say, *The beauty of dancing a pas de deux is that you are never alone. There's always a hand outstretched to accept yours. Someone's eyes seeking yours.*

But you must never forget, a pas de deux is also about power, gaining it, losing it, giving it away.

How can it be both those things? Dara used to ask. *How can it be both?*

Why, Dara, their mother replied, *it's always about both.*

* * *

It was fast, so fast. Like a pointe shoe slipping, a wrist softening, a body lurching, a knee thundering down onto the stage floor.

Charlie and Derek interlocked, and the loud squeak of Derek's mud-stippled boots against the steps, Derek trying to right himself, freeing one arm, clambering for the stair rail, its spokes bending like matchsticks.

"Stop!" a voice cried out. Dara looked up to see Marie descending from the mouth at the top of the stairs, wrapping her jonquil arms under Derek's arms, pulling him back, Derek's boots clattering, his legs giving out from under him.

Later, Dara would remember Marie's face, how it was as wild and strange as Charlie's. Marie and Charlie, those two childlike faces, twinning in her head.

It was fast, so fast. Marie's and Charlie's arms extended, four marble spires. Almost like they were one pair of arms, one pair of hands, their faces red and vivid, wild-eyed and avid.

The heels of Charlie's hands on the dark expanse of Derek's chest, Marie's hands under Derek's arms, small and clawed, Derek losing his footing, dropping to one knee. Their arms, those spires, were they pushing him away or pushing him over? How could you ever tell?

Derek stutter-stepping backward, his boots sliding, his body bending over the railing, so low and treacherous, his body twisting over the twisting staircase.

It was fast, and then it was slow, so slow, time stretching out infinitely. This monster, this Big Bad Wolf, this bloodsucker who never should have been let in, this stranger who never belonged, falling, falling to the floor.

His body larger, it seemed, than the staircase that held it, the kick-kick of his sliding feet and the force of their arms, thick with blasted muscle, fired by feeling. Some feeling.

Over the railing, he fell, his body spinning, and his head hitting the corner of the desk below, a muted crack.

His face catching something, a whistling sound in the air, his breath leaving him.

A hot spatter of blood and the mortal thud of his body landing on the floor below, his body curled like a cat, small and shabby. His body twitching, then still.

Later, Dara would remember this: Derek's eyes catching hers, catching Dara's, as it happened. As he fell.

Looking out at Dara, as if asking, begging for something.

As if warning her, as if saying, *Wait, wait*—

I don't know how . . ." Charlie was saying, his voice low and foreign. "It happened so fast and I didn't . . . I didn't . . ."

They were all standing over him now, standing over Derek, a crumpled heap on the floor, legs going the wrong ways. Charlie's eyes glazed, his face stiff.

It was only after they'd turned him over they saw it.

Marie made a keening sound, like a fox, trapped.

Like a carnival trick, the rusted spike of the desk bill holder piercing his right eye, a starburst, a pinwheel, its center red and wet.

He needs an eyepatch, Dara thought, her brain not working, *like Herr Drosselmeier.*

It gave him the look of a perpetual wink, an eternal one. But the blood was dark and final.

THREE

THE NUTCRACKER

I t was impossible to remember Christmas without it.

This is how we keep the lights on, their mother always told them. *Those dreams of Clara are how we keep the lights on.*

The Nutcracker, a young girl's dream of peering over the precipice into the dark furrow of adulthood and finding untold pleasures. Of the eye, of the mouth.

Because, foremost, *The Nutcracker* was a dream of hunger, of appetite.

Consider the exquisite torture of all those little girls never allowed to eat dancing as costumed Sugar Plums, as fat Bonbons gushing cherry slicks. Tutus like ribbon candy, boys spinning great hoops of peppermint, and everywhere black slathers of licorice and marzipan glistening like snow.

When they were too young to dance it, too young even to play a Candy Cane or one of the darling Polichinelles, their mother read them the E.T.A. Hoffmann story *Nutcracker and Mouse-King.* An old book that smelled like must and was illustrated with gaudy, frightening images—rodents with fierce claws, the Nutcracker's teeth long and sharp.

A young girl named not Clara but Marie becomes fixated on the wooden doll her seductive godfather gives her. In bed with the doll, she drifts into a fantasy world of her own making and, at the end of her nocturnal adventures, is forbidden by her family to speak of them again.

You have to dance it long before you understand it, their mother always said.

But Dara could never remember a time she didn't understand all of it.

It was a warning for those who become lost to desire. Because, at the end of the story, Marie awakens from her dream, changed. No one believes her when she tells her tale. They say it's a fantasy and it's time to let it go. And, at the end, she is unable to live in reality. She is lost in her dream.

In the ballet, though, the story ends with Clara still in her fantasy world, her dream world. She never has to come back at all.

M arie's favorite part of the book was when the little girl sees a spot of blood on the Nutcracker and rubs it with her pocket handkerchief.

How, slowly, as she rubbed the Nutcracker, he grew warm under her hand and began to move. How his mouth began to *work and twist, and move up and down* until he could speak. Until he could tell Marie what she needed to do.

No picture books! he insisted. *No Christmas frock!*

Instead: *Get me a sword—a sword!*

In their bunkbed at night she'd make Dara read it to her.

From below, Dara could see Marie's girlish arm swing out and grab for the bedpost, to rub it like the Nutcracker, to summon it to life.

Dara would read and read and Marie would say *again, again* until Dara felt her stomach turn and flip, to work and twist like the Nutcracker's mouth.

Oh, Dara, Marie would say, her fingers working the bedpost, *we must get him his sword!*

HE DIDN'T GO HERE

The police detective was waiting for her but Dara wasn't ready yet.

Instead, she was standing in front of the dust-daubed mirror in the powder room.

This isn't a matter of life or death. That's what she used to tell herself back in her dancing days. Before a big performance, or after one. Before an audition, a solo. *But your body doesn't know the difference.*

Because it was true. Those moments just before, standing in the wings, the floor humming from the orchestra, breath heavy and body heavy and how will it ever happen?

But it does, the body going into flight-or-fight mode, summoning all its energies to defeat the threat, to conquer the danger.

The body knows so much better than you do what it needs to survive.

In the seven, eight hours since it had happened, she hadn't stopped moving, nor had Charlie.

Instead, she'd gone into the adrenaline-fired, cortisol-seething space of performance. A space of needle-sharp concentration, boundless energy, nerves jangling, senses elevated, her body taking over, her brain blank.

One breath, two breaths, she took a paper towel from the roll on the sink—

That sink, wobbling on its pedestal, flashes of Marie pressed up against it, the rutting bull, tearing it loose from its screws, tearing Marie—

Tank top stripped to her waist, she wet the paper towel, rubbing it across her skin, across the three sheets of sweat, the oldest now-gray flakes. The sweat like the sweat after a performance, three skins to shed to make oneself new again.

Somehow, all those hours had gone by. Seven, eight hours since they'd all stood over the fallen contractor, his body twisted and broken. Since Marie began moaning, her hair in her hands, her hands shaking against Charlie's chest. Since Dara watched the two of them clinging to each other, assuring each other (*it was an accident, oh god, he slipped, he fell*), while Dara looked down at the contractor, at Derek's face, the spiral of his ruined eye. The other eye vacant and heaven-tilting. Reminding her of something she couldn't quite name.

Now it was only when Dara closed her eyes that she saw him. Derek. The sprawl of his body, his ankles twisted upon themselves on the bottom step, almost daintily, almost like a *sur le cou-de-pied*, one foot wrapped like a scarf around the other.

His body in death had been surprisingly graceful. The fall like the descent of a majestic animal, a panther, a condor, its wings spread. The descent of a dancer from a *grand jeté*.

But then he was just dead, his shirt pulled up above his belly, his face like stiff paper, the awful red slick of his right eye, its jellied center.

He was dead and there was nothing they could do about it.

It was an accident, after all. And, as they would tell it, it was an accident he'd had alone.

If they stuck to the plan, everything would be okay.

* * *

That moment, staring down at him, had been the only pause. The only time Dara had given herself before she took a breath, turned to Charlie and Marie, and told them both there was no time for anything but *correcting this.*

Spine straight, chest lifted, eyes up, breathe, breathe, breathe. Make it perfect. Make it right.

"We're going to take care of this," she'd said. That was what you did. You kept it behind closed doors. Peeping Toms, voyeurs, their mother used to call them—neighbors, truant officers, social workers, police officers. It was no one's business. No one else would ever understand.

"We were never here," Dara had said to Charlie and Marie. "When it happened. We were never here and that's all we know."

Best to keep it simple. To keep themselves out of it. Dara made the plan in an instant. Someone had to.

They both looked so relieved. They looked so grateful.

Moments later, at three A.M., Charlie and Dara had climbed that same staircase to the third floor.

No one can know about Derek and Marie, Dara kept saying. *No one.*

It would draw suspicion. It would complicate things. It might make Marie look guilty. It might make them all look guilty.

Swiftly, they'd gathered Marie's belongings—a fistful of tank tops, a dark knot of tights, a mound of elastics, a pair of tangled, torn underwear that made Dara gasp—and thrown them into a garbage bag.

They'd folded the futon upon itself, and unplugged the windup Cinderella record player, wrapping its extension cord around it, stuffing it under the futon frame.

She had so little.

They took the sheets, the pillowcase with them.

Later, Dara would run them through the washing machine three times, putting her hands on them, scalding, after. Looking for any signs of him. A hair, a stain.

On her hands and knees, Dara scrubbed the shoe prints, which were everywhere.

Downstairs, Marie was throwing up in the powder room. Throwing up until the vomit came up red, sticky.

I can't, she whispered when they told her she was coming home with them.

Too bad, Dara said, grabbing her coat, shoving one of the garbage bags in her hands.

As they'd turned down Sycamore, their breath fogging the old car, Marie covered her face in her hands.

At first, she wouldn't go inside, her head tilting up like a child at a haunted house. Then, Dara shoving her across the threshold, she wouldn't go upstairs. Finally, she disappeared soundlessly into the den, their father's old domain.

In the bathroom, Dara examined Charlie's face, neck, arms, body, for any marks from the struggle. A bruise was blossoming on his upper arm, but that was all.

For the next three hours, Dara and Charlie sat at the kitchen table, thinking it all through with cigarettes and instant coffee, waiting for dawn.

Once, Dara squinted through the den door crack to see Marie curled in their father's recliner, sunk in some impossible sleep, her face so innocent and pure it nearly made Dara scream. And then it nearly made her cry.

"It was an accident," Charlie kept saying, his neck clammy with sweat, his hands doing that trembling thing. There was something intent and feverish about him. Something punch-drunk, as their father used to say, beerily recalling getting his clock cleaned in his hockey days until he couldn't count his fingers.

"It was an accident," Dara repeated. Over and over again. "We found him there. We don't know how it happened. But it did."

They couldn't bring Marie to the studio.

Dara had tried, coaxing her to the bathtub, pushing her head under the running spout. Trying to clean her up, get her straight. But Marie wasn't making sense yet, her teeth chattering, talking ceaselessly about the Fire Eater at the carnival who swallowed a neon tube and lit up like a glowworm. (*That was the Sword Swallower,* she told Marie. *You always get everything wrong. You always ruin everything.*)

Marie was not okay. Marie, could she even be trusted?

Charlie told Dara to stay home with her sister. He would make the discovery, call the police.

Marie could not be trusted.

Charlie returned to the studio at six A.M. At seven, he called Dara at the house. She could hear police radios buzzing in the background.

Dara, something happened, he said. *The police are here. They think our contractor fell down the stairs. . . .*

Charlie's voice was shaking.

He was very convincing.

Oh my god, Dara said, even though no one could hear her but Charlie. *Oh my god.*

Now it was nearly noon and Dara had spent all morning with the paramedics and the police, then with Benny and Gaspar, who exchanged glances when Charlie told them the news. Both were surprised and Gaspar took his hat off, crossing himself. *We didn't know him well,* Benny said vaguely. *But it is very sad.*

Charlie had done everything right, posting the signs, calling the parents of students scheduled later in the day. Saying the right things. (Still, they came. Charlie told them not to come, but they came. Half grim curiosity, half *Nutcracker* panic.)

Charlie was sharp and focused with the police, with everyone. It was only Dara who saw his shaky hands, the tremor in his wrist, the spasm at his neck.

Somewhere in the back of her mind, she was wondering: *Is he okay? Would he be okay after what he'd done?* But there wasn't any time.

A nd when you arrived, you saw him at the foot of the stairs?"

Dara had finally emerged from the powder room and joined the detective in Studio C.

In the back office, a woman was taking pictures, writing things down, showing things to the medical examiner, who couldn't stop coughing, red-faced and wheezing from construction dust. Earlier, Dara had seen the woman leaning over the contractor's muddy shoe treads, the tight triangles of his natty boots.

"Yes," Dara said. "My husband called me after he called you. Like I said."

The police detective, a creasy-eyed white man of indiscriminate middle age, wore a tan trench coat like a detective in a movie. He had, Dara noticed, a smear of toothpaste on his shirt collar.

"Was it typical of your contractor to be working already at that hour? What, six A.M.?"

"They'd fallen behind. They were trying to pick up the pace," Dara said. "We're very busy here. We need that space."

"How about back there?"

"There?"

"In the office. You weren't having any work done there, correct?"

"Correct."

"What about upstairs, that attic? You keep equipment, a fuse box, something, up there?"

"No. My husband showed you. He—"

"So any idea what the guy might've been up to? He was either going up or coming down. Looks like coming down based on the angle of the body."

"I don't know. Maybe . . ."

"Maybe?"

"Maybe he heard a sound, or something. We didn't know him very well."

We didn't know him very well. But there you go.

The detective looked at her, nodded.

"Well," he said, shrugging, sliding his notebook into his pocket, "do any of us really know anyone?"

The medical examiner came out, a dust mask pressed to his face, and the woman who took all the pictures followed, a heavy case in her hand.

It was all ending, nearly. Or at least this part was.

The body was gone, carried out in that big black bag with a zipper. Dara and Charlie had both turned their heads.

"Someone should've torn out that staircase years ago," the medical examiner said to no one in particular. "Death trap."

The detective spoke to Benny and Gaspar, but not for long. Everything seemed pro forma.

After, Dara told them they could go home for the day.

"Thank you," Benny said, standing in the middle of Studio B, his hand tentatively touching the saw bench.

Gaspar began packing up, but Benny didn't move at all for several seconds.

"Benny," Dara said, "we're all so sorry. About the accident."

Benny looked at her and Dara found herself looking away.

"It's very sad," he said finally. "But we keep going." Taking off his cap, he slid in his foam earplugs and reached for the table saw. "That's how we get paid."

I don't know," Dara said to Charlie later. "I think it's fine."

"But they probably knew. About Marie."

"Maybe," Dara said, pulling her hair back into a bun.

"We should," Charlie said, "make sure they got paid."

All the younger girls were crying in little clumps across the studio. The five- and six-year-olds, tugging at their leotard crotches, whimpering softly, sneaking glances at the door to the back office, the police tape criss-crossed.

The older girls were, as ever, dry-eyed, cool. Speculating, whispering in corners to one another, guessing about canceled rehearsals, biting their fingers and cracking their toes.

Older than most of their fathers, the dead contractor was only a voice through the walls, a constant obstruction as they navigated the makeshift path through Studio B. A dad type, with a thunderous voice and a mercurial schedule, strolling past everyone in his shiny boots, shouting to Benny every time a circuit broke.

They'd likely noticed him far less than Benny, who arrived every day on a candy-orange motor scooter and was always so nice, even when he unclogged the toilet for them, and Gaspar, who was charming with his little habits, like setting a jug of milk on the sill of the open window, not drinking it until it was icy, or the time he played Crazy Eights with a few of the younger girls, their carpool parent late for the day's pickup.

They had no feelings for the dead contractor and, besides, *The Nutcracker* began in ten days.

* * *

Everything felt surprisingly normal, even as both students and parents were in a frenzy. Perhaps because they were in a frenzy. The turbulence of the contractor's death in these very rooms merely seemed an extension and an intensification of the turbulence of *Nutcracker* season. Gossip, anxiety, paranoia churning, and two six-year-olds vomiting in the powder room, one in the sink, after another girl claimed there was still blood on the floor where the contractor's body had fallen. *It was terrible!* she kept saying. *I can smell it!*

If only, Dara thought, they'd seen the back of his head when the paramedic turned him over, spongelike and ravaged from hitting the desk's sharp corner, the unforgiving floor. If only they'd seen the dark hole where his eye had been.

I was scared of him," Chloë Lin confided at one point to Dara.

"Why?"

Chloë took a deep breath, her eyes dragging to Studio B once, then twice.

"I don't know," she said. "He didn't go here."

"Go here?"

"He . . . he didn't belong."

No, Dara thought, momentarily gratified. *He didn't.*

Few of the students could conjure any specific encounter with the dead contractor, other than Ivy Neuman's long recounting of the time he helped her untangle her wool scarf from the power cords stretched across Studio B.

Of all the things competing for their students' attention—which were almost entirely the varied and countless ways they could fail disastrously and on an epic scale onstage—Derek was the least.

Still, everyone had taken notice when they'd carried the body through the studios, the clatter of the gurney, the black monolith of the contractor, the body bag zipper glistening.

Everyone had stepped out of the way, the students grim-faced, hands folded, heads down as if for a fallen solider.

Charlie was steady and reassuring with the parents. Promising them that, while this surely was not ideal timing, in some ways it would have been worse if it had happened a few weeks ago. Now they were nearly ready to move to on-site rehearsals at the Ballenger and maybe they could even expedite the process. Move off the premises until everyone felt comfortable again. You see, it was a very sad thing—tragic, really—but they all knew how much *The Nutcracker* meant to the students and how hard they'd been working. The show must go on, to coin a phrase.

Finally, everyone was gone, the parents having stuffed their children back into overheated cars, the back office emptying out after being swollen for hours with detectives, with the medical examiner and his watering eyes, with the woman taking photographs, scraping the floor, that thick smear of blood, brown like a coffee rind. Putting things in paper bags, sealing them, packing them in her kit. Metal fragments from the bent and buckled stair rail. The bill holder, its newly bent spike.

All of it was gone now.

There was nothing here to see.

It was all going to be fine.

In a few days, the swirl of *Nutcracker* madness, everyone would move on.

Dara found Charlie seated at the desk, staring at the worn and pitted floor, the fresh gouges in the wood. A stray glove, acid blue, like a deflated balloon.

"They said we can clean it up now," Charlie murmured. "They took all the pictures. They took all the statements."

The stoic face he'd worn all day had vanished. He looked hollowed out, raw.

"So that's it," Dara said, reaching for him. "It's over."

Charlie didn't say anything. He just opened the closet, reached for the gallon of peroxide, and began pouring.

The yellow stain on the hardwood after—a wobbly shape like a giant puzzle piece—would stay forever. They could sand it away, brush it with darker stain. But, with the volcanic force of *The Nutcracker*, there was no time for it, so they left it, tiptoeing around it.

The next day, Charlie would drag the desk over the spot, even though its diagonal meant there was no way to move comfortably in the space.

The police told them not to use the spiral staircase, stretching hazard tape across it. It rattled dangerously with any weight at all, the force of the fall yanking the center pole loose from its moorings.

You couldn't go up or down safely, so Marie would have to stay with them.

It all made Dara remember the car accident, her parents. How the police department impounded what was left of their father's Buick, its twisted, zigzagging frame, its ashy center, like one of their mother's Gauloises, bent and crumpled in her tin ashtray.

After, they kept the ruin on display in the lot as they did all the drunk-driving fatalities, their own vehicular Death Row. It was meant to be cautionary, which Dara supposed it was. Not just for drunk driving, though the heavy, liquored smell of the wreckage made that clear, but for everything else. For all the damage two people staying together can do. Two circling rivals locked in an endless, fatal embrace.

Years later, Dara asked Marie if she remembered all that time the

Buick remained in the lot's center spot before being dethroned by a pulverized stretch limousine, prom corsages exploded across its dashboard and the cloying smell of Southern Comfort, cheap weed.

I remember, Marie had said. *I remember everything.*

It turned out Marie had snuck out of the house one night, late, in those strange months following the accident.

She'd walked all the way to the police lot, where she could run her hands all over the car, its pocked and blistered metal. She even climbed inside and sat on the front seat, bisected, its stuffing shaking loose. She put her hand in the hole in the windshield where their father's head had landed.

It was, she said, *the closest I ever felt to them. To him.*

Everyone had assumed their father was behind the wheel, and drunk. Dara assumed it, too, even after Charlie explained what the police said. Even when Marie told her how she could tell from that visit to the car, the driver's seat thrust forward for their mother's petite frame, the long strands of their mother's hair caught in the windshield.

It was her, Dara. It was Mother.

Sometimes what happened just doesn't feel like what really happened.

Behind the wheel and drunk, too, the end of a long tear, late for their anniversary dinner, to celebrate twenty years of tumult and terror, their mother refusing to leave for hours as she slowly, vengefully drained his holiday-bonus scotch.

Dara, don't you see? It was her. It was always her.

No, Marie, she wanted to say. *It was them. It was always both of them.*

That night, the house felt different, drafty and forlorn.

They hadn't slept or eaten or groomed themselves since it happened.

At last, the flood of feeling, the hard push of nerves had ended, had reached its end. Dara felt like a shell, a husk, the feeling after a performance, the dread sinking with the final curtain, settling inside her.

For Charlie, too, it seemed. When Dara watched him march up the carpeted stairs like the steps to the guillotine, he looked so much older than he'd ever looked before, drawn and bony and blue. For a second, a brief second, as the ceiling light hit him, he looked like their mother in those last few weeks, drinking all the time, slamming doors, and the heavy glass ashtray their mother threw, hooking their father in the chin, the mouth, knocking two teeth loose.

Oh, that, Dara thought. *Remember that.*

She was remembering so many things lately that she'd packed away long ago.

Without saying a word, Charlie disappeared into the upstairs bathroom, filling the claw-foot tub until the floor bulged with its weight.

Dara thought she could hear him talking to himself in there.

She climbed the stairs and put her ear to the door, wet from the steam.

His whisper, rising and falling, and all she could make out was *it's over, it's over, it's over.*

All evening, Marie left the den only once, appearing in the kitchen, looking for matches. She left as soon as she saw Charlie.

He was standing at the stove, making tea for the toddies, and he pretended he didn't see her either.

As the tea steeped, he counted softly to himself, something he hadn't done in years. The way, as a barely pubescent dancer, he couldn't stop himself, his voice cracking slightly, his Adam's apple rising and falling, a tremor as he counted off his pirouettes.

We're never going to talk about it, Dara realized at some point. Neither Charlie nor Marie seemed strong enough to talk about it. To face it.

She felt, obscurely, like Clara in her nightgown, alone on the dark stage.

In the end, their mother used to tell her, hands on Dara's shoulders as she waited in the wings, *it's only you out there.*

In the end, you only have you.

It wasn't until the final hour of that endless day that was really two days that it all fell on Dara. She lay in bed and her thoughts flung back to the things he'd said, the insinuations, the accusations, the lurid pictures he'd painted. But most of all the looks on Charlie's and Marie's faces as it happened.

It was a look that was uncannily familiar though she couldn't place it.

She was touching the corners of something. She could feel it. She wasn't sure she wanted to.

She didn't cry, not once. And she felt very strong, somehow. Something had happened at last, she thought. A pressure released. A valve turned, a window thrown open.

Marie was back home. They were all here again.

Everyone could forget.

DON'T LOOK

Once in the night, Charlie sleeping beside her, his throat thick with sleeping pills, breathing funnily, she woke to a piercing sensation beneath her right brow.

A flash came of some murky nightmare of eye sockets, rolling eyeballs, her slipper slipping over a jellied orb.

A flash then of another, Derek running up the spiral staircase and suddenly their mother running down, darkly luminous in a nightgown as white as Clara's.

Their mother, her long hand twined around the iron railing, and then Derek was gone, their mother falling. Falling, slumping, her nightgown mounded around her like a sunken flower.

Don't look, Charlie was saying. *Don't look at her eyes.*

In the kitchen, she poured a splash of the cream brandy their *Nutcracker* lighting vendor gave them every year into their morning coffee and watched Charlie shuffle around numbly.

At some point in the night, he'd slunk out of bed, down the hall, down the stairs to the sofa bed where she found him, mummy-tight in the old afghan, crocheted snowflakes yellowed with age.

"We can do this," he kept saying, but he seemed less sure today. No longer fired by adrenaline, the snaky spring of fear.

The blue of the veins at his temple, his skin nearly translucent in the morning light.

She would never not want to touch him, to stroke his skin, to fondle and caress. He was too beautiful and also half-forbidden, that half-broken body.

Charlie, Charlie, she thought and remembered their mother once saying, *So beautiful, like spider silk, and not strong enough by half.*

They had both heard Marie at four A.M.

"I thought I was dreaming," Charlie said, rubbing his eyes, "that she was coming after us with a hammer."

It was a hammer, pounding, pounding. That singular cacophony of her sister taking what sounded like a ball-peen to a pair of pointe shoes.

Waking them both up, keeping them up.

"Are you going to stop her?" Charlie had asked.

"No," Dara had replied tiredly, wanly. "Let her. Let her."

The ritual would soothe her. Soothed all dancers, Dara thought.

The shoes, the shoes. The shoes were everything.

Pink satin fantasies from afar, from the audience, enthralled. But if you moved too close, you'd see that they'd already been battered, scored, disemboweled.

Those shoes, so intimate, soaked with your sweat until they sealed themselves to your feet, until, soon after, they fell to pieces.

Pink satin fantasies we beat into submission so they can be used and then discarded.

Pink satin fantasies created to give pleasure but destroyed in the process.

This, their mother said when she held out Dara's very first pointe shoe, *is what we are.*

This, she said, handing her the shoe, Dara's stubby nine-year-old fingers touching it, feeling a static charge, *is you.*

S he's in no condition to work today," Charlie was saying as they finished their coffee. "We can't have her in front of parents."

Dara didn't say anything, holding on to the last sly tang of brandy, trying to calm herself, when Marie appeared in the kitchen doorway.

Hair glossed back wetly and wearing an outsize oxblood cardigan sweater Dara recognized as their father's, she held a pair of gleaming pointe shoes, Freed of London, size four, toe glue-slicked, shank cut, sole scored, satin hardened, their toes mysteriously crusted with dirt.

"Marie," Charlie said, "are you okay?"

Because Marie's feet were bare and red, like little stumps.

"I was dancing," Marie said, setting the shoes on the table. "I forgot what it felt like. I can't believe I forgot."

"Where were you dancing?" Charlie said.

"In the backyard. On the icy grass, like the Waltz of the Snowflakes. I danced until my feet were on fire. I was on fire."

Her voice high and faint, a voice that had always meant bad things. Meant Marie not sleeping for days, making bad choices like running their car into a guardrail, booking a last-minute trip around the world.

"Marie," Dara said, "you can't do this, not now. I can't worry about you right now."

"I'm not doing anything," Marie said, blinking at Dara. "I'm here, aren't I? Back in this house. I'm here."

The way she was blinking, eyes glinting, Dara was worried her sister might start crying. It was enraging.

"Like you're doing us a favor," Dara said. "Marie, do not forget: You got us into this. You're here because of you."

"Dara," Charlie said. "She's . . . she lost someone."

There was a heavy silence. They both looked at Marie, hands dug deep into the cardigan's pockets. Dara wondered if those pockets smelled like their father's cigarettes.

"There's no time for that," Dara said. Her own voice so like her own mother's in that moment she felt a chill drag up her spine. "That's a luxury we don't have."

"Listen," Charlie said, even as he let his head drop, averting his eyes. "What happened—that fight—it got out of hand, but I shouldn't have . . ."

Marie looked up at Charlie. "It was an accident," she said softly.

"Those things he was saying," Charlie said, his eyes fixed on Marie's now. "He never should have said those things."

"I told him things," Marie blurted. "And he . . . twisted them. I told him things he couldn't understand."

Dara watched them, the two of them, how they worked it out for themselves. Neither of them really taking responsibility, but instead feigning at it, fluttering past it.

Watching them, she didn't know how she felt herself yet.

Accident, yes. Sort of. Not precisely. Not fully. And these two . . .

"We don't need to talk about fault," Dara said. Not wanting to look at either of them suddenly.

"I'm sorry," Marie said, "I'm so, so sorry. I was . . . I thought he . . ."

"It was an accident," Charlie said, more firmly now. "Those stairs— those stairs were dangerous from the start."

Yes, Dara thought, remembering her own insistence that they stay. *They were.*

"We're all sorry," Charlie said, reaching for Dara's hands, then Marie's.

It happened slowly; all of them moved closer together, forming a huddle. Something old and childlike. Their heads brushing against one another like tentative animals, like feral creatures exiled and now returned.

Their faces all pressed close, like long ago, ages thirteen, fourteen, bodies entwined in a *pas de trois* on the studio floor, their mother watching from the corner, a dark shadow, a raven hovering.

"Can we never talk about it again?" Marie asked, barely a whisper. "Can we?"

"We can," Charlie said, his voice rough and urgent. Then, turning to Dara, "Can't we?"

Dara looked at them, their twinned faces.

"What," she said, her voice a smooth assurance, "is there to talk about?"

ALL RISK

It all felt right, natural. Pretending nothing had happened. Keeping secrets. Hiding everything. They'd been doing it their whole lives.

And there was too much else to consume them. Hours went by held captive by rehearsals and one-on-one sessions, by meetings with the prop master, costume fittings, wig fittings, by long trips to the Ballenger to work with the musicians, to approve the final backdrops, the Land of Snow, twenty-five feet high and glistening hotly like those old Christmas cards with the sparkles that shook loose in the envelope.

Dara spent the better part of an hour working with the stagehands and Bailey Bloom in her Clara costume—that ghostly white nightgown—on the crowd-pleasing moment when Clara's bed glides across the stage thanks to "bed boy" hiding beneath: her youngest male student, a ginger-haired nine-year-old who'd practiced crawling swiftly under the bed so many times he'd skinned his elbows red.

She did all these things, including unpacking the six Nutcracker dolls they'd rotate throughout the performances, each one identical, Santa-red uniforms, glossy black boots, mustaches swooping over those colossal teeth.

Everything was the same as it had been every year for all the years of her life. Nothing had changed. Nothing.

O n her way back to the studio from the Ballenger, she stopped at the bank so she could pay Benny and Gaspar. A large sum, larger than they seemed to have expected. It turned out, Charlie told her, Derek hadn't paid them in weeks.

"It's okay, ma'am," Gaspar kept saying as she counted out the cash. "Everything's fine."

M s. Durant," Benny said, organizing his bills, folding them neatly into his wallet, "we can still complete the work. We know what to do."

"I know you do," Dara said. "But we've got a lot going on here now and—"

"Ms. Durant," he said, then paused, as if deciding something. "I hope you know you don't need to worry."

"Worry?"

"About all the questions. I mean, we don't have anything to say."

Dara looked at Benny, who wouldn't quite meet her eyes.

"Are the police still asking you questions?" she asked. "Were they here today?"

"Just the lady," he said. "From All-Risk."

"What? Someone was here—"

"She's in the back office now," he said. "Your husband let her in."

R andi Jacek," the woman in the navy pantsuit said, a tape measure in her hand. "All-Risk."

She was a bright-eyed woman of middle age, the yellowed fingers of a smoker, and she had the office to herself, her left shoe treading slightly on the bleach stain on the floor.

Reaching into the pocket of her pantsuit, she pulled out a card, its corner slightly bent: RANDI JACEK, CLAIMS INVESTIGATOR, ALL-RISK INSURANCE.

"Ms. Jacek, I think you've made a mistake," Dara said. "We're not All-Risk. We're Consolidated Life."

"You are. But your contractor was All-Risk."

"Oh."

"I explained to your husband—"

"And where is he?"

"Don't tell him I ratted him out," the woman said, lowering her voice conspiratorially, "but I think he went for a smoke."

"Was there something you needed you didn't get from the police?" Dara said. "They were here all day yesterday. They told us they were done."

The woman looked at her, squinting slightly.

"You know, I love those guys. Cops. Overworked, underpaid," she said, removing a small digital camera from her pocket, rubbing its lens with her cuff. "The thing is, Ms. Durant, they'd just as soon I do their work for them. And it just so happens it's my job."

"You must be very busy then," Dara said, her voice clipped. None of it sounded right. "Going to every place someone took a bad fall."

The woman smiled. "You got me," she said. "We don't usually make house calls. But I knew him a little. Derek."

Dara felt her chest pinch. Folded her arms. "Really?"

"Everyone knew Derek," she said, eyes dragging around the office. Scanning the windows, the floor, settling on the staircase. "You know."

"I don't," Dara said. "We didn't. I mean, he was overseeing this project, but—"

"We go way back. De La Salle, Class of mumble-mumble-mumble," she said, turning to the staircase, eyeing it again. "And he took out a lot of policies with us. The nature of his biz. We used to call him D-Wreck. Hey, how many contractors does it take to change a lightbulb?"

"What? I—"

"Two," Randi said, snapping a photo of the staircase railing. "One to screw it in and another to knock over the ladder and file an accident claim the next day."

Dara didn't laugh.

"Well," Randi said, "probably not funny to his family either. You kinda get a gallows humor in this line of work."

"His family?" Dara said, her eye twitching. Derek's family. Who? His brother? The one in the upper bunk? If that story had even been true.

But Randi wasn't listening, still focused on the staircase. Dara didn't like it. She also didn't like looking up the staircase. She didn't like remembering anything that had ever happened on the staircase, or through the mouth into the third floor.

"See, this is what I mean," Randi said, lifting the drooping hazard tape from the railing. "Police photographs, measurements, they don't tell the whole story. But if you can get in there and see the space, lay your hands on it, sometimes things become instantly clear."

She reached out and grabbed one of the balusters, hard.

Dara watched the stairs shiver.

"These," Randi said, shaking her head at the staircase as if it were a disobedient child, "are accidents waiting to happen."

"Yes," Dara said, exhaling at last. "We should have torn it down years ago."

When Charlie eventually returned, cigarette stub between finger and thumb, his face red from the cold, he looked surprised to see her.

"You left her in there alone," Dara said tightly, shutting the door behind him.

Charlie stopped. "I thought it would be better. She wouldn't ask me questions."

"So she asked me questions instead," Dara said, then a low hiss: "She knew him."

"Oh," Charlie said, sinking down into the desk chair. "Oh."

"It seems like she was satisfied," Dara said. "I guess she's just doing her job, investigating the claim."

Charlie threw the stub in the trash can, head down. "So someone filed a claim already?"

"I guess so," Dara said. "His family must have."

She'd forgotten how it all worked with her own parents. Getting the death certificate, the police report. Waiting for the check to come. How long it took and why.

"But she didn't get into that with you?"

Dara shook her head.

"I think it's okay," she added, because Charlie was still looking at her expectantly. "She wasn't here long. That's probably the end of it."

"Right," Charlie said tentatively. "Construction workers get into accidents all the time, right?"

"Right," Dara said.

The way he was looking at her. His heavy-lidded eyes blinking slowly, tenuously. Waiting for assurance, comfort.

It reminded her of Charlie years ago, barely fifteen, his skin like the skin of a peach, that dazed look he'd have in his eyes whenever he wasn't dancing. How when he was dancing, he seemed to go some other place, exalted and forbidden. How when he stopped, he looked immediately lost and forlorn. Showing him where the towels were when he first moved in, showing him how to light the oven burner, to call his mother overseas on the landline.

Like a boy in a painting, their mother used to say, looking at him. *Caravaggio.*

It made her want to put her hand on his forehead, to put him to bed.

"Dara," he said, "can we go home now?"

He drew his hands inside his sweater cuffs, rubbed a cuff against his face. Those tremulous hands.

She was the only strong one of the three of them.

* * *

That night, she sat at the kitchen table a very long time, alone.

Her head kept vibrating, her teeth. It was that woman, Randi Jacek, her hand on the staircase.

She was remembering something. Something that had been hovering there for days, weeks. Hovering just beyond reach, like a flicker in the corner of her eye.

At first the memory came in fits and starts, her hand on the railing, music floating from her mother's radio on the third floor.

Crying out, *Mother! Mother!*

A feeling in her chest, an echoing in her ears.

Back, back, start again: Age fifteen, long-legged, coltish, running back late to the studio to tell her mother she'd been cast as a Dewdrop in the exalted Waltz of the Flowers for the Eastern Ballet Company's regional production.

Age fifteen and puffed up with her triumph—a role earned, and all hers—she called out for her mother as she bounded through the dark and dust of Studios A, B, and C and to the back office, the opening to the third floor glowing, like the cutout mouth in a jack-o'-lantern.

Gripping the rail of the spiral staircase, she whipped around its three hairpin turns and emerged on the third floor, the smell of their mother's black currant tea and the fuzz of her battered radio, tinny jazz, and it took a moment, a long, flickering moment, for her eyes to adjust to the darkness, the only light an old gooseneck lamp, curled and lying on its side, its narrow glare illuminating their mother on the futon.

Their mother half-reclining, her head thrown back and her legs flung apart, that bright blue vein snaking up her inner thigh. And something, someone kneeling before her, the soft blond thrush of his hair and the princely profile.

"Charlie," Dara had said, the first time her voice full of wonder still.

"Charlie," she'd said seconds later, watching their mother thrust the boy aside now, wrapping her legs back around herself, drawing up the tights that had slithered to her ankles.

"Charlie," she'd said a third time, her voice changed now, changed forever. "Mother."

Later, much later, Dara would wonder if it even happened. It felt more like a picture she'd once looked at in a book. It had happened, but had it happened to *her*? And what had she seen, really? What was their mother really doing with her fifteen-year-old student, with her own daughter's beloved, what was she letting him—having him—do to her other than nestle his fevered head against her warm belly, her lovely thighs?

But at the time, it felt like everything. Because it was, of course.

None of them spoke of it in the days that followed. She never told Marie, or anyone.

That first night, Charlie slept on the sofa downstairs, but by the second, Dara had snuck down and climbed beside him, his body so hot on her skin and eager for forgiveness. Her hands gathering him hungrily, she found herself wanting him to forgive her, to forgive them.

Two days later, she and Charlie began making plans to leave, together. It was just too unbearable, all together in the studio, at that house. It was unbearable to pass one another in the hallway, at the bathroom, over the kettle on the kitchen stove. Dara couldn't look her mother in the eye. Charlie couldn't sleep or eat, taking long, scalding baths in the claw-foot tub. They had to go. Maybe to Charlie's mother in England, or Charlie could take that apprenticeship in the Sarasota Ballet.

Immediately, they began paperwork, made calls. Tried to find out about passports, licenses. They'd even secretly lugged their mother's rolling trunk from the basement and begun packing.

Maybe it's too quick, Charlie said, watching her.

It's not, Dara insisted. It was like one's first *grand jeté*. How students were never ready until suddenly they were and they had to do it right away, or the moment would pass.

We have to go now. We have to.

Three days later, it was their parents' twentieth wedding anniversary and their car careered into oncoming traffic and they were dead.

The morning after the funeral, Dara unpacked the trunk, Charlie watching. Down the hall, Marie was crying, had been crying for days. She couldn't sleep, wouldn't eat, her body like a broken bird. After, Dara dragged the rolling trunk back down to the basement, where she wouldn't see it again for more than a decade, when Marie heaved it back up the stairs for her trip around the world.

See, Dara thought, *I tried to leave once too, Marie. Long before you. It's harder than it looks.*

UNHEALTHY

Charlie's back felt hot under her hand when she woke.

She felt a tickle in her throat, a feeling of something. It had hummed in her all night. All those conversations with Charlie, with Marie. Those half-conversations, all the past stirred up again. And now it wouldn't leave her.

And she kept thinking about that word *accident*. What it meant, what it contained. *They were killed in a car accident. He fell down the stairs in a terrible accident. I didn't mean to do it. It was an accident.*

And when she reached out again Charlie's back was hot, tortured. It felt like putting your hand on a tangle of lighting cables, illuminating everything.

Today was the first on-site rehearsal. Normally, Dara and Marie would focus on the stage, on the performances, while Charlie did everything else. Overseeing the backdrop load-in, meeting with the stage crew, making sure the snack packs arrive on time, corralling the hectic parent volunteers and managing their access to their nervous children.

But there was nothing normal about today, and Charlie could barely move from the bed, his body like a fallen statue, his face taut with pain.

"I don't know how I could have done it," he said. "I've been careful."

But Dara knew. Those mad minutes the other night, she and Charlie scurrying around on the third floor, heaving the futon mattress in half, snapping the frame shut, hoisting garbage bags, wiping the place clean of Marie, of the contractor. All while one floor below the contractor's lifeless body stiffened, his skin turning cold. All while Marie sat in their car, where they'd stowed her, her head resting against the window like a child waiting, waiting forever for her parents to remember she was there.

L ie back," she said to him now. "Stay home. I'll take care of it. And Marie . . . Marie will do her best."

"Not a chance. I'm gonna rally here," he whispered, even as his body was sinking back, his face contorted in pain. "I just need a few minutes. It's just, with the cold weather, it . . ."

Slowly, slowly she let her hand drop away.

It would be her and Marie. It would have to be.

I 'm gonna be all right today," Marie said as they walked to their separate cars. "I promise."

"Okay," Dara said. "Okay."

T he Ballenger Center—a sleek, featureless lightbox of a building—had undergone its annual transformation. Wrapped in thousands of white lights like lace, dotted with shimmering gumdrops the size of church bells, trimmed with bright candy canes big as coat stands dangling from its roof.

Inside, the theater volunteers had clearly spent hours draping boughs and garlands in every corner. A fleet of the familiar two-story-high *Nutcracker* banners hung from the ceiling, swaying with each burst of forced heat.

Marie stood in the lobby's center, in front of a brand-new decoration: a fifteen-foot-high Nutcracker statue of resin and fiberglass, his face a glossy rictus.

Gazing upward, Marie couldn't take her eyes off it, not even noticing as all the students began tumbling in, tearing off wool hats, chattering softly, reverently, smoothing their hair back into their tight buns.

"Are you ready?" Dara asked, stirring Marie from her reverie.

Her sister turned and looked at her and smiled.

In seconds, the lobby was filled with students, the youngest ones nearly squealing as they moved through the carpeted space.

It was the first time at least a quarter of them had ever been behind the scenes at the Ballenger, a theater they'd all sat in, enthralled, their whole lives, tucked since ages three or four in the red plush seats, their candy- and saliva-coated palms pressed on the wooden armrests, their eyes un-blinking, struck.

"I'm so nervous I could die. I could throw up and die."

"Shut up. You're making it worse."

"What if Oliver drops me? Did you see his arm—"

"You-know-who makes me sick. Her toes curl under like claws."

For the next four hours, as Dara stalked the stage, the theater aisles, it was a ceaseless assault: pitched laughter, stifled screams, and the teary strains of forgotten slippers, the tragedy of monthly bloat, a blackened toe-nail hanging by a strip of withered skin, and their Clara, Bailey Bloom, missing for a perilous half hour. Finally, Madame Sylvie found her locked in a lightless custodial supply closet, hysterical with fear.

"She said someone blindfolded her and locked her inside," Madame Sylvie told Dara. "Some shadowy 'they.'"

But Dara knew just who the "they" was, looking across the stage at all the unchosen Claras—Pepper Weston, Gracie Hent, Iris Cartwright—waiting to rehearse the Waltz of the Snowflakes, their faces aloof, watchful.

"The little darlings," Dara said, sounding more like their mother than ever before. "I suppose they hoped we wouldn't find her until after opening night."

D id you see it?"

"Shhhh . . ."

"Let me look."

Midway through the Waltz of the Snowflakes run-through, the energy corkscrewed, a scattering of students hovering over their phones in the dark wings.

It was a news article. The Durants hadn't received a newspaper in twenty years, since the *Tribune* strike began and their father, a union man, called to cancel his subscription, harrumphing that he was no scab.

Dara got a copy from a stagehand perusing the sports page while, onstage, two dozen Snowflakes flitted and leapt.

CONTRACTOR KILLED AT AREA BALLET SCHOOL, the headline noted grimly, the photo of the studio just as grim, the weather-beaten sign, its brick streaked with salt.

"Higher!" she could hear Madame Sylvie calling out. "In a week, you'll be doing those *assemblés* in fifty pounds of snow!"

Behind the curtain, she read the article once, then twice.

> *Authorities are investigating the death of an area contractor whom police said died early Sunday after apparently falling down a staircase.*
>
> *Police were called to the scene after the owners of the Durant School of Dance reported discovering Derek Girard, 49, of Roseville, at the foot of the staircase and unresponsive. Police arrived to*

find the man lying on his back, with visible injuries and his head
surrounded by blood. He was reported dead on the scene, according
to police reports.

A preliminary autopsy revealed that the cause of death was a
complex skull fracture due to blunt force head trauma from the
elevated fall, internal bleeding, and major intracranial bleeding
due to eye perforation, according to the county coroner.

A final determination of the manner of death is pending toxi-
cology and histology results. The police investigation is ongoing.

There really wasn't any new information in the article, she decided. Everything was falling in line as it should. It would all be over soon.

Except: those words. *Autopsy. Pending. Manner of death. Ongoing.*

I thought autopsies were only for murder," Liv Lockman was whispering.

The acoustics of the Ballenger were unforgiving and Dara could hear all of it, each little rosette of Snowflakes assembled, waiting, chattering, eager to hurl their minds to something other than their rigid and anxious bodies.

"It's any unnatural death," announced Gracie Hent, from some mysterious well of knowledge. "They do autopsies for any unnatural death."

"What's unnatural about it?" Liv Lockman said, her voice even lower, her eyes shining with excitement.

"Because it wasn't supposed to happen," Gracie said, looking less sure now. "But it did."

Unnatural. The word like a cold lash. Once, twice, three times.

Later in the afternoon, when the parents began arriving, it seemed to be everywhere: the dreary gray page-three article, a few column inches but also a photograph of their studio, dark and stark as a crime scene.

"What are we going to do about this?" Dr. Weston said, looking dreary and gray himself as he approached Dara. Dr. Weston, there for rehearsal again. How did a doctor have so much leisure time?

"About what?" Dara said, playing distracted, focusing instead on a group of the Level IVs trying to hide in a lobby alcove, bent over a plastic tub of contraband rainbow cookies. *Come try one, Bailey,* someone was saying. *They're so good.*

"This article. The picture." He shook his head. "Aren't you concerned?"

"It has nothing to do with us," Dara said, feeling her face grow hot, avoiding his heavy gaze, watching as Madame Sylvie scolded the girls for their cookies. *Do you think I don't see, mes anges? I see everything.*

"But it does," Dr. Weston insisted, moving closer toward her.

Jesus, Dara thought. *What could he know?*

"I don't see how . . ." she started.

Then, leaning even closer, he lowered his voice, pointing at the paper, "I mean, they haven't even given us coverage for *The Nutcracker* yet. What kind of crap is that?"

Dara felt a hard smack of relief. *The Nutcracker,* what else was there?

"I have to get back," she said abruptly, backing farther away.

"Well, it's the world we live in," he said, his voice echoing through the lobby as Dara turned and began walking away. "Sick, sick."

Back in the cool dark of the theater, she tried to settle into the work, watching Corbin onstage donning the Nutcracker Prince mask, lurid and startling under the lights. The tufts of white hair on either side. The grin manic, the teeth two perfect lines.

While the lighting engineer made adjustments, bringing up the blue, Dara called Charlie, but there was no answer.

"Just checking in," she said into the voicemail. "Call me."

Behind her, she heard a voice, Marie. One row back, leaning close to Dara's ear.

"Is he coming here?" she asked. "Charlie?"

"No," Dara said. "But we should talk."

"Okay," Marie said.

The stage was flooded violet, Corbin adjusting the mask on his head.

Behind her, Dara could hear Marie breathing. Fast, then more slowly. Slower still.

I t doesn't mean anything," she told Marie as her sister read the article, her fingers smudging.

They were in a dressing room, backstage. A half-dozen mouse heads perched on stands, the room smelling of glue, rubbing alcohol, cold cream, vomit.

"It's okay," Marie said, twisting her thumbnail between her teeth. "I'm okay."

"They do them for everyone. Autopsies," Dara said, even as she knew they didn't.

Marie held out the newspaper, offering it back to Dara, her grip tentative, like it was a carton of eggs, or a box of firecrackers.

"I keep thinking of his face," she said. "At the end. How surprised he looked."

"Why are you doing this?" Dara said, letting the newspaper fall to the vanity. "We said we weren't ever going to talk about this."

Marie looked into one of the cloudy mirrors. "On the stairs. He looked so surprised."

In that instant, Dara wondered if she'd looked surprised, too, watching Marie and Charlie on those stairs, their strange faces. She knew she had. It was the same.

"Surprised like he didn't recognize us," Marie said, eyes on the mirror. She and Dara twinned there. Dara was cool, but Marie was hot. Dara was dark, but Marie was light.

"Like we were these alien things."

* * *

It was nearly seven. Everyone was tired. All the excitement eaten away by the rigors of the day, its small victories and humiliations.

The stage was bare except for Bailey Bloom, an unlit taper candle in her hand, gazing into the darkness. Though no one else was in costume that day, Bailey was wearing her Clara nightgown for the lighting crew. For the important moment Clara leaves her bed in the blue-black night to retrieve the Nutcracker, her longing for him so immense.

From her seat, Dara watched as Bailey, her pale tights glowing, bounded across the stage over and over again as they adjusted the fly rigs.

"Slow and big, Mademoiselle Bloom," Dara called out. "The audience needs to be able to feel everything."

Nightgown ballooning, Bailey streaked across the stage, scooped the abandoned Nutcracker into her arms. Sleeves like white wings, she hoisted it into the air like a totem, a godhead, then lifted herself into an elegant arabesque, her neck so long and her leg so high in the way you can when you're fourteen, fifteen, your body both feather-light and molten, and everything is forever and nothing ever changes.

Dara felt her eyes fill. No longer thinking of articles, or autopsies, or Charlie, or even Marie, she was giving herself over to Bailey, who'd earned it, who needed it. As their mother so often gave herself over to her students. The gaze, hot and relentless, felt like love. It was love.

Bailey onstage, so small amid the darkness, her body whirling antically, seeking her Nutcracker, braving the unknown.

It was so beautiful, like the grainy production they used to watch on their mother's portable black-and-white set. Their favorite Clara, a big-eyed waif, petal thin but impossibly strong. It was years before Dara realized they were watching their mother, recorded on videotape twenty years before.

"Bravo!" Madame Sylvie called out.

Onstage, her arms in a perfect *port de bras*, cradling the Nutcracker between them, Bailey looked out into the dark theater, her face blue in the spotlight. Her eyes wide and face open, with all Clara's fear and wonder.

That's it, Dara thought. *That's Clara.*

"Shall we move on?" called out Madame Sylvie from the back of the house. Wanting to go home.

Dara looked up at Bailey, her chest still heaving, her collarbones pulsing.

"Not yet, please," she said, her voice surprisingly strong.

Bailey, who hadn't left the stage in hours, was lathered with sweat, the sweat of a longshoreman, the heels of her pointe shoes flecked with blood.

Bailey who said, "Once more, please?"

Dara nodded.

You had to let them keep going. Bailey knew to stop if she needed to. She knew to ask for first aid, to ask for Anbesol to numb her toes, to say she needed to rest.

But Bailey didn't want to rest—*I don't have it yet. Please, one more time*—and she kept going again and again, her face blazing under the lights, strands slipping from her immaculate bun. Chasséing across the stage again, one foot chasing the other, feet skimming the floor.

Dara heard the dull crack of feet pressed against seatbacks and turned, spotting the same spiky thicket of fellow Level IV girls—Pepper Weston, Gracie Hent, Iris Cartwright—their legs hanging over the seats, their heads dipping up and down from their phones to the stage. Pepper silently stitching elastic bands to her slippers and occasionally yawning.

They weren't making any noise, but they were still asserting their presence and Bailey's eyes kept flitting to their corner.

"Our Clara is relentless," Madame Sylvie whispered over Dara's shoulder.

"She's sending a message," Dara said.

The light board operator called for a pause and Bailey stopped a moment, hands on her hips, catching a breath, bending at the waist to steady herself.

From the thicket came the abrupt screech of a quickly suppressed laugh.

"Bailey," Dara called out, "do you need five?"

Bailey paused, trying not to look at the Level IV girls, their low whispers, their prison-yard stares, Pepper's slit-eyed gaze lifting to the stage.

"No," Bailey insisted, lifting her body back in her arabesque, one impossibly long arm up, one out, holding the Nutcracker, her left leg in the air, her right leg planted still.

"Bailey," Dara repeated, rising, moving down the aisle, thinking of the dazed, glassy look on the girl's face after her time locked in the supply closet, after the pins in her shoes. "Let's take a break."

You have to leave them to it, their mother used to say about the plight of Claras every year. *It's jungle logic. You have to let them handle it amongst themselves.*

"I don't need it," Bailey insisted, teeth gritted as Dara approached the lip of the stage. "I'm really fine."

With that, her arms fell, the Nutcracker slipping from her hands, clattering to the stage floor just as Bailey leaned over at the waist and vomited.

You'll be okay," Dara said, both of them bent over the stagehand's bucket, deep in the wings now. "Let's take you to the restroom."

Bailey didn't say anything, her hands on her hips, taking long gulping breaths.

"Maybe it was something she ate," someone said.

Dara turned and saw Gracie Hent lingering in the shadows, her face dark.

"Someone brought cookies from the deli at break," Gracie added coolly, her eyes on Bailey. "The cookies had mold."

There was such a boldness to the girl, a barbarism to her. This pink waif, her tidy bun.

"And how do you know that, Mademoiselle Hent?" Dara said sternly, moving toward her.

"It doesn't matter," Bailey blurted, reaching for Dara. "Forget it." Clearing her throat, lifting her voice. "I'm fine now."

Dara looked at the girl, her face wet and her eyes glittering, wiping her mouth with her sleeve.

This was, Dara had to remind herself, the same girl who once burst into tears over a correction (*Elbows ups! No chicken wings!*), who had, for years, fretted openly over her body, the length of her neck, and burst into tears again when girls started calling her *stub neck, nub neck*. The girl who, just six weeks ago, had wondered over Clara, over her own talents—that girl was gone.

Good for her, Dara thought. *Good.*

Everyone was exhausted and they'd dismissed half the cast, Marie ordering a sheaf of pizzas for the rest, the smell of grease and cardboard and little-girl burps everywhere, because the six- and seven-year-old mice still needed to rehearse, which they should have done hours ago when they were still pitched and excited, stroking their acrylic mouse paws and dying to get onstage. Now they looked greasy, bloated, their bellies like pigeon breasts.

Dara slumped in fifth-row center as Marie and Madame Sylvie tried to rouse them, clapping and calling out the steps.

It was funny seeing Marie onstage, her fists sunk in the pockets of their father's cardigan, her bleached hair the same whiteness as her face, her long, mottled neck. Mottled with brown bruises that lingered past the life of their maker, his thumbprints still on her somehow.

It was funny to see her up there, working, but it also felt natural, right.

Dara's phone lit up and it was Charlie.

"I should be there," he said. "I thought I'd feel better after I took the baclofen. I just . . ."

She started to tell him about the news article but somehow she couldn't, his voice so fragile and eager.

"We're nearly done," Dara said, her eyes on the stage as "mice," their wrists bent for flat paws, scurried under the lights more antically now, the recorded music booming. "Let's try it with the heads now!" she shouted to the stage.

On the phone, Charlie was still talking.

"But I think I can still get a PT appointment," Charlie was saying. "A late one. Nine o'clock."

"Pay the extra," Dara said. "Helga's worth it."

"Follow my voice," Marie was saying onstage.

The mice were putting on their mouse heads, Marie standing over them, helping them with all the foam and fur. The heat underneath, which Dara still remembered from the years she was a mouse, blind and breathless.

"I miss you," Charlie said, sounding so far away.

Onstage, all the little girls bobbing against one another, the mouse heads too big for their little bodies. *Follow my voice.* She remembered what it was like, your big moment and you're missing everything.

"Me too," Dara said into the phone, her eyes unaccountably filling. "Bye."

It was over, everything. For the day. Until tomorrow, the stakes higher, higher every day until after opening night.

The students were packing up wearily, their limbs loose and lifeless. Backstage, Madame Sylvie was nipping at her annual "Nutcracker nog," a pint tucked in the pocket of her tunic. Parents were arriving, the parking lot glowing with headlights.

The Level IVs carpool had, mysteriously, left without Bailey Bloom.

"It's okay," Bailey said. "My mom will text me back eventually."

"No," Marie said, sweeping her arm around Bailey, shepherding her through the darting mass of wool and fleece. "I'll take you, honey. But first, ice cream."

* * *

I never knew Marie drove," Madame Sylvie said.

"She's full of surprises," Dara replied as they watched them disappear inside Marie's creamsicle of a car.

Marie being so helpful, Marie being a grown-up, responsible. Was this what it took?

"Seat belts!" Dara called out. Then, more softly, "We need our Clara alive. We need both of you alive."

Back in the lobby, Dara found herself stopping in front of the giant Nutcracker. The one Marie had been so transfixed by that morning.

He was so jolly, the brightly colored uniform, the handlebar mustache hanging over the tidy row of chunky teeth, its hinged jaw, the heavy lever of the mouth.

But her eyes kept landing on that black slash of his eyepatch. She'd never thought about it before, how his eyepatch matched the eyepatch of Drosselmeier, the sinister and seductive godfather who gives the Nutcracker to Clara and sets her on her adventure.

The eyepatch dominant, his other eye was colorless, the pupil swimming in the milky white.

There was something almost familiar about it, and then, the longer she looked, something upsetting. But she couldn't put a name to it.

Until the picture came to her: of Derek, at the end. The dark pinwheel of Derek's iris, red swirling from the center, filling his eye. The pupil punctured, the spike of the metal bill holder snug in its center.

"Ms. Durant. At last. We've been looking for you."

Dara turned and saw the detective approaching.

THE COUNT

It was the same one from before, from that first morning, wearing the same tan trench coat like a Hollywood private eye.

He moved toward her as arriving and departing parents swirled past, trailing winter scarves, grabbing sparkly backpacks abandoned in the lobby's corners, as their daughters and the few scant sons, exhausted, struggled to put on their heavy coats, unbearably hot against their sweat-stuck bodies.

He moved swiftly, easily, as if no parent could touch him, as if he didn't even see them, not even the half-dozen with the enormous mouse heads hooked under their arms, handing them to Madame Sylvie's assistant for safekeeping.

"Ms. Durant," the detective said.

Another man, slightly younger, with a brush cut and a ski vest, joined from a nearby water fountain, rubbing his mouth on the back of his sleeve like a teenage boy.

"Can I help you?" Dara said as they approached.

"Maybe," the detective said. "Let's see."

* * *

Everything about it felt wrong, the way the older one, a Detective Walters, was looking at her, tapping his pen on a flip notebook in his hand. His face, up close, reminded Dara of a baked potato.

His partner, Mendoza, looked uncomfortable, eyes darting from the older girls, a few stripped down to their dance bras as they waited in the overheated lobby.

"We went by your studio first," Detective Walters said. "Finally tracked you down by the trail of tutus."

Dara didn't smile. Trying to avoid the eyes of any stray parent.

"We're very busy right now," she said to Walters. *"The Nutcracker."*

As if on cue, both men looked up at the towering statue behind her, suddenly more sinister-looking, its clownish colors, the hard spikes of its gold crown.

"You know," Detective Walters said, tapping his pen again, an old Bic with a chewed blue top, "I never really got the *Nutcracker* thing until I had a daughter. Girls love that shit."

"So is that what this is about?" Dara said. "Comp tickets for your daughter?"

Detective Walters grinned, his potato face crinkling.

They had a few more questions, that was all. Some clarifications, mostly. Maybe there was a quiet place they could talk?

Dara led the way, vining them through the swarm, the air muzzy with that familiar studio mix of sweat, funk, hairspray, camphor oil, urine, vomit, this grand and stately theater completely contaminated by the Durant School of Dance in just six hours.

She used the three- or four-minute walk to try to center herself. To bring herself together the way one did before performing, drawing all one's energies and spiky fears into one sharp point, a mighty saber, an immutable and unfeeling thing.

Everyone loves a pretty dancer, their mother used to say. *But strong is better.*

They crowded into the lighting booth, away from the whir of the custodial staff working below. Through the window, you could see them clearing away all the dirty Band-Aids, the browning apple cores, the frills of torn elastic straps, errant toe pads and toe pouches like pale rose petals gathering, the stray ruffs of lamb's wool like the aftermath of an animal fight, a beast and prey standoff.

"We told you all we know," Dara said. "But go ahead if you must."

Walters and Mendoza exchanged looks.

"Most people," Walters said, a grin back in his voice, "are a little intimidated by the police."

"Most people are guilty," Dara said. "Of something, at least."

Walters looked at her, that pen out again, the mangled cap. "Clean living for you, huh?"

"That's the way our mother raised us."

Below, onstage, one last custodian swirled a giant tentacled mop like a sailor swabbing a deck. The puddled remnants of Bailey Bloom's fluorescent vomit, like a gasoline rainbow, disappearing. The creamy brown of the stage turned dark, luminous.

The two detectives were asking her the same things as before, the contractor's schedule, his comings and goings, and was it typical for him to be there at such an early hour and alone, and why might he have ended up in the back office, the staircase. Wasn't that all a bit strange?

"Maybe," Dara said. "I didn't know him."

Mendoza threw Walters a look, but Walters didn't blink, his eyes on Dara.

"I just don't see the point in all this," Dara said. "The insurance investigator already came by."

"We know."

"She seemed satisfied."

"The bulldog," Walters said to Mendoza, with a wink.

"Pardon?"

"Never mind. We love Randi."

Dara began doing eight-counts in her head—*six, seven, eight*—her tongue tapping on her palate like a metronome. Counting off imaginary *piqué* turns. Keeping her cool. They didn't know anything. They couldn't.

"And you said the third floor—what did you say you used that for?"

"Storage," Dara said.

"And this . . . *accident* with the contractor," Walters said, a definite pause in the middle. *Cinq, six, sept, huit*—"that's the third recent incident on the site. Is that correct?"

Dara stopped her silent count. "I'm sorry?"

"Let's see. You had a flood on October thirtieth?"

They hadn't asked about that before. Why would they ask about that? *Dix, onze, douze.*

"Well, yes," Dara said. "That was related to the renovation. They hit a pipe. How did you—"

"And the contractor—he was injured, correct?"

"No," Dara said. "I mean, I guess. Some minor burns. He was fine."

Walters looked at her a moment, then looked back down at his notepad.

"And then a fire on September fifteenth?"

The fire. Dara tried not to look at them. Tried to concentrate only on the steadiness of the voice.

"The fire, yes, but that was before the construction. That's why we hired him. To repair the damage."

"Right," Walters said, nodding, an opaque expression on his face. Mendoza's eyes wandered to the stage below.

Dara looked too. Other than the lone custodian, his trailing bucket, the stringy spill of his mop, all was still below, the black maw of the theater.

There was a pressure at her temple, the detective's talc tickling her nose.

Dara looked at her watch. "Excuse me," she said abruptly, "but what does this have to do with what happened?"

Walters looked up from his notebook. Even more interested now.

"Maybe nothing," he said. "Space heater, right?"

Dara could feel her spine tighten, like a crank turning. *Cinq, six, sept . . .* "Yes."

"Call came in . . . your sister called it in to nine-one-one. Four A.M.?"

"I don't know. I—"

"What was she doing there at that hour?"

Dara took a breath. "Marie goes in early, stays late. We don't punch a clock."

"Report says she'd been sleeping there that night," Walters said, flipping his notebook shut.

Dara paused. Mendoza turned and looked at her.

"She'd camp out in her studio once in a while," Dara said, "if it was late. But not recently. With the construction, there's always dust, noise."

"How about on the third floor?" Mendoza said abruptly. It was the first time he'd spoken since they'd begun. Walters looked as surprised as Dara. "She ever camp out up there?"

Dara paused again, thinking. Remembering squinty-eyed Pepper Weston, her impudent mouth: *Is it true that Mademoiselle Durant sleeps in the attic now?*

"That was our mother's space," Dara said carefully. It wasn't an answer but sounded like one. "It was just for her."

There was a brief silence, the booth so small, the smudgy black console, fingerprints glowing in the light. Making Dara think of prints, evidence. A feeling in her chest like a valve tightening. *What was behind these questions? And all this attention to Marie . . .*

"Okay. Now if we can have a word with her," Walters said. "Your sister."

Mendoza was looking at Dara, a long, uninterrupted gaze.

"She left," Dara said. "Look, what's this about? I read the paper. The autopsy's done. The man fell. Accidents at construction sites—that has to happen, right?"

"Sure," Walters said, nodding. "All the time."

"So—"

"That's why contractors tend to load up on insurance policies," he added, looking at Mendoza with something like a wink. "Especially if they have a family."

"Well," Dara said, watching them, "it's a dangerous business."

"For some," Walters said. "Look, we're doing our due diligence. Don't like to get shown up by a claims man. Or woman."

Dara got it suddenly. "This is about that Randi woman."

"Bulldogs gonna sniff," Mendoza said, smiling at Walters.

"She's just doing her job," Walters said. "Insurance companies, they're crap shooters. They make a bet with you and, most of the time, they win. But once in a while, the dice come up snake eyes for them. Suddenly, all they wanna do is slow the roll."

Mendoza nodded. "That poor guy probably paid those premiums for, like, decades. Now he takes a header on the job and they hold out on his grieving widow—"

Dara looked up. "Widow?"

"Sure," Walters said, closing his notebook. "And widows like to get paid."

The widow. Derek's widow. Derek's wife.

DEATHLESS

Part of her must have known.

He'd never talked about a family, a home to go to. He'd stayed over so many nights on the third floor.

He'd never worn a wedding band, but not all married men did. Their father didn't, not after one of his electrician colleagues was working on a hot panel with his ring on and a jolt tore right through him. *Professional hazard*, he always told them, showing them the band once, tucked beneath a pile of handkerchiefs in the top drawer of his dresser. *So he claims*, their mother always added, under her breath.

Still, someone who lies so freely, who hustles so ceaselessly . . .

Part of her must have known, but had Marie?

Dara didn't remember saying her goodbyes to the detectives. Didn't remember them shuffling ahead of her back down the stairs from the light booth. The stairs like the spiral stairs at the studio, shuddering under their weight, the thick-soled shoes of the policemen.

She was thinking of this wife, this mysterious wife. *What kind of woman would be married to Derek?* But then she started to create a picture in her head, a passive hausfrau, a doormat. Or, she thought, maybe a former stripper, a pole dancer on the decline.

But what mattered, she reminded herself, was the threat this posed. Someone new to reckon with. Someone who wanted things, wanted money. Another intruder in their lives, another hostile invader. First Derek and now Derek's wife. Another stranger who could ruin everything for all of them.

C harlie," Dara said into his voicemail, wondering if he was already on the way to his PT. "I have to talk to you. Call me."

She tried Marie next, and her sister answered amid a blast of noise—wind rushing, radio panting, Bailey's chirping voice.

"What is it?" Marie kept saying, but she couldn't hear Dara at all and instead started explaining that Bailey had never been to the Chocolate Shoppe and had never had a hot fudge cream puff, could you believe it.

"Call me after," Dara finally said, thundering into the phone. "Call me."

I t doesn't matter, she thought. The fact of the wife. It didn't change things. All it proved was what she already knew. The contractor was bad. A liar. A dangerous person.

But there was something behind it. Something she couldn't quite put her finger on.

After their parents' deaths, the life insurance money came through quickly, but their father's accidental death benefit payout took months and months. The attorney they'd hired told them the insurance company had to make sure it wasn't suicide, or murder-suicide. Because, he told them, some people will in fact run their cars into buildings, off cliffs, into other vehicles. And then there was the role of alcohol in the crash.

But, in the end, the money came.

In the end, no one could prove their parents had wanted to die. *Didn't everything prove that?* Marie had asked. *Didn't their whole lives prove that?*

The money came because their father hadn't been driving drunk. Their mother had. That was something Dara was told, but she couldn't make it fit. So she chose not to remember it at all.

The money came, but only once the insurance company was satisfied that the death was an accident.

There she is!"

Dara looked up with a start.

At the far end of the emptying lobby stood a Nutcracker Prince—not the statue, but the Prince himself, in tunic and tights, his papier-mâché head large and impossible, the jabbing mustache, the teeth big as playing cards, the eyepatch severing his face.

"Madame Durant!" the voice came again.

And, as if in a dream, he lifted his own head free, revealing Corbin Lesterio, his rosy face and that lustrous forelock, raking his fingers through it as teenage boys have done throughout time, spurring the deep, low-down sighs of all admirers in sight.

"Madame Durant," he said, then whirled himself into an impromptu pirouette. "It was better, right? It was good? I was good today? *Un gentil prince.*"

As she moved closer, the sounds of his breath, the breathlessness of beautiful young boys—it made her forget, just for a second—an exquisite, piercing second—the low hum of death in her ear.

Here was this young and perfect thing, and the way he looked at her, his eyes bright with awe and desire—what could ever go wrong? What could ever be ruined or die? Everything is as it should be forever, no snakes in the garden, no temptation, no loss.

That's what it does, their mother always told them. *Ballet. It stops death.*

* * *

S he walked Corbin to his father's car, the rush of the boy's words spilling into her hands.

"I've never been so excited," he was telling her, his breath a silver cloud. "This is the best thing that ever happened to me."

Dara smiled and waved to Mr. Lesterio, seated snugly in his overheated Plymouth.

"I guess I better enjoy it," he said, moving to the passenger door, his face falling so fast. "Like you always tell me, there's only one first. You never get it back."

Dara looked at him, struck.

She didn't remember saying that. She didn't remember saying that at all.

B ailey!" The voice tight and humming like a violin string. "Are you here, Bailey?"

Dara turned and saw a figure shimmering through the cascade of white lights, the enormous Christmas wreaths hanging from the lobby windows.

"Madame Durant! I'm late. Did I miss her?"

The princess coat, seal gray, the dark glasses, the shining bob. The careless mother. The contractor's former client. *He has something he wants. He'll hold it close until he's ready.*

It was Mrs. Bloom, the elusive Mrs. Bloom, looking for her daughter, and Dara would not let her get away this time.

YOU WOMEN

Mrs. Bloom didn't want to talk in the lobby, or her car, or a nearby diner.

She didn't want to talk at all, but Dara was insistent.

"It's very important," she said. "About your daughter."

Finally, she said Dara could follow her home. They could speak there, in private.

It was four miles away, a large brick house with the gleaming white columns of a wedding cake.

There wasn't much time. But Bailey would be at least an hour with Marie.

Marie, Dara thought. *Marie*. Suddenly, she had this memory of her sister, age three or four, her music box open, reaching for the pirouetting ballerina, the net of her miniature tutu. And then snapping the ballerina loose. Staring at it in her dimpled hand.

* * *

They sat in the Bloom living room, cream-colored and feminine with candles everywhere and the smell of crushed flowers.

They both held thick-banded glasses clinking with vodka and ice from the bar cart.

It burned Dara's throat, reminded her of the Fire Eater. Everything did lately. *Those ladies*, Dara had thought the first time they'd seen the Fire Eater, the Sword Swallower, *they're not afraid at all.*

"Tell me about Bailey," Mrs. Bloom asked, leaning back on her sofa, her eyes glassy and her head bobbing slightly. "I must admit, I haven't been as attentive as usual. I've been dealing with some personal issues."

"She's coming into her own. She's going to be a very fine Clara."

"She will be, won't she?" she said softly, a sip from the rattling glass. "But that isn't why you're here."

"No."

Mrs. Bloom set her glass down on the sofa arm, a ring forming immediately, and spreading.

"You came about him," she said.

"Yes."

She took a breath. "I heard what happened to him. Bailey told me. Then I read it in the paper . . ."

"That time I saw you at his truck," Dara said abruptly, "you had an envelope you left there."

"I owed him some money," she said coolly. "But I don't see how that's your—"

"Why didn't you mail it?"

Mrs. Bloom shook her head wearily and reached for her glass again.

"Because Derek didn't operate like that," she said, her voice looser, her shoulders slumping. "He didn't want checks sent to his house. He wanted cash in hand. Haven't you figured that out by now?"

"Why were you still giving him money?"

She took a long sip. "I didn't have a choice."

"Was he blackmailing you?"

First, Mrs. Bloom smirked a little. Then she sat very still, setting her highball glass on her knee, a new water ring forming on her wool pants.

"I'm so ashamed," she said at last, nearly a whisper, even though they appeared to be alone in the house. "So ashamed."

Dara felt pinpricks on her neck, her wrists, her hips. Something was happening.

"Did you know about the wife?"

Mrs. Bloom looked up.

"That," she said slowly, carefully, "was the hardest part."

"Because he didn't tell you."

"No, because I knew her first."

It had begun nearly two years ago. She'd been having these migraines ever since Bailey was born. So bad she'd vomit, so bad she couldn't open her eyes for days. A friend recommended acupuncture. She found a woman she liked at a medical spa, a little place inside that big glass building by the highway.

"And this was her?" Dara said. "His wife?"

Mrs. Bloom nodded. "She understood my body so well. By the end of the first session, my body felt like liquid. My head felt clear and strong. Then she told me about this special bathtub that would help. Her husband could install it. I'd been thinking of a renovation anyway, so I hired him."

Mrs. Bloom took a long sip from that rattling glass, leaning back, her lipstick slightly smudged.

"But then, one day, weeks into the renovation, she shows up at my front door. In her scrubs. She looked like she'd been crying for hours. She'd found some things on his phone . . . some texts, some . . . photos. Things he promised me he wouldn't keep."

There it was. There it was. Mrs. Bloom and Derek, the furtive sex, the bleached hair, the ensnarement, the money, the manipulation, the trap.

"What did you say to her? The wife?"

"I denied it. But it was all there." Mrs. Bloom's face reddened, even at the memory. "But then she just started begging me. Telling me how she needed him. They were deep in debt, about to lose their house. She had to hide her car in a coworker's garage so they wouldn't repossess it. And then she started talking about the children."

"Children?" Dara felt the cold of her glass in her hand. She took another sip, feeling the fire again. There was always something new now. Something new and incredible.

"Four. One with some kind of . . . problem. It was all so terrible. I needed her to leave. I ended up writing her a check."

"Why?"

"I would have given her anything," Mrs. Bloom said. "Anything."

"That's when you ended it?"

Mrs. Bloom looked at her like Dara hadn't been listening at all.

They were moving soundlessly up the carpeted stairs.

"You need to see it," Mrs. Bloom kept murmuring as Dara hurried behind her, up the stairs and down a long hallway, "to understand."

The pocket door slid open soundlessly. Inside, the walls, the carpet, the towels, were all dark pink and strongly scented, such that it was like stepping into the center of a blooming rose.

"I never come in here anymore," she whispered. "I can't."

It was Mrs. Bloom's master bathroom—the one they'd heard about. The contractor's dazzling work. *Imagine what he could do for you!*

Everything looked new and shiny. All the fixtures and hardware, like the cellophane hadn't yet been pulled off. The walk-in shower with gold taps and jets studded up and down like fat jewels. A vessel sink suited for Cleopatra. Gold-plated towel warmers thick with white swaddlers. A cream-white tub shaped like an elegant slipper, curved low in the center, its ends dipping upward like a pointe shoe turned on its side.

It made her think of their mother's claw-footer, rust rings around its faucets, sides coated with lime. The only bath she'd ever known, her whole life.

"This is what he did," Mrs. Bloom said. "Derek."

It was like a little girl's fantasy of a bathroom, Dara thought. Like she herself imagined as a child, bubble baths and fur rugs to wiggle your toes in.

It made her think of Derek that first day, promising a ballerina palace.

. . . why not dream bigger? I can give you all the things you want.

"Take off your shoes," Mrs. Bloom said, her hands dancing along a control board on the rose-colored wall.

Dara would just as soon spread her legs as show her bare feet to this woman, not a dancer, and in this bathroom—his creation.

"You want to understand," Mrs. Bloom said, her tone harder, steely, an insistent mother doling out a lesson. "You want to know why, how. So take off your shoes."

Dara slid off her boots slowly, her toes like overripe cherries on the white carpet.

"Feel that?" Mrs. Bloom said.

And suddenly Dara felt something tickling the bottoms of her feet, even through her cowhide-thick skin. The carpet was humming warmly, tickling along her arches.

"Radiant heat," Mrs. Bloom said. "He insisted."

Dara closed her eyes. The feeling was too much somehow. She wanted to cover her face.

"For every pleasure," Mrs. Bloom said as if reading her mind, "we pay a price."

G et inside it," she told Dara, turning on the taps.

Mrs. Bloom wanted to show her the bath jets.

Without thinking Dara stepped in the tub, peering inside, its center pink, a blush pink like the inside of a seashell.

The water was a hot gush on Dara's feet. There was no stopping it.

Mrs. Bloom in her proper turtleneck, her blown-straight hair, sunk down to the carpet, her hand gripping the side of the tub.

Mrs. Bloom, her voice gone low and throaty, knelt against the lowest dip in its lip, running one hand, her wrist, her forearm into the water, its heat and energy.

Standing there, Dara let it happen, surrendered to it. The hot jets thundering against her blood-struck, bruise-mottled feet, she couldn't stop it if she wanted to. She didn't want to.

And that was when Mrs. Bloom told the story.

She was drawn to him that very first day. A man so different from her husband—soon to be ex-husband—with his Brooks Brothers suits, his tight shoes and cool eyes. Her husband, who traveled constantly and who hadn't held her hand in half a dozen years.

But the contractor . . .

She never thought of him as her acupuncturist's husband, not once. He erased that in an instant that very first day. He was such a big presence. And how persuasively he spoke—about what she could have, what she deserved. *This should be your most private space,* he said. *It should be classy and sensual. It should be pristine and safe.*

It was exciting having him in the house. Knowing he was down the hall. Sometimes she would even lie on her bed, under her duvet, and think about how close he was. What he was doing. The walls vibrating with him, his noise and power.

A man in her house and her husband forever out of town, like every glossy paperback on the library spinner rack. There was a reason those books were so worn, their covers peeling.

One day, she discovered him working long after she thought he'd left for the day. He was kneeling beside the tub, fondling its new gold taps with such delicacy.

To see such a big, hulking man handle such dainty things stirred something inside her. Those hands of his, great, big things like a sea captain might have. How they seemed to enclose all her small, fine things.

A man who dominated the house every time he was in it, tracking mud and leaves into her kitchen, never shutting the powder room door all the way when he used it, and never seeming to wash his hands at all, the guest towels always hanging pristinely in place.

A man who, once or twice, she caught looking at her through lidded eyes, snake eyes. Like the men on the street when she was fourteen and too big for her training bra.

She watched from a distance. If he noticed, he didn't let on.

The day he finished installing the tub, he invited her to see. There was something obscene about it, the suggestive shape and color, its fleshly pink center.

And the way he ran his hand inside it, showing her his work. His fingers.

Without thinking, she said she wondered if that was how he touched a woman.

She covered her mouth the minute she said it.

But he merely looked up and asked if she'd like to see.

The answer, it turned out, was yes.

He told me to take off all my clothes," she said, Dara listening and nodding, her ankles and feet tingling in the water, the steam making her drowsy, confused.

"I couldn't wait to do it. I was so excited. He told me to slow down because I was going too fast. I was trying to cover myself." Mrs. Bloom touched her pinkening face. "Doing all the locker room tricks."

Slow, he said, *like you mean it. Like you want me to see all of it.*

"He wanted to see it all," she said. "You know. You know what I mean."

Mrs. Bloom looked at Dara, her hand on her thighs, then one palm sliding between them.

"And I showed him," she said, staring at Dara now, eyes big and confused. "I showed him everything."

At some point, Mrs. Bloom had stopped talking. Or maybe Dara just couldn't hear her anymore over the water, see her anymore through the steam.

Closing her eyes, listening to the hissing radiant heat, she was thinking of things, her brain soft and dreamy and strange. She was thinking of the Nutcracker Prince costume at yesterday's final fitting with Svetlanka, their tailor since their mother's day. They'd spent countless hours over the years watching her sew tutus, her tarnished thimble ring, her painted nails. Yesterday, running those nails across Corbin Lesterio's chest, the deep-red waistcoat. Corbin distracted, his slender fingers stroking the gold trim, the epaulet fringe, reminding her of all the past Princes, back to Charlie even, all in the same costume, its velvet still bright and spry, sliding one finger beneath its tight, high collar, his blushing throat. There were so many of them, from their mother's hands to hers, their bodies still unbroken, still growing, waiting, begging to be shaped, smoothed, perfected. Corbin looking down at Svetlanka's silver-black hair, kneeling at his feet, needle in her mouth as she bid him to *shush, shush, it'll all be over soon.* . . .

And then, *Now show Madame Durant how handsome you look. Show her her Prince.*

Corbin looking at her, face flushed.

I wanted him here all the time," Mrs. Bloom was saying, her turtleneck hooked in her finger, her mouth still gasping for air. Just like Marie, Dara thought. *I need him here all the time, Dara.*

"It didn't matter how slow the renovation was going," she continued. "I wanted to feel him here. Don't you see?"

Dara did not see. She would never see. It was just like Marie. Worse. This woman had a husband, a house. A daughter.

"When I think of it now," Mrs. Bloom was saying. "The things I did for him. The things he made me want to do. I humiliated my husband. I humiliated myself."

Dara's eyes, the lids slick and wet, opened again.

The room was so hot, so hot like the steam bath their mother used to take them to at the Y. *How can she stand it*, Dara thought, looking at Mrs. Bloom in her wool trousers, her fuzzy turtleneck.

For a second, Dara thought she might faint. She reached for the bath tap, which came loose in her hand. It was so light, the gold peeling off in her hand.

That was when she saw the crack at the bottom of the tub. A long spiny crack like a spider leg, crooked.

She could feel Mrs. Bloom watching her.

Mrs. Bloom, her face red as a blister, looked so different, all her polish peeled off too. Her hair thicker, heavy, her hands closed into tight red balls.

"The drain leaks into the subfloor," Mrs. Bloom said. "The toilet seal leaks. The first day, two tiles came off in my hands."

"I don't know why I'm here," Dara said. Her head felt tight, cramped. "I don't understand why I'm here."

She stepped out of the tub, her legs trembling, the heat from the floor rising up. She felt herself keeling like a ship in a storm. Holding on to the wall.

"And the floors are starting to warp," Mrs. Bloom was saying.

Dara nodded drunkenly, scrambling for the dials, shutting off the radiant heat, the radiant everything.

"Once you turn it on," Mrs. Bloom said, "it's hard to get it to stop."

Dara nodded again, her eyes shut.

"I wish I could burn it down," Mrs. Bloom said. "I wish I could burn the whole place down."

* * *

Panting over the kitchen sink, downing tall tumblers of icy water. Dara's feet pulsing and damp in her boots.

"It kept happening," Mrs. Bloom said. "He'd install a floor and the heat would crack it. There were leaks, a flood. It never stopped. Before I knew it, the bills were running into six digits and my husband started asking questions."

Dara nodded and nodded, closing her eyes again, fingers on her temples.

"And Derek, he was getting more . . . demanding. He wanted things."

"Like the truck?" Dara said. "You bought him that."

"I wish it were only the truck," Mrs. Bloom said, her face still so pink and wet from the bathroom, her makeup smeary. "How about all the money orders I gave him to help his mother, who had to move into a nursing home, the six thousand dollars I gave him for his marina fees for a boat I never saw that was going to launch his new business?"

"But you could have fired him. You could have ended things. That's what I don't get about you women—"

"You women," Mrs. Bloom said, a grim laugh. "So he could tell my husband? My child? And there were all the things he had me tell our insurance company. All those lies. He warned me they might come after me. I believed him."

Dara turned, setting her tumbler in the sink. Something cold settling inside her. She wanted to put on all her clothes, even though she was fully dressed.

"He would have taken it all," Mrs. Bloom said, her voice low, her eyes black rings, like a ballerina taking off her mask. "Even the things I didn't have to give."

"But you got out. Eventually."

"Did I?" she said. "Or did he just find someone else?"

Dara turned from her, reached for a paper towel, wiped her face. All this making her feel ugly. It was like being trapped in Mrs. Bloom's life, her head. Cashmere and desperation.

"I will never understand," Dara said. "With you or her. He . . . he's just . . ."

Mrs. Bloom was watching her, her face so wet, the makeup bubbling off, the mascara blooming, smocking her eyes.

"You think I'm pathetic," she said, "don't you? You think we all are. You women."

Dara didn't say anything.

"Just you wait," she said, "until it happens to you."

They were walking to the door and Mrs. Bloom's face had changed, had gone pale and slack, a handkerchief in her hand, the slow shuffle of a much older woman.

All Dara wanted was to leave. She had to get out of the sad, big house and its plush conveniences and its cracked tub and its slowly warping floors.

But she had this feeling there was still something here. There was something here and she'd missed it. It had eluded her, a snake tail sliding back in the muck.

Passing through the living room, Dara noticed for the first time the row of jaunty Nutcrackers arrayed across the mantelpiece, every color, different heights. A fur-hatted British solider with a long sword, a hussar with a riding crop, a crowned king with a scepter. But all with the same open mouth, baring two rows of painted teeth.

She thought of Marie, standing before the statue at the theater. The sense that her mind, her thoughts were veiled, remote. That she knew things she would never say. She didn't have the words to say them.

Dara stopped, turning to Mrs. Bloom.

"Wait," Dara said, "why did you do it, then? After all this. Why did you recommend him to us?"

"Pardon?"

"To us, as a contractor."

Mrs. Bloom had a funny look on her face.

"I didn't," she said.

"You did. You showed Charlie the pictures. You . . ."

"No. You're mistaken." Mrs. Bloom kept looking at her, confused, troubled, her fingers at her brow bone. "I'm sorry."

Something faint in the back of Dara's head was slowly getting louder. The slither of that snake tail now emerging from the muck. She looked at her watch. It was nearly nine.

"I have to go," Dara said. "I have to go now."

DO YOU NEED ME

In the driveway, the sharp night air a revelation, Dara stood at her car for a minute, two, figuring something out. She smoked a cigarette on Mrs. Bloom's synthetic green lawn, scattering ash, fingers shaking.

Marie's car came like the flare of a match on the horizon. Dara let the cigarette fall to the grass, a chemical hiss.

The hiss reminded her of something, the space heater after the fire. How it looked like a lava rock, with its cord scorched, like the fuse of a firecracker.

She'd thought for so long that Marie's fire was how everything started. How it brought Derek to them. But now it seemed it wasn't the fire. There was a fire before the fire.

The car pulled up the driveway, Marie's hands on the steering wheel like little claws pressed together.

"Madame Durant," Bailey said, jumping from the passenger seat, "we had ice cream, but I only had three bites."

"And no whipped cream," Marie said, looking at Dara with a worried expression. Sensing something, seeing something on her face.

"I have to go," Dara said, moving to her own car. "Get some rest, Bailey. Kiss your mother."

In the rearview mirror, they watched her drive away, Bailey in her ski jacket, her long legs still in her pink tights, vomit or brown blood streaked up one calf.

Marie shivering beside her in their father's cardigan, her eyes like great moons.

The glass building by the highway. That's what Mrs. Bloom had said.

It turned out there was more than one, an office park cluster of five, all with sweeping windows tinted blue, green, gold, part of the area's sluggish gentrification.

Driving from one directory to the next, Dara stared numbly at the names, a distant buzzing in her brain: *Hobart Partners, Glittman Technologies, Converged Network Services, Regan Logistics.*

The lots sprawling and empty, except for the last one, a low-slung glass box, its interior blue like an aquarium. Etched across its darkened front were the words: *Verdure Medical Spa.* Beneath it, in smaller print: *Physical Therapy • Occupational Therapy • Acupuncture • Medical Massage.*

This is it, Dara thought. *The acupuncturist, the wife.*

She paused a moment. Waited. Five, ten minutes went by and then a Shamrock taxicab, bright and jolly, appeared, slowing to a halt at the front curb.

She didn't move, the sound of her own breath filling the car.

The man exited the taxi, his navy peacoat buttoned high in the cold. The blaze of his blond hair, the litheness of his movements. The cold air piping color like a painter might, along his cheekbones, his handsome brow.

He moved gracefully, if carefully, his posture straight as a sword.

Spine to the heavens, s'il vous plait, their mother always told him. *And straight down to Hades himself.*

Because it was Charlie. Of course. It was Charlie.

The glass box lit up, the lobby instantly sapphire, as a woman in a coat, scrubs came rushing forward, opening the front door to him.

Opening her arms to him.

The two of them a dark jumble of hands, of clutches, Charlie's head dipping against the woman's dark hair, pressing against her throat. The woman smiling at him with her eyes until the moment her gaze shifted, seeing something. Peering into the dark parking lot where Dara's car idled, smile fading as she pulled Charlie through the door, into the blue heart of the building.

There was a feeling inside Dara of something falling and falling as she watched.

Charlie. Charlie.

Dara stepped out of her car, the air sharp as needles, sharp as the sword.

Pausing at the sound of the car door, the woman scanned the parking lot from the doorway, her hand curled over her eyes against the streetlamps' glare.

Charlie's PT is Mrs. Bloom's acupuncturist is Derek's wife is Charlie's . . .

Bun loosening, her feet crunching on the parking lot salt, Dara began moving toward the building, the lights blotching against her eyes, her chest aching from the cold.

Ahead, the woman cautiously unlatched the door, swinging it open again, calling out.

"Are you here for me?" she said as Dara moved closer, seeing the woman, her dark hair braided, a faded parka unbuttoned over maroon scrubs. "Do you need me?"

Dara stopped and looked at her. She needed to take it all in, her frumpy coat, salt streaked, her thick-soled shoes, her strong nose and brow even stronger than their mother's.

"Are you here for me?" the woman said again, drawing the parka across herself as the wind kicked up and began moaning.

"Are you injured?" she said, or seemed to, the wind like a roar in Dara's ears now. Waving her arm out, waving her in, as Dara slowly backed away, back to her car. "Do you need my help?"

In the car, her hands red from the cold, resting on the steering wheel, Dara thought she should cry, but she felt only blankness, like a cold, smooth stone. She hadn't cried even at their parents' funeral, holding herself rigidly, her chin high and everything shuttered away. Marie had done all the crying for both of them, that angry, jagged cry. The kind when you can't tell the anger from the grief because they're the same somehow. Something ending suddenly before you knew it could ever end at all.

And, as fated as the ending feels when it comes, you still never said okay. You never gave permission and it all came crashing down anyway.

SHOW YOUR TEETH

t's not true," Marie was saying, both of them with their coats still on, seated at the kitchen table. "I don't believe you."

"I don't care," Dara said, reaching for the sour table wine, pouring it in yesterday's glasses, their bottoms a sticky purple.

Dara had told her everything briskly, matter-of-factly. She told her what the detectives disclosed, what Mrs. Bloom shared. What Dara had seen.

After, Marie made her say it again, more slowly.

"But," she said after, "it can't be. Charlie—that's not how he is. That's not—"

"You really never knew," Dara said, cutting her off, "he was married? The contractor. That he was married."

Marie looked at her, eyes milky and strained.

"No," she said. "But it wouldn't have mattered."

Her shoulders dropping, her body leaning back.

"It wouldn't have mattered at all."

* * *

A half hour passed, the wine draining from its bottle, and Marie, now in one of their mother's billowy nightgowns, went on the hunt until she found another bottle, even older and the dubious color of cranberry punch, behind the encyclopedia volumes in their father's den.

Dara never moved at all from her spot at the kitchen table, rooted there.

Dara and Marie, drinking wine and picking at Madame Sylvie's Christmas cake, given to them every year and every year more pregnant with rum, thick with figs, slithery apricots. They plucked loose the studded fruit, the butter-glossed corners until Dara couldn't bear Marie's dirty fingernails and dug out an old bread knife, dull and striped with rust, from the kitchen drawer.

Neither wanted to say it aloud, to even ask it. *Was it not an accident? Could Charlie have killed Derek on purpose? Could that have been the plan all along?*

"I was so afraid," Marie started tentatively, "that it was all my fault. That I'd made all this happen myself. That it was me. Like saying Bloody Mary in the mirror three times and then she appears."

"Who says you didn't?" Dara snapped. "We don't know. We don't know anything yet."

And Marie looked at Dara, a look of such sadness it nearly shook Dara.

"Sister," she said. "We do know. We do."

Marie was staring at the clock.

"What are you going to do," she whispered, sliding her arms inside the sleeves of the nightgown, French linen and old lace, and now half-ruined already, stippled with wine, its neck stretched. "About Charlie?"

Dara was looking at Charlie's tea mug, still sitting there from that morning. The ring on the wood. His cluster of prescription bottles, his vitamins, his methocarbamol to relax his muscles, his benzodiazepines to help him sleep, his pentobarbital when the benzodiazepines didn't work.

Charlie, his delicate body, his broken body. What does it mean to destroy your own body, to grind your bones down to soft powder? Those long-ago days when he was ascendant, before the injuries began. Those two golden years he spent as a "foot soldier" in the corps of that regional ballet company. Those years he spent rehearsing ten hours a day, performing two hundred times a year, the thousands and thousands of times he'd lifted dancers above his head, leapt and landed, on one foot, onto the hardest of floors. He was a good dancer, but he would never be a great one. Their mother admitted that once, to Dara. *Then why*, she wanted to ask their mother, *are you keeping him here so long?*

What are you going to do about Charlie?

Charlie. Her Charlie, their Charlie. Somewhere, in between everything they shared every day, their lives so utterly entwined since they were children, he'd become entangled with this woman, this married woman whom he let, over and over again, put her hands on his back, his body.

He'd lied about the referral from Mrs. Bloom. He'd brought the contractor—his lover's husband—into their lives. He'd seemingly been plotting all along with this woman, this wife.

Maybe it's a mistake, Charlie had said that first day Derek made his pitch, *to always play it safe.*

It all unfurled like a mink from a femme fatale's shoulders in an old film noir. All those tales of a taloned beauty with expensive tastes, her callow lover, the unwitting husband, a staged accident for a big insurance payout. They never ended well.

Suddenly, Dara felt a coldness inside. *It was all so tacky, so déclassé*, a voice inside said. *It was all so cheap. So unbearably sad.*

"Did you hear that?" Marie said, pulling back the window curtain. Dara took a breath before she rose and looked too.

There it was, a Shamrock taxi pulling up out front of the house, the puff of its silvery exhaust. There he was, Charlie, exiting the car, his head down, then hurrying up the front walk.

For a fleeting second, Dara pondered if he'd ever been injured at all. If she hadn't been there through the surgeries, through the rehabilitation and the experimental treatments and then the new surgeries, she would have doubted all of it. Everything he'd ever said, or done.

He had never really been one of them, she decided. And, like Marie, he'd left, abandoned her too. He'd left without ever leaving, which was worse.

The door opened with a cold whoosh, all the dust in the house unsettling and settling again.

"Marie, can you leave us—" Dara started, but Marie was already gone, disappearing down the hall, into their father's pocket of a den.

"Dara."

She could feel him standing in the kitchen doorway, but she couldn't quite turn her head. She thought if she looked, she might disintegrate.

But then she did.

The way he was standing, in his navy peacoat, his cheeks too red from the cold, his eyes too bright, she thought suddenly of the Nutcracker, of all the Nutcrackers.

For a split second, she thought he might open his mouth and show two rows of sharp white teeth.

"Is everything," he said, his breath catching, eyes darting, "okay?"

"I thought we'd let a monster in," she said, rising to her feet.

Charlie nodded. "We did," he said. "But he's gone now. He's—"

"—but it turned out the monster was you."

BAD THINGS MEN DO

Sitting across from her at the kitchen table, slowly removing his gloves, he could not look her in the eye.

The carcass of the rum cake sat between them, the saber of the rusty knife, stray maraschino studs, the wax paper oil glossed, Marie's sticky prints on the glacé.

He wouldn't look at her, and his hands looked so clean and smelled of sanitizer.

Part of her had expected he'd fall to his knees, beg forgiveness. But some deeper part of her had hoped urgently that he'd tell her she'd gotten it all wrong, that it was all a lie, a misunderstanding, a bad dream, a nightmare.

Instead, he set his gloves down, his eyes cast low and inaccessible.

Oh, she thought, watching him. It had been the last hope she'd hidden deep inside herself. It hurt so much to lose it.

But then he looked up and she could see it all on his face. He'd been hiding so much for so long, but now he looked laid bare, skinned, tender and raw and exposed.

"It wasn't like you think," he said, his voice first small and tentative and then rushing faster. "It just . . . happened and then other things happened and suddenly, everything was happening and there was no stopping it."

Which, Dara realized now, was how Charlie had viewed everything his whole life.

It began last winter, when that cold snap made Charlie's nerve pain even greater. He'd overheard Mrs. Bloom raving about her new "physiotherapist," a "miracle worker" with "magic fingertips." Charlie made an appointment, expecting very little. His body had not been his own most of his life. He'd just as soon place it in a stranger's hands.

It turned out, though, that she did have a magical touch—no, almost holy. Well, that was how it felt to him, under her hands, gnarled fingers and broad-heeled. He hadn't been shy about it. He'd told Dara. His new PT's touch had changed his life.

And her voice, there was something about her voice. So calming, assuring, nurturing. She asked him questions, worried for him. It made him feel so cared for, tended to, safe.

Gradually, their conversations before and after their sessions became just as important as the feeling of those strong hands, thick-knuckled and wide-palmed. He would tell her about his abandoned ballet career—so promising, such an ascent—and how he felt at war with his body, how it had turned on him after giving him so much. In turn, she began sharing more, too, talking about her children, little Whitney's big spelling-bee win, Sammi who was learning the flute.

And, slowly, he began to learn about her husband.

It started that day he arrived to find her crying. The sheriff's office had called late. Her husband had been arrested in a mall parking lot, caught having sex in his car with some twenty-six-year-old bank teller. But she was only the latest, usurping the nameless drywall supplier who left her threatening phone messages (*He's my man now, bitch!*), the insurance adjuster named Bambi, whose fiancé showed up at the house with a baseball bat. (She'd had to talk him down while her husband hid in the toolshed.)

He was always sorry after—splashy flowers and promises and tickets to Aruba they couldn't afford—but it always happened again.

Was that better or worse, she wondered to Charlie, than the collection service sending people to the house, or the local grocery store cutting up their credit card while her neighbors watched?

And yet she didn't know how to escape it, to escape him. There was, always, the children, and the debt, and God, and everything—not the least of which her own relentless hopefulness, not yet worn away.

When they met, high school rivals at a bonfire, foamy beer and kisses and his hands down her jeans. Even then, he had big plans, schemes. In the haze of first love, she saw them as dreams. He was gonna buy up all the old, ruined houses downriver, collect them like Monopoly pieces, renovate and sell them, and become a *billionaire off blight*. All he needed to do was attract investors and maybe even her parents might be interested?

The very things that first draw you to a person will eventually be the very things that drive you away. She'd read that once. Maybe Charlie could understand?

Now, nearly thirty years together and four kids and he's never home, off "on jobs" at least a few nights a week, and they're still renting a house and owing everyone, including the government, sixty-two thousand in back taxes, and he couldn't keep it in his pants, never could. He once told her, late one night after fighting for hours until they were hoarse, *If you knew how easy it is. If you knew how little it took. If you knew, the meaner you are, the more they want you.*

(That she knew.)

They loved all of it, he told her. Some of them even loved the way—once in a while, seven times over thirty years for her—he might backhand them, or shove them, or cuff them at the dinner table, though always apologize with flowers, deli daffodils, rejected carnations sputtering across the floor.

She should have seen it all years ago, because people never really change, and it was all still like high school, when she caught him elbow-deep up Janis Truski's jean skirt behind the batting cage. She'd long ago given up on fidelity, and almost everything else, but now they were in arrears and her little Sammi needed a special breathing machine for her asthma and their oldest needed a reading tutor or he'd be held back, but her husband kept draining their bank account and had gotten meaner, rougher, more unkind . . .

Hearing it all had affected Charlie so much.

He hated her husband, this Derek, for making her feel this way. And it meant so much how happy Charlie seemed to make her just by listening, caring—well, that was the greatest feeling. He'd forgotten about that feeling.

It had never been intimate. Not really. There were physical . . . acts. But no intercourse. They never left the privacy, the cocoon of the small treatment room, its cool blues and soft simulated wood, the diffuser huffing eucalyptus.

First, it felt like a gift. How he needed her and she needed him. But then it also felt like a burden. As he slowly realized she wanted someone to save her.

He wished he knew now how it had turned. How they'd started talking about *him* all the time. He became not so much a person as this collection of *bad things men do.*

He never seemed real, exactly. He seemed like a cartoon villain, a comic book lothario, a cheap paperback brute, a thug. She'd fantasize, they both would, about him getting arrested, sued, even, Charlie once joked, shot in the back by a jealous husband.

Somehow, someday, he would be gone and goodness could return to the land, and should we really pay the price our whole lives for bad decisions made in the heat-thick swarm of adolescence?

She got the idea from the space heater fire. She said, *Bring my husband in. Bring him in to fix your studio. Maybe the next time it will burn him to ashes.* It was a joke, a dark joke, maybe a bad one.

It was a joke until it wasn't.

Slowly, it came to feel necessary, fated, urgent. The only plan, a rescue.

But whatever notion she'd had, they'd had together, went to pieces because of Marie. Because of the thing with Marie.

He'll ruin her, she warned him. *He's done it before. One threatened to kill herself if he didn't leave me. She swallowed kitchen bleach right there on the phone with me.*

That was when they began imagining new ways he might disappear from their lives. A burst pipe, a sunken ceiling. A fall. Then there was that time a pipe *had* burst, as if all their wishing had somehow made it so, the unstoppable pressure of their need and wants. But, ultimately, it only succeeded in flooding the studio, elongating the nightmare even further.

In the end, it wasn't planned or plotted at all. At least not the specifics, that night.

Instead, Charlie found something in himself, or something inside Charlie found him. He never would have thought he could have done it. Until he did.

D on't you see?" he said to Dara now, pressing his fists onto the tabletop. "I had to. We all know I had to. He was going to ruin us. He was going to bring the whole house down on us."

It had been the sight, unbearable, profane, of seeing the contractor parade down those spiral stairs, the stairs that led to the third floor, once and always the first Madame Durant's private space. In his head—hot, jumbled—Charlie could even hear their mother calling out. He could hear her voice and she was calling to him. He could hear her calling. Calling until he came. Those stairs that carried all this meaning for him, meaning he couldn't explain.

("Don't," Dara said. "Don't bring her into this."

She remembered, of course. She remembered climbing those stairs, her eyes adjusting to the darkness, and then, a blur of limbs, seeing them both, seeing the serene pleasure on her mother's face, all her nakedness laid before Charlie, a mere boy . . .)

* * *

He never would have thought he could have done it, he said once more, shaking his head.

But it turned out he could.

And now he couldn't believe himself. Didn't understand himself.

The relief in her voice when he called to tell her what had happened, what he'd done. Her husband, the villain, was gone. It was something almost like happiness. (Even as there was a funny briskness to her after, wanting to get off the phone with him so quickly, saying she needed to start taking care of things. Reminding him they shouldn't be talking on the phone anyway but especially not now and he'd better not come around for a while. Maybe a long while.)

Two people, tightly twined, can begin to convince themselves of anything. There's reality and then there's the shared experience, which feels so much more real.

Two people, needing each other, can come to believe things. Can come to believe wanting something was the same as making it happen. That it wasn't a choice, in the end, but the right thing to do, the fulfillment of some deeper calling.

Two people, even three, a family, he said, looking at Dara, *can make their own world.*

You forgot one thing," Dara said, her fingertips tracing the cake crumbs, sliding along the wax paper, the serrations of the old bread knife.

"What?" Charlie looked at her, tender, lips like a bow. Like a little doll. A wooden doll, with pointed teeth.

"The money."

Charlie paused.

"What money?" he said finally.

Dara looked at him and he looked away. It was so disappointing—crushing, really.

"The insurance policy," she said, her voice creaking. "The fat payout you're both expecting. That you'll share, I guess."

Charlie paused again. Then, his expression dazed, impenetrable, he said, "I don't know about that. We never talked about that at all."

They sat for a long moment. Dara thought she could hear someone moving somewhere. Marie. That floorboard in the front hallway that creaked all winter long.

Maybe Charlie didn't know about the insurance. The payout. Or maybe he did, but only in part.

She didn't care, not now. She didn't care and he could see it on her face.

"Dara, you have to understand," he said, voice high and desperate now, "it's not my fault."

Dara's eyes lifted toward him, not even quite believing that he'd said it.

"Don't you dare," Dara said, her voice such a boom that Charlie nearly jumped.

"I mean, it is. It is," he said, reaching for her hand before she pulled it away. "But, Dara, please."

"You need to leave," Dara said. "Leave before I scream *fire*. Before I start a fire right here."

She could hear Marie breathing from the hallway, shallow, fast breaths like a little girl.

"We've all been trapped here and I never even asked," Charlie was saying, softly, fumblingly, his head in his hands. "I never asked to be here forever. I was just a kid and your mother, she . . ."

The only thought in her head: *He has to leave, he has to.* The things he was saying, like a stain spreading. In this house, their home.

"Don't. Don't," she said.

"But, Dara," he said, head lifting, eyes searching again for hers. That wet-eyed-waif look she knew so well. The same one he had when he first arrived, nearly twenty years ago. When he *was* that wet-eyed waif, uncorrupted and hungry for love. "She was your mother. You saw what she was doing."

"Don't you dare talk about her. Don't you dare bring our mother into this—"

"I don't blame you," he said, his voice speeding up now. "You were afraid of her. Afraid of both of them. We all were. We wanted to leave, remember? You and me. And then they were gone, so we stayed. But they were still here, weren't they? They're still here now. And we just live inside it."

"Stop—"

"You forgot somehow. You forgot why you wanted to leave, why we had to leave if we wanted to live. You forgot and just kept going. But I couldn't. *Marie* couldn't—"

"Get out!"

Charlie rose abruptly, his chair skidding back, and faced Dara.

But looking at him was impossible. That face, like a statue, hopelessly perfect. That body, how precious it was. And how rarely he offered it.

"Get out," came a voice and it was Marie standing in the doorway. "Get out. Get out. Get out." Over and over again, rising to a scream.

Charlie turned to Dara, panicky now.

"But," he said, and his face, his voice—suddenly he was thirteen years old again, "where will I go?"

Looking at him, that boy face, Dara felt a well of feeling—messy, tangled—rise in her. *Don't*, she told herself. *Don't*.

"I don't care," Dara said, Marie walking over, reaching for her hand, and adding, "We don't care at all."

He was gone. Charlie was gone, but something he said kept vibrating through her head for hours, all night.

I could hear her calling, he'd said about their mother. Their mother waiting for him on the third floor, her voice tantalizing, insistent. *I could hear her calling. Calling until I came.*

And, secretly, Dara knew what he'd meant. In some ways she could hear their mother calling too. Could always hear her calling, her whole life.

When did it happen?" Dara said to Marie later that night, both of them huddled in Dara and Charlie's bed, the emptying bottle between them and Marie with a spooked look about her. Maybe it was being in their mother's domain again. Even before she moved out, she rarely set foot in this room, saying it gave her hives.

"When did it happen," Marie repeated, her mouth purple from the old wine.

"When did he become this . . . other thing."

For so long, he'd been one of them. *We three.* For so long she thought it would be forever. But then, without her ever knowing, he'd turned into . . . But she couldn't finish the thought, her eyes blurred.

"Sometimes," Marie said carefully, "you get desperate. Trapped. Sinking. It's like quicksand in your mouth. You have to do whatever it takes to get out."

Dara looked up at Marie, her eyes dry in an instant.

"No, you don't," she said. "You can just leave."

COLD, COLD

When she woke, her brain felt thick, wiry, an old scouring pad. Her phone was ringing. Her hand was tangled in Marie's hair.

Missed call and it had to be Charlie, but it wasn't. She was relieved for a second, then, obscurely, sad.

The voicemail clicked and beeped, and then a flinty voice began talking and talking and Dara felt the stir of old wine in her belly.

"*. . . All-Risk Randi here, remember me? I'm like a bad penny. I was hoping you might be able to make time for me this morning. Planning to swing by, say, nine o'clock? Maybe I can speak with your sister too. So I'll see you then if I don't hear from you. Same address, same spiral stairs?*"

Dara put her hand over her mouth. She thought she might be sick.

Pulling back the bedspread to rise, she saw Marie's bare legs and arms covered in lurid rosy hives.

She guessed Charlie had spent the night nestled in the contractor's marriage bed with his PT, the wife. In other rooms, there were children sleeping innocently. Everywhere, there were Derek's things, the smell of his aftershave, all his shiny boots. Charlie, she thought, in the same bed, on those same sheets as Derek.

What did it matter, she thought. *How different is he from Derek?* She might never know.

Once, in the night, she had woken with a jolt. *Derek's injury, the pipe spraying hot water on him, the flood.* Had that been Charlie's first, failed attempt?

She might never know.

I dreamt about that old-timey dancer last night," Marie said, her face puffy and voice scratched. "The one who caught fire."

"I remember," Dara said, trying to make the coffee go down, the instant crystals sludged at the bottom of the mug from the day before.

That story their mother used to tell—the dancer whose tutu brushed against the footlights and burst into flames. Whenever she heard it, Dara couldn't help but feel herself burning. She was feeling it now, her feet tingling. Marie standing before her like a clean flame.

"She refused to wear the skirts that were safe," Marie said, rubbing her face. "She only wanted to wear what was light and beautiful."

Dara turned to the stove, her hand over the stove burner, lighting the jet for more coffee.

"She wanted what she wanted," Dara said, the words tipping from her mouth, which felt hot, too, felt thick with hot water.

"But in my dream," Marie said, "I was the one onstage. And it was my skirt that went up, up, up in flames." She turned and looked at Dara. "And you were there."

Dara didn't say anything, watching the kettle.

"You saw me and you cried out," Marie continued, her voice urgent and pained as if she were dreaming it now. "You threw Mother's rabbit blanket over me and smothered the flames."

That blanket again, Dara thought. The one she'd left moldering in the basement the other day.

"The flames ate the fur," Marie said, rising and walking toward Dara. "But they never touched me at all."

"Marie," Dara said, turning off the stove.

"He set a fire in me—Derek. No, I set it in myself. But I'm burned through now, you see," Marie said, her voice quivering but strong. "I'm burned through and now it's over. It's over."

She reached out for Dara's hands and held them in her own, hot as a burner coil. Dara swore she could feel Marie's blood rushing under her skin.

It was like Marie was awake. Awake for the first time not just in six weeks—the sex haze and humiliations, the impulsivity and retreat—but in months, years maybe.

It was like seeing someone who's been away so very long, their face changed, the shadows heavy now, but in the eyes a flash of something ancient and pure.

Oh, Marie, she thought. *I've missed you for the longest time.*

S he told Marie to go straight to the Ballenger.

"I have to meet with the insurance lady," she said. "She wants to talk to you, so you can't be there."

"No," Marie said, pulling their father's sweater over her shoulders, "I'd rather not."

"We can't let her in," Dara said firmly. "We have to get her out."

They'd had invaders enough.

A s they put on coats, gloves, silently, the shush of their shoes, the scatter of bruises on Marie's neck as she threw a scarf around it, Dara kept thinking of what could happen. All-Risk Randi suspected it wasn't an accident. The likeliest and most convenient suspect? The wife with the big, fat insurance policy her bosses will have to pay out. But how many steps might it take to find out about Marie? About Charlie? There were things investigators knew how to find out. There were cameras everywhere now, the parking lot, the traffic lights. Phones told them everything. There was no private world anymore. The larger world had turned itself inside out, was seeking to infiltrate every smaller, private one. The home, the family.

Seeking to pass judgment. To prod and probe at a safe remove.

No one wanted to face the truth. That every family was a hothouse, a swamp. Its own atmosphere, its own rules. Its own laws and gods. There would never be any understanding from the outside. There couldn't be.

"Are you going to tell the police?" Marie asked suddenly. "About Charlie?"

"No," Dara said. "Not now."

They both paused. It was one of those moments—they'd had them before, the night their mother struck their father in the head with the cast-iron pan and he dropped to the floor so fast Dara and Marie both burst into tears. For a long moment wondering what to do, like all the times their father had chased their mother around the house or that time he locked her in the garage overnight and Dara and Marie only found out in the wee hours, her screams finally frenzied enough to wake them from their sleep. They didn't ever call anyone. That was not something any of the four of them ever did. It wasn't what you did. You kept going.

Driving into the lot, she looked up at the third-floor window, which was dark, its glass smeary.

Randi Jacek was waiting at the front door in a pantsuit and puffy vest, palming a vape pen. "Terrible habit," she said. "But we all can't be as healthy as dancers."

Inside the studio, there was a chill in the air, as if the furnace had broken in the night.

When they stepped inside, Dara had the thought: *What if Charlie is here?* She couldn't see him, not now.

But as they moved through the studios, the coolness sinking in their bones, there was no sign of him.

"I'm sorry about all this," Randi was saying, following Dara to the back office. "I know you have your show coming up."

"Performances. Sixteen performances," Dara said, her voice tight. "The detectives said you might be back."

"Like a bad penny," Randi Jacek said, repeating the same joke.

"Or a bulldog."

Randi smiled. "My reputation precedes me. Detective Walters?"

Dara nodded, pulling her coat tighter, setting her hand on the radiator. But Randi Jacek didn't seem to notice the cold, or the smell in the air, like an electric iron left on the pad too long.

T he back office was warmer, its door shut overnight, trapping the last of the heat. But everywhere else, the floorboards and ceiling beams were creaking and popping from the cold.

"All yours," Dara said, stepping back. "Though I can't imagine what there is left to look for."

Randi nodded distractedly, her eyes back on the staircase. "And your sister? She'll be here soon?"

"She's at the theater. You know, our 'show.'"

Randi looked at her, smiling generically.

"Ms. Durant, you know what?" she said. "Last night, my husband made chicken riggies for me."

"Pardon?"

"Chicken, rigatoni, peppers. We had it on our first date. We've made it together on anniversaries, special occasions. And last night, out of nowhere, chicken riggies. I got the point. Fella can't come out and say he misses me, but . . ."

"Ms. Jacek, I have to get to the theater," Dara said.

"The son of a gun even put out place mats," she said. "Cloth napkins.

Extra-hot cherry peppers, just like I like it." She smiled, shaking her head. "But I couldn't eat a thing."

"No?"

"No. Because you know what I was thinking about?"

"Ms. Jacek, I—"

"*Why*. Why was my friend Derek—old D-Wreck—going up the stairs? At that hour? What sent him up there?"

"A noise," Dara said quickly. *Here we go again. Here we go.*

Even empty, the studio was full of noises, buzzing lights, a scurrying mouse or two, birds flapping against the gutters, clanking pipes, the furnace wheezing.

Even now, there was that whistling sound that had to be from the radiator, though the pipes were cold to the touch.

"The thing is," Randi said, "if there's one truth you learn after fifteen years in this business: People mostly behave in completely explicable ways. Until they don't."

"Maybe the power went out," Dara continued, her voice speeding up, taking on a tone. "Maybe he thought the fuse box was up there. Maybe he just wanted to snoop, to pry. Who can say what went on in that man's head."

Dara closed her mouth a sentence too late. She was so tired, so tired.

Randi's eyes were fixed on her now.

"He was just another contractor to you—someone to take up your time and take your money. But I knew him back when he was eleven years old, that great curly mane of his. All the girls loved him. I remember my friend Carla Mathis telling all of us how he'd accidentally touched her hip in gym class and she nearly passed out." Randi laughed. "*An ache that was not an ache*. That's what she called it."

Randi seemed, maybe, even to be blushing.

"Look, Ms. Jacek," Dara said, "I'm sorry you—"

"But he chose me. Briefly, but he chose me. One long summer day a bunch of us ran into each other biking around town in our bathing suits, like you used to do. And somehow we ended up behind my cousin's house. Derek had stolen a Popsicle from the fridge inside. One of those twins, you know."

Dara didn't know. Dara doubted she had ever had a Popsicle in her life.

"Broke it in two with one hand! And gave me half. Midway through, he leaned in and kissed me right on the mouth. Tasted like grape soda. The Popsicle melted all over my hand. I still can't drink grape soda and not think of him."

Dara was listening, but she wasn't listening. She was thinking of something. Of Charlie, the year he was the Nutcracker Prince. Age fourteen, cheekbones like knives. That feeling when she first saw him in the costume, so unbearably handsome in the crimson tunic with the brass buttons, the epaulets, and their mother draping the gold sash across his chest, pressing her palm on the velvet. *Look*, she said, seeing Dara in the mirror. *Look*. And Dara understanding, somehow, that their mother, like Drosselmeier in the ballet, seemed to be giving him to her. Passing him to her, the most special gift. *An ache that was not an ache.* And yet now it was.

"When you know someone before," Randi said and she had moved to the spiral staircase now, her hand resting on the railing. "The Big Before. Before things happen. Before all the adult stuff—the disappointments, the broken hearts, the missteps, the scars. Then you know the real person. Before everything happened to them and they became what they became."

"You don't have to let it change you," Dara said. "The adult stuff. That's a choice. These are all choices."

"Maybe," Randi said. "But the thing is, how often do you realize something's a choice when you make it?"

Dara started to open her mouth, but no words came out.

"Sometimes," Randi said, shrugging, "choices feel a lot like surviving."

She only knew the second before she saw him.

Oh, Charlie, her voice a whimper.

* * *

Do you mind?" Randi Jacek was saying, starting up the stairs, her breath little puffs now.

"The police said it's dangerous," Dara warned, moving toward her. "They're not safe."

But Randi was already heading up the steps and there was that sound, that lonely whistle she kept hearing, hissing harder now as they ascended.

"I just want to get a look up there," Randi said, reaching the top as Dara stood tentatively on the bottom step, "to understand what he might have . . . Maybe that's the sound he heard? Do you hear it?"

The rafters squeaking, squeaking and popping so loudly, and what was that whistling sound and why was it so loud here?

"Ms. Jacek, it's not safe. . . ."

But Randi Jacek was already disappearing into the dark at the top of the stairs. Dara followed quickly now.

As she made that last turn onto the third floor, the cold coming hard as an ice sheet, Randi started screaming, really screaming, even as her mouth let forth only the smallest sound.

Her lips gone white and Dara pushing past her, and knowing suddenly, and how hadn't she known before?

Oh, Charlie. Beautiful Charlie.

Charlie, hanging there, long and lean, his blond head dipped, his face hidden.

An orange cord was lassoed around one of the heating ducts and around that lissome neck of his, his weight dragging the duct to a silver V, dragging his body down so far his knees nearly brushed the floor.

When Dara put her hand on his neck, cool and smooth as ever, and impossibly lovely, it reminded her of the snowy neck of a swan, exquisite and impossible.

Behind her, Randi was on the phone and the bent heat duct was dipping lower and lower, the cord squeaking and Charlie's body turning so Dara couldn't avoid his face, a white smudge.

She was thinking of that moment in *The Nutcracker*, the book. The part that made her stomach tighten, that gave her an ache that wasn't an ache. How the heroine sees a spot of blood on the Nutcracker's neck and begins rubbing it with her handkerchief until he suddenly grows warm under her touch and begins to move. How she brings him back to life.

But Charlie wasn't going to move at all and was only cold, colder than ever before. Cold as the radiator below. Cold like marble church steps, Midnight Mass. Cold as a star.

Randi was saying something beside her, reaching out, then stopping, wanting to touch Dara, something.

B ut Dara didn't want to talk, to move. She only wanted to stay in this space a moment longer with this boy, this poor broken boy, the red-rimmed furrow she'd see on his neck once they lifted the cord loose, once they let her touch him, that swanling neck. He'd given her so much, after all. More than he had to give. But he'd ruined everything all the same.

A DISPUTE

Everything happens three times. Three times, the wicked queen tries to kill Snow White. Three times, Christ asks Peter if he loves him. Three times, Rumpelstiltskin spins the wheel.

Three times, police officers filled the studio. The fire, the fall, and Charlie.

Detective Walters, this time in a thick shearling overcoat, and Detective Mendoza talking to Randi and all of them talking to the medical examiner, wheezing and whistling once more into a mask clamped over his face.

Dara watched through the doorway as a gloved woman slipped the orange extension cord into a paper bag. The same cord that, the other night, they'd unplugged from Marie's lamp and Charlie had wrapped it around and around the lamp base, like bright circus taffy, before hiding it away.

It turned out there was a note. Shoved in Charlie's pocket, written on a Post-it, a word more than a note, written in Charlie's cramped hand: *Guilty.*

The detectives were puzzling over the reverse side, another single word: *Snow.*

Only Dara knew that it was Charlie's to-do list. More snow for *The Nutcracker.* Always more snow.

*I*s it possible your husband had a confrontation with the contractor?

They were trying to be gentle, respectful. She was the grieving widow, after all.

Inside, though, she had such clarity. The grieving, complicated as it would be, could come later.

In the end it was Randi and the police who gave her the head start.

Earlier, she'd overheard Randi saying that in the end it's always two men throwing themselves at each other. An accidental shove at a bar. An argument over a bill.

Aren't there some states, she'd heard Detective Mendoza joke to Walters, *where murdering your contractor is a misdemeanor?*

We were both frustrated," Dara admitted. "Everything was taking so long. Charlie was very upset. The tension kept building."

"That morning, did your husband say he was going to confront the contractor?"

"No. He was just going to work."

"Can you guess why one or both of the men might have been on the third floor?"

Dara paused. "Charlie suspected the contractor was using the third floor, maybe to entertain a date. You know. We were concerned. The students . . ."

It all came naturally, like smoke ribbons from her mouth. It was true, after a fashion. Nothing was ever simple.

"We found cigarette butts up there," one of the deputies said, as if on cue.

"If they'd caught fire . . ." Dara said, shaking her head.

Yeah, I like it. It tracks, she heard Mendoza saying to Walters. *Fella's pissed. Work's not getting done. Can't even find the contractor. Thinks the guy's up to no good.*

So maybe he gets here, tries to catch him in the act? Walters said. *Or hears him and charges up the stairs—*

—just as the contractor's coming down. They struggle on the stairs, a do-si-do and BAM . . .

There would be more questions, she knew. They asked for samples of handwriting, they took more prints, put things in bags, took fibers from her shirt and Randi Jacek's, scrapings under nails. They still wanted to talk to her sister. But at the end of it, they let her go home, Detective Walters offering to drive her himself.

She declined.

It never crossed her mind to tell them the truth. Telling them about the contractor's wife would mean telling them about Charlie and about Marie, all the private things.

It wasn't their business, any of it. It was hers and Marie's, all of it.

She called Marie at the Ballenger and told her to go home immediately. To lock up the house and wait for her.

Then she told her about Charlie.

The call was brief and awful.

Marie kept crying. She couldn't stop crying and Dara had to hang up or she'd never make it.

* * *

'm so sorry," Randi Jacek said, touching Dara's arm as she moved to leave. "If I hadn't made you come here, you wouldn't have had to see—"

Dara felt something stir in her chest, against her heart. She moved quickly past and heard a sound in her throat that felt like a scream.

In the stairwell, in the parking lot, in the car, she tried to let it out, the scream, the cry, the breath. It never came.

THRESHOLD

She was pulling into their driveway when she saw the car out front, a weathered minivan, rust-dimpled and sputtering exhaust.

Dara could make out two girls' heads in the backseat, both swathed in winter hats, one plain purple pom-pom and the other shaped like a unicorn, a silvery horn bopping to and fro.

It was only then that she saw the figure on the front porch bouncing on her feet to keep warm. Sunglasses, a hood, but the same faded parka from the night before. Was it only the night before?

Exiting the car, Dara approached the woman without knowing what she was going to do, with no idea what was inside her.

The woman, her face weather-beaten, looked tired, frightened, her head darting from her minivan to Dara and back again.

"Do you know who I am?" she asked.

"I guess so," Dara said. A curtain twitched in the bay window. *Marie,* Dara thought, *watching. Hiding.*

The woman shook her head, pressing her mittens over her ears.

"The detectives called," she said. "They told me about Char—your husband."

"Why did they tell you?" Dara snapped.

"They were asking questions. About my husband mentioning any trouble at work," she said. "I'm so sorry for your loss."

Dara said nothing, staring into the woman's sunglasses—oversize, bottomless—and seeing only the dark flutter of her own eyes reflected there.

"I don't know what Charlie told you. Or if he told you anything."

"I know more than he did," Dara said coolly. "I know you used him."

"No," the woman said, shaking her head again, the vast abyss of her sunglasses. "No."

"Charlie could never do anything like that. Not on his own. He had trouble doing anything at all," Dara said, her eyes pinching suddenly, upsettingly. "So it had to be you. You wanted out. You wanted the money—"

"Is your sister inside?" the woman said suddenly.

"You're not talking to my sister," Dara said, stepping forward, a feeling in her chest, a ferocity, something she hadn't felt in years, since they were small and their father sometimes sent them both to the deli to buy beer for him, three ragged blocks, and sometimes the cashier who leaned down far too close to her sister and once asked her if she had *polka dots on her panties.*

"Okay," the woman said. "But maybe she wants to talk to me. Maybe I can help her. About Derek."

"That's not going to happen," Dara said.

They both looked at each other a long time. It reminded her of playing board games with her sister, the few soggy ones her father kept in the basement. How it was impossible to play with Marie because she never cared about losing—paper money, game pieces, pride. It only worked if you both cared. If you both had the power to wipe out the board.

"So are you going to tell them?" the woman asked finally. "The police. Are you going to tell them about Charlie and me?"

Dara peered into her sunglasses, one lens smeared. This woman, this woman. With a hunch to her posture and a spray of gray at both temples. This woman. Who was she.

"No," Dara said. "I'm not. But not for you."

The woman nodded, breathing softly now, her shoulders sinking. "Would you believe me," she said, "if I said I didn't know Charlie was going to do it? That night. Would you believe me?"

"I wouldn't," Dara said, "believe anything you said at all." Looking past her toward her minivan, sludge-colored. The two girls in the backseat, the sway of their winter hats listening to some song on the radio as the car fogged up.

"Those are your girls," Dara said, her voice small and strange.

"Yes," the woman said, a stitch of caution on her face. "The boys are away at school."

They were both looking now, at their winter hats bopping through the window, purple and plush, the unicorn horn slightly bent, pressed against the roof of the car as the girls played.

The woman's body twitched suddenly, as if remembering something, and she covered her mouth with a stiff mitten. Dara knew what it was. She'd felt it a dozen times that day already. The body remembering, contorting. *He's gone, he's gone.*

For a moment, only a moment, Dara felt sorry for her.

As if sensing it, the woman looked at her and reached for her sunglasses, removing them at last. Her eyes heavy, swollen.

"I wish I could explain," she said. "You build this family. And it's perfect. It's everything you wanted. And then something goes wrong. Slowly or all at once. It was good and now it's so bad, and it's his fault. Or he started it. All the ripples from his bad behavior."

Dara didn't say anything. The woman kept going.

"So, in some private part of your head, you start thinking up fantasies of escape. You tell yourself: If only he were gone, if only a heart attack, a lightning bolt, a car crash . . ."

"I have to go," Dara said, turning.

"Sometimes," the woman said suddenly, her voice choked. "Sometimes, you think you'd do anything to get out, to be free."

They held glances a long moment. Dara could feel Marie behind the glass. She could feel her as if they were one. She could feel Marie's little rabbit heart beating fast. *Oh, Marie . . .*

"You're never free," Dara said, realizing it as she said it.

When something goes wrong in a family, it takes generations to wipe it out. Those words came to Dara, something from a history book, a book about kings and queens she once found in the den long ago.

Marie, Charlie, they thought they could escape it, through leaving, or trying to. Through other people, lovers. But they both ended right back where they started. In their mother's house, her third-floor hideaway.

"I guess you're right," the woman said. "You blame everything on that one person. You think if that one person is gone, everything will be perfect and good." She slid her sunglasses back on. "But in the end, that person is you."

WE TWO

I t was late, very late when Dara woke with a start.

She'd barely fallen into a tingly pitch-black sleep, her face pressed on the pillow beside her, which still smelled like Charlie and like Marie, when she heard something,

A slither of slippers along wood.

Charlie, she thought with a start.

S quinting down the long hallway, she spotted her sister at the far end.

Ghostly in their mother's nightgown, Marie hovered at the threshold of their old bedroom, the very spot the contractor had stood less than a week ago.

She looked tentative, unsure, her face bright under the moon.

Dara moved toward her, gliding down the hall, her own feet seeming to make no sound.

It was almost as if she were sleepwalking, still dreaming, or they both were, and together, clasping hands, they stepped inside.

* * *

This room," Marie said, the whiskey on her breath, coming off her skin now. "I hate this room."

Dara didn't say anything, her gaze snagging on things, the nicks in the paint where they'd whacked their pointe shoes into submission, the worn spot on the carpet from the time they spilled varnish for their pointe shoes, the smear on the bedpost where the contractor's hand had been.

"It's just a room," Dara said, even as she remembered everything, remembered sneaking Charlie in here that first time, curled around her in the bottom bunk, the smell of sex and saliva everywhere, the damp bedspread.

"It wasn't healthy here," Marie whispered, shuddering in her nightgown, all her bruises illuminated by the streetlamp shining through the window. She looked, Dara thought, like the illustrated lady at the carnival. The ladies of the carnival.

"It wasn't healthy for me," she said again. "It wasn't healthy for any of us."

Reminding Dara of the day nearly ten months ago when Marie moved out, milk crates tattooing her arms, her eyes covered by sunglasses though it was the middle of the night. How she passed Dara on the way to her waiting cab and whispered, her chin dipped to her shoulder, *You can't even breathe in here. How can you breathe.*

The house that was their childhood. The house they never left.

"We've always lived here," Dara said. "We've lived here our whole lives."

Are you remembering?" Marie was saying. "All those nights."

"Which nights?" Dara asked, but she knew. She knew before Marie began.

"How we'd hide under the covers to make it stop," Marie said. "Our hands pressed against our ears when the screaming started. Remember how she screamed at him? *You are nothing to me. You mean nothing to me. You touch me and I feel nothing.*"

"Why are you talking about this?" Dara said, moving for the door. The carpet smelled of old glue, felt like sandpaper under her feet.

"She got worse and worse," Marie said, turning around and around in the cramped space. "She wouldn't stop. Drinking almost as much as he was, that glass always curled in her hand. How she raged at him—"

"You mean how he raged at her," Dara said, bristling. "How he pushed her, choked her?"

"She pushed him," Marie said, eyes fixed on Dara with a look she'd never seen before. Determined, resolute, grave. "She slapped him. She tore out a hank of his hair. That time. Other times. She did things behind his back. You know."

You know. It seemed cruel to say it now. It felt cruel with Charlie's slippers still on the floor of their bedroom. Charlie who, three days before, had scrubbed this carpet for her, for them . . .

Dara's head throbbed, Marie too close and smelling like the rancid whiskey, like old sweat. Dried spit.

There was something Marie was going to say. Dara could feel it. A thing that could never be unsaid. Maybe it was time.

"She never should have been driving that night," Marie said.

"He always drove," Dara said. "He always drove. I think he was driving."

But he wasn't. Everyone had told her that. Her mother flung up against the steering wheel so hard its shape tattooed her chest.

The day of the accident was a blur to Dara. Was lost to some furrow of her brain. She only remembered the night before. How her mother had sat her down on the bunkbed and tried to explain that what Dara had thought she had seen on the third floor—what she *thought* she'd seen her doing with Charlie—well, it wasn't like that.

Dara didn't say anything, a feeling in her chest like a sharp stone. It had been four days since she had walked in on them, four days in which she and Charlie plotted and schemed an exit, an escape. The impossible confidence of youth.

I need you to promise you won't tell anyone, their mother said. *Because other people might not understand.*

Dara promised. Who, after all, would she tell.

And I need you to promise you understand. And forgive me.

Her mother's voice breaking over the word *forgive.* A word Dara couldn't remember her mother ever using before. Along with *sorry.*

Now is the time, Dara had thought. To tell her she was leaving, with Charlie. But she couldn't make the words come, the stone in her chest now in her throat.

Dara, her mother said, more firmly now, *I'm your mother.*

But Dara couldn't speak.

Dara, tell me you understand. Tell me you forgive me.

But Dara couldn't and she started to feel sick, her body keening over.

You have to leave.

The voice wasn't her mother's but Marie's. Marie standing in the doorway.

Mother, you have to leave.

The look on her mother's face, so surprised. So full of wonder.

Marie Durant, their mother said, her voice trembling, *this is a private conversation.*

Mother, you have to leave. Marie so stoic. So certain. The certainty of the Sword Swallower, lifting her blade.

The look on her mother's face—like a queen dethroned.

And then that next night, their anniversary. The only time their parents ever went anywhere together and alone. They'd both been drinking and her mother had locked herself in the bedroom, refusing to put on her dress until he nearly tore the door from its hinges, threatening to drag her out in her nightie to *pretend this one night a year that you're my wife. My wife.* And that tomorrow she could go back into her playroom *with the children, with all the pretty little boys.*

Dara and Marie were hiding in their bedroom, in this room. Dara and

Marie wanted it to be over and they were glad Charlie was still at the studio and couldn't hear.

You can't drive, their mother was saying. *Give me those keys. Give them to me. I know where we're going.*

Eventually, they heard the car engine shudder and spurt.

I know where we're going.

Peeking out the bedroom window, they'd watched the car lurch out of the driveway and into the blue night.

N ow, more than fifteen years later, Dara stood at that same window, looking at Marie.

"Dad mostly drove," she said finally. "But that night she wanted to."

Marie looked at her, her eyes blue and limpid.

"Yes, that night she wanted to," she whispered. "So she did."

W ithout either of them deciding, Marie followed Dara into the master bedroom, sidestepping Charlie's slippers and climbing into bed after her.

"I'm sorry," she whispered to Dara.

Marie smelling like toothpaste, pushing gently against Dara's back, little scratches, hands tangling, like when they were kids.

"It's okay," Dara said. Somehow, she was glad to feel her there. To smell her smells—the Band-Aids and baby powder and the sweetness of her sweat.

She was finally starting to slip to sleep when—

"Where's Mama's blanket?" Marie whispered. *Mama.* She hadn't called their mother that since they were very little. "Mama's fur blanket. The rabbit blanket."

Dara's eyes shuttered open.

The rabbit blanket. It wouldn't go away, would it, like seeing it in the basement only days before, kicking it across the floor toward the furnace.

She'd made it come to life and then Marie had dreamt about it and now it was back again.

"You hated it," Dara said. "And it gave you hives."

Marie had wanted to throw it out when their parents died. She thought it looked like an animal hide left behind by a hunter. Which it was, really. Later, she'd claim it gave her hives and then, suddenly, it did. Pink wheals across her belly, on her thighs.

"What did you do with the rabbit blanket, Dara?" Marie asked, clutching at Dara's back. "Do you and Charlie still take it out? Remember that blanket, how electricity would run through it. How it would hold it and spark?"

Dara could feel what was coming, could feel it vibrating in the air, and it was more than she could bear.

"We loved that blanket," Dara said, even as she saw herself kicking it across the basement floor.

Marie was crying now and she was always so lovely when she was crying, her skin flushed and downy like a baby's, her lashes fluttering.

"Dara," she said, and kept saying it. "Oh, Dara. It was wrong. It was wrong and as long as we stay here we'll never escape it."

But there was nothing wrong with it. Sisters often slept together. And Charlie was like a brother to Marie.

They'd all known one another since they were children. That's what someone like the contractor, or a detective, or the police could never understand. The innocence of children. The specialness of their special family.

It started on one of those *Nutcracker* nights, the first with Charlie in the house. After closing night, their mother invited all three of them into bed with her, under the rabbit blanket to watch grainy videocassettes of old Alberta Ballet performances, to watch their mother's Clara, grave and perfect and wise beyond her twelve years.

Their mother clasping their hands under the blanket, cuddling tight, eventually taking Dara's tiny hand and placing it on Charlie's, like a blessing, or something.

It was all so intense and overwhelming, age thirteen, fourteen, fifteen, being so close to a boy, a boy whose body she longed for, whose touch made her feel warm all in the center of her.

And Marie, whose body she knew as well as her own and who loved to nuzzle up to Charlie as she nuzzled up to their father, the only man she knew. It all made Marie feel cozy and loved, a cat squirming with pleasure. And then a fox.

Marie, whose curiosity was even greater than Dara's own, but confusion the next morning far heavier. *What did we do, Dara. I feel so strange*, and her legs trembling, and her wrist sore.

We didn't do anything, Dara would tell her, her body still throbbing from it, feeling so spent from Charlie's fingers, her own.

This was after their mother stopped joining them at all. Instead, she would drift down the hall, running a bubble bath. Leaving them alone to play.

After their parents were gone, there seemed no reason to end the tradition. In fact, it felt especially meaningful to sustain it, to honor it.

These were rare events, only on special nights. Marie's twenty-fifth birthday, or maybe Charlie recovering from his latest surgery. A summer storm knocking the power out. The three of them in that old king-size, the blackened brass headboard and the drooping box spring. They felt so close, and would sometimes even whisper ghost stories to drown out the howling wind. Or on hot nights, the ceiling fan, the desk fan, the rotating floor fan, all the fans in the house arrayed around them. Charlie with his arms around them both and Dara not minding it at all. In fact clasping Charlie's hand onto Marie's arm, her belly.

They all needed one another and this was the way.

No one could say that it wasn't natural. And pure. Three bodies all three knew so well, limbs interlaced by morning. Warm breath and giggles. Dara never felt jealous, nor ashamed. It didn't seem like sharing Charlie, it seemed like an extension of their childhood, under that rabbit blanket big enough to contain them all, including their mother, whose hard, long hands would draw Charlie toward her. Who would encourage Dara to close her hands around him.

It was about play, comfort, escape. Soothing one another, and oneself. That childhood feeling of body pleasures that's so pure, and natural, and right.

The next day, there was no need for bad feelings. Sleepily, a little bashfully, at the kitchen table, sneaking winks at one another over coffee, robes pulled tight.

It was like a dream in that you could never recall specifics after. You could only recall, dimly, how it felt: like family, like home.

Dara never felt jealous because Marie was part of her in ways deeper than feelings, attachments, rules. Marie was a part of her until she wasn't.

Until she moved out, rejected them.

Dara had loved giving each to the other, the feeling of it, like their mother, taking one in one hand, and the other in the other. Joining them, laying her hand on him or his on her. Their lovely bodies so close to her as to be part of her. Family.

She was only doing as their mother had done, their mother had shown them, directed them, her greatest ballet yet.

This, she seemed to say, *is beautiful and ours.*

Some people liked to make everything dirty.

Some people liked to ruin everything.

Dara," Marie was saying, her face gone so soft and her hand on Dara's arm, "it's not our fault. It's not our fault."

It wasn't wrong, Dara wanted to say but couldn't make the words come. It felt so strange, lying in the same bed, all the memories flicking around her, sly little flames.

"I know," Dara said finally. "I know it's not our fault."

Marie paused, then said, as if just realizing it herself, "I think you wanted to leave even before I did."

Dara looked up. It was true, of course. It was true. She had wanted to leave. She'd almost made it once, right before the car accident. Charlie was right about one thing, about that. They'd almost made it together, packing that rolling trunk, her chest jumping, imagining a world beyond that paint-thick front door. That house, this house. The house that was her childhood.

A n hour passed, sleep tugging on Dara but never taking her.

A memory kept rising up, of Marie, age ten or eleven, squirming in her bunkbed above and insisting, *I have something no one else has.*

We all have it, Dara had said, dismissing her. But she'd never really been sure. Dara was dark, but Marie was light. Dara was cool, but Marie was hot. Marie, the wild child, the sword swallower, the illustrated lady, the freak.

"Marie," she found herself whispering now, feeling for Marie behind her, her halting breath. "Do you remember the carnival? The one Dad took us to every spring at St. Joan's?"

"Yes," Marie said sleepily. "I remember."

Dara didn't know what made her think of it. Maybe it was Marie's feet brushing against her feet, trying to stay warm.

"The Fire Eater was my favorite," Dara said, pressing her arches against Marie's hard skin. "And the Sword Swallower was yours."

"They were the same," Marie said softly.

Dara's feet went still. "What?"

"They were the same woman," Marie said, her sleepy voice, the words coming slowly and never quite finishing.

"What?" Dara asked, wondering if she was dreaming.

"I saw her once," Marie said, her feet wrapping around Dara's, warming them. "Changing her costume behind the stage."

"They were the same?" Dara repeated, needing to be sure.

"They were the same."

FIRE, SNOW

The dream came fast—moments, it seemed, after she closed her eyes, Marie curled up beside her. They were at the carnival, watching the Sword Swallower in the sideshow tent.

She was tall and grand, with scars around her mouth like hatch marks, like tribal signs.

The *swoosh* as she raised the sword, hoisting it high above her head. Then, bending her knees, springing herself into a spin, head whipping around in a pirouette.

One turn, two turns, then suddenly the sword became a torch and, stopping, she was no longer the Sword Swallower but the Fire Eater, scars around her mouth like hatch marks, like tribal signs.

Her arms mighty and rounded, lifted up over her head, forming a perfect oval. Her arms corded red and invulnerable, holding the torch high, so high it reached the sagging top of the tent.

The canvas, scarlet and gold, above them and suddenly shuddering with fire.

Dara, we have to go! We have to go! It's time!

How she reached for Marie's hand but couldn't find her, the heat coming down like a vibration.

Opening her eyes, she thought she could still see it.

Waves of fire rolling across the ceiling, fingers of fire stretching to all corners.

I'm burning. My body is burning.

*I*s it morning, her eyes pinching, the room bright as noon but the clock saying four A.M. And then remembering the bedroom window faced west and dawn never came in there.

"Dara, we have to go! We have to go! It's time!"

It was Marie, her hands on Dara, lifting her.

And she was on her feet and the room suddenly fell dark and her mouth filled with stench. The door open, the hallway black and her hand on the wall, her palm sticking to the hot plaster, and Marie pulling her, pulling her so her arm felt it might leave its socket.

The floorboards burned under her feet and she was running, Marie's hand clamped to her wrist, pulling her down the stairs, stumbling to the entryway and the *jusssssh* of air sucking them in, gasping to hold them, and Marie nearly dragging them forward, nearly yanking Dara's arm from its socket, across the threshold and out the door.

A swarm of fire trucks, a police car, outside, a neighbor must have called, great white tides of smoke, rolling across their house, swallowing their house, swallowing everything.

*I*t might have been fifteen minutes or two hours, the hushed awe of neighbors in flannel pajamas, a little boy in mouse-paw slippers crying loudly, mournfully, the whine of sirens, a chemical smell in the air of singed metal, melting plastic, burning foam, but the fire was gone, leaving a heavy black streak up the center of their house.

What was left of their house, its center sunken, its cavity exposed: buckled floorboards, snaky wires, a few remaining rafters like fingers pointing and white ash like confetti shaking from its rafters.

Shivering under a heavy blanket someone had draped over her, Dara stared at it in wonder. How small it looked, how diminished. Like looking at a fuzzy Polaroid from childhood, like stepping into your kindergarten classroom again, its furniture like matchsticks under your feet.

"You're so calm," a neighbor was saying to her.

"She's in shock," whispered another.

She turned and looked at them, a white-haired couple in matching robes. Holding hands, their bony knuckles knocking against each other.

"I'm okay," she said. Because she was, though she couldn't say how, or why.

But she was looking past them at Marie in the distance.

Marie, except her blond hair was black, black streaks running up one arm.

Sitting in the back of the fire truck, an oxygen mask over her face, mottled legs dangling, she was waving at Dara, waving her over. *Come here. Hurry. It's time!*

Dara waved back and began walking toward her, the blanket falling from her shoulders.

Breathe. Breathe.

T he firemen were talking about the gas furnace, the flue. *Years of junk caught in there. Old leaves, a bird's nest, dead mice.*

Flame rollout, they were calling it. Flue gets jammed up, flames escape and roll out like a great wave.

It's a shame how much junk people keep in their basement, right by that combustion chamber and *I always tell my dad, the flame should be clean and blue.*

Dara was listening, sort of, but she was mostly listening for Marie's breathing, her mask fogging up. It was so soothing, like a metronome, like a promise.

A firefighter appeared suddenly, his face glistening with soot, holding something on a stick.

"I was worried it was a pet at first, or something," he said. "A dog or cat."

"No," Dara said, looking at Marie. "It's just an old blanket."

"Rabbit fur," Marie said, the oxygen mask off now, cradled in her blackened hand. "Vienna Blue."

"Found it halfway up the basement stairs," the firefighter said. "The force of the flue must've sent it flying. You'd be surprised how often it happens. Crowded basement, old house. Bad luck."

"Yes," Dara said looking at it, the sooty and wet pelt in the man's hands. "Bad luck."

She looked at Marie, who looked at her, a sneaking smile there.

They made Dara sit in the truck and take the oxygen, the smell even stronger now, the strongest she'd ever known. Burning plaster, carpet glue, dry wood, mildewed crates.

Breathe, breathe, she told herself until she could again.

Until she heard Marie again.

"Dara," Marie was calling out, running toward her on the blue-black street. "Look! Look!"

Her voice was high and light like a bell.

Looking up at the streetlamp above, Dara saw how there were suddenly snowflakes everywhere, swirling everywhere, dappling the asphalt, their hair.

Marie stepped backward, the fireman's blanket falling to the ground, her nightgown drenched, and her body turning, twirling, her bare feet on the pavement, her long neck, her arms like white birds, and the snow falling and falling.

"Save a few," Dara found herself saying, her eyes filling, her face hurting from her smile. She was smiling. "Save them."

Marie smiled, lifting her arms into the air, Dara lifting hers too.

And as they landed in her outstretched palm she saw they weren't snowflakes at all but ashes, pale and bright, falling silently over everything that had been theirs.

It didn't matter if it was snow or shredded paper or ash in her hands, because she could breathe and Marie was dancing under the streetlamp and it was over, over at last.

FOUR

EDEN LOST

One Year Later

You've never seen true longing until you've seen a theater of young girls gaze upon the opening moments of *The Nutcracker*. All in their holiday best, their red velveteen dresses, their glitter-threaded tartan jumpers, pearl headbands, flocked hair ribbons, their mouths open, agape, their eyes hard dots of wonder.

But it wasn't only the little girls. It was their mothers in their beaded sweaters and sweeping skirts, their heads heavy from to-do lists, from cleaning the snow off the car. It was their fathers in their navy blazers, maybe a tartan necktie, their faces red from the cold or the quick scotch before heading out the door.

In moments, they'll all be transformed, Dara thought, standing in the wings, watching the Ballenger Center fill with wool and glitter and Christmas plaid.

In a few minutes, the music would start. Audiences always forgot how well they knew it until it began. From those first strains of the overture, their bodies would begin to shift and lift, their eyes opening wider, a glimmer there, something stirring inside, a holiday long ago, an aching memory of a broken toy, the smack of a chocolate orange on the tabletop, a parent after too much eggnog crashing into the Christmas tree, the forever-feeling of standing at a church pew, the candle melting off its paper collar into your hand. Watching the audience, you can see them tunneling back, the ache of it all. Their hearts opening. And then Clara appears, in her party dress.

Clara, who is us, Dara thought.

She hovers anxiously behind a pair of enormous drawing room doors, waiting for permission to enter as her parents prepare for the holiday celebration.

She tries to peep into the keyhole, into the adult world beyond. *Let me in*, she seems to say, frantically climbing on the chair, pressing her ear against the door. It's ecstatic and unbearable and it makes everyone in the audience lean forward, clamp their fingers, hold their breath.

Everyone remembers that feeling, Dara thought. The tortuous waiting of childhood. Waiting for parents, forever, waiting while adults do their adult things. Wanting to understand, the doors always closed. Until the adults finally decide to open them and then there's no shutting the door again.

There was something so astonishing about Clara's hunger, Dara thought, a pinch over her chest. She's so eager, desperate even, to escape her safe, warm, cloying home, overstuffed with things. With history, the past.

All she wants is what's behind the doors. Beyond the doors.

The Nutcracker and *The Nutcracker* grants her everything. Her fantasy takes over the ballet. A dark and sumptuous world where she's a hero and a queen. Where everything is new and strange and waiting for her.

And home and family are now the foreign country and she need never go back.

* * *

Everyone was moving through the dark behind her. Backstage whispers and sweat and glitter and terror. It was happening, it was finally happening. And Dara felt her breath catch with excitement for the first time in more *Nutcracker*s than she could recall.

But where was her Clara?

Searching the shadowy masses of girls in party dresses, of boys in stiff suits, she couldn't find her. Instead, there was Marcus, this year's Nutcracker Prince, sneaking past the curtain, waving to his parents in the front row, his Adam's apple dancing with fear.

He would do well, Dara knew, but she felt a twinge remembering Corbin Lesterio, who had succumbed at last to his father's pressures and quit ballet not long after the cancellation of last year's performances.

Over the summer, she'd been driving by the high school football field when she saw him. She might not have even recognized him—already so changed, from the football, yes, but also from time. But though that particular fleeting beauty was gone—the beauty of boys before their necks thickened, their features coarsened—she could still see the ghost of that boy inside him.

Her foot gently on the brake, she took a moment to watch him jogging to the sidelines under the bank of lights. Glowing like an old painting. He stopped and seemed to see her. Seemed to move toward her, toward the fence.

Just as she began to pull away, he stepped forward, pulling off his helmet with such grace, such gentility, like a medieval knight lifting his vizor.

The same way Marcus now cupped the Nutcracker mask in the crook of his arm, his face clear and soft and impossibly young.

Dara, darling, I have something for you."

It was Madame Sylvie sailing over with her trailing scarves.

"Better late than never," she said, handing over a bright foil tin. Her annual rum cake, slick with glaze.

"You didn't need to," Dara said.

"But I did, my dear," she whispered, a hand on Dara's shoulder, the smell of her "Nutcracker nog" on her breath. "We must keep up traditions. They make us who we are."

The entire time Tchaikovsky was composing *The Nutcracker*, Madame Sylvie told Dara once, he was mourning his beloved sister Sasha. He reanimated her through Clara. It explained the strange heaviness of the ballet, its grand melancholy, its piercing nostalgia. And the deathlessness of its vision of childhood, of innocence and escape. Our almost unbearable awareness that everything we're seeing is disappearing even as we watch, fluttering past us as the dancers do, slipping away like smoke.

Every year, when the grand *pas de deux*—the Sugar Plum Fairy and her Prince—begins, the audience's eyes fill with tears. Those shimmering sounds of the celesta, like bells clear and pure, and we are flung backward. Time is conquered for a brief, luminous moment. Dara remembered one parent telling her that prayers from the Russian funeral mass were hidden in its opening bars. *We don't hear it,* he told her. *But we feel it nonetheless.*

Just like that moment, her favorite moment, Clara on the stage alone, nightgown, like a white flower, like a handkerchief caught in the wind.

Spot one on Clara . . . go.

Clara searching, darting across the stage . . . alone but brave.

Clara, golden under the lights, her head lifted, throat glowing like a torch, like the Fire Eater.

Marie," Dara found herself whispering, her hand on her chest. She turned to look for her, as if expecting to see her sister's foxen face.

But, of course, Marie wasn't there. She'd left two months after Charlie died, after they'd walked through the ash-shook carcass of their house, the sky white and pure. She'd stayed, Dara knew, as long as she could, longer—until finally she couldn't wait anymore. The day she left, she'd thrown herself into Dara's arms with such force it took her breath away. Standing on the front lawn, Dara watched her drive away in that vivid flame of a car. The one, it turned out, she hadn't bought for him at all. She'd bought it for her new life, for her beyond.

The most recent sunbaked postcard came from Greece, which she'd found her way back to, to the beginning of civilization, before history, but not before family.

The photo was of some kind of statue, a soldier, or an angel, arms raised above the head, hands grappling a magnificent flaming sword.

"Marie," Dara whispered again, her eyes filling. Loving her. Loving her sister who had carried everything for all of them. What a terrible burden. What an albatross to free herself of. How glad Dara was that she had.

"Marie," Dara whispered once more, her hand on her chest, "can I too?"

Madame Durant."

Dara turned and it was Bailey Bloom. In the smoky half-light, her hair slicked and gleaming into its bun, her face painted, her doll lashes affixed, her brows a slash. The pearlescent white of her face.

"Mademoiselle Bloom," Dara said, nodding approvingly. "Clara at last."

Bailey in Clara's party dress, forest green and darted, sequins sewn into the trim.

Bailey, finally getting to dance Clara a year late, the burgundy sash on her dress lowered to accommodate her new breasts.

What a difference a year had made. The Bailey of last fall, suffering through the pins in her pointe shoes, the tainted cookies, the dead rat. And then the canceled *Nutcracker* performances after the fire, after Charlie.

How strong Bailey had been, how stoic. And now this year, unshaken by anything, she stood before Dara so poised, so eager, so hungry to get out onstage.

Behind her in the audience, Dara spotted Bailey's mother in the front row. Mrs. Bloom, dear Mrs. Bloom with all her loneliness and her ravenous longing—a longing that felt like an X-ray into herself that she never wanted to see.

But she looked so proud now, seated in the front row, with her hound's-tooth scarf and her square-toe pumps, and the bouquet of pale roses tucked beside her, waiting for her daughter's final bow.

"Madame Durant," Bailey repeated. "I just—"

"Shouldn't you be on your cue?" Dara said.

"I have ninety seconds," Bailey said, biting her lip, white teeth sinking into the dark red of her painted mouth. "Madame Durant, I wanted to thank you."

Dara paused, her throat tightening.

"Don't thank me," she said. "You did it. You did it all yourself."

A smile flitted across Bailey's powdered face.

"Lights, warning on cue one. Curtain up—now." The stage manager was calling, her headset sliding down her face. "Is she ready?"

Bailey turned to her and nodded, her back straightening, her sash shushing, the soft thump of her feet in her pointe shoes.

But then Dara saw it: the slight furrow of her brow as Bailey stared out into the darkness.

"You're ready," Dara said, her own voice throaty, shaking. "You are."

Bailey looked at her. Held her gaze, the floorboards beneath them vibrating, the buoyant overture, like the winding of a music box.

"I am," Bailey said, and then, inexplicably, putting her slender hand on Dara's. Dara felt it, the heat of her touch, the beating of her heart, both of theirs. "I'm ready."

"Lights, cue one—now. Spot one, be ready to pick up . . ."

Dara watched, holding her breath, as Bailey flew from the wings onto the stage. The gasps of excitement from the audience, the music sweeping over them, all eyes on the girl, the hero, at last.

ACKNOWLEDGMENTS

Boundless thanks are due to my brilliant editor, Sally Kim, for her masterful eye and ear and especially her true-blue readerly heart.

To the peerless Sylvie Rabineau at WME and Maja Nikolic at Writers House. To Bard Dorros and Robyn Meisinger at Anonymous Content.

Thanks also to Mikaela Vidmar-Perrins, for her invaluable fact-checking and question-answering.

As always, such gratitude to my mom, Patricia Abbott, for all her support and, in the last few years, bravery and resilience. And to my stalwart family: Josh Abbott, Julie Nichols, and Kevin Abbott, without whom, and to the Nases: Jeff, Ruth, Steve, Michelle, Marley, and Austin.

And I'm forever in debt to genius and muse Alison Quinn, to Darcy Lockman, and to Lisa Lutz. And heart-in-throat gratitude to Jack Pendarvis and my beloved Oxford, Mississippi, friends: Theresa Starkey, Ace and Angela Atkins, Bill and Katie Boyle, and Jimmy Cajoleas.

And to Dan Conaway, to whom I owe the whole enchilada.